UPPER HOUSE CONSPIRACY

ROBERT GODDARD

UPPER HOUSE CONSPIRACY

Hope you enjoy Bill,
Robert Goddard
3/28/06

THE BEALL TOWER PRESS, INC.

UPPER HOUSE CONSPIRACY

Published by
The Beall Tower Press, Inc.
www.bealltower.com

This is a work of fiction. Names, characters, places, and incidents either are the product of the author's imagination or are used fictitiously. Any resemblance to actual persons, living or dead, events, or locales is entirely coincidental.

All rights reserved.
Copyright © 2006 by Robert Goddard

No part of this book may be reproduced or transmitted in any form or by any means, electronic or mechanical, including photocopying, recording, or by any information storage and retrieval system, without the written permission of the publisher, except in the case of brief quotations embodied in critical articles or reviews. For information, address The Beall Tower Press, Inc., 106A Office Park Drive, Brandon, MS 39042.

ISBN 0-9771429-0-6

Library of Congress Control Number 2005910330

Printed in the United States of America

First edition: May 2006

Acknowledgments

Thanks to my wife, Priscilla, who has all the patience in the world, and thanks to Thomas Beall, her brother, who spent a few days showing me around Washington, D.C. Also thanks to Judith Myers, my editor, who knows far more than I about punctuation and did a marvelous job for me.

PROLOGUE

It is early September in Washington, D.C. The Republicans control the White House and House of Representatives, but the Democrats control the Senate by a one-seat majority. President Thompson, a Republican, is in his first term. Midterm congressional elections are coming up in November.

Conditions in the Middle East are extremely unstable. The United Nations has been unable to prevent Iran from pursuing development of nuclear weapons and the new governments in Afghanistan and Iraq are in danger of failing without continued U.S. support.

President Thompson wants to maintain the current level of U.S. involvement in the Middle East, but the Senate has blocked the necessary funding, just as it blocked his attempts to fill two vacant Supreme Court positions with conservative judges.

Polls indicate the Republicans will win control of the Senate by at least one seat and maybe more. Much is at stake and the world is watching with baited breath.

Wednesday Evening
Early September

1

O'Brien flattened his chubby frame against the wall by the hotel room door, and tensed his body, ready to leap in front of the door if the bellhop could con the occupants into opening it. The bellhop would force the door wide open and O'Brien would snap a couple of quick shots for his tabloid, hopefully catching the senator lying nude on the bed. Then a shot of the broad, and he'd run for cover. O'Brien took a deep breath, checked his camera, and nodded to Reggie, his reluctant accomplice.

The bellhop's Adam's apple hitched as he took a hard swallow. He raised his hand to rap on the door, but the door was snatched open and a wild-eyed young blonde in a low-cut blouse and dark pants burst from the room, carrying her high-heeled shoes in her hand.

"*Merde!*, she screamed, then rammed into the bellhop, who stumbled backward and stepped on O'Brien's toes with his heels.

Off-balance and unable to move his feet, O'Brien tumbled to the floor with Reggie on top of him. The blonde danced over their bodies like a running back going through a tire drill, and scampered down the hallway.

With Reggie on top of him and his camera out of reach, O'Brien watched helplessly as the blonde disappeared into the elevator. As the elevator doors closed, her slender arm snaked through the narrow slit and retrieved a shoe she'd dropped.

O'Brien shoved Reggie aside, rose to his knees and reached for his camera, lying several feet away.

"Damn!" gasped Reggie, standing in the open doorway. That dude's done had a heart attack and died!"

"What?" O'Brien struggled to his feet and pushed past the skinny bellhop. He saw Senator Pearson's naked body sprawled face-down across the king-sized bed.

"Senator Pearson?"

The senator didn't respond. O'Brien entered the room and sidled around to the far side of the bed for a better look. The senator's sightless eyes stared at the wall and his mouth sagged open.

Low, throaty moans drew O'Brien's eyes to the TV, where he saw a surgically enhanced blonde and a young stud entwined in an exotic Kama Sutra position. Apparently, the aging senator had needed a little inspiration. O'Brien shook his head. "Looks like he bit the weenie all right."

"What we gonna do, man? What in the hell we gonna do now?" whined the bellhop.

"Go down to the front desk and call the police while I get some photos."

"What am I gonna tell them?"

"Say there's a dead man in 822 and it looks like he had a heart attack."

"Won't they ask me how I found the body? Won't they ask me what I was doing in the dude's room? What am I gonna say then?"

"We haven't broken any laws I know of, so stick to the truth—both our stories will match and the cops will be happy."

"They're gonna fire me, man! They're gonna fire me sure as hell!"

"You can't worry about that now. Just go on and call the police. We don't want them wondering why we hesitated, do we?"

The bellhop's shoulders slumped in resignation. "No, I guess not." He shuffled slowly through the doorway, like a little boy called to take a dose of bitter medicine.

O'Brien surveyed the room. Bedcovers lay in a pile on the floor at the foot of the bed and the senator's clothes draped over the back of a straight chair by a small writing desk in the corner. The night stand displayed what appeared to be the contents of Pearson's pockets.

After taking photos of the dead senator from different positions around the room, O'Brien moved to the night stand for a close-up shot of Pearson's pocket items: keys, money, a pocket knife, some little blister tabs holding pills, a tiny brown bottle with a screw cap, and an open pack of condoms. O'Brien smiled. Another good front-page shot.

Using a tissue from his jacket pocket, he lifted the brown bottle and read the label aloud. "Nitroglycerin Sublingual Tablets." Figured, since Pearson had a history of heart trouble. What a way to go—stroking out while banging a twenty-something blonde. A fitting end, considering the old rake's history.

O'Brien replaced the bottle and picked up one of the little blister tabs. An inch long and a half-inch wide, it contained a yellow, football-shaped tablet under a plastic bubble—the kind that could be pushed with a thumb to pop the tablet through the paper on the back. It looked like NazinX, the over-the-counter allergy medicine O'Brien used on occasion. In fact, he was carrying some in his pocket at that very moment. He turned the blister tab over in his hand and saw the familiar brand name on the paper backing.

A hair-thin slit in the backing caught his eye. Had the paper been cut open? He probed at the slit with the tip of his fingernail, but couldn't pry it loose. "Bizarre," he mumbled to himself. Had someone cut a slit in the backing and glued it back in place?

O'Brien replaced the tab on the night stand and picked up the other two. The second tab bore the same signs of tampering, but the third tab was empty. He assumed Pearson had taken one after checking into the hotel—or possibly he took one earlier in the day and simply stuffed the empty tab back into his pocket. O'Brien pushed the yellow tablet through the paper backing with his thumb and held the bare tablet up for inspection. The NazinX brand name was pressed into the tablet, just as it was on the ones in his pocket. This particular tablet felt a little different though, softer.

O'Brien fished a bubble pack from his jacket pocket and pushed the tablet out into his palm beside the senator's for comparison. The senator's tablet was the same size and shape as his, but it lacked the hard, shiny surface of his tablet, as though it was unfinished. He rubbed the senator's tablet between his thumb and forefinger and noted some of the material came off on his fingertips.

O'Brien weighed the tablets on his open palm. The senator's NazinX tablet appeared to be a crude imitation of the real one from his pocket. Had someone made these tablets and switched them with the senator's real ones? Did the bogus tablets contain poison? Had Pearson been murdered?

A spark of ambition kindled in O'Brien. It would take the cops several days to perform an autopsy and analyze the senator's medicine—several days he could use to maximum advantage. Jason, his drinking buddy, was a chemist and worked at a research lab. If he could persuade Jason to analyze the tablet and verify it contained poison, he could scoop the big-time news media.

His spirit soared. His breaking of the story might be big enough to re-establish him as a legitimate investigative reporter. With visions of a comeback dancing in his head, he slipped the fake tablet into his shirt pocket.

Suddenly, a pang of conscience stabbed him; removing evidence from a possible homicide scene was surely a felony. He dug the tablet out of his pocket and gazed at it apprehensively, pondering the possible repercussions should he be found out.

Deciding the potential reward was worth the risk, he shoved the tablet back into his shirt pocket. The police would still have the other tablet for their lab to analyze and that was all they needed.

Satisfied he had enough photos, O'Brien stepped into the hallway, pulled the door closed behind him, and waited for the cops.

2

Zalva sat up, startled out of a nightmare in which someone was trying to kick her door in. A quick glance around the room reminded her she'd fallen asleep on the couch again while reading. She breathed a sigh of relief at being rescued from the dream, then almost jumped out of her skin when someone pounded on her door. So that's what caused the nightmare. Someone had knocked on her door and to avoid waking, her mind tricked her by telling her it was a dream, albeit a bad one.

She rubbed her face vigorously, trying to come fully awake. She checked her wristwatch and saw it was a quarter past nine.

More banging on the door.

"Zalva! Wake up!"

"Oh, hell," she muttered. It was her partner, which could only mean one thing: someone had been killed and she'd have to go back to work. She stumbled to the door, unlatched the deadbolt, opened the door, and stood to the side.

With a scowl, Archie slipped by her, towering over her with his six-foot three-inch frame. "Why didn't you answer your cell phone?"

She closed the door and leaned her back against it. "I must've left it on vibrator mode when I took it out of my pocket."

"Vibrator mode, huh?"

She ignored his snide attempt at humor. "How did you know I was home?"

"Saw your car in the parking lot."

He obviously knew her too well since he hadn't assumed she might have a lover in her apartment. She winced inwardly at that thought. Why wasn't she in the sack with a lover? Hah! No mystery there. She hadn't met anyone but cops and criminals since coming to D.C. a year ago, and she'd had her fill of muscled-up, steroid-taking, macho-men.

She forced her thoughts back to the matter at hand. "What's the deal?"

"We've got a dead senator at the Palmyra Court Hotel."

"No kidding? Which one?"

"Pearson, from Michigan. Appears he croaked from a heart attack while humping a young blonde."

"If he died of a heart attack, why send homicide?"

"Since it's Pearson, Captain Thurman wants to play it safe—in case somebody decided to shut him up before he ratted them out on a plea bargain."

"Let me wash my face and comb my hair. I won't be but a minute. Ginny's crew already there?"

"They're on the way."

They picked up coffee en route to the hotel, and Archie ran over a rough spot as Zalva took a sip. "Ouch!"

"What's wrong?"

"Scorched my lips when you hit that last pothole."

"Hmpf. Life is tough."

She let his remark go unanswered and gingerly licked her wounded lips. Partners since her first day with the department, she'd grown accustomed to his sarcasm. He griped and grumbled about everything and though he never said it, she suspected he bitterly resented having a female partner.

Only fifty-five, he appeared much older due to the tight carpet of curly white hair covering his head and the haggard look on his face. Woefully out of shape and more than fifty pounds overweight, he'd almost stroked out earlier that day when they climbed two flights of stairs in search of a witness.

Archie drove in silence until they reached the hotel. "Two people found the senator's body. One's a bellhop. The other's a sleaze-ball reporter from the *National Probe*."

"That grocery-store tabloid?"

"Yep."

"A sleaze-ball, huh?"

"Slimy as a slug dipped in oil."

"How is it he was there when Pearson's body was found?"

"Bellhop spotted Pearson sneaking into the room with a young blonde and called the reporter."

"To sell him the info?"

"Probably. Anyway, I'll grill the reporter. You talk to the bellhop and the people at the front desk. When you've got their statements, come to Room 822 and we'll compare notes."

In a corner of the lobby, Zalva found a uniformed officer talking to a rangy bellhop—presumably the one who had reported finding the body. She joined them, confirmed her assumption, and relieved the officer. The bellhop jerked and twitched as he gave his account of finding the body. He explained he was nervous over the prospect of losing his job for tipping off the tabloid reporter about the senator's rendevous with the blond. She figured it'd be justice if he did, given his attempt to exploit the situation.

Zalva took Reggie's written statement and approached the registration desk staffed by two young women of Asian descent, dressed in dark green pant suits with the hotel logo printed over the left front jacket pocket.

"Which of you checked the woman into Room 822?"

"I did," answered the taller of the two women. Janet, according to her name tag, stepped over to face Zalva across the counter.

"The woman paid for the room with cash, right?"

"Yes."

"Did she fill out a check-in card?"

"Oh, yes. It's required of everyone."

"I'm taking the card as possible evidence."

"Evidence of what? Didn't the old guy die of a heart attack?"

"We won't know for sure until the autopsy is performed. In the meantime we have to gather potential evidence, just in case."

With a sour expression on her face, Janet opened a drawer and began flipping through a card file.

"Don't touch it," warned Zalva. She reached into her pocket, brought out a pair of tweezers, and handed them to Janet. "Use this."

Janet took the tweezers and continued scanning the cards. "Got it." She pulled the card from the drawer with the tweezers and offered it to Zalva.

Zalva held a clear plastic evidence bag open and Janet dropped the card into it. After scribbling a label on the bag, she read the name and address on the card. "According to this, her name is Marie Antoinette and she lives at the White House."

Janet smirked. "We don't have to verify what guests enter on the cards."

"No, you don't," Zalva replied curtly. "But it wouldn't hurt to check ID on guests. Be a big help in cases like this."

Janet pouted at the mild rebuke but said nothing.

Zalva called in the tag number scrawled on the registration card and repeated the result aloud for Janet. "Tag's bogus."

Janet gave her a blank look, shrugged her shoulders, and remained silent.

"Well, she probably left a print on this card. We might have some luck with that. In the meantime, give me her description."

Janet leaned on the counter with both hands and rolled her almond eyes at the ceiling, trying to recall the details of the woman's appearance. "Mid-twenties, curly blonde hair, not quite long enough to reach her shoulders. About five and a half feet, medium build, well developed, with sky blue eyes."

"Any moles, tattoos, scars or other distinguishing marks?"

"No . . . not that I can remember . . . but she had a French accent."

That jived with what Reggie told her about the woman yelling something in French when she fled the room.

There was no vehicle make or model on the check-in card. Zalva looked over her shoulder and through the front doorway. Hotel guests had to drive in off the street, park by the front door while registering, then drive straight into the parking garage. "Did you see the woman's car?"

"Yes. It was white. I don't know what kind . . . but it had . . . like some linked circles on the trunk, like this." Janet drew in the air with her finger, and Zalva recognized the Audi logo.

Zalva pulled out another evidence bag and held it open in front of Janet. "Now please be so kind as to use those tweezers to take the bills she gave you out of the drawer and put them in this bag."

"Can you take hotel money for evidence?"

"You bet."

"Won't there be lots of other fingerprints on the bills?"

"Yeah, and one of them might be hers. Now cough it up."

With a sour look on her face, Janet opened the cash drawer. "I'll need a receipt for the money."

"No problem."

Reluctantly, Janet handed over the bills. "Is that all?"

"Not yet." Zalva motioned with her head at the security camera mounted high up in the far corner behind the counter. "I need the tape from that security camera, too."

"I'll have the bellhop get it for you."

After the bellhop fetched the tape, Zalva signed receipts for Janet and took the elevator to the eighth floor.

She found Archie in the hallway outside Room 822 with Sleaze-Ball, who looked to be just past forty. He was about six feet tall, broad framed, and a slight paunch overhung his belt. Not obese, but a little pudgy, with a wide face and bushy eyebrows. A tangle of unruly brown hair poked out from underneath his military-style campaign hat. He wore baggy khaki pants and an old army field jacket. As he talked, he made a lot of hand gestures for emphasis, and his face and eyes were in constant motion.

Sleaze-Ball's eyes roamed her body as if surveying a buffet table loaded with desserts. She scowled at him in and he grinned at her like a thirteen-year-old boy who'd lifted his first girlie magazine from the corner convenience store. Suddenly her face was hot with anger and her legs trembled. What arrogance! She stopped a few inches short of arm's reach from him, defeating the urge to slap the grin off his face.

Sleaze-Ball turned away from Archie and offered her his right hand. "I'm Will O'Brien."

She ignored his hand and replied in a stiff voice, "I'm *Detective* Zalva Martinez—Detective Wilson's partner."

"Yeah, the badge on your belt was the third or fourth thing I notic—"

Archie stiff-armed Sleaze-Ball in the back, propelling him across the hallway where he bounced off the far wall. "Get your sorry ass out of here!"

The reporter regained his balance, turned toward them with a sneaky-looking grin, bowed, made a sweeping gesture with his arm, and began backing away from them as if they were royalty. About twenty feet away, he straightened up, spun around, and hustled off toward the elevator.

Zalva shook her head as she watched him depart. "What a character!"

"Hmpf! A couple of good licks with a night stick would straighten him out."

Zalva rolled her eyes at Archie then stepped into Room 822. She found little Ginny, the lead crime scene investigator and handed her the evidence gathered in the lobby. "How about it? Heart attack?"

"Yes, I'd say that's pretty much it," replied Ginny. She placed the evidence from Zalva in a large satchel on the floor, and pulled out a brown evidence bag. "Take a look at this."

Zalva opened the bag and peered at the contents: a triangular-shaped, green tablet and two pieces of wadded-up aluminum foil. The tablet bore the name JUNO, meaning the tablet was manufactured by JUNO Pharmaceutical. She rolled the tablet over and saw MXL100 imprinted on the flip side. She passed the bag to Archie. "What is it?"

"Don't know what the MXL stands for but the 100 means it contains a hundred milligrams of whatever active ingredient it carries," answered Ginny. "I found the pill wrapped in aluminum foil in the outside pocket of his suit coat, along with the other wadded-up piece of foil. He could've had two of these, taken one, and kept the piece of foil—like maybe he wasn't near a trash can." Ginny took the bag from Archie, swapped it for two others from her satchel, and handed them to Zalva.

One bag contained a small brown bottle and the other held two blister tabs, the kind that could be torn off a card for carrying convenience. One tab was empty and the other contained a yellow, oval tablet about twice the size of the green one found in Pearson's coat pocket. "What are these?"

"An over-the-counter allergy medicine called NazinX. Looks like he took one, either here or somewhere else, and like the aluminum foil, kept the empty blister tab. Supposedly, the brown bottle contains nitroglycerin sublingual tablets."

"So, pending lab and autopsy reports, we've got a natural death?"

"Appears so," replied Ginny.

Zalva and Archie left Ginny and descended to the lobby where there was coffee, settled down on a corner sofa, and compared notes on their respective interviews of Reggie and O'Brien. They found no conflicts in the stories, agreed Zalva would write their official report in the morning, and departed.

3

O'Brien trudged back to his ancient Volvo, got it started after several tries, and chugged off toward his place. A couple of blocks from the hotel, his thoughts drifted back to the female detective. He whispered her name aloud, "Zalva." It sounded mysterious, sexy, and she looked it, with her dark hair and eyes. Five feet and a half, athletic body, full, sensuous lips, and maybe a little over thirty—quite a package. Not a heart-stopper, but pleasing to the eye, and intelligent. He wondered what it would be like to have a lasting relationship with someone possessing both good looks and intelligence.

He heaved a deep sigh, banished Zalva from his thoughts, and checked his watch. A quarter past eleven. When he left Finigan's with Wendy during happy hour, Jason was in the back playing snooker. Maybe he could still catch Jason at the pub and give him the tablet. Otherwise he'd have to wait until Thursday night and lose a day, missing the Thursday afternoon deadline for the weekend issue of the *Probe*. He snatched his cell phone off the passenger seat, punched in Jason's phone number, and looked up at the road in time to narrowly avoid running over the curb.

Jason didn't answer but that didn't mean he wasn't there. His cell phone might be in his coat hanging on a peg near the snooker table. Might as well check out the pub before heading home he thought, just in case Jason was still hanging around. Besides, he needed a cold brew after the hotel episode.

• • •

O'Brien stepped through the doorway into his favorite place in the world, Finigan's Pub, near George Washington University in Foggy Bottom. This was his safe-house, his island fortress, his Gibraltar in a sea of troubles. No matter how bad the day had been, he always recovered his spirit when he stepped through the portal.

He stood just inside the doorway, admiring the richly decorated mahogany bar with its white marble counter top, the twenty-foot mirror behind the bar, and the heavy mahogany cabinets and shelving that framed the mirror. His mind wandered briefly to thoughts of all the women he'd made eye contact with in that mirror. Eye contact that had occasionally led to brief affairs. He inhaled deeply, savored the familiar smell of food, beer, and booze for a moment, then allowed his gaze to roam away from the bar.

About forty feet wide, at least a hundred feet deep, and with a high ceiling of fourteen feet or so, the pub was divided into three sections. The bar and customer tables occupied the first section, with the bar on his left and tables on his right. The middle section was for darts, and the third section contained a single snooker table. A row of billiard chairs lined the wall to the right of the snooker table and a row of pinball machines and stools stood against the opposite wall. A five-foot-high, mahogany wainscot graced the walls and was complimented by darkly stained, plank flooring.

The front section also contained a small stage large enough for three musicians and their instruments. Mary Kate popped for professional musicians on Friday and Saturday nights during the tourist season, but the rest of the year it was left to amateurs. Anyone could mount the stage and play or sing, the only requirements being an audition for Mary Kate before five and the music had to be Irish, blues, or jazz. And there was no shortage of people who qualified although most were not overly polished.

Occasionally, one of those brave souls would turn out to be first-rate and bond with the houseful of patrons. On those nights, O'Brien usually stayed longer, imbibed to excess, and rode home in a taxi. But at this late hour the stage was empty and the lilting Irish music came from a CD player.

Mary Kate O'Hurly, an Irish immigrant who had become a U.S. citizen, owned the place. She'd bought the pub while O'Brien was a student at George Washington University, and since he'd been a regular for all but his few years in New York, they had become friends. A tall, pug-nosed, large-boned blonde, with curly hair beginning to turn gray, and light blue eyes, she wasn't beautiful by any stretch, but her heart was in the right place.

She spied O'Brien, grabbed a mug from the rack, and began drawing his Guinness Stout. The crowd had thinned since he'd left earlier with Wendy, leaving him room to walk right up to Mary Kate at the bar.

With a crooked grin, she handed him the full mug. "Didn't expect you back here tonight. What happened? Wendy kick your arse out of bed?"

Actually, he'd been about to crawl into bed with Wendy when the bellhop called with the tip about Pearson at the hotel. He couldn't pass up the chance for some juicy photos for the front page of the tabloid, and left, promising Wendy he'd be right back. He'd never admit that to Mary Kate, though.

"Why Mary Kate!" He grabbed his belly with both hands and jiggled it. "Would a woman kick this All-American dream body out of bed?"

Mary Kate rolled her eyes at the ceiling and shook her head. "I don't know what those young women see in you. It sure as hell ain't obvious."

"It's my technique."

"Ha! You couldn't handle her. Come on and admit it."

"You got it all wrong, Mary Kate. She's so satisfied she won't wake until dawn, so I'm here for a fill-in."

She uttered a harsh cackle and waved him off with both hands. "Go on and swill your Stout."

"Jason still here?"

She scowled and nodded toward the snooker room. "He's back there losing his arse on the snooker table."

O'Brien pushed away from the bar and took a step toward the rear.

Mary Kate called out after him, "You forgot to close your tab when you left here earlier. Don't you leave again without checking in with me."

O'Brien ignored her and kept going. He'd walked out more than a few times, forgetting to clear his tab for the night—unintentional of course, but she always remembered to get it the next time he came in, so she'd never lost anything.

He sauntered to the back and found Jason dropping a few crumpled bills onto the snooker table. A slender young brunette in her late twenties, dressed in a white silk blouse that clung to her nipples, faded blue jeans that looked like they might've been spray-painted on her, and tennis shoes, scooped the up bills with an exaggerated sweep of her arm and with no small effort, stuffed them into the front pocket of her jeans.

With the cash finally tucked away, she looked up with emerald eyes and caught O'Brien admiring her. Her lips parted in a smile, their moistness glistening in the intense light from over the snooker table. She winked at him and grinned. He pretended to get weak knees, bringing a broader grin to her face. Suddenly he felt the urge to whip out his cell phone, call Wendy at his place, and tell her to catch a cab home.

Composing a line to pitch, O'Brien started toward the brunette but pulled up short when she turned to a young lawyer-type who challenged the table. With the brunette now occupied, he cursed softly and glanced around for Jason.

He spotted Jason replacing his cue in the wall rack, shaking his head in disgust. Jason noticed O'Brien and lurched toward him on wobbly legs. Jason was tall and slender, maybe six and a half feet, with a thin face, sandy hair, and close-set eyes, now carrying a look of stunned amazement.

He hovered over O'Brien, swaying slightly. "She cleaned me out, man. How can a sexy broad like that be so good at snooker?"

"Her dad probably owned a pool hall and she grew up in it," said O'Brien. He put an arm around Jason's shoulders and ushered him toward the front of the pub. "You shouldn't gamble when you're drinking anyway."

Jason gave him a puzzled look. "Didn't you leave earlier . . . with Wendy?"

"Yeah, but I had to go out for a story. Tell you about it in a minute."

They found an empty table along the wall and O'Brien slipped onto one of the hard wooden chairs while Jason went to the bar for a refill. O'Brien looked back toward the snooker room and caught a fleeting glimpse of the brunette through the milling patrons playing darts. Too bad Wendy was waiting for him at his place. Otherwise, he'd be back there pitching lines at the brunette like a New Orleans street barker on Bourbon Street.

Jason returned empty-handed and sagged into his chair, looking like he'd bought a beer at last call and spilled all of it.

"What's wrong with you?"

"My only credit card was declined and Mary Kate wouldn't let me slide until tomorrow."

"What? She wouldn't trust you for one more beer?"

"Hell, no. She's pissed."

"Over what?"

"She asked me why I was broke. I told her about losing my money on the snooker table and she went berserk, like it had been her money or something. Said I could damn well do without for gambling my money away." He turned baleful eyes toward O'Brien. "Buy me a beer."

O'Brien caught Mary Kate's attention and motioned for her to put one on his tab for Jason. She screwed up her face, but jerked a mug off the rack and began drawing the beer.

He turned back to Jason and motioned for him to lean over, so they could talk without being overheard. "You want to pick up two hundred bucks on the side?"

Jason's eyes widened at the mention of money. "Yeah—long as it's legal."

"It's legal—sort of."

Jason's glassy eyes crossed for a second and his brow knitted in consternation. "Didn't I just hear you say *sort of*?"

"Well, yeah, it's sort of legal." O'Brien brought out the tablet from the hotel room and held it out on his open palm for Jason to see. "I want you to run some lab tests on this, find out what it's made of."

O'Brien caught a movement out of the corner of his eye, closed his hand over the tablet, and sat back in his chair while Sheena served Jason's beer. He waited until she pranced away from the table before opening his fist to display the tablet again.

Jason leaned over the table, his face within a couple of inches of O'Brien's open hand, and studied the tablet for several seconds, tentatively poking at it with his index finger as if it were a poisonous spider. Finally, he sat up and gave O'Brien a disdainful look.

"I don't have to analyze this. It's an over-the-counter allergy medicine called NazinX. Can't you read?"

O'Brien snatched the real NazinX tablet from his shirt pocket and put it in the palm of his hand next to the homemade one. "Compare these, smart ass."

Jason took the two tablets from O'Brien, rubbed each tablet with his fingertips, then gave the real one back to O'Brien. He held the other one close to his eyes with the tips of his fingers, and studied it like a jeweler inspecting a stone for an obvious fault. After a few seconds, he cut his eyes toward O'Brien and arched an eyebrow. "This bad boy is a fake, right?"

"Just as sure as that green-eyed babe took all your money."

Jason winced and shifted uneasily in his chair. "You got that right. Now where'd you get this?"

After swearing Jason to secrecy, he described the events at the hotel, while sipping lightly at his mug of Stout.

"You think somebody poisoned him?"

"Why else would somebody make a fake pill that was supposed to pass for a real one?"

Jason studied the tablet again, twisting his mouth from side to side as he concentrated. Suddenly, he made a choking noise, dropped the tablet onto the table top, and gaped at O'Brien with eyes widened. "You mean this could be some kind of poison, and I've been handling it?"

The possibility of being poisoned by handling the tablet hadn't occurred to O'Brien and it startled him, but he shrugged it off. "Don't sweat it, man. I handled it an hour ago and haven't noticed any ill effects. Wouldn't hurt to wash your hands though."

Jason lifted his beer mug, snatched the damp napkin from under it, and swabbed his fingers vigorously. Finished, he scowled at O'Brien and took a heavy pull on his beer.

"Look, Jason. I've got an ordinary scandal story here, with some great pictures, but it'd be a blockbuster if I could say Pearson was murdered. If you could confirm this tablet is really poison, by my mid-afternoon deadline tomorrow, I'll scoop everybody else because the official lab and autopsy reports won't be out for several days."

Jason studied O'Brien through half-closed eyelids. "You stole this from the crime scene. Isn't that illegal?"

"Maybe. But there were two of these on the night stand by the hotel bed and I left one for the police to analyze, so they won't miss this one. And hey, no harm, no foul, right?"

"I guess not," said Jason. With a sigh, he picked up the tablet with a bar napkin, held his shirt pocket open with one hand, and slipped the tablet into it with the other. But he leaned too far to his right, his chair shot out from under him, and his butt hit the floor with a loud splat.

O'Brien rose and pulled Jason to his feet.

Swaying on unsteady legs and red-faced, Jason looked down at O'Brien. "You reckon I've had too much?"

"Too much to drive for damned sure." He patted Jason on the back. "Sleep on my couch tonight. I'll bring you back here for your car in the morning. Okay?"

Jason agreed, so they downed the rest of their beer and departed for O'Brien's place.

· · ·

After settling Jason on the couch in the den, O'Brien slipped into his bedroom and felt his way to the bathroom in the dark to avoid waking Wendy. He brushed his teeth, washed his face, stripped, and slid into bed expecting to snuggle up to Wendy's warm body, but she wasn't there.

He stretched out his arm and groped across the bed, finding nothing but bedcovers and mattress.

"What the hell?" He rose up on one elbow, flipped the switch on the bedside lamp, and confirmed she was gone.

"Damn!" She must've lost her patience and left in a taxi. O'Brien let out a long breath in frustration, and dropped his head back onto the pillow. Good and bad, he thought. Bad she's gone, but good too, because it left him free to romance the green-eyed brunette.

He settled himself under the covers and fantasized about the snooker-playing brunette. Before long, his thoughts drifted back to the events at the hotel and the female detective. He thought about her name again. *Zalva*. What an exotic name. She seemed to exert a special attraction over him. Was it her obvious intelligence? Was it the aura of mystery around her? Or was it the age-old 'forbidden fruit' syndrome? Did he subconsciously know she was out of reach for him, causing him to desire her all the more ardently?

He gave up on self-analysis and wondered what it would be like to have a woman like her. Eventually, though, he pushed her out of his mind and concentrated on the article he hoped to write. Finally, sleep overtook him, and with it, came the recurring nightmare that had haunted him since his disaster in New York.

Thursday

4

On her way to the station, Zalva stopped at a convenience store for her morning coffee and noticed a newspaper rack by the cash register, containing the daily issue of the *Post* and several tabloids. Normally she wouldn't give the rack a second look, but her cursory glance revealed a copy of the *National Probe* among the tabloids. She picked up a copy of the *Post* for reading at the office and as an afterthought, grabbed a copy of the *Probe*, to see what one of Sleaze-Ball's articles was like.

She arrived at the station at her normal time, even though she could've come in later, since she and Archie had worked a couple of hours the night before. She made her way past the front desk and through the main office space, cluttered with cheap desks and chairs, to the break room. Most of the desks were unoccupied this time of the morning, as this area belonged to Vice and they often worked well into the night and came in late. She and Archie were lucky enough to share one of two cubicles in a small room toward the rear of the building.

In the break room she picked up a mug of coffee and a couple of doughnuts from a platter provided by some would-be politician.

Archie wasn't at his desk and his coat wasn't hanging on the coat rack in the corner, confirming her suspicion he'd be in late. She settled down at her desk and pulled out the copy of the *National Probe*, expecting to find a big spread on Pearson's death, but saw nothing about it on the front page. She glanced at the top of the front page and discovered the *Probe* was a weekly publication and she had the previous week's issue. The next issue wouldn't be on the news stands until tomorrow afternoon.

The tabloid contained a couple of local D.C. scandal articles and several more articles describing ridiculously unlikely events: an Elvis sighting in Valdosta, Georgia, an alien abduction in Pearl, Mississippi, and a wolf-boy running wild somewhere in Indiana. Two of the articles were written by Will O'Brien.

Zalva sat back in amazement. How could an educated man sign his name to such garbage and still show his face in public? Disgusted, she tossed the rag into the trash can under her desk and reached for the real newspaper.

She found it interesting to read about one of her cases in the paper and often marveled at how badly the press could screw up the facts. She studied the report for several minutes, saw nothing she didn't already know, and spent another ten minutes flipping through the pages, scanning other articles.

After finishing the paper, she took a call from an assistant D.A. regarding the upcoming trial of someone she'd arrested six months earlier. Unable to remember the specifics, she had to refer to her notes. Eventually, the attorney was satisfied with her answers and let her go.

She spent the next hour writing her report on Senator Pearson's death and wrapped it up a few minutes before eleven. With nothing else to do, even though she believed it premature to expect results, she left her desk and stepped back to Ginny's lab: two small offices to the rear of the building where the dividing wall had been removed. At least she could find out whether Ginny had lifted any fingerprints off the sign-in card or the cash taken from the hotel desk clerk.

Zalva found Ginny sitting with her feet propped up on her desk beside her keyboard, sipping coffee, and peering over the rims of her glasses at the computer screen. Less than five feet tall and approaching fifty, Ginny couldn't weigh more than eighty pounds. She wore the customary white golf shirt with the department's logo, khaki pants, and loafers. Her gray-streaked, blonde hair was pulled back behind her ears and tumbled down to her shoulders. Her pale blue eyes, along with the corners of her mouth, were lined with wrinkles she made no effort to hide, disdaining makeup. With her slanted eyes, long ears, and tiny body, she resembled a little elf. Maybe she really was an elf—that would certainly explain how she sometimes produced results that seemed so magical.

Absorbed with the image on her computer screen, Ginny didn't notice her standing in the doorway. Zalva rapped softly on the open door to get her attention. Ginny glanced up from her coffee, saw Zalva, and swung her feet off the desk.

"Get any good prints off the sign-in card from the hotel," asked Zalva.

Ginny set her coffee cup on the desk and wiped her forehead with the back of her hand, like a field hand who'd been toiling in the noonday sun. She puffed up her cheeks, blew the air out, and shook her head as if defeated. "This is a tough one for sure."

Disappointed, Zalva leaned against the door frame. "No luck, huh?"

Ginny eyed her blankly for a second before allowing a broad grin to spread across her face. "Would a name and address do?"

Zalva's jaw dropped. "Don't tell me you've already matched her prints!"

"Her name is Lezette Demornay, she's a French citizen, and she's currently assigned to their D.C. embassy."

"For real? But how . . . how did you figure that out so quickly?" She checked her wristwatch again. "It's only eleven o'clock."

Ginny leaned back in her chair with a smug look on her face and clasped her hands behind her head. "Piece of cake."

"Enlighten me, please."

"Well, she had a French accent and the largest French embassy in the world is here, so I decided to check with the State Department. They maintain computer files on all foreign staff personnel assigned to embassies in the U.S. I scanned the prints and the image from the video tape and e-mailed them to the State Department first thing when I came in. The return e-mail identifying her came in right before you did."

"And she works for the French government—at their embassy?"

"Yep. Give me a minute and I'll print out the file they sent me. It'll have her photo, age, height, weight, and anything else you might need."

After getting the printout, Zalva found Archie, who'd arrived while she was in Ginny's lab. She filled him in on the identity of the French woman and explained how Ginny had gotten the ID so quickly. They reported to Captain Thurman, who made a phone call to the State Department, which arranged for them to make an official visit to the French Embassy, on Reservoir Road.

5

They were met at the main entrance by Jacques Lucet, a tall, thin man with an extraordinarily long nose and weak chin. He reminded Zalva of a French comedic actor who had starred in a couple of movies during the nineties. He wore a double-breasted, dark blue suit with pin stripes, a silk tie—pink with white polka-dots—and combed his wavy blonde hair straight back.

Jacques spoke fluent English and presented himself as a personnel liaison responsible for assisting embassy staff members cope with life in the U.S. After a brief greeting, he escorted them to a small ante-chamber containing a Louis XV couch and three matching side chairs arranged around a coffee table of the same period.

A china coffee urn and cups, all bearing the French Embassy logo, and a platter of French pastries adorned the coffee table. Zalva accepted a cup of coffee, gave the pastries a wistful look, regretted eating the doughnuts earlier, and sat on the small couch indicated by Jacques. Archie eased down beside her, a cup of coffee in one hand and a plate of pastries in the other.

Seeing they were comfortable, Jacques spoke crisply. "I was not told precisely why you wished to speak to Ms. Demornay. Would you please explain the purpose of your visit?"

Zalva had intended to let Archie do the talking, but a quick glance revealed his mouth was full of pastry. "Have you heard about Senator Pearson's death last night?" she asked.

Jacques put both hands to his cheeks in surprise. "*Mon Dieu!* You suspect Lezette Demornay was the woman who fled the hotel room?"

"More than just a suspicion. She's on video-tape, we've got eye witnesses, and she left fingerprints."

"I see," said Jacques. His face took on a puzzled expression. "But the press reported his death natural . . . heart failure . . . *non?*"

"Far as we know, but we still need a written statement from her—for the record, you know," replied Zalva.

Jacques sat back with an arm draped over the back of his chair and exhaled before speaking. "Confidentially, Ms. Demornay has been an embarrassment to the embassy since her arrival. I requested she be withdrawn—obviously without success. Perhaps this episode will convince my superiors."

Clearly, Jacques didn't approve of Lezette, but he still hadn't produced her. Zalva sneaked another glance at Archie, noted his bulging cheeks, and continued. "Mr. Lucet, are you going to allow us to interview Ms. Demornay?"

Lucet gave her the typical European palms-up gesture with shoulders hunched. "Unfortunately, Ms. Demornay neglected to appear or report in this morning—a frequent occurrence in recent weeks."

"Could you tell us where she lives? Maybe she just overslept, or is simply afraid to come in."

Jacques pulled a Palm Pilot from his inside coat pocket and punched a few keys. "She lives in quarters provided by the embassy, at 4150 Massachusetts Avenue. I believe it's called the Regal Arms, Apartment 703."

"Does Lezette have a roommate or perhaps a friend who might know how we could reach her?"

Jacques took another peek at his computer. "Yes, her roommate is also on the embassy staff."

"Would you allow us to interview her while we're here?"

"Of course." He stretched his arm out for the phone on the coffee table between them, pushed a couple of buttons, and spoke tersely in French. "Michelle will be here momentarily." He gestured toward the refreshments. "Would you care for more coffee?"

Zalva reached for the coffee urn but Jacques waved her off. He stretched out an arm, lifted the coffee urn, and refreshed her cup. Archie helped himself to another pastry while Jacques refilled his cup. Jacques lifted his eyebrows slightly at Archie's lack of restraint with the pastries, noticed Zalva's grin, and matched it with his own.

A young, redheaded woman in her late twenties, entered with a look of apprehension on her face. She was dressed in a light green suit, wore her hair in the style Audrey Hepburn made famous in her heyday, and had a wistful air about her.

Jacques spoke a short phrase to her in French, and her look of apprehension was replaced by one of relief. Jacques introduced her as Michelle Gambon and she sat in a chair next to Jacques, across the coffee table from Zalva and Archie, with her knees together and her hands clasped over them. "What do you wish to know?"

"Michelle, I understand you share an apartment with Lezette Demornay. Is that correct?"

"Oui."

"When did you last see Lezette?"

"Yesterday evening, a little before seven."

"Where?"

"At our apartment."

"Did she leave at that time, or did you leave first?"

"She left first."

"Do you know who she went out with?"

"Non."

"Did she say anything about her plans for the evening?"

"She mentioned a party."

"Did you hear her come in last night?"

"Non. I knocked on her door this morning, to wake her, but she wasn't in."

"How do you know that for certain?"

"I opened the door to wake her, and saw the bed covers had not been disturbed."

"Do you have any idea where she might be?"

"Non."

"You mean the two of you live together and you don't even know the names of her friends?"

"Lezette spent little time in the apartment. Even when she did, she kept to herself. I barely knew her."

"Well, she's not a suspect or anything. We simply need her statement since she was with Senator Pearson when he died. If you see her, will you tell her that? Tell her it's a formality, and nothing more?"

"Oui, mais certainment."

Jacques dismissed Michelle, apologized for Lezette's absence, and promised to notify them when Lezette returned to the embassy. They thanked him for his cooperation, and departed.

• • •

As Archie drove off the embassy grounds, he darted a sidelong glance at Zalva. "It must've shaken that little French girl up good when old Pearson bucked off. She's probably hiding with a friend somewhere, trying to figure out what to do."

"Let's get on over to her apartment anyway. Maybe she decided to come home after Michelle left for work."

Archie grunted an okay, then lapsed into his customary silence while driving, lost in those mysterious thoughts that turned him into a zombie when behind the wheel. Zalva's own thoughts turned to Lezette and the aged Senator Pearson together in bed.

"Archie, I just can't bring myself to believe Lezette went to that hotel room with Pearson out of lust for his body—not with him more than sixty years old, pot-bellied, and with heart problems."

"Hmpf. Women go to bed with older men for all kinds of reasons— money, power, prestige." He gave her a wide grin. "Why do you think so many old farts keep working past sixty-five?"

She mulled the matter over in her mind for a couple of minutes. "I know there are women who use older men as stepping stones, but how could Pearson help her career in any way? Wasn't he about to be voted out of office and prosecuted for fraud? It just doesn't smell right."

"He might've paid her for sex. Or maybe she wanted to brag about screwing a U.S. Senator. Regardless, the old fool took on more woman than he could handle and his ticker gave out under the strain. You'll see, when the autopsy report is in and we get the lab report on those pills and tablets."

"How long will that be?"

"For a U.S. Senator? Forty-eight hours, max."

They passed the rest of the time to Lezette's place knocking the types of articles she found that morning in the *Probe*. Eventually, they arrived at the apartment building and, as expected, found she wasn't in, or least not answering the door.

Archie wrote a note asking Lezette to call them when she came and wedged it between the door and door frame. Then they started back to the station, with Archie hunched over the steering wheel, deep in thought.

Suddenly, he broke the silence with a grunt. "Hmpf. I'll bet after that little French girl left the hotel, she drove to the airport and grabbed the first plane back to Paris."

"Hey! Whose Audi was she driving at the hotel?"

Archie darted a glance in her direction. "Yeah . . . that's a good question. Call that *Lucy* guy at the embassy and ask him about it."

Unfortunately, Jacques said she didn't have a vehicle, nor did Michelle. They rode to work in an embassy van driven by a staff chauffeur.

Back at the station, they reported to Captain Thurman, who told them to cool it until the autopsy and lab reports came in. In his opinion Pearson's death was from natural causes, which he was sure the reports would verify. No point in wasting time chasing the French girl when there were so many other things to do. Besides, he felt she'd show up on her own, eventually, since they'd explained the situation to the embassy.

6

O'Brien worked feverishly all morning putting together a scandal article, sans the allegation of murder, about Pearson croaking in the hotel room. Not the article he hoped to write, but he doubted Jason could complete his analysis of the tablet in time for Friday's issue of the *Probe*. Without Jason's confirmation of poison, his article would only mirror those in the daily papers, but with his exclusive photographs as a bonus.

After lunch, he sat with his feet propped up on his desk, reviewing the stack of photos he'd taken at the hotel, hashing out a selection for the front page. The phone on his desk rang, interrupting his contemplation. He stretched out an arm and picked up the phone.

"O'Brien here."

"Hey, man."

It was Jason, but the background noise sounded like street traffic. "Where are you?"

"I stepped outside the lab to call you—didn't want to take the chance I'd be overheard."

"You analyzed my tablet yet?"

"Just finished."

"How did you do it so quickly?"

"Well, if I wanted to kill a man with a heart condition and make it look like an accident or a simple heart attack, I'd poison him with something a heart patient wasn't supposed to take. So, I made a list of medications that would cause adverse reactions if combined with nitrates and started testing for them."

"But wouldn't that still take a lot of time?"

"Look, man. We've got the best equipment and computer software in the world, except for that disease control center in Atlanta."

"Well, let's have it."

"It's saldenafel."

"Saldenafel? What's that?"

"Ever heard of Maxual?"

"Yeah, that's the pill some guys take when they can't get it up, right?"

"You got it. Saldenafel is the active ingredient in Maxual. It's sold in fifty and one-hundred milligram tablets."

"I had expected cyanide."

"The saldenafel might as well have been cyanide, because that's what did him in. It interacted with his heart medication and, combined with the physical stress of screwing the blonde, made him a tad too *rigid.*"

"So, somebody did murder him, because if he wanted to take Maxual, he'd just take the straight pills right out of the bottle."

"That's logical."

"How much saldenafel was in the tablet?"

"Approximately 200 milligrams."

"How many Maxual tablets would that be?"

"Two of the big boys."

"How do you know it was two?"

"Because the fifty and one-hundred milligram tablets are the same size. The fifty milligram tablets just have more filler material. Since the tablet contained about two hundred milligrams of saldenafel, it had to be two of the big boys."

"How do you remake a tablet like that, after it's been crushed?"

"Hmm . . . I guess you'd make a mold . . . out of clay . . . or maybe some sort of poly-resin stuff. Something soft enough to take an impression of a real tablet, then harden to hold the shape after the real tablet is removed."

"How could they make the crushed powder bind together?"

"Probably used water mixed with corn starch. Look, I gotta get back in the lab. Check you out at the pub tonight, okay?"

"Yeah, sure. And thanks for the help. I owe you one."

O'Brien dropped the receiver back onto its hook, leaned back in his chair with his hands clasped behind his head, and savored the moment. Pearson had been murdered and no other paper knew it. What a scoop! It was big. Maybe even big enough to overcome the stigma from his New York disaster.

An exclusive story on the murder of a U.S. senator by poisoning him with a sex drug. And he had real, unaltered photos, too. They'd sell at least a million copies of this weekend's issue for sure. He might even get a decent bonus. With that inspiration, he shot out of his chair and headed for Slick's office.

Slick was editor-in-chief for the *Probe* and one of the slimiest character he'd ever known. He would print anything if it would sell papers; exactly the trait required to be an editor of a tabloid like the *Probe*.

He found Slick sitting with his back to his desk, feet propped on the window sill, studying one of his weekly tipoff sheets. Hooked on sports betting, Slick subscribed to several such sheets published by shady characters supposedly in the know. No one at the *Probe* knew how much Slick won or lost each week, but on Monday morning, you could certainly tell which way the action had gone.

O'Brien stepped through the open doorway and cleared his throat to announce his presence.

Slick pushed off the window sill with his feet, spun his chair around to face O'Brien, and tossed the tipoff sheet on his desk. A dozen years older than O'Brien, he was a thin man of medium height and he combed his long, black hair straight back and plastered it down with mousse. His pencil-thin eyebrows and mustache looked like they'd been drawn on his narrow face with a brush. Swap his white shirt and red tie for a black shirt and a white tie, and with his black suit and pale complexion, he'd be a dead ringer for one of the pool hall denizens O'Brien had seen in reruns of the B-movies of the 40s.

Slick scrutinized O'Brien for a moment before speaking. "What's up?

"I've got a new story for the front page."

"Kinda late to be changing isn't it?"

"But it's real."

Slick's thin lips twisted into a cynical smile. "*Real* is for the newspapers and TV. Our readers don't want *real*. They like the stuff we give them and the weirder it is, the more they eat it up."

"Wait until you hear the details. It's hot."

Slick waved his hand at a chair for O'Brien to take a seat, folded his arms, and twisted his mouth from one side to the other. "Okay, shoot."

"You heard about Senator Pearson?"

"Yeah, they found him dead in a hotel room last night."

"Yep. And I'm the one who found him."

"You? The TV news said the hotel clerk found him."

O'Brien related the events of the previous night, but omitted the part about removing evidence from the scene and Jason's subsequent report. He tossed Slick a large envelope containing his photos.

Slick took the envelope, shook the photos onto his desk, and studied them, running his index finger along each eyebrow in turn. Abruptly, he looked up at O'Brien and tossed the photos back to him.

"So, we've got photos and the newspapers don't. Big deal! They've already reported he croaked from a heart attack while banging the young broad."

"Right. But what we know and the rest of the media doesn't, is that Pearson was murdered."

Slick regarded O'Brien with eyes that had become dark slits. "Says who?"

"Says I."

"And how exactly, does '*I*' know that?"

O'Brien told Slick about finding the suspiciously crude NazinX tablets and taking one from the hotel.

Slick shot out of his chair as if he'd been slapped. "What? You removed evidence from the scene of a murder? Don't you know that's a felony?"

"Chill out, man. Besides us, nobody knows about it but Jason."

"Jason? Who in hell is Jason?"

"A friend of mine—a chemist."

Slick made a face that would've stopped a nuclear clock and slouched back into his chair with arms folded. O'Brien told him about giving the tablet to Jason and the results of Jason's analysis.

Slick's jaw dropped so far it almost bounced off his desk. "Well, I'll be damned."

"And we've got the exclusive story, if we can get it in this week's issue, because the cops won't have the autopsy and lab reports until sometime next week at the earliest. And nobody's ever going to know I took the tablet. Jason won't tell a soul, for fear of losing his job. And you and I sure as hell won't tell anybody."

"Oh, yeah? The cops will see your article and when they get their lab reports, they'll know you took the tablet from the hotel room."

"Not necessarily. They'll probably think somebody from the medical examiner's office leaked it to me, since we don't have laboratory facilities. They'll question me about it though."

"And you'll tell them what?"

"I'll tell them I spotted the tablet as a fake and made up the part about Maxual just to add pizzazz to the scandal part of the story."

Slick twisted his mouth back and forth and nodded his head several times. "They just might buy it. Anybody with a lick of sense knows we make things up all the time."

Slick leaned over his desk, and wagged a finger in O'Brien's face. "But if they ever find out you removed evidence from the scene, you're on your own and your ass will wind up rotting in jail."

"I'll take that chance."

Slick stood and gazed over O'Brien's head with a far-away look in his eyes. "We need a snappy headline—big as this." He spread his hands a yard apart, exaggerating the size of headline he wanted. "Murder by Maxual! Pearson Poisoned! Something like that, big print, at least half the front page. I want people to notice it from fifty feet away." He cut his eyes back to O'Brien. "Got it?"

O'Brien rose to leave. "Got it."

Slick leaned back in his chair in with a smug grin on his face and chuckled softly.

"You find Pearson's death amusing?" asked O'Brien.

"No, but I'll bet the Democratic Party big-wigs danced in the street when they heard about it."

"Why?"

"The charges of bid rigging and bribery against Pearson surfaced right after his primary. Once that came out, the prostitutes and bimbos opened up on him. He nose-dived in the polls, and it looked like the voters were going to dump him for a novice Republican in November. The party tried to get him to resign, but he wouldn't give in—out of spite I suppose."

"But it's too late to qualify another candidate, so won't they lose the seat anyway?" asked O'Brien.

"Hell no! Remember in 2002, a New Jersey senator resigned just five weeks before Election Day. The New Jersey Supreme Court ruled that having a choice on the ballot overrode the qualifying deadline and allowed the Democrats to make a last-minute replacement on the ballot. The Republicans appealed the matter to the U.S. Supreme Court which refused to hear the case. The Democrats chose a well-liked former senator who walked away with the election."

"Yeah . . . I do remember that. Now, they'll slip somebody else in on the ballot for Pearson, and since the state's dominated by Democrats, they'll keep the seat."

"Exactly!" agreed Slick. "And this break may allow them to hold on to control of the Senate."

"You know, that sounds like a possible motive for murder."

"Absolutely!"

"I'll make sure the benefit to the party is in the article."

"Don't point a finger though. Just dance around the edges of it. Better to give the readers a little info and let them jump to conclusions on their own."

"How about his wife? Since he ran around on her, she had a motive too."

"Same thing. Don't point at her either. Just lay out the facts."

"How much time I got?"

"No later than six. Can you make it?"

"No problem." With that, O'Brien left Slick's office and hurried back to his desk to rewrite the article.

Monday

7

Zalva and Archie worked a shooting late Sunday night, so she slept in on Monday morning and didn't make it to the precinct station until ten. She grabbed a cup of coffee and strolled to the small office she shared with Archie, where he sat with his feet propped up on his desk, reading a newspaper.

"Morning Arch."

Archie made a sound she took to be a greeting, without looking up.

"How long you been here?"

"About ten minutes."

Zalva eased into her chair, craned her neck to read the name on the back side of the newspaper, and saw it was the latest issue of the *Probe*. "Why you reading that rag? Sleaze-ball write anything about Pearson?"

Archie refolded the tabloid and tossed it across the two desks to Zalva. "Look at the front page."

Zalva snatched the paper out of the air, unfolded it, and gasped at the bold headlines on the front page. "Pearson Poisoned! " The subheading under that, half as big as the headline, stated, "Senator Pearson Murdered!" A large photo of Pearson's nude body stretched across the hotel bed and a close-up photo of Pearson's personal items atop the night stand accompanied the article written by Will O'Brien. A superimposed arrow pointed to the allergy tablet.

According to O'Brien, the NazinX tablet was a fake and contained Maxual instead of allergy medicine. He offered no proof of any kind, other than alleging the tablet was a crude, homemade imitation of a real NazinX tablet, although he hinted at a reliable source. O'Brien speculated the sex stimulant, heart medication, and stress of sexual activity had triggered a stroke or heart failure.

Toward the end of the article, O'Brien pointed out Pearson's troubles with the law and women, and how he was trailing in the polls and likely to lose his office in the coming election. He discussed how convenient Pearson's death was for the party, since it would now be able to appoint a substitute candidate who, even at this late date, would most certainly win the upcoming election—possibly enabling the party to hold their slim, one-seat majority.

The next paragraph delved into Pearson's philandering and how disappointing that must have been to his wife. And, with the probable loss of his office and the impending legal action against him, her status in life had been about to drop like a dot.com stock. His legal defense would surely have cost them most of their net worth, without changing the outcome. Certainly, his untimely death had saved her from being a pauper and a social outcast.

She finished the article and looked up at Archie. "Wow! This guy's a loon."

"Hmpf. He fabricated the sex stimulant angle to sell papers—and the wilder the story, the more papers they'll sell."

Zalva tossed the paper back to Archie, who stuffed it into the trash can beneath his desk. "But he claims the senator was murdered and as good as pointed the finger at the Democratic Party and Pearson's wife."

Archie chuckled. "Yep. He stuck his neck right out there, and the Democrats will take his head for sure."

Zalva imagined O'Brien on his knees, with his head on a chopping block, and a burly, bare-chested executioner standing over him with one of those medieval-style, curved-blade axes raised high in the air.

The phone on Archie's desk rang, bringing her back to reality.

Archie answered it, listened for a second, and hung up. He swung his feet to the floor, stood up and straightened his tie. "The boss beckons."

At the Captain's door, Archie knocked twice and entered after a gruff invitation from within, with Zalva trailing him.

Captain William Harvey Thurman, six-four and weighing close to three hundred pounds, stood behind his desk with hands in his pants pockets, gazing out the window. African-American and nearing retirement, he'd served nearly thirty years with the D.C. Police Department. Per Archie, Thurman had a quick temper in his early years, which had cost him promotions several times. Eventually, he learned to control his temper, and now kept his emotions in check, smoldering inside.

Thurman had been a professional boxer in his younger days and his facial features showed it. His eyes were set deep beneath a prominent brow, his naturally broad nose looked as though it had been broken at least once, and his ears were slightly caulliflowered. Dozens of boxing posters and photographs decorated the walls of his office. Zalva's gaze roamed the walls and locked on a poster of Thurman in his early twenties, dressed only in boxing trunks and gloves. He'd been an awesome specimen in those days, and still intimidated the hell out of her.

Captain Thurman turned, nodded for them to sit down, and took his seat at the desk. A four-inch-high stack of official-looking reports squatted in the center of his desk like a solitary mesa in a vast plain. Obviously, he didn't do paperwork.

He leaned back in his chair and folded his arms. Ignoring her, he looked straight at Archie and spoke in that deep, growling voice that made her think he'd explode any second.

"We got the autopsy on Senator Pearson this morning, along with the lab report on his medications. Seems he died of cardiac arrest brought on by a combination of saldenafel, nitro-glycerin, and exertion from sexual activity."

"What's saldenafel?" asked Zalva.

Thurman shot her a menacing glance and continued speaking to Archie. "It's a drug for old men who have trouble getting it up or keeping it up long enough for a climax. It's marketed as Maxual."

"You're shitting me!" blurted both Zalva and Archie in unison.

"I'm not shitting anybody, and nobody's shitting me, either. That green tablet Ginny found in his coat pocket was Maxual."

"Surely, he knew that might kill him," said Zalva.

"Hmpf. With a pretty young girl like that, he probably figured it was worth the risk," added Archie.

"He didn't know he was taking Maxual," growled Thurman.

"Didn't know? But why did he have one in his jacket pocket?" asked Zalva.

"A decoy," replied Thurman. "Somebody tried to be real slick with us. Remember the NazinX tablet and the empty blister tab found on the hotel night stand?"

Archie nodded with Zalva, and Thurman continued.

"The NazinX tablet was a fake. It was Maxual disguised to look like NazinX, so the one he took probably was, too. The lab concluded that somebody crushed Maxual tablets and molded them into the shape of NazinX tablets.

They slit the backing on the blister tabs, took the real NazinX tablets out, put the fake ones in the bubbles, and glued the paper back in place. We're figuring Pearson didn't notice the slit on the paper backing because he pushed the tablet out from the other side.

"The NazinX tablets are good for eight hours at a time, so Pearson probably took two with him when he left home or his office that morning. The killer either figured we'd never check the NazinX tablets or figured Pearson would take both of them during the course of the day, thereby eliminating the evidence. The single Maxual tablet wrapped in aluminum foil and the wadded piece of foil found in Pearson's outside coat pocket were meant to trick us into believing he took the stuff on his own. I believe Pearson must've crossed the perp up, skipped taking a NazinX tablet that morning, but remembered to take one before going to the hotel—probably to clear his sinuses so he wouldn't have trouble getting his breath while humping the French girl."

"Leaving us with evidence of a murder," added Zalva.

Thurman nodded. "It had to be somebody close to him—maybe his wife, or one of his playmates, like the French girl, or maybe someone on his staff with access to his medicine and coat."

"Someone who knew he screwed around," said Zalva.

"And someone who knew he'd never look in the outside pocket of his coat," said Archie.

"Right," said Thurman. "They were counting on it."

"Hmpf. You haven't seen this week's issue of the *National Probe*, have you?" asked Archie.

Thurman's eyes almost bulged out of his head and Zalva fully expected lightning bolts to shoot out of both eyes and skewer Archie in his chair. "What in the hell do you think?"

Wisely ignoring Thurman's question, Archie glanced at Zalva, winked, and motioned toward their office with a jerk of his head. She jumped up, ran back to their cubicle, and returned with the trashed copy of the tabloid, which she straightened out and handed to Thurman.

Thurman laid the paper on his desk, pushed his chair back so that his arms were fully extended, tilted his head back, and unfolded the paper with a frown of disgust—as if he expected to find a dead fish. His frown became a sneer when he took in the headlines. He leaned forward and, as he read the article, his eyes narrowed, his brow furrowed, and the paper crinkled as his fists clenched. The corners of his mouth twitched and he hitched each shoulder in turn, fighting for control.

Thurman finished the article and tossed the paper back to Zalva. He then kneaded the back of his neck with a huge paw and twisted his neck to release his tension. After his struggle for self-control, he folded his hands on the desk in front of him and broke the silence.

"Forget O'Brien's slur on the Democratic Party. Most times, when poison is involved, it's the spouse, so we're starting with her. I had a discussion with the D.A., this morning, after I read these reports. On his advice, I called Mrs. Pearson and she agreed to be interviewed at two this afternoon, here at the station."

Thurman rose from his chair and the two of them stood up with him. He picked up two bound reports from his desk and handed them to Archie.

"These are extra copies of the autopsy and lab reports. You two do a quick study on these and draw up the questions for her interview."

"How about a search warrant for her house?" asked Zalva.

"Being done right now. The house will be searched while you two are interviewing Mrs. Pearson. Drag it out as long as you can. Maybe the search team will find something and we can arrest Mrs. Pearson while she's at the station."

Zalva and Archie turned and were almost through the doorway when Thurman called out to them. "And after you arrest Pearson's wife, find that sneaky bastard O'Brien and get the name of the asshole at the crime lab who leaked information to him, got it?"

They both mumbled acknowledgments of his order and returned to their cubicle to prepare for the interview.

8

At precisely two o'clock, the door to the interrogation room opened and Captain Thurman escorted Mrs. Pearson, nearly sixty and still attractive, into the room. Tall and thin, she wore a black dress that buttoned down the front. Her light brown hair, obviously dyed, was pulled into a chignon, and she carried herself with an air of aloof dignity.

Zalva had expected Mrs. Pearson to show up with an attorney, and craned her neck to look around her through the open doorway. To her astonishment, Mrs. Pearson came alone. On second thought, maybe the lack of an attorney shouldn't be a surprise. If Mrs. Pearson had murdered her husband, she'd want to appear to them as a poor, unsuspecting widow. Showing up with an attorney might belie that.

They rose and Captain Thurman introduced them. "Mrs. Pearson, this is Detective Sargent Wilson and Detective Martinez. They investigated the scene at the hotel where your husband was found." With that, Thurman excused himself and exited the room.

"Please have a seat," said Zalva.

Mrs. Pearson frowned disdainfully at the battered straight chair for a moment, before she eased down on it as if she expected it to collapse and dump her on the floor. Seated at last, her gaze darted from Zalva to Archie, and back to Zalva again. "What . . . what exactly, is this interview about?"

Archie responded. "We'd like to ask you some questions about your husband's death."

"Why ask me about his death? Didn't he die of heart failure while having sex, like the *Post* reported?"

Without answering, Archie pulled a tape recorder from a drawer in front of him, placed it in the middle of the table, and turned it on.

Mrs. Pearson's eyes widened at the sight of the recorder. "Oh, my goodness. Are you going to record everything I say?"

"It's routine," answered Archie. "Anytime we interview someone at the station, we tape the interview. It's for your protection as well as ours."

Mrs. Pearson's lips twitched at the corners and her eyelids fluttered. "Is there something wrong? Am I under suspicion? Didn't my husband die of cardiac arrest?"

Zalva thought it best to speak a half-truth to allay her suspicions. "Mrs. Pearson, as you might expect when a high profile person like your husband dies under unusual circumstances, the media sometimes go into a feeding frenzy. In fact, one of the tabloids has suggested the senator was murdered because he wouldn't resign and save his seat for the party."

Mrs. Pearson placed both hands on her cheeks. "Murdered? Someone . . . someone . . . claims my husband was murdered?"

"Yes, the *National Probe*. You haven't heard about it?"

"No. I don't read trashy tabloids and I haven't watched TV news since my husband's troubles began. I . . . I . . . couldn't take the stress."

"Well, as a result of the *Probe*'s allegation, Democratic Party officials are demanding an investigation in order to clear the party, and Republican Party officials are demanding one hoping the Democrats *are* implicated. With both parties clamoring for an investigation, we can't sit on our hands, can we?"

Mrs. Pearson fumbled with the buttons on her dress, raised her eyes, and looked into Zalva's. "How can the tabloid get away with printing such lies?"

"Hmpf! Freedom of the press," answered Archie.

"You understand why we have to do this?" asked Zalva.

"I suppose," muttered Mrs. Pearson.

Archie began. "Mrs. Pearson, you have the right to remain silent. You have the right to have an attorney present during this interview. If you can not afford an attorney, the state will appoint one for you. If you choose to answer our questions, anything you say can be used against you in a court of law. Do you understand what I've said?"

Mrs. Pearson's face paled and she nodded.

"Please answer yes or no. Do you understand what I've said?"

"Yes, I understand what you said. But I don't understand why you feel the need to advise me of my rights. Certainly, you don't think I murdered my husband, do you?"

Archie ignored her question and pressed on. "Do you agree to proceed without an attorney?"

Mrs. Pearson shrugged her shoulders in resignation. "I suppose so."

They began with questions about her husband's politics and possible enemies who may have wanted him dead. They asked about trusted members of his staff and friends who might have had access to his office or personal effects and would have had an opportunity to switch the NazinX tablets for fake ones. She knew little about his friends or staff members and offered up no potential suspects.

"Mrs. Pearson, did the senator have any life insurance?" asked Zalva.

Mrs. Pearson gave her a leaden stare for a few seconds before responding. "Of course. Doesn't everyone?"

"What's the face value?" asked Zalva.

"You mean how much will it pay?"

"Yes."

"If I'm not mistaken, I believe it's two million."

Certainly enough to kill someone over, thought Zalva. "Are you the beneficiary?"

"Yes. We have no children."

"How long has the policy been in force?" asked Archie.

"I don't remember exactly when we bought it...possibly when he was elected to his first term as a state senator...more than twenty years ago."

"What's the name of the insurance company?" asked Archie.

"I believe it's Northern Liberty Life—or something similar."

"Where is the policy?" asked Zalva.

"In our safety deposit box at the bank—with our other important papers, I suppose."

"Have you contacted the insurance company regarding your husband's death?" asked Archie.

"No, I . . . I haven't tended to anything like that yet."

"Can you give us an estimate of your husband's estate, combined with your net assets?" asked Zalva.

"Oh, dear, let me see. There's our home in Michigan—might be worth a hundred thousand net of the mortgage . . . around ten thousand in cash . . . nearly fifty thousand in stocks . . . and that's about it."

Zalva was shocked. With all the fuss in the newspapers and TV about Pearson's graft and corruption, she was expecting their net worth to be several million.

Mrs. Pearson read her face and added, "We've always lived on the edge of our means and my husband had invested heavily in the energy and communications companies that crashed."

Ironic, thought Zalva. Pearson's ill-gotten wealth from fraud and corruption had been invested in stocks that crashed due to fraud and corruption. Maybe there was a higher justice than the courts after all. She then realized Mrs. Pearson had omitted the house on Massachusetts Avenue.

"How about your current home here in D.C.?" she asked.

"Oh, my. We couldn't afford to own that. We're only leasing it."

"Mrs. Pearson, did you realize your husband wasn't going to be re-elected?" asked Archie, switching the angle of attack.

"Of course. I'm not an idiot, you know."

"What were your plans for after the election?"

"My husband lived in a state of denial. He wouldn't admit defeat—wouldn't even discuss the possibility with me."

"Hmpf," grunted Archie. "Don't expect us to believe you two didn't even talk about what you were going to do after the election."

"You obviously didn't know my husband, Detective Wilson. If he said he didn't want to discuss something, he meant it."

"How about his indictment and the upcoming trial? He wouldn't discuss that either?" pressed Archie.

"Absolutely not!"

"Nothing at all? He didn't even try to convince you of his innocence?"

"Of course he denied the charges, but that's as far as he would go with it."

"Weren't you worried about the future?" asked Zalva.

Mrs. Pearson's shoulders slumped at Zalva's question. "Yes, I feared he would be convicted." She dropped her eyes and fiddled with the buttons on her dress again. "And I was worried about what would become of me if that happened."

"How did he plan to pay for his legal defense?" asked Zalva. "From what you've told us, your cash and investments wouldn't make a dent in the legal fees on a high-profile case like his."

"He planned to cash in his life insurance policy," she replied in a voice barely above a whisper.

Her words hung in the air, vibrating in Zalva's head like the sound of a large, Chinese gong. Mrs. Pearson had revealed her motive, just as surely as gravity causes things to fall to earth. She'd killed Pearson to keep him from squandering the cash value on a hopeless effort to stay out of jail. And now the motive was documented on the interview tape. Still, for the moment, they had no evidence to use against her, short of a confession.

They started over again, repeated questions, asked the same questions in different ways, dwelled on details, and dragged the session out for another thirty minutes, in an effort to give the search team time to find evidence. Zalva wished Ginny would report in, as they had stretched the session out as long as possible without making a direct accusation, which they didn't want to do without concrete evidence.

Mrs. Pearson sat with her hands folded on her lap and her head lowered, gazing absently at the table top. Evidence or not, Zalva sensed the time had come to put a little pressure on her. "Mrs. Pearson, were you aware your husband was seeing other women, that is, before it became public knowledge?"

Mrs. Pearson jumped as if startled from a daydream and turned her eyes toward Zalva. "Of course I knew. I couldn't do anything about it though, so I begged him to be discreet."

"Why didn't you divorce him?" asked Archie.

"You must understand that I still loved him. He was my life, you know. We met and were married while attending college. I devoted my life to helping him with his political career." She paused for a moment, wiped a tear from her cheek, and continued. "And he still loved me, too."

"How can you say he still loved you, when he ran around like that, and didn't care if you knew it?" asked Zalva.

"Oh, he loved me . . . and if he was still alive, he'd tell you that."

"Then why did he run around on you?" asked Archie.

She lowered her eyes. "It was my fault. I had a hysterectomy when I was fifty-five . . . and lost all ability to enjoy sex after that."

Zalva forced sympathy for the woman aside, cleared her throat, and plowed on. "I know this is unpleasant, but we have to tie up all the loose ends. Please explain what you mean by that."

Mrs. Pearson breathed deeply and her gaze met Zalva's. "The operation resulted in a lot of nerve damage. I became unable to enjoy intercourse . . . because . . . I had no sensitivity. We tried everything . . . drugs . . . exercise . . . all the different positions . . . but nothing worked." She sighed and lowered her head. "Once he realized I felt nothing, he couldn't enjoy it either. Eventually he quit trying and began seeing other women."

"Did your husband need a sex stimulant in order to perform?" asked Zalva.

Mrs. Pearson's back stiffened. "I . . . I . . . really don't know. But . . . it . . . it wouldn't surprise me if he did. He liked younger women—girls, actually. Perhaps . . . perhaps . . . he resorted to a sex stimulant in an effort to keep up."

Zalva pushed on. "Did you ever see anything like Maxual or one of the other new pills in his possession, or lying around on his dresser?"

"I . . . no . . . no, but that . . . that—"

"Have *you* ever had any Maxual in your possession?" asked Zalva.

Mrs. Pearson's face flushed. "Well . . . I . . . I . . ."

"Come on, spit it out!" demanded Archie.

She took a deep breath and let it out slowly, composing herself before responding. "As you may have heard, a recent report stated Maxual had been effective for some women with my problem. A friend of mine told me she tried it and said it really helped her. I was desperate enough to try anything, so, about a month ago, I asked my doctor about it and he gave me a sample pack."

"Fifty or one-hundred milligram tablets?" asked Archie.

"One-hundred milligrams, I believe."

"How many did you take?" asked Zalva.

"I took one, but I got a migraine headache from it and didn't get a chance to see if it helped."

"How many were in the pack?" asked Archie.

"Twelve, I think."

"What did you do with the rest?" asked Archie.

"I was going to throw them in the trash last week, but when I looked in the drawer they were gone."

"Gone? What happened to them?" asked Zalva.

"I . . . I don't know. That's why it surprised me when you asked if my husband was taking a sex stimulant. Maybe he found them and decided to use them."

"Hmpf! And him with a heart condition?" sneered Archie.

"You didn't know my husband. He thought he was bullet-proof."

"Was your husband taking any allergy medication?" asked Zalva.

"Why, yes—regularly."

"What kind?"

"NazinX. I had Sylvia, our housekeeper, buy him some every week when she went grocery shopping."

A sharp rap on the door interrupted them. Zalva opened the door and found Ginny, who motioned for them to step into the hallway.

They advised Mrs. Pearson they were taking a ten minute break and left the room to join Ginny.

"Find anything?" asked Zalva.

"Take a gander," said Ginny. She opened a woman's expensive-looking leather handbag and held it out for Zalva and Archie to inspect.

"We found this on the top shelf in Mrs. Pearson's closet in the master bedroom, tucked away in the far corner behind some hat boxes."

Archie looked inside the purse first. "Hmpf. She really did kill the poor bastard."

Zalva looked into the purse and saw a small cereal bowl, two of the fake NazinX tablets, a pestle, and several pieces of hardened clay.

Ginny pointed at the fragments of clay. "That's the clay mold she used to shape the crushed Maxual into NazinX tablets."

"Why is it in pieces?" asked Zalva.

"Who knows? Maybe she dropped it or had to smash it to get the molded tablets out. Doesn't matter which. It's obvious it was a mold and that's good enough."

Ginny shifted the contents of the purse around, revealing a sample pack of Maxual underneath the other items. She reached into the purse with her latex-gloved hand, pulled the packet from underneath the bowl, and held it up for Zalva to inspect.

Zalva saw that the sample pack had twelve little bubbles for tablets. Ten were empty and two still contained green tablets.

She counted off the tablets known to have been used. "Two to make the fake NazinX tablet taken by the senator; two more to make the fake NazinX tablet found on the hotel night stand; one whole tablet found wrapped in aluminum foil in his coat pocket; one whole tablet taken by the senator's wife, if you could believe she actually took one; four used to make the two bogus NazinX tablets found in the bowl, and two still on the card. That's it, all twelve tablets are accounted for."

Ginny slipped the evidence back into her satchel and followed them into the interrogation room.

Sitting with her shoulders slumped and her head lowered, Mrs. Pearson jerked erect upon their return. A puzzled look crossed her face when she saw Ginny. The three of them took their seats around the table.

Archie began without introducing Ginny. "Mrs. Pearson, the autopsy report indicates the senator's heart attack resulted from a large dose of saldenafel, the active ingredient in Maxual, combined with his heart medicine and the physical exertion of sexual activity."

Mrs. Pearson arched an eyebrow at them. "So, he *was* taking Maxual."

"Yes ma'am," replied Archie. "According to the autopsy report, he'd taken more than two hundred milligrams of Maxual shortly before engaging in sex, but he didn't know it."

"Didn't know it?" Her gaze darted from Archie to Zalva to Ginny and back to Archie. "How could he not know it?"

"The saldenafel that killed him came from a fake NazinX tablet," answered Zalva.

The color drained from Mrs. Pearson's face. "He . . . he *was* murdered?"

"Absolutely," replied Archie.

"Who would do such a thing?"

Archie continued. "Apparently, someone close to the senator crushed up several Maxual tablets, molded them into the shape of NazinX tablets, and switched them with his real ones."

Mrs. Pearson gasped and moved her lips to respond, but no words came out. Finally, she overcame her shock enough to speak. "Surely you don't think I did that, do you?"

"Did you?" asked Archie, peering into the depths of Mrs. Pearson's eyes.

She shot out of her chair, no longer timid and frightened, but angry. "I most certainly did not!"

At a signal from Archie, Ginny produced the purse from her satchel. Zalva kept her eyes on Mrs. Pearson's face, expecting to see Pearson's eyes widen or her face pale, or maybe both. Instead, Mrs. Pearson's brow knitted in a puzzled expression.

"Do you recognize this purse?" he asked.

She stepped forward to get a closer look at the bag. "It looks like my Gucci leather handbag. Where did you find it?"

"On the top shelf in your closet, tucked in behind several hat boxes," replied Ginny.

Mrs. Pearson's mouth gaped wide open. "My closet! You . . . you've been in my house?"

"We had a search warrant," replied Ginny. She dumped the contents of the handbag on the table.

Mrs. Pearson sucked in her breath and clapped her hands to her cheeks when she saw the Maxual packet, the fragmented mold, and the bowl.

Archie tried to press on. "Mrs. Pearson, do you—"

"No!" shouted Mrs. Pearson. She grabbed her own shoulders, dug her fingernails into her flesh, and backed into the far corner. "I'm not saying another word without my attorney."

Archie rose from the table. "Mrs. Pearson, you're under arrest for the murder of your husband. You can call your lawyer after we book you."

9

O'Brien left his office in mid-afternoon, happier than he'd been in several years. It was only Monday, and last Friday's issue of the *Probe* had sold out, even though Slick had ordered a double quantity printed. Slick even awarded him a five grand bonus, which he wouldn't get until next payday, of course.

For the first time since New York, he felt like a legitimate investigative reporter again. As expected, there was fallout from his article, including an angry call from Walker Gibson, Executive Director of the Democratic Party, livid about O'Brien's insinuation the party might be behind Senator Pearson's death.

There were dozens of other irate callers, most of whom weren't as politely indignant as Gibson. In fact, there were some rather explicit suggestions about what O'Brien could do with his article and how he could entertain himself. There were even a few calls from right-wingers congratulating him on his insight. But the calls he wanted never came: calls from the *Post*, or the *Times*, or maybe a major TV network.

So he'd come to Finigan's early, to escape the crank calls and to celebrate—to prolong his feeling of elation. At the moment, he was engaged in his favorite pastime; playing the old-style pinball machine and swigging Guinness Stout. The flashing lights and dinging of the machine had a pleasing rhythm, almost hypnotic, as the steel ball caromed from the flippers onto the electronic sensors and back to the flippers again. He played on in a trance, oblivious to all around him.

With his mind dwelling on his scoop, he played the pinball machine on instinct, flipping the steel ball back up the playing surface of the pinball machine, where it struck the extra-points bumper and ricocheted back toward him at blinding speed. Another push of the right flipper button and the steel orb split the air with a loud smack against the underside of the glass on its way back up the board, interrupting his reverie. He leaned over and gave the glass a quick once-over, amazed it wasn't cracked.

O'Brien's fourth ball finally bit the dust, gobbled up by the gaping maw between the last pair of flippers at the bottom of the playing surface. He lifted his beer mug from the glass, turned away from the pinball machine, raised the mug to his lips, and checked out the action at the snooker table.

Jason had arrived earlier in the afternoon, to get the two hundred from O'Brien for his lab analysis, and was now in the early agony of losing it all in a rematch with the brunette who had robbed him the other night.

O'Brien watched the brunette pocket a tough shot on the five ball, sending the cue ball off three rails to a dead stop in excellent position for a cinch shot on the six ball. Jason hurled his cue chalk against the wall and cursed—a sign he needed both the six and seven balls to win, but the six ball was now easy pickings for the brunette.

While Jason fumbled in his pocket for cash, O'Brien took another sip of his beer and studied the brunette. Tonight, she wore a simple white T-shirt, tight jeans and, as the bouncing of her breasts attested, no bra. She wasn't hustling Jason by barely winning, but was knocking his dick in the dirt. Still, Jason played on out of stubborn pride.

Oh well, it was Jason's money. He turned, set his mug back on the glass, pulled the plunger back and let it rip, playing his fifth and last ball. He only needed 75,000 more points to break the house record—a cinch for him.

Suddenly, someone reached from behind him and hammered the corner of the pinball machine with the heel of his hand, bringing the clanging of the bells and bumpers to an abrupt halt. O'Brien's heart sank as the feared word *TILT* lit up across the scoreboard. He spun around in anger, ready to lash out. "Who in the hell—?"

He found himself staring up into the dour face of Detective Wilson. His surprise at seeing the detective shifted back to anger. "Why'd you do that, man? I had the record for sure."

"Hmpf. Just be grateful I didn't tilt your head."

The good-looking female detective stepped from behind Wilson. "It's almost six. Let's get over to the table in the corner where we can catch the news."

Wilson draped a massive arm around O'Brien's neck and pulled him along with them toward the front of the pub, as if they were shipmates on leave in Hong Kong. "You will have a sociable drink with us, won't you?" he growled into O'Brien's ear.

O'Brien twisted his neck so he could see Wilson's face from the corner of his eye and grinned. "I'm always ready for a sociable drink—but I gotta tell you, I don't put out on the first date."

Wilson jerked his arm from around O'Brien's neck, slapped his meaty paw down on O'Brien's back, and shoved hard.

The force sent O'Brien stumbling, and he collided with a haughty blonde in a dark business suit, who frantically clutched at him to keep from falling down. Her hand caught him by the belt, just under his overhanging paunch, and snatched his pants down to his crotch.

The move kept her from falling, but she stumbled a few steps backward, dragging O'Brien with her. Her knuckles against O'Brien's dick sent a tingle through his scrotum and brought a grin to his face. The astonished woman saw his grin, realized what it was about and, with face aghast, snatched her hand back as if she'd touched a hot light bulb. She gave him a fierce scowl, turned her back, and stalked off, cursing him over her shoulder.

Wilson clamped an iron grip on his shoulders with both hands and steered him toward the front of the pub.

Zalva led the way to a corner table and pulled out a chair for O'Brien. Wilson slammed him down on it like a weight lifter dropping a set of barbells after a clean-and-jerk, then eased his large frame onto the chair on his right. Zalva slipped into the chair on his left. In that position, they could all see the TV mounted at the ceiling in the nearest corner.

Sheena appeared at their table and O'Brien ordered a round for them on his tab. He stuck with his Guinness Stout and the two detectives ordered Killian's Red.

After Sheena left for their drinks, O'Brien looked from one detective to the other. "What's this all about?"

"Shut up and watch the news," snapped Wilson.

O'Brien directed his attention back to the TV, then sneaked a sidelong glance at Zalva. She had a beautiful profile, a bit of an up-turned nose, and full sensual lips. She turned as if sensing his eyes on her and her gaze met his for a brief second, before she looked back toward the TV. Aha, he thought, as his pulse quickened. She'd sneaked a peek at him and he'd caught her at it. He smiled to himself. Maybe he ought to pursue this a little further.

The first item on the evening news was the arrest of Senator Pearson's wife for the murder of her husband by poisoning him with Maxual. The news anchor reported that the police declined to speculate on her motive, but the network's talking heads had no such qualms, and proffered several motives: infidelity, insurance proceeds, and the potential squandering of their assets on his legal defense.

O'Brien gaped at Wilson and Zalva with wide eyes. "Can you beat that? She really did murder the old boy with Maxual—just like I said!"

Wilson laid his heavy right arm across O'Brien's back, squeezed his shoulder hard, and leaned over until his nose almost touched O'Brien's. "You see, that's the problem."

"What problem?"

"You knew about the bogus tablet before we got the lab results back. That's the problem."

Zalva pitched in. "How did you know that? You got a friend in the crime lab?"

O'Brien tried to look innocent and shocked at the same time. "Gosh, I don't even know anybody at the crime lab—medical examiner's office either."

"Well golly gee," mocked Zalva. "Just how *did* you know?"

"I didn't know. I saw that NazinX tablet on the night stand and noticed it looked different than the ones I had in my coat pocket, like maybe it was homemade. I figured somebody switched the homemade one for real ones to poison him. Since he was screwing a broad when he tapped out, I just made up the part about Maxual to sell more papers. You know we make up stuff all the time."

Wilson pounded his fist on the table, bouncing the beer mugs, spilling beer all over the table. "That's bullshit!"

"You wouldn't make up something like that. Your editor would be afraid of lawsuits," said Zalva.

"Law suits are no big deal to the *Probe*. We get sued all the time—even got a special fund for lawyers."

They pressured him for another half-hour, during which he popped for another round of Killian's Red for them. Finally, they realized he wasn't about to admit having an inside source for his information, knocked down the last of their brew, and departed.

He watched them exit before turning to look for the brunette, heartened by her long, lingering glances and playful smiles that hinted at more than a passing interest.

10

O'Brien sauntered by the bar to get a fresh mug of brew before going back to the snooker room to hit on the brunette.

Mary Kate set his beer on the counter before him and spread her arms out on the bar. "You in trouble with the cops?"

"How'd you know they were cops?"

"The big guy swaggered up to the bar with tight jaws, flashed his badge in my face, and asked if you were here."

"They're just pissed about my article on Pearson."

"You pulled a coup, didn't you?"

"Yeah. Just a lucky guess though."

"That what you told them?"

"Yeah."

She arched an eyebrow. "And they bought it?"

"What do you mean by that?"

She gave him a twisted smile, straightened up, and threw a bar towel over her shoulder. "Honey, I saw you and Jason at that table over there last week, and I know what he does for a living."

Her remark struck home. If Mary Kate had already put it together, it wouldn't take Wilson and Martinez long to figure it out either—if they found out about Jason. He rubbed the side of his nose with his finger and winked at her. "Our little secret, huh?"

She cocked her head to one side and studied him like a school teacher eyeing a student she suspected of firing a spit-ball. "You're gonna get your butt in a sling, screwing around with the law like that."

O'Brien took a heavy pull from his mug and wiped his mouth with the back of his hand. "I'm a risk-taker and a heart-breaker."

She shook her head, rolled her eyes, and sidled down the bar to serve other customers. He turned and meandered back to the snooker room.

Jason and the foxy brunette were still battling on the snooker table, so O'Brien settled for an empty stool where he could sit and watch the brunette play. He rested with his back against the wall and his elbows and beer on the narrow ledge that ran all around the snooker room at a convenient height.

Within seconds, the brunette was standing in front of him, leaning on her cue and sipping her drink, waiting for Jason to complete his turn at the table.

The move wasn't lost on O'Brien. She'd used a pool chair on the other side of the room all night. This was certainly looking promising. Jason missed a shot and the brunette turned to place her glass on the narrow ledge behind O'Brien.

"Well, hey there," she said. "I thought you left an hour ago."

"No, just went up front to watch the news with some friends."

"Friends, huh? Didn't look very chummy to me."

"Just a little misunderstanding."

"If you say so" She offered her hand. "I'm Carla."

He shook her hand. "Will O'Brien."

"The Will O'Brien who won a Pulitzer Prize?"

"Yeah, that's me. How'd you know about the Pulitzer?"

"We talked about you in my Ethics in Journalism class."

"Damn! I suppose you know all the sordid details then."

She patted his arm and smiled. "Don't worry about it. I think you were unfairly treated—and so does most of my class."

O'Brien shrugged his shoulders. "No matter. It's ancient history now."

Behind them, Jason pounded the butt of his cue on the wood floor to get her attention. "You gonna play or not?"

She winked at O'Brien and turned back to the snooker table. He watched her move around the table, studying the angles, making the shots. Her body was perfect, and the tight jeans and clinging T-shirt revealed her charms to full advantage.

In between turns at the snooker table, he learned she'd married while in college and dropped out to work while her husband finished law school. Things didn't go well for them and the marriage ended in a divorce. Twenty-eight and single again, she'd returned to George Washington University to complete work on a degree in journalism.

O'Brien passed an hour drinking beer and admiring Carla as she pranced around the snooker table. He figured Jason would be broke, in one more game, and he'd make his move on her after that.

He felt a soft touch on his arm and turned to find an attractive African-American woman of about thirty-five, dressed in a dark pant-suit. "Are you Will O'Brien," she asked.

"The one and only," he quipped.

"I must talk to you—it's very important."

"About what?"

"Can't we find a table? Please."

He decided to humor her, thinking it could lead to a new story. "Okay, okay. Follow me." He slid off the stool, took her by the hand and pulled her behind him as he worked his way back to the front room. They found a table, but instead of sitting across from him, she took the chair next to his.

"Can I buy you a drink?" he asked.

"Oh, no. I don't drink, smoke, or take drugs."

"Damn! That's a bit extreme, isn't it?"

She ignored his comment, leaned toward him, and spoke in a lowered voice. "My name is Shaunda Rogers. I work at the Washington office of PMC."

O'Brien's head snapped back as if she'd tossed cold water in his face. PMC stood for Pavilion Media Corporation, a media conglomerate that owned several big-city newspapers, including his former employer in New York, a television network, cable movie and news channels, publishing companies, magazines, recording companies, and no telling what else. Her connection with PMC made him a tad suspicious.

"Who told you I'd be here?"

"I called your office just before five and they told me you usually came here at night—the woman at the bar said you were in the back."

"Okay. So, what's this all about?"

"Like I said, I'm a secretary at PMC. About two weeks ago, I was in the library adjacent to Mr. Marchant's office, filing some reference books. I had to get on a ladder to put some books on a high shelf and I heard voices coming from the air conditioning vent in the ceiling."

"Coming from the adjacent office?"

"Yes." She wrung her hands as if they were numb with cold and sneaked a quick glance over each shoulder. "I thought surely I'd misunderstood what I heard until I read your article in the *National Probe*."

"Which article?"

"The one about Senator Pearson being murdered."

"The conversation you overheard had something to do with the murder of Pearson?"

She put a finger to her lips and shushed him. "Please, Mr. O'Brien. Speak lower. I'm afraid someone will overhear you."

Humoring her, he leaned toward her and lowered his voice. "I'm sorry. Now tell me what you heard."

She glanced over both shoulders again and whispered. "I heard them plotting to get rid of Senator Pearson so they could put someone else on the ballot."

"Who was in the conference room?"

"Donald Marchant, Walker Gibson, and another man."

"The Walker Gibson who's the executive director of the DNC?"

"Yes."

"You sure about that?"

"Absolutely. He's visited Mr. Marchant often."

"Who is this Marchant guy?"

"His title is senior vice president."

"Isn't PMC's headquarters in New York?"

"Yes."

"What's a senior vice president doing with an office in D.C.?"

"I've only been working there for about three months, but from what I've seen and heard, everything he does is political."

"Like a lobbyist?"

"Sort of . . . and like a strategist, too. And he gives away tons of money."

"To politicians?"

"Yes, and to all kinds of organizations."

"Like what?"

"Just all kinds of activist organizations, like the ACLU, Pro-Choice, Rainbow Coalition, anybody that's against restricting immigration, Amnesty International, several anti-gun groups, and of course, the Democratic Party. And lately, a couple of the groups opposing the president's appointments to the Supreme Court."

"And the third man?"

"I don't know. He spoke in a slight French accent though, and seemed to be in charge."

"Okay. We've got the scene set now, so tell me exactly what you overheard."

Shaunda covered her eyes for a moment, apparently trying to recall. Then she took her hand away from her eyes, sighed, and said, "I can't remember everything exactly, and I didn't hear everything they said. But I did hear Mr. Gibson say it looked like the party was going to lose a net of two seats in the Senate, which meant they were going to lose control for sure."

"How did the other guys take that?"

"The French guy asked Mr. Gibson how Pearson had responded to their latest offer."

"And?"

"Mr. Gibson said, 'The recalcitrant old fool is determined to hang on to spite us for not helping him quash the investigation in Michigan.' "

"Ah, so that's why Pearson wouldn't step aside. He had a grudge against the party."

Shaunda nodded. "Apparently."

"Okay, keep going."

"Mr. Gibson said he didn't know what else could be done. Said there wasn't time to turn the tide for the other seats that were going to be lost. That set the French guy off, and he chewed Mr. Gibson out."

"Chewed him out? How?"

"He pitched a tantrum and called Mr. Gibson, 'an incompetent old fool.'"

"How did Gibson take that?"

"He yelled some curse words at the French guy. Then I heard the door slam."

"Gibson walked out?"

"He must have, because I didn't hear his voice again."

"What happened after that?"

"Mr. Marchant moaned about it being too late to change things, but the French guy told him not to worry. He said something about Plan B being set in motion already."

"Plan B? Did he elaborate on that?"

"Mr. Marchant sounded like he was surprised. I think he said, 'You're really going to get rid of him?' And the French guy said, 'Yes, we have to do it while there is still time for a replacement.'"

"And you assumed he was referring to an assassination?"

"What else could it mean?"

"It does sound ominous. What else?"

"The voices dropped off, like maybe Mr. Marchant and the French guy were huddled close together. I could hear them talking but couldn't make out the words."

"Did you go to the police?"

"Not at first."

"Why not?"

"At the time, I didn't know what to think. Later, I learned about Senator Pearson's death on TV, and when I read your article at lunch today and saw he'd been murdered, I almost died."

"Did you go to the police or FBI after that?"

"Yes. I called the FBI from my office after lunch."

"What'd they say?"

"They treated me like a crackpot."

"Why come to me? Why not go to one of the real newspapers?"

"And take a chance on it being owned by PMC?"

O'Brien chuckled aloud at the irony in that. Shaunda glared at him. "Surely, Mr. O'Brien, the assassination of a U.S. Senator is no laughing matter."

"Oh, I agree with you, Ms. Rogers. But I gather you didn't watch the six o'clock news, that right?"

"I didn't have time."

"Senator Pearson *was* murdered, but not by your boss or Frenchy. His wife poisoned him."

"His wife?"

"Yep. The police searched the house and found evidence she tampered with his allergy medicine. They arrested her early this afternoon."

"Why did she do it?"

"Who knows? Jealousy, insurance money, pride, hate—pick one."

Shaunda covered her face with her hands. "Oh, I feel like such a fool. And I even called the FBI."

"Don't worry about them. They probably get thousands of calls like yours."

"And I've been terrified, afraid those men would discover I overheard them and murder me, too."

O'Brien dismissed her concern with a wave of his hand and rose from the table. "They might have wished him dead, but I don't believe high-ranking people like Marchant and Frenchy—whoever he is—would have a senator murdered just to hold on to his seat."

Shaunda had risen with him. "I feel so silly now. But, you know, with all the politicians at each others throats the way they are, and the bickering and name-calling . . . and lawsuits, and allegations of voter fraud . . . and calls for impeachment, it's enough to make anyone afraid of what people might do if they become desperate."

"Well, at least in this case, it looks like a simple murder by the guy's wife, so you can sleep well tonight."

"And I've worried myself sick over the other ones, trying to figure out who they were and how to warn them."

O'Brien had turned to walk away, but spun around to face Shaunda again. "Others? They talked about other senators?"

"Yes. They didn't mention names though. They used nicknames."

"You didn't say anything about that earlier."

"I thought I did. Did I really skip them?"

"Yeah, you did skip them." O'Brien didn't think the men had been plotting political assassinations; however, the names of senators they'd like to see replaced intrigued him and might even be fodder for another article. "Who were they?"

Shaunda clasped her hands together and bumped them against her lips while she tried to recall the exact words she'd overheard. "Let me see now . . . I think the French guy said something like, 'We'll take care of the old Satyr first, then get the Traitor and the Rogue.'"

"Ah, the *Satyr*, the *Traitor*, and the *Rogue*. Has kind of a poetic ring to it. You sure they didn't mention any real names, other than Pearson?"

"I didn't hear any. I think they moved across Mr. Marchant's office to the bar after that. I could hear them putting ice into glasses, but I couldn't make out anything they said."

O'Brien looked into Shaunda's eyes and shook his head. "I wouldn't doubt there's a couple of other senators they'd like to see replaced, but I don't believe they'd turn to assassinations to achieve it—especially now that we know Pearson's wife murdered him." He put his arm around her and patted her on the shoulder. "You can rest easy now."

She took a deep breath, let it out slowly, and thanked him. He watched as she threaded her way through the patrons to the door; then he headed back to the snooker room for Carla.

Two guys were playing snooker, and Carla was nowhere in sight. Jason slouched on a stool in the corner, staring forlornly into his empty beer mug.

O'Brien sidled around the snooker table and approached Jason. "Hey, man. Where's Carla?"

Jason raised his head and gave him a blank stare for a few seconds before responding. "You blew it with her when she saw you walk off with that other woman."

O'Brien left Jason and pushed his way through the crowd back to the front room. Maybe she hadn't left yet, and he'd have a chance to explain that the other woman was just business. He found Carla standing at the bar sipping a drink and talking with a well-dressed lawyer type. She glanced in O'Brien's direction, made brief eye contact with him, and moved closer to the other guy, pressing her breasts against his chest.

O'Brien's heart plunged, his shoulders sagged and, like a boxer who'd been slugged so hard he'd forgotten he was in the ring, turned and stumbled back toward the snooker room. He slumped into the chair beside Jason, caught Sheena's attention, and signaled for another round.

With a fresh mug of Stout, he reconsidered Shaunda's words. Was it possible such a conspiracy existed? Had the police arrested an innocent woman? Were other senators likely to be killed?

No, too improbable, he decided. He slid off the chair and sidled around the snooker table toward the pinball machines, but he still couldn't help wondering who the Traitor and the Rogue might be.

Tuesday Morning

11

Zalva and Archie briefed Captain Thurman on their conversation with O'Brien, and Archie remained in Thurman's office afterwards for a personal matter. Zalva detoured by the break room and picked up a fresh cup of coffee before returning to her desk.

Assuming Archie would be in Thurman's office a while, she settled in at her desk to read the *Post*. Her peace was soon interrupted by Archie's deep voice.

"Put the paper down. You've got another corpse to check out."

She looked over the top of the newspaper at him. "What is this? Were you watching from around the corner, waiting until I got comfortable? And don't you mean *we* have a corpse to check out."

"Nope. I don't feel well—going home to bed."

"What's wrong?"

"Just tired and worn out. Must be coming down with something."

"Get a flu shot this year?"

"Nope. Never had one. Had a relative take one, back in the seventies—got paralyzed by it."

"How long since you had a checkup?"

"Years. This is nothing, though. Don't worry about it. I just need a little more rest. Didn't sleep good last night."

"You ought to see a doctor. At your age, it could be more serious than you think."

"Hmpf. I might just do that. In the meantime, you're on your own."

"Who's the corpse?"

"The missing French girl. Her roommate called it in, this morning."

• • •

Thirty minutes later, Zalva stepped out of the elevator on the seventh floor of Lezette's apartment building. Michelle was in her bathroom, crying, so Zalva made her way back to Lezette's bedroom, where she found Ginny examining the body.

She spotted a box of latex gloves on a chair by the door and paused to don a pair. Ginny noticed her come in, nodded to her, and continued with her work.

Zalva approached the bedside and looked over Ginny's shoulder at Lezette's fully clothed body sprawled across the bed, face down. She didn't see any blood on the corpse or the bed.

"What's the verdict?"

Ginny rose from her squatting position with a grunt. "Well, I found traces of white powder around her nostrils and under her fingernails, so it's likely a cocaine overdose."

"That's odd. Neither Michelle or Lucet said anything about her using drugs when we talked to them last week."

"Maybe this was her first time," offered Ginny. "Could've had an adverse reaction, or maybe the stuff was contaminated."

"Let's see what Michelle has to say now," said Zalva. She went back to the living room to interview Michelle, assuming the young woman had regained control of her emotions.

She found Michelle, dressed in blue jeans and a T-shirt, sitting on the living room sofa, with her face buried in her hands. Zalva pulled out her notebook and eased down beside her.

"Michelle, I know how you must feel, but I've got to ask you some questions. Are you up to it?"

Michelle shifted her position to sit facing Zalva; she wiped her eyes, sniffed back a few tears, and nodded her head. *"Je pense que oui."*

"Good. Now, can you tell me about finding Lezette?"

Michelle patted around her eyes with a tissue, using the time to gain a little more composure. "A friend and I were sitting on the couch last night when we heard someone fumbling with the door knob. It sounded—"

"A friend? Who?"

"Must I say? It was Philippe, one of our military men assigned to guard the embassy."

"What time did she come in?"

"Around eleven-thirty."

"Are you sure of the time?"

"Oui. The evening news had just ended."

"So, you heard someone fumbling with the door knob . . ."

"Oui. I went to the door and looked through the peephole. It was Lezette. She seemed too drunk to . . . to . . . manipulate her key, so I opened the door for her."

"Did she come in by herself?"

"Oui. She entered the apartment and went straight back to her room."

"Did she seem okay?"

"Non. She stumbled through the living room and had to prop herself up in the hall doorway for a moment before going back to her room."

"Did she say anything?"

"Non. She completely ignored us. When she stopped in the hall doorway, I could see she needed help and went to her. I asked her what was wrong, but she pushed me off with her hand, and stumbled back to her room."

"Had she ever come home intoxicated before?"

"Mais oui. She became wild here in D.C."

"When you approached her in the hallway, did you smell alcohol?"

Michelle paused for a moment before answering, and tears ran down her cheeks again. *"Non . . .* I didn't. I should have known something was truly wrong . . . shouldn't I?"

Zalva patted her on the back. "Don't blame yourself, Michelle. What happened to her is not your fault."

"But I could have called for help. I . . . didn't think about it . . . didn't notice the absence of alcohol on her breath."

"Let's concentrate on what you did notice. Did you or Philippe hear voices in the hallway, before you opened the door?"

"Non . . . I don't recall any voices."

"Did you look down the hallway when you let her in?"

"Oui. There was no one."

"Do any of the men she's been seeing drive a white Audi?"

Michelle shook her head. "I don't know who she has been seeing."

"Come on Michelle! I know how girls are. Didn't the two of you ever talk about men or date some of the same men?"

"Non. Lezette didn't come here until recently. She seldom spoke to me, even at work, and she never brought anyone to the apartment."

"Did she get a lot of phone calls?"

"Only on her cell phone."

"Okay. Lezette made it to the hall doorway and pushed you away when you tried to help. What next?"

"She went back to her room, bouncing from one hallway wall to the other, and closed the door. We didn't hear anything after that, and I assumed she had passed out."

"Did she ever say anything to you about drugs?"

"Non. She didn't confide in me at all."

"Did she ever appear to be strung out on drugs, here or elsewhere?"

"She came in drunk several times, and we could smell the alcohol. Of course, she could have been taking drugs and we wouldn't have known. Is that what happened to her? Did she die of an overdose of something?"

"We won't know how she died until an autopsy is performed."

"But . . . but why are you asking me about drugs?"

"Just to cover the bases."

"Pardon?"

"To cover all possibilities."

"I see."

"So, you heard nothing and saw nothing of her after she made it to her room?"

"C'est vrai."

"Pardon?"

"We saw and heard nothing more."

"Tell me about this morning."

"Since she hadn't been to work in several days, I decided to wake her and make her go in, or at least call. I knocked on her door at seven this morning, and called out her name. She didn't answer, so I banged on the door a little harder. When she still didn't answer, I went in to shake her awake. But when I touched her arm, it felt cold . . . and her eyes were wide open. I realized she was . . . was . . . dead, and I called *les gendarmes.*"

Zalva asked Michelle to put her statement in writing and went back to Lezette's room, where she was unable to find a cell phone. A check with the officers who had canvassed the neighbors yielded no witnesses who had seen a stranger in the hallway the night before, and Ginny had nothing new to offer.

Zalva picked up Michelle's signed statement and left for the station, saddened by the loss of such a young life and frustrated that it seemed to have happened so invisibly.

12

O'Brien spent the first two hours at work taking the usual phone calls about Elvis sightings and alien abductions. But today, instead of listening patiently, he was brusque. Why couldn't one of his lunatic callers report a conversation with the ghost of Abraham Lincoln, or maybe Attila the Hun, or even Hitler? He sat back with a sigh and rubbed his face with both hands. Maybe the years of writing this crap were finally getting to him.

A rumble from his stomach reminded him he'd skipped breakfast, and a glance at his watch confirmed it was time for a break, so he left the office for the coffee shop across the street.

In the coffee shop, he bought two banana-nut muffins and a mug of Mocha Java, and settled down at a table near the front window. From there, he could observe the women walking past on the sidewalk, or having coffee and sweet rolls in the shop, as well as the TV mounted on the wall in the corner.

O'Brien leaned back in his chair, took half a muffin in one bite, and glanced up at the TV. A breaking news story was in progress on CNN. The scene was an upscale convenience store with a black limo parked in front. He leaned forward and squinted at the screen, at least twenty feet away, but found he couldn't read the caption at the bottom.

He moved to a table nearer the TV and saw the caption on the screen: "Shooting in Alexandria, VA ." The limo at the scene boded ill for some noted personage.

Management kept the sound muted. O'Brien caught the cashier's attention and motioned for her to turn up the sound, which she did with a disapproving scowl.

The scene shifted back to Rich Shelton, one of the dynamic, young-gun, daytime anchormen at CNN, and the TV came alive with his voice in mid-sentence.

". . . shot to death this morning when he stopped for cigarettes and coffee at an upscale convenience store near his residence in Alexandria, Virginia." Shelton put a hand on his earphone and listened in concentration for couple of seconds.

"Hold, on. We're sending you back to the scene in Alexandria where Lindsey McMichael is about to interview the senator's driver."

O'Brien shot out of his chair. "What senator?" he yelled.

The face of a nice-looking, young brunette with brown eyes appeared on the screen. "Lindsey McMichael here, with an update on the shooting in Alexandria." A large, broad-faced, square-jawed man in his mid-thirties, wearing a black polo shirt and black slacks, stood next to her. "I have Mike Rollins, the senator's driver and bodyguard, here with me. He's agreed to talk to us about this startling event."

Lindsey looked up at the huge man's face, more than a head above her. "Mike, could you tell us why the senator stopped here?" She stretched her arm out and held the microphone in front of his mouth.

"We always stop at this store for cigarettes and coffee," answered the big man. His voice was curiously hoarse and strained, as if he'd taken a hard blow to the throat at some point in his career. "The senator liked to have his coffee and cigarettes before he got to the Capitol, but his wife wouldn't let him have any at home—his health you know."

"This was a regular stop?"

"Yeah, every morning when he went to the Capitol."

"Mike, where were you when the senator was shot?"

Mike's face reddened and he hitched his neck before answering. "In the restroom."

"Did you hear anything?"

"Yeah, I heard a woman scream and somebody started shooting."

"Could you tell how many shots were fired?"

"It had to be seven or eight shots. Just bang, bang, bang, like that—one after the other—real fast; like firecrackers going off, only louder. Only took two or three seconds."

"What did you do?"

"I pulled my gun and came outta that restroom, low and fast."

"You always carry a gun?"

"Yeah, and I know how to use it."

"Did you use it this time?"

"Damned straight!"

"You shot at the killer?"

"By the time I got around the aisles between the restroom and the counter, he was already out the door. I ran outside and put three slugs through his back windshield before he got away though."

"Did you hit him?"

"Hard to say."

"Did you get his tag number?"

Mike grimaced and his eyes darted to the side. "No, I didn't think about it."

"What did you do after that?"

"I went back inside to check on the senator."

"What senator, damn it?" muttered O'Brien, growing more irritated by the minute.

"What did you find?" asked Lindsey.

"Everybody was dead."

"Not just the senator?"

"No, everybody. The clerk, the senator, and two other customers."

"Do you think it was a hit on the senator?"

"No . . . I don't . . . not now. I did at first, but after seeing all those other bodies, I think the guy tried to rob the store and panicked."

"Care to speculate on the type of gun the killer used?"

"It had to be a semi-automatic, 'cause of the rapid fire and the number of shots. Not a nine millimeter though—way too loud. I'd put my money on it being a forty-five."

"Have the police interviewed you yet?"

"Yeah. I had to sign a written statement."

Lindsey darted a glance to the side, then back at the camera. "Rich, I see the detective in charge coming back out of the store. I'm going to try to interview him now."

The face of Rich Shelton reappeared. "We'll get back to Lindsey in a moment. Hopefully, she'll have an interview with Detective Oscar Sims, the man in charge at the scene. For those of you who missed the earlier part of our telecast, I'll recap the breaking news for you. At approximately eight forty-five this morning, Senator Roland Gunter and three others were shot to death during the robbery of an upscale convenience store in Alexandria, Virginia.

"For the moment, it appears an unidentified assailant wearing a black ski-mask and a green army field jacket, attempted to rob the convenience store while Senator Gunter was waiting at the counter to pay for coffee and pick up a pack of cigarettes. At this point, no one knows for certain exactly what happened. Maybe the store clerk or one of the customers resisted, or maybe someone said something that set the killer off.

"One thing is certain, though. Four people are dead, including one of the most respected senior senators ever to serve in the U.S. Senate. A man who, it is believed, had absolutely no enemies."

Shelton continued. "We're going to Eric Stallings, our analyst in D.C., for his take on this shocking event."

The wrinkled, wizened face of Eric Stallings appeared on the screen. The corners of the silver-haired man's mouth drooped, and he peered at the camera with faded blue eyes. "Rich, I'm deeply saddened by the news of Senator Gunter's untimely death, as everyone else around the country will be as the news circulates. The nation will feel the loss of Senator Gunter, a moderate who helped keep the country in the middle of the road."

Stallings' brow knitted and his tone became graver. "As much as the country will miss him, the more severe impact will be felt by the Republican Party."

"Could you elaborate on that for the viewers?" asked Shelton.

"As you may recall," replied Stallings, "Senator Gunter was originally elected to the Senate as a Democrat. Before this current term began, he switched to the Republican Party, apparently disappointed by his party's shift to the left. Even though his district has a heavy Democratic majority, he was popular enough to be re-elected as a Republican. The latest polls showed him a cinch to be re-elected in November. Now, with him gone, the Democratic Party is certain to reclaim his seat."

"Excuse me Eric," said Shelton. "Could you explain to our viewers why the loss of that one seat is so critical for the Republicans?"

"Rich, it's a crushing blow. The Democrats will likely retain Pearson's seat and will almost certainly pick up Gunter's seat, virtually assuring them control of the Senate for the foreseeable future."

The news program switched to a commercial break and O'Brien slumped into a chair, the strength suddenly gone from his arms and legs as if he'd been sitting in a 747 that had just dropped four thousand feet in an air pocket.

Two senators killed within six days! Could it be mere coincidence?

He thought about last night's meeting with Shaunda Rogers at Finigan's. The plot she allegedly overheard included three senators: the *Satyr*, the *Traitor* and the *Rogue*.

The philandering Pearson was undoubtedly the *Satyr*, and since Gunter had switched parties while in office, he was almost certainly the *Traitor*. And per his driver, Gunter regularly stopped at that particular convenience store at about the same time every day—a situation made to order for someone planning an assassination.

If the men at PMC had really been plotting murder, they had done a good—if heartless—job of it, because the deaths didn't look anything like assassinations, but like the murder of an innocent bystander during an armed robbery and the poisoning of a man by his wife.

O'Brien stuffed the remainder of the second muffin into his mouth, grabbed a go-cup of coffee, and left for his car, cheeks bulging with food.

He had to find Shaunda and get confirmation that the meeting had actually taken place. He needed the time, date, and the identity of the guy with the French accent.

A plot to assassinate senators? What a story! And if he was the one to break it, he'd be on top again. Might even get signed up by a major player again, like the *Post*.

Spurred on by visions of fortune and glory, he hurried across the street to the parking garage for his Volvo.

13

O'Brien parked his old Volvo on a side street near the PMC offices on K Street, a couple of blocks off Pennsylvania Avenue. He reached for his camera on the back seat, thought better of it, and pulled his tiny digital camera from the glove compartment. Wouldn't do to go wandering around the PMC offices with a professional-looking camera slung over his shoulder.

To his surprise, he found the building being picketed by a handful of solemn-looking men wearing gray suits and carrying signs. Protestors were a common sight in D.C., but they usually picketed government buildings, not businesses.

He glanced at one of the signs, which proclaimed in large, bold lettering, "PMC IS EVIL."

Old habits die hard. Even in his rush to find Shaunda, O'Brien sensed a good story for the *Probe*. He caught the arm of one of the men.

"What's your beef with PMC?"

Tall and gaunt, the elderly man turned and looked down at O'Brien with deep-set, faded blue eyes. Wispy strands of silver hair framed his deeply lined face and lifted slightly with each breath of wind. He resembled John Carradine, the old character actor who played Moses' brother Aaron in Cecil B. De Mille's *Ten Commandments,* only needing a robe and a staff to look like he'd just stepped off the movie set.

He spoke in a deep, haunting voice. "Stopping Satan, Brother."

"What does PMC have to do with Satan?"

Aaron looked down at O'Brien as if pitying him. "Have you no eyes, Brother? Can you not see?"

"Come on, guy. I'm a reporter. Give me a straight answer for my paper."

Aaron lifted an eyebrow. "Do you work for PMC?"

"No. I work for the *National Probe*, a weekly paper."

Aaron grabbed O'Brien by the arm with a strength belying his gaunt frame and obvious age, and pulled him aside, like a carnival con-man working a mark. "Know this, Brother. PMC is preparing the way for Satan."

This guy's got some shorts in his circuits, thought O'Brien. But what a great article for the Probe. "Now how exactly is PMC doing that?"

"By promoting evil and criticizing the way of Jesus. Have you not seen the movies PMC makes? Have you not listened to the gangster rap PMC produces? Does PMC not stand against Christianity at every turn, in our courts, in our schools, and in our government?"

"I don't go to the movies or watch much television," admitted O'Brien.

Aaron rested his sign against the building, placed his hand on the wall, and leaned over O'Brien. "We have studied the movies PMC shows on its cable TV channels. Movies made by PMC companies and movies made by others. They follow a definite pattern."

"Pattern? Like what?"

"They glorify murder, adultery, drugs, and alcohol, in all their movies, on television, and in the music they produce. All are full of profanity, hate, and devil worship, and they belittle or ridicule those who follow God. They consistently show authority figures, like elected officials, policemen, detectives and FBI agents, as foolish, evil, and corrupt, while making heros out of those who murder, rob, steal, and sell drugs."

"To what end?"

"They're deliberately trying to destroy respect for traditional authority figures, like government officials, law officers and parents—particularly fathers, by showing them as corrupt and unable to control their emotions, flying into rages when the least little thing doesn't go their way, and by portraying them to be stupid, close-minded, and lazy. All this is calculated to make our youth have nothing but contempt for authority—authority of the church, of government, and of the family.

"And they're getting bolder. PMC or its subsidiaries produces many of the cartoons children watch on television—cartoons in which the heroes are vampires, werewolves, and other demon-like creatures, while the evil doers are ordinary-looking people. It's all designed to get our children accustomed to accepting demons as good instead of evil."

"So that's what you meant when you said, 'paving the way for Satan.'"

"Yes, Brother."

"Very interesting," said O'Brien. "But I've got an appointment. Can I get a photo of you with your sign?"

"Of course, Brother." Aaron picked up his sign and held it against his chest.

O'Brien pulled out his digital camera and snapped several pictures of Aaron and his disciples.

"Take this, Brother," said Aaron. He handed O'Brien a pamphlet. "Read it and be enlightened."

"I'll read it tonight, and thanks for your time." O'Brien stuffed the pamphlet in his coat pocket, stepped around the gaunt lunatic, and entered the building.

14

O'Brien cleared the security station just inside the main door and stepped into the cavernous lobby. He spotted a lone pylon in the center of the vast space, as conspicuous as a pyramid at Giza. He assumed it displayed a directory, as everyone in sight checked it out before proceeding to the elevators.

He strode toward the pylon feeling a little self-conscious at the incongruity of his squeaking tennis shoes contrasting with the clicking of the leather soles and heels worn by the other visitors.

The pylon was indeed the directory and showed PMC to occupy the entire top floor.

O'Brien rode the elevator to the top and stepped out into a much smaller lobby with a cherry-stained, wood floor. A long hallway ran off the lobby to his left and a formal reception counter loomed behind a wall of glass bearing the PMC logo in gold, to his right. He stepped into the reception area and his feet sank into the plush carpet.

A beautiful woman of about thirty, with long, blonde hair and blue eyes, smiled at him over the receptionist's counter. "May I help you?"

"I'd like to see Shaunda Rodgers, please."

"Do you have an appointment?"

He gave her his best imitation of a warm smile. "No, but I believe she'll be happy to see me."

"Your name?"

"Will O'Brien."

She gestured to the sofas and side chairs that lined the walls of the waiting area. "Please have a seat, Mr. O'Brien, while I ring her office."

Before taking a seat, he wandered around the lobby and examined the movie and music posters that decorated the walls. Judging from the subject matter of the posters, Aaron just might be on to something after all, he mused. After a quick review of the posters, he picked up a magazine and eased into one of the side chairs.

Several minutes passed before a statuesque, African-American woman stepped into the reception area. She had prominent bone structure and wore a black pantsuit, with her hair braided tightly against her skull. She went straight to the counter and spoke to the receptionist. O'Brien couldn't make out their conversation, but they looked in his direction and *Blondie* nodded her head toward him.

The tall woman approached O'Brien and stood before him with both hands on her hips. "You asked to see me?"

O'Brien stood and found himself on eye level with her. "I asked to see Shaunda Rodgers."

The woman frowned. "I am Shaunda Rodgers. What do you wish to see me about?"

"No . . . you're not the Shaunda Rodgers—"

"I am most certainly Shaunda Rodgers!"

"Please, I didn't mean to offend you. It's just that I met a woman the other night who said she was Shaunda Rodgers and worked for PMC in this office."

"Well then, surely you're the victim of a hoax, as I'm the only Shaunda Rodgers working in this office and, I dare say, the only Shaunda Rodgers in D.C."

O'Brien held his hands up, palms out, in an effort to put her at ease. "The woman must've used your name instead of her own. Is there an African-American woman, early thirties, about—"

"Obviously, I'm not the person you're looking for and I don't have time to waste like this." She turned her back to him and strode quickly across the lobby, whispered something to Blondie, then disappeared down the long hallway.

The woman who'd met him at Finigan's had apparently used Shaunda's name, but the question remained whether his informant really was an employee of PMC or had merely been acting as an intermediary for a friend who actually did work at PMC.

He noticed Blondie eyeing him warily, and stepped over to her counter.

The woman assumed a rigid posture. "Yes?" she asked in an icy voice.

He gave her what he hoped was a disarming smile. "I met a woman who said she worked for PMC in this building and had a car for sale. I've misplaced her card and can't remember her name. I'm serious about the car, but I don't know who to ask for. Perhaps if I described her . . . tall, good-looking, African-American, say about thirty-five, with— "

"We don't give out information about employees, sir. I'm afraid you'll just have to find her some other way."

"But she may sell the car to somebody else before I find her." That didn't move Blondie, so he gave her an even broader smile. "Maybe if I wandered around the office for a couple of minutes, I'd see her."

He didn't give her a chance to object, and walked quickly through the doors, across the lobby and down the hallway where the real Shaunda Rodgers had disappeared.

Blondie yelled out after him, but with the glass door closed, her words were muffled. He shot a glance over his shoulder and saw her waving for him to come back.

O'Brien turned his attention back to where he was going and collided with two men hurrying down the hallway in his direction. The unexpected impact knocked him to the floor and before he could recover, the larger of the two men reached down, grabbed O'Brien by the front of his jacket with both hands, and snatched him to his feet. O'Brien struggled to break free, but the huge brute twisted his right arm behind his back and slammed him, face first, against the wall with such force that his teeth cut his cheek. He ran his tongue over the cut and tasted blood.

"Damn! Why in hell did you do that?"

"We'll ask the questions," said the thinner of the two men, with a French accent. "Hold him, Roscoe, while I frisk him."

Roscoe pressed O'Brien against the wall as if trying to push him through it, and squeezed his arm hard, cutting off the circulation. He stood almost a head taller than O'Brien, not counting the matt of curly, black hair that topped his great head, and looked like he was all muscle. His eyes were coal-black and set far apart, on either side of a broad nose that had obviously been broken more than once. His mouth was a cruel gash across his broad face, and he looked like he could drive railroad spikes with his chin.

The thin man searched him for weapons and took his billfold. O'Brien watched him go through it out of the corner of his eye, and frowned when he didn't stop with his driver's license but kept plundering the contents.

They didn't appear to be run-of-the-mill security, as both were handsomely attired in dark suits: Armani for the thin guy, and something from Omar, the tent-maker, for Roscoe. Both wore dark gray, knit shirts and shoes that looked European. Could the thin one be the guy with the French accent Shaunda, or whoever she was, overheard?

O'Brien studied the thin man's face. From a broad forehead it tapered down to a sharp chin. His hair was dark as night, combed straight back, and shiny with mousse. There was cunning in the tiny, dark eyes which darted from the contents of O'Brien's billfold up tp O'Brien, then back to the billfold. The look of a merciless predator. O'Brien labeled him *Snake Eyes*.

Snake Eyes found one of his business cards and studied it for a moment. Suddenly, he jerked his gaze back to O'Brien's face. *"Merde!* You're the tabloid reporter who said the Democratic Party killed Pearson."

"I didn't say the party—"

"Shut your face!" bellowed Roscoe. He jerked O'Brien away from the wall and slammed him against it again.

"That'll do, Roscoe," ordered Snake Eyes. He put his face close to

O'Brien's. "Why are you here?"

Roscoe gave O'Brien's arm another savage twist. "Yeah, just what in hell *are* you doing here?"

O'Brien's arm throbbed with pain, but he managed to gasp out a protest. "Hey, take it easy, man! You don't have to break my arm. You know I'm not going anywhere."

Roscoe eased his grip slightly. "Damn straight you're not going anywhere."

O'Brien twisted his head to make eye contact with Snake Eyes. "I was looking for a woman who told me she worked here. Why am I being treated like this?"

"We'll ask the damn questions," retorted Roscoe.

"What woman?" asked Snake Eyes.

"A woman I met at a pub the other night who said she had a car for sale."

"What's her name?"

"Shaunda—at least that's what she told me."

Roscoe slapped him lightly across the back of his head. "Bullshit!"

"What kind of car?" asked Snake Eyes.

"A white Audi," he blurted. He realized his mistake as soon as the words left his mouth, and winced. The hotel bellhop had told him the French girl in Pearson's room had arrived in a white Audi, and that was what popped into his mind.

Snake Eyes studied O'Brien for a couple of seconds with narrowed eyes. His thin lips twisted into a sadistic grin and he stuck his face inches from O'Brien's again. "You don't really expect us to believe you're here looking to buy a car from an employee, do you? You being such a high-powered tabloid reporter and all?"

O'Brien let out a long breath. "Okay, you got me. I came here chasing pussy."

"But you specifically asked for Shaunda Rodgers, who says she's never seen you before. Explain that," hissed Snake Eyes.

"I met a good-looking African-American woman in a bar, a couple of nights ago. I wrote her name down on one of my business cards but I guess she gave me Shaunda's name instead of her own." He grinned and glanced from Snake Eyes to Roscoe and back to Snake Eyes. "Broads do that, you know. When I discovered she'd given me the wrong name, I thought I'd poke around in the building—maybe luck up on her."

Snake Eyes allowed a sly grin to creep across his narrow face, but his eyes told O'Brien he wasn't fooled at all. Not now. Not with O'Brien's blunder about the white Audi. Snake Eyes moved back a couple of feet and slapped O'Brien's billfold against his palm a couple of times, appearing to ponder alternatives. "Roscoe, hold him in the little conference room while I check with the boss."

Snake Eyes handed the billfold back to O'Brien, but kept one of his business cards. Roscoe waved a huge paw at a doorway, inviting O'Brien to enter. As O'Brien stepped through, Roscoe shoved him into the room where he fell across the table. He shook it off, debated making a run for it, remembered Roscoe's strength, and decided against it.

Long, agonizing minutes passed with Roscoe leaning against the closed door, staring down at O'Brien with a malicious grin on his face. Finally, he spoke. "You know, Henri probably won't mind if I bust you up a little bit while we're waiting. Be pissed he didn't get to watch, though. He's like that—digs hurting people." Roscoe stepped away from the door and reached for O'Brien, but stopped short when the door opened behind him and Henri entered.

O'Brien figured even if they suspected he knew something about the conspiracy, they weren't likely to do anything here, or else they wouldn't still be talking. He decided to go for broke, put his hands on the arms of the chair and started to rise. "I haven't broken any laws that I know of, so I'm out of here."

Roscoe clamped a heavy hand on O'Brien's shoulder and slammed him back into the chair. "Sit your ass back down!"

"That'll do," ordered Henri. "Marchant said to let him go." He looked at O'Brien with leaden eyes and hissed, in a soft, sinister voice, "You come back, and we'll let Roscoe sort this out in his own special way—know what I mean?"

O'Brien grunted at the threat and shouldered his way past them, out the door and down the hall, followed closely by Roscoe. They rode down in the elevator together, a tense and silent trip.

Out on the sidewalk, O'Brien glanced back over his shoulder at the front door of the building, saw Roscoe standing inside the doors with hands on his hips, watching him, and gave him the finger. Roscoe's face contorted with rage; he caught the automatic doors in the process of closing, pulled them apart with his massive arms, and stalked through, heading straight for O'Brien.

O'Brien quickened his pace and made it to his car before Roscoe caught up with him. He jumped in without looking over his shoulder and locked the doors. Thankfully, the old Volvo came to life without skipping a beat, and he drove away from the curb with Roscoe reaching for the door handle.

He glanced over his shoulder and flipped Roscoe off again before he turned to watch where he was going, then snatched his hand back at a sudden horrible thought. What if the light on the corner turned red and he had to stop within sight of Roscoe?

He held his breath, gripped the steering wheel until his knuckles ached, praying the light would remain green.

Luckily, it did. Realizing he had the green light made, O'Brien rolled his window down, stuck his arm out, and flipped Roscoe off one final time, for good measure.

15

O'Brien navigated his Volvo through traffic, chewing on the words of his mysterious PMC informant and the treatment he'd received at PMC. Two senators murdered and both named by his informant—too damned much to be pure coincidence.

The assassination of politicians wasn't supposed to happen in the good old U.S., was it? He recalled Kennedy, Lincoln, Garfield, and McKinley, had been assassinated, but all those had been carried out by radicals acting alone, hadn't they? Well, maybe not the Kennedy assassination. The jury was still out on that one—at least in the minds of a few million conspiracy nuts. But why assassinate lowly senators? After all, there was only one president compared to a hundred senators. Those guys were a dime a dozen, weren't they?

He dredged up what he could remember about American government from his college political science course. Congress was patterned somewhat after the British Parliament, with the Senate being the upper house—like the House of Lords, and the House of Representatives being the lower house–like the House of Commons. But instead of representing the noble aristocracy, the American upper house represented the states—hence the equal representation regardless of population. And until the Constitution was amended in 1918, Senators had been elected by the various state legislatures.

Senators were widely regarded as powerful people, yet one senator acting alone had little power. But what about the Senate as a whole? The Constitution vested some pretty important powers in the upper house. The president could appoint federal judges, including Supreme Court justices, but only with the *advice and consent* of the Senate. In addition, the president could make treaties with foreign nations, but only with the *approval* of the Senate.

Both houses of Congress had to pass a bill before it could go to the president for his signature, meaning that a Senate in the control of one party could block all legislation passed by the House, which might be in the hands of the other party. The Senate also had broad powers of investigation, and could even try the president in impeachment proceedings.

Taken as a whole, the Senate was powerful indeed. And in recent years, with the balance of power in the Senate swinging back and forth between parties by as narrow a margin as one seat, the importance of an individual seat was magnified. The gain or loss of two or three—or perhaps even just one—Senate seat could have a significant bearing on the course of American history.

This was especially true now, with the Republicans in control of the White House and the House of Representatives, and the Democrats with a slim margin of a single seat in the Senate. The Republican president had been in office for less than two years, and the Democratic majority in the Senate had already successfully blocked his attempts to appoint several hard-line conservatives to federal judgeships, and had stalled all bills passed by the House.

According to the polls, the mid-term elections in November were likely to give the Republicans control of the Senate by one vote. The president's approval rating exceeded sixty percent, so unless something drastic occurred, like a severe plunge in the economy or a major disaster in foreign affairs, he was a lock to be re-elected in two years.

The Democrats were facing the prospect of a Republican Congress and presidency for the next six years. Six years during which important judicial positions would be filled by conservatives. Six years during which much of the liberal social legislation spawned during the years when Johnson had a rubber-stamp Congress could be reversed.

And even if the Democrats regained control down the road, the effects of the judicial appointments would carry on for decades, since federal judges were appointed for life.

O'Brien shook his head at the implications. The stakes were high indeed. And, with the stakes that high, might not one party or the other resort to extremes to stave off elimination of all it had accomplished? Or, if not a party, perhaps someone who had devoted a lifetime to scheming and pushing the country in the direction he wanted, only to see it beginning to slip away from him, could lose his grip and take matters into his own hands.

Perhaps even two or three such individuals could form a conspiracy for such a purpose. A handful of well-placed individuals, rich and powerful, could use other people in such a cause without those others ever fully realizing they were involved.

And that's what Shaunda, for the lack of another name for her, had laid out for him: three well-placed and powerful individuals, meeting and conspiring to take drastic actions so their party could hold on to power. Well, not three, because she said Gibson walked out of the meeting.

He didn't know the identity of the third man in the alleged meeting, but Marchant certainly qualified as being well-placed and powerful, with the financial and mind-shaping resources of the world's largest media conglomerate at his command. And Shaunda said Frenchy was apparently in control of the meeting. O'Brien gnawed his bottom lip over that thought. More powerful than the chairman of the DNC and the president of PMC? Just who was this mysterious *Frenchy*?

A cacophony of automobile horns from the cars behind him broke his concentration. Apparently, the traffic light had turned green while he was lost in thought. He released the brake, pressed the gas pedal, and eased the Volvo through the intersection. The vehicle behind him at the light swerved into the adjacent lane and, as it passed, the burly driver glared at him, yelled obscenities, and flipped him off.

Normally, O'Brien would've returned the greeting, but not today. He had a bigger game to play. Having rationalized that the conspiracy was plausible, he decided to lay it out for the FBI, even though they hadn't believed Shaunda—or whatever her name really was.

16

Within minutes, he found himself going through a metal detector at FBI headquarters. He asked to see an agent and told the receptionist it involved a matter of national security. After filling out a form and a twenty-minute wait, a secretary escorted him to a tiny conference room, presumably to meet with an agent.

The room contained only a small, rectangular table about four feet long, and four straight chairs. The gray walls were bare except for a large mirror on a side wall, which he assumed was a two-way mirror for observation, and a video camera mounted in one corner near the ceiling. His escort asked him to take a seat and advised him an agent would be with him shortly.

Five more minutes passed before two men, dressed in dark suits, white shirts, and drab ties, entered the room. Both were six feet tall with medium builds. Typical agents he thought, average height, average build, average weight, brown hair of average length, and average looks.

The agent on O'Brien's left spoke first. "Mr. O'Brien, I'm Special Agent Barnes and this is Special Agent Peters."

The two agents ignored the hand O'Brien extended and took seats across the table from him. Once they were seated, he noticed Agent Barnes had a small earphone in his right ear.

Agent Peters clasped his hands behind his head and surveyed O'Brien skeptically, as if expecting to hear a story of alien abduction. "You said you have a matter of national security to discuss with us?"

O'Brien told them all he knew, starting with Reggie's phone call and ending with his failed attempt to locate his informant at PMC, but omitting the part about stealing the fake NazinX tablet. Since they took no notes, he assumed they were recording the session. Nor did they ask any questions, simply allowing him to run on uninterrupted. At times, Agent Barnes appeared to have tuned him out, listening to someone on his earphone instead.

When O'Brien finished his story, Peters stared at him with a blank face. "That's it?"

"Well, yeah. That's it."

"Didn't the D.C. police arrest Pearson's wife and charge her with the murder of Senator Pearson?" asked Barnes.

"Yeah, that's true. But I believe she was framed."

Barnes rolled his eyes at the ceiling. "And you maintain Gunter's death was a contract hit?"

"Well, it surely is a strange coincidence that two of the senators mentioned in the meeting were killed within a few days after the meeting."

Peters leaned forward with an incredulous look on his face. "Do you seriously think someone planning an assassination like you proposed would hire a low-level crack head to carry out a hit?"

"Has Gunter's killer been identified or caught?" asked O'Brien.

"Don't think so," answered Peters.

"Then how do you know he's a crack head?"

Peters' jaw muscles tightened at O'Brien's remark, but he remained silent.

Barnes asked, "And what's the name of the PMC employee who overheard this so-called conspiracy?"

O'Brien shrugged his shoulders and shook his head. "I don't know. Like I said, she used someone else's name and they wouldn't let me look around the building for her."

"And that brings up another point. Why did she come to you in the first place?" asked Peters.

"I already told you, she called here yesterday, and didn't get anywhere with you guys. She came to me because she read my article about Pearson and thought I knew something."

Barnes shook his head. "There's no record of any such phone call. It's been checked out while we've been sitting here."

"I can't help that. All I know is she said she called here and spoke with an agent."

Barnes leaned back in his chair again and folded his arms. He studied O'Brien for several seconds, while apparently listening to someone on his earphone. He smirked and shook his head from side to side while listening. He pulled the earphone off and tossed in on the table. "You've got a history of having trouble with the truth, haven't you?"

"What are you talking about?"

"That Pulitzer-Prize-winning hoax of yours in New York."

Damn! Would he ever be rid of that accursed ghost from his past? "I was the victim on that deal, but nobody would believe me."

"And look at you now. A *reporter* for the mighty *National Probe*. Don't you fabricate most of the crap that rag publishes?"

"That's different. Everybody knows it's phony to some extent. I wouldn't invent something as serious as this."

Peters shot from his chair. "To hell you wouldn't!" He put his hands on the table and leaned over in O'Brien's face. "Didn't you just tell us you invented the story about Pearson being murdered with Maxual just to sell papers?"

"Yeah, I said that, but—"

Barnes stood up abruptly, interrupting O'Brien. "And I think you made this conspiracy crap up, too, just to sell more papers. Only, this time, you're trying to pull the FBI into it for credibility."

"That's a—"

"You're lucky we're not going to throw the book at you. Just get your lying ass out now, while you've got the chance," said Peters.

"What about the senator they called the Rogue? You're just going to let him die?"

"Nobody else is going to die, because there's no conspiracy," replied Barnes drily.

Stunned, O'Brien looked from Barnes to Peters and saw it was a lost cause. He snorted in disgust, turned, and left, never looking back.

17

O'Brien left the FBI office, feeling as low as a college football coach with back-to-back winless seasons who'd just come under investigation for alleged recruiting violations—not because the FBI wouldn't believe him but because they'd reminded him how low he'd sunk: writing for a grocery-store tabloid—if you could call it writing. He remembered his early years after school, his eagerness, his innocence, his great expectations. Now look at him. Over forty, overweight, no real career, and no soul mate to share his life.

Thoughts of a soul mate brought back memories of his ex-wife, the college sweetheart he'd lost soon after he lost his job and the Pulitzer Prize. As a journalist caught in a lie, no reputable paper or magazine would touch him. The love affair that began in college had been hounded away by the financial disaster that followed his scandal.

He shook his head to drive away the sad thoughts of his past, and focused on the plot again, and the questions posed by the FBI agents. Maybe he was gullible . . . too eager to work on something real, something meaningful. Maybe there really was no conspiracy. Maybe the woman who came to the pub was using him to get back at PMC for some damage done to her in the past by the media giant. Maybe Pearson's wife really did kill him. Maybe the guy who killed Gunter really was just a crack head robbing a convenience store for money to buy drugs. However unpleasant the thought, he had to face the fact that he might be falling into the same trap that ruined his career in New York.

In no mood for lunch or the office, O'Brien called the *Probe* and told the receptionist he would be out for the rest of the day. Said he didn't feel well, which was true. He was about as depressed as the Dow. But instead of going home, he opted for Finigan's, where he'd have a few early brews while he gathered his thoughts, and maybe grab some grub if the mood struck him.

. . .

Over the next couple of hours, he chased his depression away with several mugs of Stout, a corned-beef sandwich, and a long chat with Mary Kate. When Mary Kate became too busy to linger with him, he took a deep draft from his mug, set it down on the bar, and turned around on his stool to survey the joint.

The pub had livened up considerably since he arrived. Possibly the pre-happy hour crowd had begun arriving. Had he been here that long? He glanced at his watch and saw it was half past four.

He got a roll of quarters from Mary Kate, grabbed his mug of Stout and wandered back to the pinball machines, pausing to trade insults with some of the late afternoon regulars. Finding his favorite machine idle, he set his mug on the glass and slipped two quarters into the slot.

An hour later, he noticed Carla strutting into the snooker room. She perched on a stool against the far wall and pretended not to notice him, obviously still angry about him leaving her to talk to Shaunda, last evening. He kept tabs on her out of the corner of his eye and caught her looking his way a couple of times. But when he checked her out again, he saw a clean-cut, well-dressed, young broker-type hitting on her.

O'Brien's gaze drifted from the broker guy back to Carla, and their eyes met. She waved excitedly at O'Brien, as if she hadn't noticed him until that moment. She said something to the young guy that made his face pucker, hopped off the stool, and started across the room.

O'Brien turned his attention back to the machine and within seconds found Carla standing next to him.

"You don't mind if I watch you play, do you?" she asked.

"You can play, too—that is, if your date doesn't mind."

Carla made a face. "Don't get cute now."

With his concentration broken, O'Brien lost his last ball and cursed softly. He turned to Carla. "I bet the guy's a broker, right?"

"Yes. How did you know?"

"He looked it. I see his type in here all the time. Drinking a wine cooler, wasn't he?"

"So what's wrong with that?"

O'Brien hitched up his pants, shook his jowls, and assumed his Falstaff face. *"There's never none of these demure boys come to any proof, for thin drink doth so overcool their blood, and making many fish meals, that they fall into a kind of male greensickness, and then when they marry, they get wenches."*

Carla giggled softly. "Is that from Shakespeare?"

"Yeah, one of Falstaff's lines I happen to like."

"You certainly are an amazing guy, O'Brien." She took a sip from her glass, eyeing him over the rim. "Where's your girlfriend tonight?"

"What girlfriend?"

"The woman you were with, the other night. I saw you go up to the front with her and sit down at a table."

"Oh, you mean Shaunda—or whatever her name really was. That concerned a story for my paper. Strictly business."

"Oh yeah? Didn't look like business to me. Every time I looked over there, you two were huddled up like lovers."

"She was afraid somebody would overhear us and wouldn't speak up, so I sat close to hear her better."

Carla's face relaxed. "A story for your paper?"

"Yeah, just another gossip story for the tabloid."

Seemingly satisfied with his explanation, Carla sipped her drink and studied him. A mischievous smile tugged at the corners of her mouth.

"You want to go a couple of rounds with me?" she asked.

Stunned by her unexpected proposition, O'Brien gaped at her, speechless. He'd been around aggressive women before, but never one so direct. With his mind reeling with images of her nude body crawling into bed with him, he gained enough control to act. He reached around her waist, pulled her body against his, and looked deeply into her green eyes, "My place or yours?"

She grabbed his hand, twisted it off her waist, and pushed him back. "I mean on the pinball machine, silly!"

"I . . . I knew that." With face and ears burning, he fished four quarters from his pocket and, with a flourish, stuck them in the coin slot. He moved aside and motioned for Carla to take his place. "You go first, so I can study your style."

She gave him a wry smile as she took his place. "My style, huh?"

"Yeah, your style. Body English."

"Body English?"

"You know, the little twists of your hips and shoulders that help guide the ball while you're playing. Here, watch me." He moved back in front of the pinball machine, put his hands where he could reach the flippers on each side, and pretended to be playing, twisting this way and that, as if guiding the ball with his hips.

Her eyes lit up, and the corners of her mouth curled up in a knowing grin. "Oh, I get it. I think I can do that."

O'Brien ran his eyes down her slim body, lingering on her sensuous curves. "I'll bet you can, at that."

She began playing, twisting her hips seductively. She turned out to be proficient at the machine and ran up a decent score with her first ball.

He gave her a smug grin. "You think that's pretty good, huh?"

She smiled up at him as she moved over to allow him access to the machine. "I'm just getting warmed up."

As O'Brien stepped around her, she moved back slightly, just enough that his dick brushed her ass as he slid past her. It felt good. Was the move accidental or carefully planned? Planned, he decided after a couple of minutes, because as he played his turn, she leaned forward to see the action better, pressing her right nipple into his left arm, which he couldn't move without losing his ball in a trap. When he didn't move his arm, she pressed in tighter and he felt her nipple harden.

The intimate contact distracted him, and he watched in dismay as the ball vanished down the maw of the ball-return. He glanced at the scoreboard and saw his point total was less than half of hers.

"Crap! I usually get four times that many points."

She giggled like a teenager and slid behind him, putting a hand on each side of his waist, pressing firm nipples against his back. He let out a low whimper and she playfully elbowed him in the ribs.

They played the pinball game out to its conclusion, with her beating him handily and teasing him with her body all the while. He turned, intending to raise an arm to flag Sheena for another round of beer, but Carla grabbed his arm.

"I'm starved. Have you had dinner yet?"

"No, have you?"

"No, and I don't feel like eating here, do you?"

Taking her cue, he smiled down at her and asked, "Why don't you come over to my place? We can pick up a couple of steaks and a bottle of wine on the way. I'll grill steaks and we can watch an old Bogart DVD afterward."

She bounced on her tip toes. "Sounds great. I'm ready."

He grabbed her by the hand and led her through the mob and out the front door. A front had moved in, bringing with it an early darkness due to the heavy clouds. He looked up at the dark sky, and a light drizzle of cold raindrops pricked his face like needles.

Carla snuggled against him. "I'll follow you in my car. That way you won't have to drive me back here later."

"Fine with me, as long as you don't chicken out."

She pinched his belly playfully. "Not a chance."

He walked her to her vehicle with his arm around her shoulder and her arm around his waist. She opened the door and slipped onto the seat. He leaned into the car and gave her a long kiss.

Carla broke off the kiss, pushed him away, and closed her door. O'Brien turned and headed for his car parked across the street. Half way there, he heard car tires spinning on the wet pavement, looked up, and was blinded by a pair of headlights bearing down on him out of the darkness.

18

Late in the afternoon, Captain Thurman appeared in the doorway of the small office Zalva and Archie shared. "Archie's wife just called me from the hospital. They're going to do an emergency by-pass on him tomorrow."

"He's got blockage?"

"Yeah, pretty serious. That's the bad news. Good news is, he went to the doctor in time to do something about it."

"He seemed tired all the time, but I thought he was just out of shape. That's what he thought, too."

"He'll be okay now, but it'll be a while before he can come back here and do anything but a desk job."

"You giving me a new partner?"

He shook his head. "Don't have one to give. We're undermanned. Been that way for over five years. You're going to have to go it on your own for a while."

"That won't be all bad."

Thurman frowned and pointed a finger at her. "Just you be careful out there. Don't get in over your head. I mean with the physical stuff."

"I can take care of myself. Been trained, you know."

"Yeah, that's right. You *have* been trained. But this is real life—not the movies. No matter how well-trained you are, you're no match for a two hundred-plus guy, or even a little guy strung-out on dope. So, don't tackle anything physical."

Zalva frowned at his warning. She'd handled large men in her martial arts classes without difficulty.

"If you don't believe what I'm saying, you need to watch a few of the video tapes in my office," added Thurman, as if he'd read her mind.

When she didn't protest, he continued. "When you get into a situation that might become physical, call for uniforms and wait till they get there. And by God, I mean it. You got that?"

"Yeah, I've got it. When the situation could get physical, call for uniforms."

He cocked his head to one side and studied her for a second, as if trying to decide if she was mocking him. "Good. We're too shorthanded to lose another good detective."

Now that they were past Thurman's concern, she thought about Archie again. "What hospital is he in, and what's the room number?"

Captain Thurman gave her the information, and she left work early to pick up a card and flowers for Archie.

. . .

Zalva made it to her place a little before five, collapsed on the couch, and closed her eyes for a nap. Almost immediately, it seemed, her cell phone rang. She sat up and looked at the caller ID. It was a New York number—Dwayne again. She sighed in exasperation. It had been almost a year since she walked away from him. Any reasonable man would have realized their affair was over and given up by now, but not Dwayne. Somehow, he'd learned her new cell phone number after she moved to D.C. and began calling her. She never answered, but the calls still kept coming, although with less frequency. She assumed he only called now when feeling sorry for himself, or drunk, or both.

She turned the phone off, rubbed the sleep from her eyes, and checked her wristwatch. Almost seven o'clock. She'd been out for about two hours, although it only seemed like a few seconds. She stood up, stretched her arms, legs, and back to get the kinks out, and heard a deep rumble from the pit of her stomach.

After rummaging through the kitchen and finding nothing that could be easily prepared, she decided to go out for a couple of cold beers and some potato skins, or maybe a platter of beefy nachos. Normally, on an evening like this, she'd go to Murphy's. She pictured the usual crowd of off-duty cops that hung out at Murphy's and grimaced. Tonight, Murphy's didn't appeal to her—possibly because Dwayne's call reminded her why she'd left New York.

Nope, definitely not Murphy's. After years of running with Dwayne and hanging around other cops after work, she'd grown tired of putting up with guys pumped up on body building, steroids and testosterone. She needed a change of pace, an ordinary watering hole where she could meet ordinary people again.

She thought about the pub where she and Archie had questioned the tabloid reporter. An upscale clientele, business and lawyer types; not the kind of place where she was likely to meet other off-duty cops. She'd go there.

19

Zalva parked well down the street from Finigan's and walked back. As she approached the pub, she noticed a man standing next to a car parked down the street from the pub, talking to the female driver. As she watched, he leaned into the vehicle and kissed the woman, then turned and lurched across the street, presumably toward his own car.

From behind her, the deep growl of a car engine erupted and she heard tires slipping and squealing on the wet pavement as they picked up traction. A black BMW sedan flashed past her and bore down on the man, who stood mesmerized, as if unable to comprehend the danger—like a deer that had wandered onto a highway.

"Lookout!" she screamed.

Her warning was drowned out by the whining engine of the BMW, and she watched helplessly, expecting to see the man go sailing over the top of the car. But at the last possible second, he lunged aside, barely avoiding being run down. The BMW roared past him, clipped the front of the car of the woman who was just pulling out, and roared off into the rainy night.

Zalva rushed to the man, who was now picking himself up from the pavement and discovered that it was O'Brien, the tabloid reporter. He appeared uninjured, so she hurried over to check out the woman. Once she'd verified that the woman was unharmed, she stepped away to report the accident on her cell phone.

At the sound of shoes shuffling on the wet pavement, she turned to find O'Brien standing behind her.

He glared down the street after the BMW. "Did you see that? The son-of-a-bitch almost killed me!"

"I thought you were a goner," said Zalva.

"You get the tag number?"

"Happened too fast, and my eyes were glued on you."

O'Brien looked into her face for the first time, and realized who she was. "What you doing here? Come to roust me again?"

"No, I came here to eat and relax with a drink. You sure you're okay?"

"Banged my knee pretty hard, but I don't think I broke anything. He came within a gnat's ass of hitting me, though."

"Why did you stand there like a zombie? Got a death wish?"

"Not lately. I heard it coming—saw it coming, but couldn't move."

He stepped past her to talk to his woman, still sitting in the vehicle with her feet on the pavement and her head in her hands. Zalva moved away to give them some privacy. She watched them from a distance of thirty feet and noticed the woman didn't appear to be interested in what he was saying, as she shook her head and held her hands up as if fending him off.

A patrol car arrived and after giving them a report, Zalva entered the pub. She found an empty stool at the bar between a slender, silver-haired, well-tanned executive type of about fifty and a much younger, dot.com-looking executive with a buzz-cut. She ordered a mug of Killian's Red, a patty-melt sandwich, and a large platter of potato skins.

When the beer came, she picked up the mug, swung around on her stool, took a heavy sip, and scanned the crowd.

O'Brien stumbled through the front doorway, spotted Zalva and limped toward her, trying to walk without bending his right knee. He made it to the bar, wedged in beside her, and called out to the bartender. "Mary Kate! How about a mug of Guinness?"

A woman Zalva took to be Mary Kate stalked over to the bar in front of O'Brien and leaned on the counter with both hands.

"You left here again without closing out your tab, didn't you?"

O'Brien's face went blank as he struggled for an excuse. After a few seconds, he spoke in a wheedling voice. "Jesus, Mary Kate. You know I didn't mean to. I just forgot about it. You know, I had a lot on my mind."

"I know exactly what you had on your mind. She's got green eyes and brown hair. Now, give me your card so I can clear your old tab."

O'Brien reached for his billfold, whipped out a credit card and, without a word, tossed it on the counter. Mary Kate, also without a word, picked up the card and stepped over to the cash register.

The silver fox on Zalva's left said something witty that seemed meant for her, so she casually turned to face him. They struck up a conversation in which it only took about a minute for him to let her know what an important man he was in his law firm and how many high-placed members of the current administration didn't make a move without consulting him first. Silver Fox was handsome, intelligent, physically fit for his age, and obviously well-heeled. If he hadn't been such an egotist, she might have been interested.

She let the conversation tail off and turned back toward O'Brien in time to see Mary Kate lean over the counter, holding his credit card with the tips of her fingers as if holding a dead mouse by the tail.

O'Brien gave Mary Kate a puzzled look. "Where's my beer?"

She dropped the card on the counter. "Declined," she replied in a reedy voice.

"What? I sent them a payment."

"Yeah, yeah, it must've gotten lost in the mail."

O'Brien picked up the card and pulled his billfold out, a little more slowly this time. He stuck the declined card back into one of the slots in his billfold and drew out a second card, which he tossed onto the counter, giving it a spin like a professional blackjack dealer might do. "Use this one. I know it's good."

Mary Kate picked up the credit card with a sweeping motion, turned, and stalked off toward the cash register. O'Brien gave Zalva a weak smile, and limped off toward the back of the pub.

The young dot.com guy with the buzz cut gave her the once-over, met her eyes for a moment, and nodded, but turned his attention away without venturing a line. She smiled to herself. He must've thought her too old for him.

A few minutes later, O'Brien appeared beside her at the bar again. He leaned on the counter with his right elbow, facing Zalva, and didn't see Mary Kate coming at him with fire in her eyes. Zalva watched as Mary Kate placed the credit card in the palm of her hand and, with a great looping motion, slapped it down on the counter with a loud splat, like an obnoxious bridge player trumping a trick.

O'Brien spun around to see what caused the noise, and found Mary Kate glaring at him. "Did you do that?"

Mary Kate put her index finger on the card and pushed it across the counter. "This one's no good either."

"Damn! That can't be—"

Mary Kate held her hand up, signaling for him to stop. "Save it, O'Brien."

"That card's a new one. I must've forgotten to acti—"

"Let it go! If you want anything to drink, you're gonna have to pay cash."

O'Brien stuck both hands in his pockets and fumbled for cash, muttering softly under his breath with his brow furrowed. After a couple of seconds, he drew empty hands from his pockets and looked up at Mary Kate like a little boy who'd lost his lunch money. "I forgot to go by the ATM, this afternoon."

"Yeah, right! Like you had money in your account."

"Come on, Mary Kate. I'll pay my tab in cash tomorrow. Just let me have one more brew tonight."

"I don't have any sympathy for you, Will. You shouldn't have loaned Jason two hundred bucks to gamble with, yesterday."

O'Brien looked at her in surprise. "I didn't loan Jason any money."

"He told me he blew two hundred on the snooker table and said he got it from you."

"But that came from—"

"If you can loan money to Jason for gambling, you can certainly pay cash for yourself."

O'Brien glanced at Zalva, looked back at stone-faced Mary Kate for a couple of seconds, and shrugged his shoulders in resignation. *"I can get no remedy against this consumption of the purse. Borrowing only lingers and lingers it out, but the disease is incurable."*

Mary Kate flipped a bar towel over her shoulder and scowled at O'Brien. "Don't think to soften me up with that trick, Will O'Brien. Quoting Shakespeare won't get you any more free rides from me."

Zalva recognized the line O'Brien quoted as one of Falstaff's from *Henry IV*, which she'd worked on as a crew member while in college in New York. Feeling sorry for O'Brien, she decided to help out. "I'll buy the fat knight a tankard of ale."

Mary Kate raised her eyebrows at Zalva; then, with a twisted smile and a shake of her head, she began drawing O'Brien a mug of Guinness Stout.

O'Brien gave Zalva a broad grin. "Thanks. I really need another brew, after what I've been through today."

"Well, you can pay me back one day."

O'Brien shook his head emphatically, causing his jowls to quiver. *"Oh, I do not like that paying back, Tis a double labor."*

Another of Falstaff's lines. Zalva combed her mind, trying to recall something from the play, and came up with only one simple line. *"Sir John, you live in great infamy."*

He hitched up his pants, and grinned at her. *"He that buckles him in my belt cannot live in less."*

His grin was contagious and drew a smile from her. "You must've played Falstaff once, to remember lines like that," she said.

"Played Falstaff for a year with a touring company—still have dreams about it. You know Shakespeare?"

"Just enough to recognize it when I hear it."

Mary Kate set a mug on the counter and slid it down the bar toward O'Brien. He caught the mug, turned it up, and drained a good third of it. Short on air, he brought the mug down on the counter with a bang, and let out a long sigh. He smiled at Zalva, but his smile turned to a grimace, and he flexed his injured knee again.

She watched as he bent over and massaged the knee. "You'd better get that checked out. Might be something broken in there, after all."

"Let me see how bad it looks," said O'Brien. He raised his right foot to rest it on the rung of Zalva's stool, but his foot slipped through and, with his leg tangled in the stool, he fell against the bar. He lifted his leg over the rung of the stool and, red-faced, turned to Zalva. "Didn't hurt none."

"I didn't say anything—but you still might need to see a doctor about that knee."

"I'll take care of it when I get home."

His mention of going home and his lack of coordination unsettled her a little. "How long you been here?"

He wrinkled his brow in concentration. "Since about one . . . I think."

"And you've been drinking all that time?"

O'Brien gave her a *how stupid can you be look*. "Of course. That's what one does in a pub, you know."

"Yeah, and you've had too much. I'm an officer of the law and I can't let you drive off, knowing what I do."

O'Brien gaped at her with a look of disbelief. "You gonna make me take a taxi home?"

"Get a ride with your girlfriend."

He frowned at her mention of the woman. "Carla? Her car was towed away and she left in a cab."

"That BMW ruined your evening, didn't it?"

"You might say that."

"Well, I'll give you a lift home, but you'll have to get a taxi back here for your car in the morning."

"I can handle that," he replied.

"I've got to eat first, so nurse that beer for a while."

Zalva's food arrived and ,while she ate, O'Brien wandered back to the pinball machines.

After finishing her meal, Zalva rounded O'Brien up and they departed for his place.

20

On the way, Zalva decided to probe a little. "Where'd you go to school?"

"George Washington University."

"Degree?"

"Journalism."

She shot him a quick glance. "You've got a journalism degree from GW and you're working for a grocery-store tabloid?"

After a moment of silence, O'Brien replied in a flat voice, "That's right. That's what I do."

"Why not a real newspaper?"

O'Brien folded his arms and looked out the passenger window. "Tried it once. Didn't like it."

Zalva sensed a lot more to it than that, but decided not to press it. "What a waste."

He turned in his seat and looked at her. "I've got a plan to do better."

"Yeah? What's that?"

"I'm going to be a novelist."

"Genre?"

"Mystery. My protagonist is an investigative reporter who solves murders."

"You said *is* and not *going to be*."

"That's right. I've finished my first manuscript."

"That's great. Tried to publish it yet?"

"No. Still polishing it."

"Anyone read it?"

"No, only got one friend. Been reluctant to inflict it on him."

"I love to read. In fact, I fall asleep on the couch every night with a book in my hand."

"Want to read my manuscript?"

"I'd love to."

"Come in when we get to my place and I'll find it for you."

He broke off the conversation and pointed to the street ahead. "Turn right at the corner. My house is the third one on the right."

Zalva turned onto P Street and saw it was lined with rows of well maintained, two-story Federalist-style townhouses. She parked in the empty space in front of his house but, instead of getting out right away, Zalva sat in the car, looking up and down the street at the well-maintained townhouses and brick sidewalks.

"I don't know much about real estate in D.C., but houses in this area are awfully expensive, aren't they?"

O'Brien squinted at the houses through her windshield. "I suppose."

"No wonder you're writing for a tabloid, if it pays well enough to buy one of these."

"Didn't buy it. Inherited it from my grandmother."

"Was she wealthy?"

"Not hardly. Worked for the Library of Congress forty years, though. And my late grandfather retired from the State Department."

They left the car and made the short walk to his porch. O'Brien had difficulty on the steep steps with his stiff knee and had to use her shoulder as support. A ruse, she suspected, to get his arm around her shoulder. She played along and helped him into the house.

The front door opened into a small foyer which led to a moderately sized den with a large brick fireplace and plank flooring—the original flooring, judging by its condition. A matching wainscot wrapped the lower third of the walls, and the first floor ceiling appeared to be at least twelve feet high. One wall of the den contained shelves loaded with books, a small computer desk, and a printer. She pushed a pile of old newspapers aside and sat down on the sofa across from his computer, while he searched for his manuscript; which he apparently hadn't touched for some time, as he seemed not to know where it was.

As he rummaged through the shelves and desk drawers, she realized she hadn't told him about Lezette. "You remember the woman who ran from Pearson's hotel room?"

He stopped his search and looked over his shoulder at her. "Yeah. You find her?"

"Her roommate found her body in their apartment."

"Dead?"

"Yeah. Accidental overdose of cocaine."

"No accident," sneered O'Brien. "She was murdered."

"Murdered? Why would anybody murder her?"

He shuffled across the room with his manuscript and slumped down on the couch beside her. "They hired her to seduce Pearson, so he'd have a heart attack and die. They probably planned to kill her all along."

"What do you mean *they*? Pearson's wife killed him. You think she hired Lezette to seduce him?"

"Pearson's wife didn't kill him."

"Of course she killed him. We found the evidence hidden in her closet."

"Planted."

"What? By who?"

"That bunch down at PMC."

"Are you out of your mind? What bunch at PMC?"

She listened with growing amazement as O'Brien told her about the mystery woman's story of the conspiracy, how he linked Gunter's subsequent death to her story and the results of his visits to PMC and FBI headquarters.

He finished his tale and paused a moment before continuing. "And because of my article and my poking around at PMC today, they suspect I know about the conspiracy, and tried to kill me tonight."

"That's incredible."

"Well, it's true."

"The FBI didn't think so."

O'Brien threw up his hands in a gesture of hopelessness. "I can't help that. It's still true."

"Why wouldn't they just assassinate the president? That would accomplish their mission, wouldn't it? And be a lot simpler, too."

"Lots of reasons. Access for one thing—plus everybody would take a harder look at that, even if it looked natural. Besides, the vice president would take over and still make conservative appointments and pursue the same foreign policy."

"Sounds like one of your hokey tabloid stories to me."

"Then why'd they try to kill me?"

"That was likely some drunk feeling his oats. He probably never even saw you."

O'Brien wasn't convinced, and after arguing with him for about ten minutes, she realized it was pointless. She bid him a good night, and left for her apartment, taking his manuscript with her.

Wednesday

21

O'Brien squinted at the clock on the bedside stand and groaned. Late again. He sat on the edge of the bed for a moment, with his elbows on his knees and head in his hands, waiting for the pounding in his head to taper off. After several agonizing minutes, the pounding eased. He rose from the bed and shuffled stiff-kneed to the bathroom, like Boris Karloff in one of his old mummy movies.

He turned on the shower, stripped off his underwear, and waited for the water to get hot before he stepped in. After lathering up and rinsing off with hot water, he stood with the water beating down on the back of his neck and gradually turned the control all way to cold.

Invigorated by the shock of the icy shower, he dressed and made a phone call to activate the new credit card. He then called American Express, inquired about the status of his payment, and learned it had been received the day before, but not posted in time to clear the hold for that day. The hold was gone now and he could use the card again.

He gobbled down a couple of Pop Tarts, right out of the box, and stepped out onto his front stoop, where he surveyed the neighborhood, then casually glanced toward his parking space. His car was gone!

"Damn it! They've stolen my car!" he yelled. Enraged, he jammed his hand into the pocket of his field jacket and grabbed his phone to call the police.

Suddenly, it hit him: Zalva had brought him home. He let out a long sigh of relief, turned and went back inside, rummaged through the pants hanging in his closet until he found enough cash, and called for a taxi. Normally he'd be annoyed at having to call a taxi, but not this time. The opportunity to get better acquainted with Zalva had been worth the inconvenience.

Forty-five minutes later, O'Brien slumped in his chair at work and sipped thoughtfully on his first cup of coffee. Yesterday, he'd left the FBI office, full of doubt about the conspiracy. Today, with the gimpy knee reminding him of the incident with the BMW, and Zalva's revelation about the French girl being killed, his belief in the conspiracy had grown stronger.

He took another sip of coffee and tried to remember all of his conversation with the woman who had called herself 'Shaunda.' According to her, the conspirators had named three men: Pearson, (the Satyr), Gunter (the Traitor), and the Rogue. He pondered the last nickname. Who could the Rogue be? Maybe a senator from their party who didn't always follow the party line, perhaps voting with the opposition a little too frequently to suit the conspirators.

With that in mind, O'Brien got on the internet, found a site on the U.S. Senate, and printed a report listing every bill the Senate had voted on in the last four years, and how the individual senators had voted. He scanned the voting records, noting and highlighting the few votes that didn't fall along party lines. He found that Senator Scott of Maryland appeared to lean toward the conservative side of issues, having voted contrary to party lines about half the time. Scott was in his third term, up for re-election in November, and had a predominantly Democratic constituency.

O'Brien reared back in his chair, with his hands clasped behind his head. Now that he had a line on who the Rogue was, what could he do about it? After mulling it over for a while, he decided to contact the FBI again. Even though Agents Barnes and Peters had refused to believe his story about the conspiracy, he felt obligated to advise them that Senator Scott fit the profile of the rogue senator mentioned by Marchant and Frenchy, and could be in grave danger. Even if they didn't believe him, they might be afraid to completely ignore his warning, since heads would surely roll in the event Scott *was* murdered and the press later discovered the Agents had ignored his warning.

Agent Barnes accepted O'Brien's call—reluctantly judging from the sound of his voice—listened to what he had to say, thanked him politely, and hung up.

"Up your ass, too," muttered O'Brien. He doubted Barnes would take any action based on his call, but at least he'd made an effort.

O'Brien made a quick run to the coffee pot and returned to his desk, where he sipped his coffee thoughtfully. His conscience wouldn't let him rest—not with his suspicion that the FBI wasn't going to follow through on his warning. What else could he do, though? His intended front-page article for the coming weekend's issue of the *Probe* would deal with the conspiracy and the danger to Scott, but Scott might well be assassinated in the meantime.

He could warn Scott himself, of course. He smiled to himself at that thought. His chances of getting through to Scott were only slightly better than hitting the New York lottery. Still, he had to try. Maybe he'd at least be able to sleep at night, knowing he'd done what he could to warn him.

He called Senator Scott's D.C. office and spoke with a secretary who refused to pass him up the line to someone in authority without knowing the reason for the call. About to tell her Scott's life was in danger, he pictured her dropping the phone before he could complete his message and running around the office like *Chicken Little*, screaming about a caller threatening Senator Scott. Alarmed at the probable outcome of that misunderstanding, he broke the connection.

He needed to speak to someone not likely to go bananas in the middle of his warning. Since the secretary wouldn't pass him up the chain of command, he sent an e-mail message instead, describing the overheard conspiracy and the tie-in to the deaths of Pearson and Gunter. At least if anyone read the e-mail, they were likely to read the entire warning and not go running around Scott's office in a panic.

Having done all he could about warning Scott, O'Brien began to think about the woman who said her name was Shaunda. She probably *was* an employee of PMC, but he wasn't about to try sneaking around in the PMC building looking for her. He'd just as soon not have to deal with Snake Eyes and Roscoe again. His best shot at finding her was to observe the main entrance to the PMC building from a distance, with a pair of binoculars. If he did that around quitting time, he might get lucky and spot her leaving for the day.

He leaned back in his chair, placed his feet on his desk, and wondered where he could buy a small pair of binoculars. Just as he got comfortable, the phone rang. He stretched out his arm and grabbed the phone. "O'Brien here."

"Mr. O'Brien, it's me, Shaunda," responded a soft female voice.

O'Brien swung his feet off the desk and sat up in his chair, with his heart racing. What a break! If he could just get her real name and phone number . . .

"You sound like the woman I met at Finigan's, but you're not Shaunda Rodgers."

After a pause lasting several seconds, the woman replied. "Who I am isn't important. What's important is that you realize I'm right about the conspiracy."

"I'm afraid who you are *is* important, and I'm not going to have anything else to do with you until you identify yourself."

After another long pause, the woman yielded. "Okay, my name is Monique Norris and I really am an employee of PMC."

"Home address, home phone, and cell phone number—now."

"You sure you need all that?"

"Absolutely! I've got prior experience in this sort of thing."

"Okay, but don't give it to anyone else, please?"

"On my honor as a journalist."

That seemed to satisfy her, although he couldn't fathom why, and she rattled off the information. O'Brien jotted everything down, then had her verify it. "Okay, Monique. I believe you about the conspiracy, but I need–"

"I've got to go."
"Wait! Can you meet me for coffee?"
"I can't leave the building right now."
"How about lunch?"
"It'll have to be nearby. I can't be late getting back."
"Name the place."
"There's a small deli about two blocks east of here."
"On K Street?"
"No. It's on Connecticut Avenue, a block up from K Street."
"Name?"
"Sly's Deli."
"What time?"
"Ten after twelve."
"I'll be there."

She hung up without replying. He laid the phone on his desk and pulled a thick phone book from the bottom drawer. He leafed through the pages, found the PMC main number and punched it in. When a woman answered, he asked to speak to Monique Norris.

"One moment please."

After thirty seconds of gangster rap music, produced by PMC he assumed, Monique picked up her phone. "This is Monique, may I help you?"

He hung up without a word. All he wanted was confirmation Monique Norris worked for PMC and that he could recognize her voice. Now he had it.

22

On her way to work, Zalva went by the hospital to check on Archie. She visited with him for about half an hour. He appeared to have come through the by-pass surgery without a hitch, and his prospects were good.

She left the hospital in good spirits, but in route to the station she was dispatched to the scene of a drug-related shooting to assist the two young narcotics detectives already on the scene. Familiar with the area of Anacosta where the shooting occurred, she found the right neighborhood without difficulty, and turned up the street where the body had been found. The street looked much like one from the TV series *Cops*, with trashy yards, run-down houses, broken-down cars parked in yards, and seedy characters loitering on porches, steps, and corners.

Eventually, flashing blue lights came into view. She drove as close to the scene as possible, parked and approached on foot. Uniforms had cordoned off the immediate area, but let her pass when they saw her badge. As she walked toward what she took to be the victim's car, two men carrying a full body bag passed her on their way to their van.

Zalva found the two narc guys, Dodson and Beall, huddled on the sidewalk near the victim's vehicle. Both looked to be in their late twenties, but the similarity ended there. Tall and wiry, Beall wore a Redskins wind breaker, dirty T-shirt, faded blue jeans with holes in the knees, and tennis shoes. Stringy red hair hung down to his shoulders, and he sported a matching soul-patch under his bottom lip.

Dodson, an African-American, stood six feet even, with a stocky build like a college running back. He wore oversized jeans that hung low, exposing his underwear, and a baseball cap bearing a rap band logo, turned sideways on his head.

Beall spotted her and frowned. "What you doing here, Zalva?"

She tried a disarming smile. "I'm from home office and I'm here to help." Beall's frown didn't go away. "No kidding, Captain Thurman sent me over to see if you guys needed any help."

Dodson also appeared irritated that Thurman had thought they might need help, and gave her the sort of look an assembly-line worker might give an efficiency expert. "Don't know why 'big daddy' Thurman sent you over here. Not a whole lot to it. The Dude just tried to cheat the wrong people and they capped his silly ass."

"How you figure?" she asked.

Dodson motioned for her to follow him. "Get that good-looking ass over here, momma, and see for yourself."

She followed Dodson around the vehicle, a late-model, bright-red Ford Mustang. Both doors on the passenger side of the vehicle were standing open, and a chalk outline on the sidewalk denoted where the victim's body had been found. Blood and white powder covered the area around the chalk outline. A ruptured plastic bag, still containing a considerable amount of powder, lay nearby.

"Cocaine?" she asked.

"Yep. Been cut way too much though," answered Dodson. "Looks like his buyer tested the bag and trapped his ass."

"They put a bullet in his brain and threw the bag on his corpse as an insult and a warning to other would-be cheaters," added Beall.

Zalva pictured the scene playing out in her mind. She imagined the horror in the victim's eyes when his buyer pulled out a test kit, and realized he was about to be found out. "They killed him right here on the spot?"

Dodson motioned for her to step closer. "Check out the top of the car."

She did so and peered over the top of the open door. Blood and brains were sprayed all over the roof of the vehicle. She suppressed the urge to retch, and turned her back to the vehicle. The urge passed and she pictured two men pinning the victim against the side of the car while another put a gun to his temple and capped off two or three rounds. "Now that's what I call 'up close and personal'."

Beall noticed a couple of uniformed officers signaling for him. "Those guys have been going door to door. I've got to see what the neighbors had to say." He turned and stepped over to where the officers were waiting.

Zalva turned to Dodson. "Any idea who did it?"

Dodson shook his head. "No, and we'll probably never find out, since we only got about twenty thousand possible suspects and I doubt if any of the neighbors will admit seeing anything."

She knew what he meant. Even if someone in the area had seen it happen, they weren't likely to admit it—knowing the killers knew where they lived. The only way this crime would be solved was for one of the perps to get caught on something else and rat the others out in a plea bargain. "Who was the victim, anyway?"

"Driver's license says Rashid Brown. Know him?"

"Yeah, I remember him. I talked to him about a murder-for-hire case, back when I first came to D.C."

"Never heard of the dude before," said Dodson. "This must've been his first deal."

"He was a 'wanna-be' hit man. Didn't take the contract on the case we had, but it was obvious he'd seriously considered it. Wasn't much doubt he'd take a contract, if the money and conditions were right."

"He was a 'wanna-be' drug dealer too, but not any more," said Dodson. His gaze wandered around the scene and back to Zalva. "I got work to do Zalva. You satisfied we know what's what?"

"Yeah, I don't see what I can add to this investigation."

"Later, then," replied Dodson. He turned and hurried away.

On her way back to her car, Zalva walked by Ginny's Suburban. The rear door was open and, as she passed, she glanced inside, spotted an old army field jacket folded up inside a clear plastic evidence bag, and stopped in her tracks.

The man who robbed the convenience store and shot Senator Gunter had been wearing an army field jacket, and the security camera had revealed a streak of white paint on the left shoulder, like he'd leaned against a freshly painted door frame.

She walked around to the side of the SUV where she found Ginny leaning over the hood, making notes. "Morning, Ginny."

Ginny looked up from her task. "Oh, hi Zalva. What're you doing here? I thought Dodson and Beall had this case."

"They do. Captain Thurman told me to see if they needed any help. I saw something in your unit, though, and wanted to ask you about it. Tell me, that army jacket in the back of your van. Did you take it from Rashid's car?"

"Yeah, off the back seat."

"If you don't mind, I'd like to take a look at it."

Ginny stood, looking puzzled. "Why?"

"You hear about Senator Gunter being gunned down at the convenience store?"

"Yeah, but what's that got to do with this?"

"You didn't see the security video on the news?"

"No, I just read about it in the paper."

"The perp wore an army field jacket and a black ski mask."

"Lots of people wear army field jackets. Anything special about the one worn by the killer?" asked Ginny.

"Looked like it had a streak of white paint on the left shoulder."

"Let's pull it out and take a look," said Ginny.

Zalva accompanied Ginny to the rear of the SUV, where they both donned fresh latex gloves before opening the evidence bag containing the field jacket. Ginny spread out a fresh evidence bag on the floor of her unit, carefully pulled the jacket from its bag, laid it on the bag on the floor, and began unfolding it.

Zalva sucked in her breath when she saw a streak of white paint on the left shoulder of the jacket.

Ginny let out a long whistle. "Well, well—looks promising."

Zalva noticed something black, just inside the sleeve of the jacket. "What's that?" she asked, pointing at the little bit of black material protruding from the sleeve.

Ginny pulled the material from the sleeve and unfolded it, revealing a black ski mask. "Jackpot!" she exclaimed.

"Lucky, lucky," gasped Zalva.

"You don't know just how lucky. If you hadn't come along when you did, this evidence would probably have ended up on a storage shelf and never been seen again," said Ginny.

"You mean it wouldn't have been examined?"

"Probably not, since there was no reason to believe his killers were ever in his car. It's pretty obvious he met someone here for a drug deal and got iced. My staff had already missed the connection of the paint on the jacket with Gunter's death, so even if they went over the jacket with a microscope, they'd probably still miss it."

"Did you find a gun on him?" asked Zalva.

Yes, but Gunter was killed in Virginia—different jurisdiction. They wouldn't think of comparing ballistics on Rashid's gun to a crime in Virginia. Now it might have been checked against some of the recent unsolved murders in D.C., but probably not in Virginia. I guess if the lab did that though, and found it matched the bullets they dug out of the senator, we'd probably go back and look at everything else found in his vehicle, including this jacket."

"That might have been months from now, right?"

"More like years, with all the unsolved murders on file."

Zalva thanked Ginny for letting her look at the jacket, and Ginny promised to notify the proper authorities in Virginia about the evidence they'd found. She left Ginny, got in her vehicle, and headed for the station, wondering if Rashid had accepted a contract on Gunter.

23

O'Brien arrived at Sly's Deli a few minutes before noon and picked up a copy of the *Post* from the rack outside the deli before entering. After buying a cup of coffee at the counter, he found a table which afforded him a good view of the entrance, and settled down to read the paper while he waited.

The wait was anything but boring. Thousands of people worked in the buildings near Sly's, so a steady parade of good-looking women marched through the front doorway. Most of them pretended not to notice him, but a goodly number gave him a knowing smile, while a lesser number saw him and put their noses in the air. O'Brien smiled to himself. How ironic, he thought, to wear lipstick, makeup, high heels, tight blouses, and split dresses, in order to make men notice them, yet act offended when men actually did just that.

O'Brien let out a long sigh. Be honest about it, he told himself. It all depended on who did the noticing. He didn't exactly fit the profile for the type of man most of these women wanted to attract, with his girth, wide face, and wild hair. Still, the few women who had come his way seemed to think him worthy enough, so he must have some redeeming features.

With his mind occupied with reading the *Post* and fantasizing about the female customers, the time passed quickly. He glanced at the front door and saw Monique enter, wearing a black suit and heels. She spotted him and headed in his direction with a worried look on her face.

After reaching his table, she glanced nervously around the restaurant. Then, satisfied with her survey, she sat down across the table from him. "I only have forty-five minutes for lunch, and it took ten minutes to get here."

"We'll get straight to it, but let's order first. We can talk while we eat. Tell me what you want and I'll get it."

"Corned beef with regular chips and iced tea."

After standing in line for only five minutes, he returned with the sandwiches, and placed both baskets on the table.

"Which one is mine?" she asked.

"Either one. I got the same thing you did. Simplified the process." Not altogether true, as he'd ordered a mug of beer for himself. A little 'hair-of-the-dog' wouldn't hurt anything.

Monique nibbled at her sandwich, while he took a huge bite of his. She swallowed her tiny bite and said, "I'm right about the conspiracy, aren't I?"

With his mouth full, he signaled his agreement with a nod.

She leaned across the table and spoke in a voice barely above a whisper. "And Gunter was the one they called the Traitor, wasn't he?"

He pushed the food to one side of his mouth with his tongue and replied, "Almost certainly."

Monique took a second nibble of her sandwich and chewed it thoughtfully. She swallowed the morsel and leaned over the table again. "Who's the Rogue?"

"I'm pretty sure it's Senator Scott from Maryland."

"Can't we do anything to stop it?"

"I called the FBI and sent Scott an e-mail. The FBI probably won't do anything, but the e-mail may put Scott on the alert."

"At least you tried."

He told her about his visit to PMC to see her and his surprise at learning she'd used someone else's name. "By the way, why did you do that?"

"I don't really know. When I opened my mouth to say my name, 'Shaunda' came out." She shrugged her shoulders. "A self-defense mechanism, I suppose."

He let it go and told her about being thrown out of PMC, his unsuccessful visit to FBI headquarters, and his near miss with the BMW.

"You think the conspirators tried to kill you?"

"Damned straight. But we won't be able to convince anybody there's a conspiracy unless we have some proof that the meeting you overheard actually took place. Is there anyone else, another secretary maybe, who can definitely confirm the time and place of the meeting and who attended?"

Monique thought about it for a moment and shook her head. "No, there's only Shaunda, and I don't trust her."

"You still have no idea who the third guy is?"

"None at all."

They ate in silence for a couple of minutes. Suddenly, her face lit up and she grabbed his arm as he raised his mug for another swig, causing beer to slosh over the rim onto the table. "I know how we can prove the meeting took place."

"How?"

She sopped at the spilled beer with a napkin. "Marchant's appointment book. I'll bet the meeting is noted in his appointment book."

"Good idea, but you think he'd record that kind of thing?"

She uttered a sarcastic laugh. "He's as anal-retentive as they come."

"Does he make entries in the book or does Shaunda do it?"

"Shaunda does. She keeps it at her desk."

"You think she has anything to do with the conspiracy?"

"I doubt it, but she's loyal to him. She'd tell him if I started snooping around."

"Can you get access to the book without her knowledge?"

"She has to leave the building occasionally and I fill in for her. And she's away from her desk running around the office a lot . . . so . . . yes. I can get to it."

"Man, it'd be great if the third guy's name is in the book."

"I'll sneak it off Shaunda's desk, late this afternoon, and photocopy the page for that day."

"Can you get away with that?"

"Probably."

"What if somebody sees you with it at the copier?"

"There's a small copier by my desk, so that shouldn't happen."

"Great, but don't copy only the page with the meeting on it. Copy the five pages before that date and the five pages after it, too."

"Why do all that?"

"In case this thing goes to trial and they substitute a bogus appointment book, without the meeting noted in it, for the real one. If I expose them, they might do that, or lose the book altogether."

"What good will that do? If they make a new book, the entries won't look exactly like the ones on our photocopies."

"No, but they wouldn't be likely to change the appointments noted on the other ten pages, just the one with that particular meeting on it. The entries might not be exactly alike, but they'd have the same appointments, which would prove the alternate book was a fake."

Her lips twisted into a wry smile. "Or that the photocopies were fakes."

He stewed over her remark for several seconds. She was right, of course. PMC lawyers could turn it into a real pissing match. And he remembered something, from a movie or maybe a book he'd read, about a court not accepting a photocopy of a document as rebuttal evidence against the *real* document.

"Why can't I just steal the appointment book?" she asked.

"That would solve a lot of problems," he conceded. It wouldn't take Marchant or Shaunda long to figure out who took the book though, and they'd come straight for Monique. He peered into her eyes, looking for signs of fear. She looked down, avoiding his gaze. "Aren't you afraid of being caught?"

She raised her head but avoided eye contact with him. "I'm going to leave my resignation on Shaunda's desk before I go home, this afternoon. I'll grab the book on my way out. If they ask me about it later, I'll just deny knowing anything about it."

"Hey! You don't have to lose your job over this. You could suggest the book got knocked into a trash can and thrown away."

"No . . . it's all right. I can't work there any longer, knowing about Marchant. I planned to hold out until the end of the month, or maybe until I had another job. Now, I want to go back to my hometown in South Carolina. I won't have any trouble getting a job there."

O'Brien didn't attempt to talk her out of it. A grown woman, she supposedly knew her own mind. "Good. Can you bring it to me at Finigan's tonight?"

"Yes, but not before seven. I have some errands to run, after work."

"Great. I'll finally have something tangible to work with."

"But what can you do? If the FBI won't believe us, what good is evidence?"

He took both her hands in his and looked her in the eyes, trying to appear confident. "With some evidence to back me up, and all the names, I'll write an article about the conspiracy for the *Probe,* and name the ones involved. I'll make such a good argument, it'll blow the roof off."

That seemed to give her hope. She gave him a weak smile, and rose to leave. He stood up with her but, as she turned to leave, she sucked in her breath.

O'Brien turned to see what had startled her, and a cold chill crawled down his spine, like a centipede with a thousand legs. Roscoe hovered in the front doorway with an armful of take-out food, like he'd been backing through the door with his arms full, spotted them, and stopped.

Roscoe's dark eyes darted from O'Brien to Monique and back to O'Brien again. He flashed a malevolent grin that said 'gotcha' and slipped through the doorway onto the sidewalk where he merged into the crowd.

24

Zalva sat at her desk, half-heartedly munching on the cold turkey sandwich she'd picked up at a deli. Despite skipping breakfast, she had no appetite. Rashid's possible connection with the murder of Senator Gunter weighed heavily on her mind.

Unable to eat, she tossed the sandwich into the trash can and began rummaging through her old case files. She remembered that when she and Archie had talked to Rashid, only a year ago, he'd expressed a bitter hatred of drug dealers for what they had done to his younger brother, who died from using crack, and for what they were continuing to do to the black community, getting them addicted to crack cocaine—destroying their minds and bodies. He'd ranted wildly about how the black drug dealers were helping to keep their own race down, enslaving them.

She found the case file and flipped through it until she found her notes on Rashid's interview. A brief review confirmed what she recalled about his hatred of drug dealers, which made his apparent involvement in a drug deal even more mystifying. What could have happened to Rashid that would've caused him to become one of the drug dealers he'd despised so bitterly? And what would have caused him to knock over a convenience store? And where did the money for the late model Mustang come from? A couple of convenience store robberies wouldn't net him that much money. Not enough to fund a drug deal either, for that matter. Convenience stores didn't keep that much cash.

According to her notes, Rashid had said he was living with his grandmother, Rachel King, at the time of the interview. She wrote the grandmother's address in her notebook and tossed the file back into the drawer. Rashid couldn't give her any answers, not with the top of his head blown off, but his grandmother might.

Before leaving the station, she called Ginny and confirmed that the address on Rashid's driver's license matched his grandmother's address in her year-old file. But that didn't mean his grandmother still lived there, since people frequently moved without changing their addresses on their documentation. Especially someone like Rashid, who probably hadn't lived with his grandmother in several years, but used his grandmother's address as a blind. Further inquiry revealed that no one had yet been dispatched to advise the grandmother of Rashid's death, so she volunteered for the job.

According to her case file notes, Rashid's grandmother raised him and his younger brother because their mother had abandoned them when Rashid was only three years old. Maybe Rashid still felt close enough to his grandmother to have visited her recently. And maybe he'd said enough, here and there, for Zalva to piece together a theory that would explain his flip-flop on drugs, or maybe confirm that he hadn't changed. And if he hadn't changed, did that mean he took a contract on Senator Gunter's life?

25

Rashid's grandmother lived in Anacosta and, when Zalva had talked to her a year ago, her neighborhood was still a fairly respectable place to live. As she turned onto the grandmother's street, she saw the neighborhood had deteriorated in the past year, but not to the extent of the area where Rashid's body had been found. She pushed the button to lower her window, grabbed her strobe light, and placed it on the roof of the car. Wouldn't hurt to let any creeps lurking in the neighborhood know she was a cop.

Zalva eased her car to a stop directly in front of the grandmother's house and found the old woman sitting on the front porch, watching two small girls playing in the yard. Dread of the task she had before her sent an involuntary shudder through Zalva's body. It was a task she'd performed all too often during her years as a cop. Resigned to it, she blew out a long breath and opened the car door.

Ms. King, dressed in a loose, flowery print dress, rose from her rocker, called the two little girls back onto the porch, and ushered them into the house. With the children safely inside, she turned and, with a hand shading her eyes from the sun, watched Zalva approach the steps. As Zalva drew near enough for Ms. King to see her face well, the old woman's jaw dropped and she sagged back into the rocker, as if she were a life-size, inflatable doll and someone had pulled out the plug.

Amazed at the ease with which the old woman read her face, Zalva ran up the steps and onto the porch to keep her from sliding out of the rocker. She knelt in front of the rocking chair and took Ms. King's hands in hers. "Are you okay, Ms. King?"

The old woman's head flopped forward, her glasses clattered to the porch, and she rolled tear-filled eyes at Zalva. She spoke in a low voice that shook with sorrow. "Rashid's dead, ain't he?"

There was no way to ease into it now, so Zalva confirmed her fear. "Yes ma'am."

"Please help me into the house," she croaked in a hoarse voice.

Zalva picked up Ms. King's glasses, and assisted her through the front doorway and into a tiny living room barely large enough for a tattered couch, a rocking chair, and a badly scarred coffee table. Ms. King pointed a finger gnarled with arthritis at the worn rocking chair. Zalva eased the old woman's frail body down into it.

"Ms. King, would you like for me to get you a glass of water?"

Ms. King's face was buried in her hands, but she nodded in reply. Zalva rose from her crouch by the rocking chair and noticed the two little girls silently watching her from the doorway to one of the bedrooms, with eyes full of fear. They could've passed for twins, except that one was obviously about a year older than the other. Had two more children been dumped on Ms. King to raise? She decided not to say anything to them, lest she frighten them more, and went into the small kitchen.

Although frail and afflicted with arthritis, Ms. King still kept a neat home. The living room was tidy and the kitchen was spotless. Zalva found the cabinet containing glasses, took one out, and opened the antiquated fridge, finding it well-stocked, and spotlessly clean, much cleaner than any Zalva had ever owned. Obviously, Ms. King had a lot of pride. People without pride didn't keep things as clean as this. She found the ice, filled the glass, and took it back to the living room. She handed it to Ms. King. "Here, Ms. King. Drink some cold water."

Zalva took a seat on the adjacent couch and watched as the old woman lifted the glass to her lips with shaky hands, not spilling a drop. She took several short sips and slowly placed the glass on the table next to her rocking chair, being careful to put it on the doily. Finished with the glass, she turned her head toward Zalva and gazed at her with glazed eyes.

"I been worried about him, ever since he called me the other day. How'd it happen?"

Zalva leaned forward, so Ms. King could hear her clearly. "It appears he was killed during a drug deal."

The wrinkles in the old woman's forehead deepened as she frowned at Zalva's words. "A *drug* deal?"

"Yes ma'am. A drug deal."

"Lord-a-mercy, that can't be right." The old woman shook her head and wrung her hands. "Rashid wouldn't never do no drug deal!"

Zalva knew why, but asked anyway, just to confirm it. "Why do you say that?"

"He hated drugs for what they done . . . for what they done to our family." Her voice began to crack and tears streamed down her cheeks. "Drugs done killed his mommy, done killed his daddy, and done killed his little brother. Ain't no way . . . ain't no way Rashid would sell no drugs."

"Ms. King, is there someone I can call to come be with you, to help you through this?"

The old woman's mind was focused on Rashid, and it took several seconds for Zalva's words to sink in. "My friend . . . Priscilla . . . lives a few houses up the street."

"You want me to call her for you?"

Ms. King nodded, fumbled with a pocket on her dress, and pulled out a cell phone which she handed to Zalva. "I have to keep this in my pocket all the time, so I can call the law when I need to. I can't read no numbers right now, though. I think she's five on the memory."

Zalva took the phone into the kitchen and called Priscilla, who said she'd be right over. She returned to the living room, handed the phone to Ms. King, and resumed her seat on the couch. The old woman had taken the news well, having been hardened by a life filled with tragedy.

"Ms. King, do you feel like talking about Rashid now, or would you like for me to come back in a few days?"

Her eyes met Zalva's and she smiled weakly with her thin lips. "I'm . . . I'm . . . fine now. I reckon I always figured this day would come, like it done for all the rest—specially after what he told me the other day. One time, I thought he'd be different. Thought he'd overcome all this." Her shoulders sagged and she sank deeper into the chair. "Reckon nothing never changes though."

"You've said he told you something the other day. Have you seen him recently?"

"He ain't been to see me in months, but he called me last week."

"Did he say anything unusual?"

Ms. King folded her hands in her lap and nodded slowly. "Said he was moving to Miami in a few days."

"For good?"

"That's what he said."

"Did he say why?"

"No, just said he was going."

"Did he have a new job to go to?"

Ms. King sneered at her mention of a job. "He said he had a big-time deal going. Lots of money. But he wouldn't tell me no details. Since he wouldn't talk about it, I knowed it was something bad. That's why I knowed something happened to him when you come up."

"Did he say anything about how much money the deal involved?"

"No. He said he got paid some in advance. Wanted to give me some of it so I could move out of here, but I wouldn't take it. I knowed it was bad money—not drug money, 'cause he wouldn't do that, but still bad money."

"How did he take that?"

"He got mad at me. Said I could go to hell like everybody else. And after I done raised him from a little boy."

"Did he ever bring any of his friends here or mention them on the phone?"

"Rashid didn't have no friends, I reckon—least none I ever knowed of."

Zalva heard someone come through the front door and looked up to see a matronly woman of about forty-five, wearing a hotel housekeeping uniform, enter the room. She nodded to Zalva and went straight to Ms. King, kneeling by her chair.

Ms. King, having a familiar face before her, lost control and began shaking and sobbing again. Priscilla patted her on the back and crooned softly, consoling her. Zalva rose from the couch and stepped out onto the porch. She leaned against one of the porch columns, with arms folded, and took a deep breath. Feeling a tug on her jacket, she looked down and found the taller of the two small girls standing beside her, eyes large with fear.

"What's wrong with Granny King?"

Zalva knelt with her face even with the little girl's and patted her on the head. "Nothing's wrong with Granny King. She just heard some bad news, but she'll be all right in a few minutes."

"She's not gonna go away is she?"

"Of course not. What's your name?"

"Regina."

Zalva smiled. "What a pretty name! And how old are you, Regina?"

A wide grin spread across Regina's face. "Six."

"Why, you're in the first grade then, aren't you?"

Regina's smile vanished and she twisted her mouth to one side. "Don't go to school," she said in a weak voice. Suddenly, she whirled around and ran back into the house.

Poor little girl, thought Zalva. She and her sister had been dumped on Ms. King, after all.

She pondered talking to Ms. King again, but decided the old woman probably couldn't tell her anything more about Rashid that would be helpful. She stepped back inside and signaled for Priscilla to come out on the porch. After giving Priscilla the details about Rashid's death and the phone number to call to find out where the body had been taken, she returned to her vehicle and started it up.

As she turned her car around in the street, her thoughts raced. The grandmother had confirmed her belief that Rashid wouldn't have anything to do with a drug deal. Could the big deal he'd told his grandmother about have been a contract hit on Senator Gunter? Had Rashid received a down payment on the contract, which he used to buy the late-model Mustang? Did Rashid's employer murder him when he tried to collect the balance due for executing the contract? A lot of questions—and she didn't have any real answers. But there was one thing she knew for certain. Drug dealers didn't make down payments!

It'd take a lot more than her hunch to convince Thurman, though. Right now, as far as the evidence showed, Rashid had robbed at least one convenience store for seed money to buy cocaine, which he cut severely, and got himself killed for it. Senator Gunter and the other convenience store customers killed by Rashid were just in the wrong place at the wrong time. A terribly unlucky circumstance.

As she pulled away from the curb, she made a mental note to check with Dodson and Beall later in the afternoon, just in case they had sorted out some additional information on the shooting and the origin of the late-model Mustang.

26

O'Brien returned to his office at the *Probe* and spent the rest of the afternoon on his laptop, writing up what he knew about the conspiracy and listing questions to research and facts he would need to document before the story could be published.

He tired of the work, leaned back in his chair, and tried to relax. His mind wandered back to the look Roscoe had given him in the deli. Did Roscoe's menacing grin at seeing O'Brien and Monique together mean he understood the implications, or simply that he relished the prospect of getting his hands on O'Brien one day? Was Roscoe in on the conspiracy, possibly as a henchman, or just a mean-spirited goon who enjoyed cracking heads whenever possible?

The conspirators would need men like Roscoe: men with few if any scruples, and even less intelligence, to do the dirty work. Men without inhibiting politics or morals. Men who could be easily led, and easily disposed of when the time came to eliminate links back to the top. Probably, Roscoe was the one who tried to run him down in front of Finigan's. Maybe that's what his grin was all about. An 'almost got you, didn't I?' grin.

If Roscoe was in on the conspiracy, he'd certainly tell his boss about seeing O'Brien and Monique together in the deli. If they didn't know who the leak was before, they'd surely know it now. And even if Roscoe wasn't in on the conspiracy, chances were good he'd say something to Snake Eyes about seeing O'Brien again, which might filter back up to Marchant, with the same end result—serious peril for Monique, and for him, too.

Monique had seemed to understand her danger when she spotted Roscoe watching them, but she didn't think they'd harm her at the PMC office, or kidnap her from there, either, for fear of being seen leaving the building with her. She planned to run her errands after work, deliver the appointment book to him at Finigan's, and leave town for her mother's place in South Carolina, without going by her apartment. Once in South Carolina, she had a raft of brothers, cousins, and uncles to protect her. So, if she could snatch Marchant's appointment book and make it home to South Carolina, she'd be safe enough. But it was a big 'if.'

27

O'Brien was playing his favorite pinball machine when Jason wandered up to stand beside him. "How you doing, Will?"

"Peachy keen. How 'bout you?"

"Can't complain. Hey, I heard you almost got run over last night, that right?"

O'Brien spoke without taking his eyes off the steel ball ricocheting around under the glass. "Yep. Had a close call."

"Was it deliberate?"

"Don't know. Could've been a drunk, or just somebody trying to show off a new car."

"Police didn't catch him?"

"No, and probably won't."

Jason flagged Sheena down, ordered two mugs of Guinness, and told her to put it on his tab.

O'Brien grunted in disgust as the last steel ball disappeared down the ball-return hole. Puzzled, he looked up at Jason. "I thought Mary Kate wouldn't let you run a tab because your card was declined."

"I paid my tab and gave her a couple of twenties in advance, so I wouldn't have to pay after every beer."

"Where'd you get the cash?"

"Sold some company stock I'd bought through payroll deductions."

"And now you're loaded, huh?"

"I mailed a check to pay off the credit card and I've got a few bucks left over."

"You gonna give the rest of it to Carla on the snooker table?"

Jason twisted his mouth to one side and shook his head. "Nope! Learned my lesson about that."

O'Brien inserted two more quarters in the machine, and started another game. A few minutes later, Sheena returned with their beer, and he paused between balls to take a heavy pull on the fresh mug.

"You screw Carla yet?" asked Jason.

O'Brien scowled at him. "Now, you know a gentleman doesn't talk about women."

Jason laughed. "Yeah, I know gentlemen don't, but how about you? You make it yet?"

"I could've last night, but the idiot who tried to run me down hit her car."

"She get hurt?"

"No, it just shook her up a little and messed up her car."

"I saw your car parked outside last night, around ten, but you weren't here. Somebody told me you left with Carla."

"She couldn't get over the wreck—caught a cab home. I got hopes she'll be here tonight, though."

"But your car was still here. How did you get home?"

"That female detective I met at the hotel where Pearson croaked wouldn't let me drive. Said I'd had too much to drink."

"You took a cab, too?"

"No, she took me home."

Jason slapped O'Brien on the shoulder and left his hand there. "Hey! You screw her?"

O'Brien brushed Jason's hand off his shoulder in irritation. "Damn it, Jason, I haven't screwed anybody. Every time I'm almost there, something goes wrong."

"Would you do her, if you had the chance?"

"The detective?"

"Yeah."

"What in hell do you think?"

Jason nodded in understanding. "Yeah, me, too." He took another swig of beer and thought for a few seconds. "Which one you rather have?"

"Which what?" O'Brien asked, keeping his eyes glued on the pin ball action.

"Which woman—Carla or the detective?"

"Both, of course."

"I mean if you had to choose between them."

The steel ball disappeared down a trap hole. O'Brien turned to face Jason before playing the next ball. "I gotta make a choice?"

"Yeah, like, if you could only have one of them."

O'Brien took a sip of beer, and thought about it for a couple of seconds. "Zalva, hands down."

"The detective?"

"Yeah."

"Why? Carla's better looking."

"Yeah, but women like Carla come and go through here, all the time." Zalva's a different kind of woman. Quieter, deeper, more mysterious."

"Good, 'cause if Carla shows up, I'm gonna hit on her," said Jason.

"Ha! You think she'd go for you, after you acted like a chump on the snooker table?"

"I think she'd go for anybody who worked at it for a while. Besides, watching her provocative little ass strutting around the snooker table in those tight jeans has been driving me nuts."

"You'll just have to deal with it, 'cause she's got the hots for me."

"Yeah, for right now. But you slip up one more time and I'm moving on her."

O'Brien turned and fired off his last pin ball. "We'll just have to see, won't we?"

After O'Brien's game ended, Jason joined him on the machine and O'Brien thrashed him unmercifully for an hour before Jason tired of losing. O'Brien finished off his mug of Stout, glanced over his shoulder for a waitress and spotted Carla. She saw him and threaded her way to the pinball machine.

When she reached him, he put his arm around her shoulder and gave her a squeeze, winking at Jason on the sly. Jason rolled his eyes at the ceiling, turned, and merged into the throng of patrons.

O'Brien looked down into Carla's sexy green eyes. "You over last night?"

She gave him a weak smile. "Just about. How about you? You weren't injured?"

"Just scraped up a bit. Nothing serious."

"I'm glad." She moved her hand up between his shoulder blades and scratched his back playfully. "You ready to take up where we left off, last night?"

O'Brien wrapped both arms around Carla and pulled her against him. "You know I'm ready, but I can't leave right this minute."

Carla pulled away from him. "Why not?"

"You remember the good-looking African-American woman I met in here the other night?"

"The one I thought was your girlfriend?"

"Yeah. She's supposed to meet me here at seven with some information."

Carla glanced at her watch. "It's seven now. Where is she?"

"Let's give her another thirty minutes. If she doesn't show up by seven-thirty, we'll leave. That okay?"

Carla pouted briefly, then shrugged her shoulders. "I guess so."

O'Brien put an arm around her shoulders and squeezed. "Come on, play pinball with me for a few minutes."

"You ready to be tortured again?" she asked with a wicked grin.

"You talking about the pinball game or something else?"

"Both."

"Why not? You're an expert at both."

And she did torture him at both, teasing him with her body when he played, and outscoring him when she played. The thirty minutes passed quickly and still no Monique. He pulled out his cell phone, found Monique's cell number, and punched it in. He let it ring ten times before giving up. He tried her home phone with the same result.

"Crap. Struck out."

Carla put her arm through his and pulled. "Let's go. You can call her again later."

Monique's failure to show or answer either phone troubled him. Had she come to some harm? Carla tugged on his arm again. He looked down into her sea-green eyes, then down to the low-cut blouse, where her nipples were barely hidden, and felt himself becoming aroused again.

She was getting impatient. If he put her off this time, he might never get another shot. He glanced at the corner by the snooker table and saw Jason watching them, like a jackal waiting for a lion to wander off from its kill.

Carla pressed her body against him, pinning his woody against his abdomen, and nipped him playfully on the neck. She whispered in his ear, "Come on, big guy. You can take care of business tomorrow."

Her hot breath in his ear pushed O'Brien over the edge. "Okay, but this time, let's both go in my car. I'll bring you back here for your car sometime next week."

She laughed. "My car's in the shop, Silly. I came in a taxi."

"Perfect." He took her hand and led her toward the door.

28

They walked down the sidewalk toward his car, with his arm around her shoulders and her arm around his waist. They went to the passenger side, where he fumbled with the key for a few seconds, trying to fit it into the door lock. He finally got the door open, let her in, and walked around the rear of the car, heading for his door.

O'Brien started to get in, but slammed his door shut when he caught movement on his right, out of the corner of his eye. As he turned, two men in dark suits stepped out of the darkness. Both had short, well groomed hair, average builds, and appeared to be in their mid-thirties. They walked directly up to him, and the one on his right spoke. "Mr. O'Brien?"

"Who wants to know?"

The man whipped out his billfold, flashed a badge, and said, "I'm Agent Fielding and this is Agent Carson. We're with the Federal Bureau of Investigation."

Still smarting over the way he'd been treated at FBI headquarters, O'Brien retorted. "So fucking what?"

"Take it easy," said Fielding. "We're here following up on a disturbing report from an acquaintance of yours."

"Oh, yeah? Who?"

"Monique Norris," answered Carson.

"Today?" asked O'Brien.

"This evening."

So that's why she didn't answer her phone, thought O'Brien. She was meeting with these guys. "Is she okay?"

"She's fine Mr. O'Brien. In fact, she's the one who told us where to find you," said Carson.

"She also told us you knew a lot more about the matter than she did," added Fielding.

"Possibly," said O'Brien.

"Mr. O'Brien, we'd like for you to come down to our office with us and help us sort this thing out," said Carson.

"Oh, yeah? The agents I talked to yesterday didn't seem interested. Even accused me of fabricating the story just to sell more papers."

The agents glanced at each other; then Carson spoke again. "Some additional information has come to our attention."

"Like what?"

"We're not at liberty to discuss it here. Please come back to the office with us," said Carson.

"Tonight?"

"Yes. We believe the matter to be urgent," said Fielding.

O'Brien wasn't about to blow his second chance with Carla; he might not get a third. "Tell you what. I'll meet you guys at the bureau office, first thing in the morning."

Fielding shook his head. "I'm afraid you'll have to come with us right now, Mr. O'Brien."

"And if I say no?"

Carson stepped closer to O'Brien and jutted his chin out so far it almost touched O'Brien's nose. "We'll cuff you and drag you in."

Not a pleasant alternative, thought O'Brien. He ducked his head and glanced at Carla, sitting on the front seat.

She leaned across in an effort to see the two men. A frown crossed her face, and she mouthed something that looked like, "Come on, now. Let's go."

He gave her an understanding wink and straightened up to face the two agents. "How long will it take?"

"About two hours, there and back," replied Carson.

"All right. Give me a couple of minutes alone with my woman, first."

"Make it quick," snapped Fielding.

O'Brien walked around the car and opened Carla's door. "Come on Carla. We're not going to my place until later."

With a puzzled look on her face, she climbed out of the old Volvo. "What's wrong?" She scowled at the two men standing in front of his car. "And who are these geeks?"

He took her hands in his and pulled her close. "FBI agents."

Carla's eyes widened with concern. "Are they arresting you?"

"No, but they want me to go down to headquarters with them. It's about the story I'm working on."

"It has to be tonight?"

"I tried to put it off until tomorrow but they wouldn't buy it."

"But what about us?"

"I'll be back here in two hours. Hang around and play snooker or something."

"You sure you'll be back tonight?"

"Absolutely."

"You'd better be," she muttered under her breath.

He pulled her against him, put his arms around her and kissed her, but she stood passively and didn't return the kiss. When he released her, she turned abruptly and stalked across the street to Finigan's without looking back, obviously pissed.

Shoulder to shoulder on either side of him, the two agents marched O'Brien down the sidewalk toward their vehicle, parked farther down the street.

"This is it," said Fielding, as they neared a bright green Buick.

The bright green vehicle seemed a little odd to O'Brien, as he thought FBI agents always drove nondescript Fords or Chevrolets. He glanced at the license plate as they walked past the rear of the vehicle, and saw it wasn't a government plate.

They steered him toward the rear door nearest the sidewalk and Agent Carson opened it for him. With his scalp crawling in alarm, O'Brien put his right hand against the open door frame and turned to face them. "Let me see those badges ag—"

Something cold and hard slammed against his temple. Stars exploded in his head, then faded as his legs went limp and he sagged to the sidewalk by the open car door. Fielding stood over him with his legs spread and spoke with a phony sounding Mexican accent: "We don't need no stinking badges."

Although O'Brien understood what Fielding said, he lay paralyzed, unable to command his arms or legs. He knew they were kidnaping him, but found himself helpless, unable to resist. Fielding grabbed him under the armpits and, with assistance from Carson, shoved him into the back seat, then slid in after him. Carson started up the engine and the car eased away from the curb.

O'Brien's breath came in quick, shallow gasps and he feared his heart would leap from his chest. He struggled against the panic and focused his thoughts. These guys were going to take him to a secluded spot and murder him. Probably already had a hole dug, out in the boondocks.

He slowed his breathing down, trying to calm himself. He'd always heard the best time for a kidnap victim to escape was immediately after capture, before being taken to a controlled environment. He remained slumped across the back seat with his knees on the floor, pretending to be unconscious, while ransacking his brain for a plan.

"You kill him?" asked Carson, from the front seat.

"No, I heard him grunt when we shoved him into the car," replied Fielding.

"Good. We've got to find out exactly what he knows and how much he told the FBI."

Lying in a position where neither of the men could see his face, O'Brien opened his eyes and studied the door, only inches away. The door handle hadn't been removed. Confident they could handle him, his captors hadn't even bothered to make the car escape-proof.

The vehicle had traveled at least three blocks from the pub, but O'Brien still felt a little groggy from the blow. Deciding it best not to try anything until he had full control of his faculties, he counted off sixty seconds silently, wiggled his toes, and flexed his fingers. Everything felt okay. Now he had to work up the courage to try an escape.

Fielding broke the silence. "Slow down a bit. Give that light up the street time to change to green before we get there. Last thing we need is to be sitting in a well-lighted intersection for two or three minutes."

Carson muttered something under his breath in response, but slowed the vehicle.

Time to act, thought O'Brien. Do it now while the car is moving slowly. He set his teeth, steeling himself for his move, and groaned as though he was still in a fog. Suddenly, he reached for the door handle and kicked out at Fielding with the heel of his foot at the same instant.

The bogus agent turned just in time to catch the full force of O'Brien's heel on the end of his nose. The door flew open and the force of O'Brien's foot against Fielding's face helped propel him through the opening. He hit the pavement with his shoulder and rolled.

The car skidded to a halt, fifty feet away. O'Brien struggled to his feet and limped quickly toward the sidewalk, looking for a place to hide— knowing that if they came after him on foot, he couldn't get away. His heart leaped with joy as the headlights of another car coming from behind them lit up the street.

O'Brien limped back to the middle of the road and began waved his hands at the oncoming vehicle. He heard the screech of tires burning rubber behind him and looked over his shoulder, fearing the kidnapers were backing up to run over him. Relief flooded over him as he realized they were going in the opposite direction.

The driver of the approaching vehicle leaned on his horn, veered around him, and kept going. O'Brien yelled a curse after him before hobbling back to the darkness of the sidewalk. Fearing his kidnapers would turn around and come looking for him, he hid behind a parked car for several minutes.

Then, satisfied they weren't coming back, he began hoofing it back toward the pub. Believing himself safe, he felt his adrenalin rush peter out, and the pain hit him. He'd skinned his right elbow, the heel of his left hand, and both knees when he hit the pavement. His knees kept getting stiffer and stiffer, but eventually he made it back to Finigan's, pushed the door open and limped inside.

29

Zalva took a long nap after work, before leaving for Finigan's for a couple of beers and dinner. She arrived at the pub a few minutes before eight and settled down on a stool at the bar. She turned her back to the bar and scanned the mob of rowdy patrons for O'Brien, but didn't see him.

"Can I help you?" asked a voice from behind her, heavy with an Irish accent.

Zalva spun around on her stool and faced Mary Kate standing behind the counter. A bar towel clung to her shoulder, and her arms were stretched out with her hands, palm down, on the counter.

"Mug of Killian's Red and a corned beef sandwich," answered Zalva.

Mary Kate's brows lifted when she recognized Zalva. "Well, looks like you're becoming a regular."

"Yeah, you've got a nice place here. A lot different than where I usually hang out."

"I bet that's Murphy's, where all the cops hang out."

"Matter of fact."

"Too many of the same kind of people, huh?"

"Yeah, it got old being around other cops all the time. Besides, with all those macho guys in there, the air was so thick with testosterone, a girl could sprout a mustache from just walking through the place."

Mary Kate laughed, grabbed a mug from the overhead rack, and drew Zalva's beer. "Cops catch the guy who tried to run over Will last night?"

"Not yet, and not likely either, since I didn't get the license number."

Mary Kate plopped the full mug down in front of Zalva, and wiped up the foam that spilled onto the counter. "Too bad."

"Speaking of O'Brien, have you seen him tonight?"

"Yeah, he was here earlier. I saw him leave with the same little brunette he left with last night. They must've had a falling out, though, 'cause a minute or two after they left, she came back in alone."

"How long ago?"

"A minute or two before you came in."

"And he didn't come back in afterwards?"

Mary Kate shook her head. "Didn't see him, if he did." With that, she sidled down the bar to draw a refill for another customer.

Zalva swivelled her stool around, leaned on the counter with her left elbow, sipped at her beer, and surveyed the patrons over the rim of her mug. She caught movement out of the corner of her eye, glanced in that direction, and saw O'Brien standing just inside the entrance.

He saw her at the bar and shuffled toward her, stiff-legged, like a zombie from *Night of the Living Dead*. Her eyes traveled down his legs and she saw his bloody knees protruding from the holes torn in his pants. She jumped off the bar stool and rushed to help him.

"What happened? Somebody run you down again?"

He reached around her and put his hand on her shoulder for support. "They moved up to kidnaping."

"Kidnaping? Somebody tried to kidnap you?"

"Yeah, right out there in the street."

"Just now?"

"Right."

"Who tried to kidnap you?"

"Two bogus FBI agents."

She helped him over to the bar. "Here, take my stool and tell me about it."

He tried to raise his leg to sit on the stool and winced when he bent his knee. "I'd better stand up."

She climbed back on the stool, put her back against the bar, and folded her arms. "Give me the details."

"I need a brew first."

Zalva caught Mary Kate's attention and signaled for her to bring O'Brien a mug of stout. When the beer came, O'Brien chugged half of it, wiped his mouth with his sleeve, and began talking. She listened skeptically as he described being approached by the two men, how he got wise to them when he saw their car, and his escape.

"You get the license number?"

O'Brien shook his head. "No, I just glanced at it and saw it wasn't a government plate."

Using her cell phone, Zalva called the dispatcher at her station and gave her a description of the vehicle and the men. Finished with her call, she turned back to O'Brien. "They'll put out an alert but I doubt if anything will come of it. It was probably a stolen vehicle and they've abandoned it by now."

"Figured that much," he muttered under his breath.

Her sandwich arrived and she fell to eating. While she ate, she studied him and reflected on what he did for a living: the outright lies in his articles and the scandals he'd disclosed. Was it possible someone he'd exposed had sent a couple of goons to work him over? And was he taking advantage of the situation to bolster his half-baked conspiracy theory?

She swallowed a mouthful of sandwich and said, "Soon as I finish this, you'll have to go down to the station with me, make a written statement, and look at some mug shots."

O'Brien made a noise of agreement and turned his gaze toward the back room, presumably looking for the young brunette. Suddenly his face turned pale and he gasped.

"What's wrong?"

"Monique! Monique is in danger!"

"Who's Monique?"

"She's the one who overheard the conspiracy."

"I thought she gave you somebody else's name, and you didn't know who she was."

"She called me at the *Probe* this morning and I met her for lunch."

"She add anything to her story?"

O'Brien described the lunch meeting, their plan to swipe the appointment book for confirmation of the conspiracy meeting, and being seen by Roscoe. "And she was supposed to meet me here with Marchant's appointment book at seven, but she didn't show up."

"Better call her—make sure she's okay."

"Tried that earlier, but couldn't get her."

"Try again."

O'Brien pulled his cell phone from his pocket and tried again. After letting it ring awhile, he announced, "No answer."

"Doesn't necessarily mean anything. She could be on the internet," said Zalva.

"Yeah, or she could be tied up somewhere, waiting to be murdered, or maybe lying on her floor, bleeding to death." said O'Brien.

"You know where she lives?" asked Zalva.

"Her place is across the river, in Alexandria."

Zalva grabbed what was left of her sandwich, took a quick bite, and spoke with her mouth full. "Come on, let's check it out."

30

O'Brien gave Zalva Monique's address and she drove in silence for several minutes. Her mind drifted to the manuscript he'd given her the night before.

"I read the first hundred pages of your manuscript, last night."

O'Brien turned to look at her. "Really?" he asked, with excitement in his voice. "Did you like it?"

"Yes. It's good. Your characters are believable, your dialog sounds realistic, and the action is fast-paced." She glanced at him and saw a wide grin on his face. "I believe you can make it as an author."

"You're not just saying that to get in my pants, are you?"

She gave him a longer glance. "I don't think I'd have to lie to get into your pants—seems nobody else has to."

He let her barb go unanswered, so she returned to the discussion of his manuscript and his ideas for future novels, which made the time pass quickly. They soon found Monique's apartment building, a converted Victorian home in an older section of Alexandria.

They climbed the exterior stairway to Monique's apartment and Zalva rang the doorbell. A couple of minutes passed without a response. She rang again, rapped sharply on the door, and placed her ear against it. She couldn't hear a radio or TV, nor did she hear anyone talking or moving around.

O'Brien reached around her and tried the doorknob. To her amazement, the door swung open. "After you," he said, waving for her to go in.

She turned and wagged a finger in O'Brien's face. "You shouldn't have done that. You might've screwed up any prints on the knob."

"Damn! I didn't think about that."

"Make yourself useful. There's a small box of latex gloves and another one of shoe covers on the back seat. Go grab us a pair of each. We'll have to put them on before we go in."

She waited by the open door while he carried out her instructions. A couple of minutes later, properly attired to inspect a crime scene, she stepped through the doorway, with O'Brien breathing down her neck.

The only light came from the vent hood over the kitchen stove, which barely illuminated the front room, casting long, forbidding shadows across the carpeted floor.

"Monique?" called out Zalva.

"It's me, O'Brien," said O'Brien loudly.

No answer. Maybe she'd gone to dinner or stepped out to the drug store. Not likely though, thought Zalva. Monique wouldn't go off and leave the door unlocked—not even in Alexandria.

She glanced around the apartment, which appeared to have only one bedroom and a large space that contained the living room, kitchen, and eating area. The bedroom door was closed. Reluctantly, she approached it, walking softly to avoid alarming anyone who might be in there.

O'Brien put his hand on her shoulder and whispered into her ear. "Maybe she and her boyfriend are in there 'making the beast with two backs'."

A real possibility, thought Zalva. How embarrassing that would be. She paused at the bedroom door, put her ear to it, and listened for a couple of seconds. She couldn't hear any snoring or other evidence of someone sleeping, nor any sounds of lovers embraced in ecstacy. She rapped on the bedroom door, just to be sure, and called out her name again. "Monique?"

She got no answer, so she turned the door knob and slipped into the bedroom. A sliver of light outlined the bathroom door, but didn't give enough light for Zalva to see if anyone was on the bed. She ran her hand along the near wall and found the light switch, flicked it, and saw a made-up bed with clothes laid out, as if Monique had planned to change clothes and go out.

Zalva crossed to the bathroom and knocked softly on the closed door. Still no answer. She turned the knob and tried to push the door open, but met resistance. Something was blocking it from the inside.

Goose bumps crawled up her arms and down her neck. "No, don't let it be," she whispered with a fearful voice. As a rookie cop in New York, she'd had this same situation and found a teenage suicide victim.

Zalva peeked through the narrow opening but couldn't see anything but the opposite wall. O'Brien pulled her aside, put his shoulder to the door, and pushed hard, creating enough space for Zalva to stick her head into the bathroom.

She saw the nude body of an African-American woman on the floor between the toilet and the partially open door. Her gaze swept the tiny bathroom and came to rest on traces of white powder and a rolled-up piece of paper on the vanity next to the toilet. "Jesus! Another cocaine overdose."

O'Brien reached over her shoulder and pushed the door hard, opening it wide enough for her to squeeze through. She quickly knelt by the body, hoping to find a pulse. There wasn't one.

Zalva looked over her shoulder at O'Brien. "This Monique?"

"It's her. She dead?"

Zalva rose to her feet and exhaled a long breath. "Yep. About two hours ago, I'd say." She pointed to the vanity. "Looks like she was sitting on the toilet, snorted some cocaine, and fell over dead, blocking the door from the inside."

She squeezed back through the doorway. In the bedroom, she pulled out her cell phone and reported finding the body to the local police department.

Two hours later, after being grilled by local detectives and giving their written statements, Zalva and O'Brien left Monique's apartment for

Finigan's, where O'Brien had left his Volvo. They rode in silence for a few minutes, then O'Brien spoke. "You don't really think her death was an accident, do you?"

Here it comes, thought Zalva. More of his conspiracy bull. "Well, it certainly looks like it."

O'Brien turned in his seat, placing his back against the door. "Didn't you tell me that the French girl, Lezette, died from a cocaine overdose?"

"Yes, she did. But that *was* an accident. Her roommate saw her come in by herself and stumble back to her bedroom."

"And you believe it's just coincidence that the only two possible witnesses in this case both died of cocaine overdoses?"

Zalva took in a deep breath and let it out slowly, gathering her patience. "Look, O'Brien, at this point, you have no case."

"What? How about my kidnaping? Did I imagine that?"

"Any witnesses see you get kidnaped?"

"How about my knees?" O'Brien leaned over and pushed his bushy hair off his forehead. "How about this knot on my head, where one of them conked me with a gun?"

She glanced at his head. "I agree it looks like somebody roughed you up a bit, but I only have your word that it involved bogus FBI agents and a kidnap attempt."

"How about Carla? She saw me leave with the kidnapers."

Zalva hadn't talked to Carla yet. It would be interesting to hear what she had to say. "If she's still at Finigan's when I drop you off, I'll talk to her." It was a small concession to make to appease him. It seemed to satisfy him, as he sat in silence for several minutes.

She studied him out of the corner of her eye. Just in case his story might be true, she asked, "If you really were kidnaped, and you think it had something to do with your conspiracy, aren't you a little worried about going back to your place tonight?"

He dismissed her concern with a wave of his hand. "I'll spend the night at Jason's. He owes me a few favors."

31

They arrived at Finigan's before it closed, but didn't find Carla. Zalva sat down at the bar and had Mary Kate pour her a cup of coffee.

O'Brien slid in beside her, leaning on the bar with his elbows. "Mary Kate, how long has Jason been gone?"

Mary Kate swaggered over to the bar in front of O'Brien, put an elbow on the bar, and leaned over in his face. "He left here about ten minutes after you did, and you'll never guess who with."

Zalva detected a touch of irony in Mary Kate's voice—enough to cause her to suspect where Mary Kate was headed.

O'Brien bit the hook. "Who?"

Mary Kate winked at Zalva. "That little brunette you've been chasing."

O'Brien's head snapped back as if Mary Kate had tossed a shot of whiskey in his face. "What? He left with Carla? *My* Carla?"

"She saw you leave with Zalva, and came running up here to the bar with fire in her eyes. She asked me if you'd just left with another woman. When I told her you had, she didn't say a word, just turned and stomped off. A couple of minutes later she strutted out of here with Jason draped all over her."

Poor O'Brien, thought Zalva. Carla just wasn't in the cards for him. First the episode with the BMW, and tonight, the alleged kidnaping.

"But it wasn't my fault," protested O'Brien.

"Woman scorned," muttered Mary Kate. She turned and moved down the bar to wait on another customer.

Zalva studied O'Brien's face from the side. His pride was shattered. The woman he'd chased, or who had chased him, was sleeping with his best friend. "I don't suppose you'll be spending the night at Jason's after all, huh?"

He gave her a dour look. "Guess not."

"Well, come on. You can sleep on my couch tonight." But to make certain he knew it was just an accommodation, she wagged her finger in his face. "You get out of line, though, and I'll cuff you to the railing on the balcony and you'll freeze your balls off."

"I'll manage with the couch."

With that settled, she drove them to her apartment, leaving his car at Finigan's, with a promise to drop him off on her way to work in the morning.

32

It was well after midnight by the time they got to her one-bedroom apartment in Adams-Morgan. After settling O'Brien on the living room couch with a spare pillow and blanket, she found a tube of Neosporin, a roll of tape, and a small box of bandages in her bathroom cabinet. She walked into the living room and tossed them over the back of the couch to O'Brien.

"Ouch! Hey, what gives?" O'Brien struggled to a sitting position, rubbing his nose where the box of bandages hit him.

"You better dress your wounds. Best not to risk an infection."

O'Brien muttered something under his breath and set about doctoring himself. Zalva returned to her bathroom and got ready for bed. Finished with her nightly toilet routine, she started for the bed, but stopped when she heard O'Brien's muffled voice through the bedroom door. Was he talking to himself?

She opened her bedroom door and saw O'Brien sitting up on the couch, muttering and cursing. As she watched, he wadded up a piece of hopelessly-tangled tape and hurled it across the room in disgust. She smiled and padded into the room.

Relief spread over his face when he saw her come around the couch.

"Can you help me with this? I keep screwing it up and wasting tape."

"I suppose I'd better, if I'm going to get any sleep." She sat at the end of the couch by his feet. He had stripped down to his maroon boxer shorts, the kind Michael Jordan once hawked on TV, in order to get at his wounded knees. She couldn't help but run her eyes over his lower body. While he was pudgy from the waist up, his thighs and calves were muscular and hairy.

She glanced up at his face and caught him eyeing her legs, and the space in between. The short nightshirt she wore reached just below her hips and had ridden up when she sat down. Blushing, she twisted her hips to the side and put her legs together.

As she leaned over to get a good look at his knees, she sneaked a peek at his face. He caught her at it and grinned.

Zalva cleared her throat and inspected his knees. The problem with bandaging knees was that every time the knee flexed, the bandage loosened. She needed Ace Bandages to hold the gauze and ointment on the wounds, but didn't have any.

"The tape isn't going to work on your knees, so I'm just going to load the wounds up with ointment for tonight. Do me a favor and sleep on your back or side, so you don't rub the ointment off on my couch, okay?"

"Whatever you say, Doc."

She spread the ointment liberally on both knees, then rose from the couch. "Sit up now, so I can do your head."

He complied, and she moved to stand in front of him. She pulled his hair back to inspect his temple and found a nasty scrape, but no gash like she'd expected. Whoever hit him with the gun knew how to use one, and struck him a glancing blow. "No need to bandage this one either. I'll just put a little ointment on it for tonight."

She leaned over him, held his hair back with one hand and squeezed the ointment onto his temple with the other. Her position put her breasts within inches of his face, and she felt his hot breath against a nipple, which hardened, to poke at the flimsy night shirt. She tensed up, expecting him to notice and take action. What would she do when he did?

Her mind raced. She hadn't slept with a man since leaving New York, and seeing and touching his muscular legs, and stealing a glance at the bulge in his shorts, had stirred a hunger in her. She realized there was no doubt about how she'd react.

She finished with his head and stepped back, disappointed that he hadn't moved on her at all. Surely he'd noticed her hardened nipples. Didn't he find her desirable?

"Thanks," he said, with a blank expression.

"Don't mention it." Her voice was weak and shaky. Embarrassed, she dropped the tube of ointment in his lap and padded back to her bedroom.

Thursday

33

O'Brien woke to the smell of fresh coffee and the tantalizing aroma of sizzling bacon. He sat up, swung his feet to the floor, and cried out in pain when he bent his knees.

Zalva called out from the small kitchen, "Hey! Come eat while the eggs are hot."

He grabbed his pants off the back of the couch and pulled them on, trying to avoid dragging the material across his knees, but failed. "Son-of-a-bitch!"

"Knees sore?" asked Zalva.

"Only when I touch them or bend them."

O'Brien shuffled stiff-legged to the counter that separated the kitchen from the living room, and eased onto one of the stools. The kitchen was narrow, enabling the cook to reach the counter while working at the stove. Zalva turned to face him, placed two steaming cups of coffee on the counter, and turned back to the range. He noticed she was already dressed for work in her customary outfit of khaki pants and, today, a turquoise polo shirt.

Zalva pulled two plates from a cabinet, divided a pan of scrambled eggs between them and added several strips of bacon from the microwave.

She snatched four pieces of toast from the toaster and threw them onto the plates. She turned to the counter with a plate in each hand and placed them on the counter. Instead of coming around the counter to sit beside him, she remained in the kitchen and began eating, while standing.

They ate in silence for several minutes. Finally, Zalva swallowed a mouthful of eggs, and asked, "You sleep okay on the couch?"

"Yeah, didn't even have any of my usual nightmares."

"You want me to drop you off at Finigan's for your car or take you all the way home?"

"Finigan's. My knees aren't so bad I can't drive."

"You coming down to the station to look at mug shots today?"

"What's the point? You don't believe I was kidnaped."

"How can you expect me to believe you if you don't even try to identify the two men involved?"

"Okay, okay. I'll come down to your station some time this morning after I check in at the *Probe*. Now what do we do about Monique, and the possibility the PMC gang of thugs murdered her?"

Zalva ran her hand through her thick black hair and frowned. "The guys we gave our statements to last night seemed to be satisfied she died of an accidental overdose. It's their jurisdiction, so it's up to them. And I don't think they're going to look for a murderer."

"Can't you push them on it?"

Zalva gathered up their empty plates, cups, and forks, and dumped them into the sink. She turned back to face O'Brien. "No, I can't push them. I've got to talk to Captain Thurman about another matter, though, and I'll mention Monique, too. Now let's get a move on. I'm due at work."

34

In route to Finigan's, Zalva told O'Brien about Rashid Brown being murdered during a drug deal, the evidence she'd found to link him to Gunter's death, and the fact he'd been a wanna-be hit man in the past.

"Aha! Just what I thought."

Zalva shot a glance at him. "Don't get carried away now. It's a huge leap from a mere suspicion to finding concrete evidence of a contract hit."

Nevertheless, her suspicion bolstered his confidence. "At least it's clear Rashid was murdered, so you guys will be looking for his killers—which is more than I can say about Lezette and Monique."

Zalva lapsed into deep thought and didn't say much the rest of the way to Finigan's, merely nodding her head or grunting whenever he spoke. As she pulled along-side his parked car, she finally spoke. "I'm going to lay out everything you've told me for Captain Thurman. He may authorize me to interview Marchant at PMC, but I wouldn't count on it."

O'Brien gave her a weak smile. "At least that's something." He opened the door and slid out. "See you at Finigan's tonight?"

"Maybe."

He closed the door and watched her drive off.

Fearing that a bomb might have been planted in his car, he unlocked the door on his Volvo and pushed the buttons for the trunk lid and the hood. After he found those areas free of explosive devices, he laid down on the pavement and slid under the vehicle. He didn't find anything there either, and pulled himself back out.

Getting back on his feet without placing his knees on the pavement was a bitch, but O'Brien finally made it, using the open driver's door to pull himself erect. He sat in the driver's seat and, with the side of his face against the steering wheel, groped under the seat, along the steering column, and under the dash, but found no wires or bombs.

He rested the back of his head against the headrest and breathed a sigh of relief. Maybe the conspirators wouldn't use something as obvious as a bomb. They'd want his death to appear accidental, like all the others. Or maybe he'd simply disappear one day, like he almost did, last night.

O'Brien inserted the key in the ignition, closed his eyes, set his jaw, and turned the key. The engine coughed and sputtered before settling into a smooth drone. He gave his shoulders a shrug to ease the tension in his spine and released his death grip on the steering wheel. For a moment, he simply sat and flexed his fingers, working out the pain from gripping the steering wheel so tightly. Fingers normal again, he pulled out into the street and drove toward his place for a shower and fresh clothes before going to the office.

O'Brien drove two blocks past his townhouse, turned around and came back to it, peering into all the parked vehicles for stakeouts. No suspicious-looking characters lurked in the parked cars or on the sidewalks. He parked in front of his place, walked up the front steps to his door, and inspected it carefully for wires. Better to be paranoid than dead, he reasoned.

He found nothing, opened the door and slipped inside. *So far, so good,* he thought, *but the day was still young.*

35

An hour later, O'Brien sat in Slick's office, sipping a cup of steaming coffee while reporting the events of the previous twenty-four hours, including what Zalva had told him about Rashid Brown: his one-time desire to be a hit man, the evidence indicating he'd killed Gunter, and the possibility he'd been executed and not killed in a drug deal, despite appearances.

Throughout O'Brien's narrative, Slick kept silent, sitting with his feet on the corner of his desk, head tilted back, staring at the ceiling and stroking his mustache.

When O'Brien wrapped up, Slick turned his gaze to him. "But with Monique dead, you've got no witnesses, right?"

"That's right. She was all I had."

"And you still don't have any proof the alleged meeting ever took place?"

"No, not yet."

Slick picked up a paperclip from his desk and toyed with it, bending it into various shapes while pondering the matter. "A lot of coincidences all right, and each one of them self-contained—like a card full of pills, with each one under a separate blister. Let's go . . . "

Slick stopped in mid-sentence as the door behind O'Brien opened and someone stepped into the office. O'Brien looked over his shoulder and saw a tall, slender man dressed in a dark suit and red tie, standing in the doorway. He appeared to be in his late forties, with hair beginning to gray at the temples, and there was a look of annoyance on his face, as if he was about to do something distasteful or beneath him.

"Meet me in the conference room," he said curtly. Then he turned and disappeared down the hallway.

O'Brien turned back toward Slick and found him standing behind his desk, staring at the open doorway with a puzzled look on his face. "Who's that?" he asked.

"Bridges, the CEO of the holding company that owns the *Probe*."

O'Brien knew that a holding company called Celebrity Press owned the *Probe*, but he'd never met any of the officers or owners. Slick usually went to the holding company's office in New York for any business meetings. Something unusual was afoot. O'Brien was convinced of it, and so, he believed, was Slick.

O'Brien picked up another cup of coffee from the break room and retired to his desk, while Slick went to the conference room for the impromptu meeting. Five minutes passed, and he glanced at the doorway just as two men in security uniforms walked past.

"What in the hell is going on?" O'Brien asked aloud. He stood and walked around his desk to look down the hallway, but was met at the doorway by the man Slick had identified as the CEO of the holding company and two more security guards.

O'Brien retreated until he backed into the edge of his desk. "What's going on out there?"

The holding-company man took a step toward him. "O'Brien, I'm Nelson Bridges, CEO of Celebrity Press, the company that owns the *National Probe*. I'm sorry to have to tell you this, but due to economic conditions, we're terminating the operations of the *Probe* as of this morning. Accordingly, your employment is also at an end." Bridges handed O'Brien an envelope. "This check includes the salary you have coming for the current pay period plus one month's severance pay."

The strength drained from O'Brien's arms and legs, and he felt hollow, as if his insides had been sucked out. He automatically accepted the envelope, and tried to speak, but no sound came out.

"You've got five minutes to collect your personal items," said Bridges. Then he turned to the security guards. "Give him five minutes. He's to take nothing with him but his personal items."

O'Brien's shock faded as he realized what Bridges had said. His ears and face burned with anger. In a voice trembling with rage, he said, "That laptop computer on my desk and that camera and other equipment on the credenza are among my *personal* items."

Bridges glared at him with eyes of lead. "That may well be the case. But some of the files in your computer, if not all, and the film in your camera are the property of the *Probe*. You can pick up your equipment in the lobby in a couple of hours, after we've had a chance to remove company property."

Within minutes, O'Brien found himself standing next to Slick on the sidewalk in front of the *Probe's* office building, feeling displaced and violated.

36

Slick appeared dazed, so O'Brien led him across the street to the coffee shop and bakery where he'd first seen the story of Senator Gunter's murder on TV.

He steered Slick to a table, then went to the counter and returned with two cups of black coffee. Slick stared silently at the mug of coffee before him, reached into his coat pocket, and pulled out a small flask. He slowly unscrewed the cap and poured a heavy shot into his mug. O'Brien shoved his mug across the table and Slick spiked it, wordlessly.

They sat in silence, sipping their spiked coffee and watching the sidewalk in front of the *Probe*, where it seemed the entire staff was milling around in confusion.

Several minutes passed and, when Slick's eyes looked normal again, O'Brien broke the silence. "I didn't know the *Probe* was losing money. I thought we were doing well."

Slick shook his head from side to side. "The *Probe's* not in any damned financial trouble."

"But Bridges said—"

"What Bridges said was a bunch of horseshit!" retorted Slick. His face had turned crimson. "In all those meetings I've been to in New York, nobody ever mentioned financial problems."

"Then why shut us down?" asked O'Brien.

"Beats hell out of me."

A possible motive began to dawn on O'Brien. "Maybe they shut us down to stop my story."

Slick peered over the lip of the mug at O'Brien. "The PMC conspiracy thing."

"You got it."

Slick slapped his mug down on the table. "Why would Celebrity Press want to block that?"

O'Brien motioned with his head toward their former office building. "Maybe PMC owns or controls Celebrity Press."

Slick rubbed his chin, considering that possibility. "Could be. PMC's got its fingers into everything else. Why not a tabloid?"

"That would explain why they confiscated my computer and camera," said O'Brien.

"They what?"

"They wouldn't let me take my laptop with me—camera either. Said I could have them back after they removed company files and film."

Slick nodded his head slowly. "That's it! PMC *must* own the *Probe*. We were going to use the *Probe* to expose the conspiracy, and now they've shut it down—cut out our tongues."

"But why didn't they just fire me, or both of us?"

"That would look like they'd singled us out. By shutting the paper down, they can cite economic reasons, or a shift in policy."

"But I can still take the story to another paper."

"Hah! Not with your background," muttered Slick. Then, he turned his mug up and drained it.

Slick's words cut deep into O'Brien's soul and he slumped back in his chair as if his spine had turned to mush. Slick had spoken the truth, and as always, the truth hurt—hurt to the quick.

Slick noticed his dejection and added, "On the other hand, I might be able to sell it to another tabloid, but we'd need something tangible to back it up."

O'Brien threw up his hands. "I don't know what that would be, unless we could get one of the conspirators to confess, or prove someone framed Pearson's wife, or maybe hack into Marchant's computer and find something incriminating."

"What about this detective woman, Zalva? Sounds like she believes there may be something to it."

"That's right. She promised to talk to her boss, see if he'd authorize her to interview Marchant at PMC."

"Good! A real detective just might spot a loose end dangling around one of these *coincidences*," said Slick.

O'Brien got to his feet. "In the meantime, I'm going to talk to Pearson's widow."

"Why?"

"If she was framed, someone had to get into the house to plant the evidence. Maybe she'll have an idea who it was."

"Isn't she in jail?" asked Slick.

"She made bond. What are you going to do?"

Slick stood and pushed his chair to the side. "I'm going home to call some of the people I know at other tabloids and magazines. Maybe one of them will have an appetite for a story like ours, and we'll still get to shove it up PMC's corporate ass."

37

Before speaking to Thurman about O'Brien's alleged conspiracy, Zalva wanted to interview Carla and see if she'd back up his version of the kidnap attempt. She didn't have Carla's number, so she called the *Probe* to get it from O'Brien, but learned he hadn't made it in yet.

She remembered that the BMW that missed O'Brien had struck Carla's vehicle. The accident report would have Carla's last name, address, and phone number. A few minutes and a couple of quick phone calls later, Zalva had Carla's cell phone number and punched it in.

After nearly a dozen rings, a female voice answered. "Hello?"

"Carla?"

"Yeah."

"Carla, I'm Detective Zalva Martinez of the D.C. Police Department. I'd like to—"

"Is this about the BMW that hit me?"

"No, I'm a detective—not a traffic cop. I need to ask you about—"

"Are you the woman Will sneaked off with last night?"

"We didn't sneak off, Carla. We left to—"

"You can tell Will O'Brien to—"

"Shut your silly mouth, Carla! This is official business. You interrupt me one more time before I'm finished, and I'll come get you and drag your promiscuous little ass back to the station in handcuffs. You got that?"

Carla paused several seconds before speaking, probably biting her tongue. "What do you want?" she asked in a frosty voice.

"Did you leave Finigan's with O'Brien, last night?"

"Yeah. We were going to have dinner at his place."

"Mary Kate said you were only gone a couple of minutes. What happened?"

"Two guys in suits came up and Will left me to go with them."

"He tell you why?"

"He *said* they were FBI agents and he had to go to headquarters with them."

"Did you see any badges?"

"No. They came up on his side of the car."

"Did you hear what they said to O'Brien?"

"No. All the windows were up."

"Then what?"

"After he talked to them for about a minute, he came around to my side of the car and told me we couldn't go to his place for another two hours."

"Is that when he told you they were FBI agents?"

"Yes."

"He tell you what they wanted?"

"He said it concerned a story for his paper."

"When he left with them, did it look like he was being forced to go?"

"No, they walked off like long-lost buddies."

"Okay, Carla. That's all for now. But you may have to come in and give a written statement later. Incidentally, O'Brien didn't sneak off with me last night. We left to try to save someone's life."

"Really?"

"Yes, really."

"Did you make it?"

"No. She was dead when we got there."

"Oh."

Zalva hung up, sat back with her arms folded, and frowned. Carla couldn't back up anything O'Brien had said about the kidnaping. No help at all. Nevertheless, she decided to lay it all out for Thurman. She gathered up the photocopies she'd made from her old files on Rashid Brown and headed for Thurman's office.

Captain Thurman sat at his desk, studying a report, and didn't notice Zalva standing in his doorway. She rapped on the open door to get his attention.

He lifted his head slightly, saw her, and scowled. "Yeah?"

"Can I talk to you for a minute?"

With a flick of his head, he motioned for her to come in and continued studying the report.

Zalva entered and took a seat in front of his desk. She sat silently for several minutes while he remained focused on his report. Finally, she cleared her throat to gain his attention again.

Thurman glanced up from the report and raised both eyebrows. "So, talk."

She repeated all O'Brien had told her about the conspiracy: his two meetings with Monique, his near-miss with the BMW, the attempt to kidnap him, and finding Monique dead of an apparent cocaine overdose.

While she talked, Thurman sat facing her, head tilted back, eyes closed, and hands clasped over his chest. He remained in that position for several seconds after she finished. Finally, he sat up straight and looked her in the eyes.

"Let me make sure I've got this straight. O'Brien, based on what this *Monique* told him, says this big-cheese guy in the largest media conglomerate in the world, along with some unidentified French guy, are murdering senators they don't like, so that their last-minute replacements can win the November elections, thereby enabling the Democratic Party to maintain its majority in the Senate. And all of that so the liberal Senate can block bills passed by the conservative House and appointments proposed by the conservative president, right?"

Zalva nodded. "That's about it."

"And you believe that crap?"

Zalva had expected his cynical response, and plowed on. "You've got to admit, too much has happened for it all to be pure coincidence."

Thurman snorted disdainfully. He leaned forward with elbows on his desk and glared at her. "If you buy any part of his story, you've got to buy the possibility that somebody framed Senator Pearson's wife."

"Maybe they did."

Thurman scooted his chair back, stood up, and waved a hand in the air. "Come on, Zalva. Get real. This is real life, plain and simple—not like in the movies." He walked over to his window, where he stood with his back to her and his hands on his hips, for a few seconds.

Suddenly, he turned to face her. "You know damned well Pearson's wife killed him. She poisoned him like thousands of wives before her have done, since the beginning of time. She had motives: insurance money, and fear of losing everything they owned trying to defend him in court. She had opportunity and the means—which you will recall we found hidden in her closet."

"It could've been planted."

"Her fingerprints were on the bowl."

"The bowl was from her kitchen—entirely reasonable for her prints to be on it."

"You think somebody broke into her house, stole the bowl, used it to grind up the tablets, sneaked back into her house, and hid it and the other evidence in her closet?"

"We can't prove the tablets were actually ground up in that particular bowl. They could've made the tablets somewhere else, and simply grabbed a bowl from her kitchen when they planted it and the other items in her closet."

Thurman screwed up his face and waved his hand in the air. "How about the little French girl? She part of it too?"

"Could be her job was to seduce him, get his heart pumping hard enough for the Maxual and heart medicine to do their worst, or maybe she slipped a crushed Maxual tablet into his wine. Once Pearson was dead, they killed her because she freaked out and they couldn't risk her being interviewed by the police—or maybe they planned to kill her from the get-go."

"And they made it look like a drug overdose?"

"Right."

"How about Senator Gunter? You think the crack head who robbed the store and killed everybody in it was a paid hit man?"

"Rashid Brown was no crack head, or any other kind of drug addict, and you know it. He was no convenience store robber, either—not his type of action. Don't you remember? He was a suspect in my first case in D.C.—a contract killing."

Thurman's brow knitted in thought. "Yeah . . . come to think of it, I do remember that."

She leaned forward and placed the photo copies from Rashid's file on his desk. "As you can see from my old notes, Rashid hated drugs and drug dealers, and for good reason. His mother, father, and younger brother all died from drug overdoses of one kind or another. I talked to his grandmother yesterday and she confirmed he still hated drug dealers. It's improbable he would've been involved in a drug deal."

Thurman walked back to his desk, reluctantly picked up the copies, and studied them for several seconds. Then he tossed them onto the corner of his desk and resumed his position at the window, with his back to her.

He hadn't told her to shut up, so she continued. "Rashid's grandmother also said he called her and bragged about a big deal he was working on—said he'd received an advance payment on it. Told her he planned on moving to Miami when he got the final payment, and offered to give her money to move out of her old neighborhood, but she wouldn't take it."

Thurman turned and waved his hand in the air. "Yeah, and his big deal was cheating somebody on a drug deal."

"That's what the conspirators want everybody to believe. I believe his *deal* was a contract to hit the senator and make it look like a simple robbery gone sideways. When he went to collect the rest of his fee, they executed him and made it look like a drug deal gone bad. And since when did drug dealers start making advance payments?"

That made Thurman rub his chin in thought for a moment. He moved to his desk and resumed his seat. "Well, who's the third senator supposed to be?"

"O'Brien thinks it's Senator Scott from Maryland. The 'Rogue' label fits him because he votes with the Republicans about half the time."

"Didn't you say O'Brien went to the FBI?"

"They didn't believe him, but that was before Monique was murdered."

"If she was murdered, which nobody can prove." He studied her for a few seconds before continuing. "If the FBI won't buy it, what can we do?"

"Go to FMC. Confront Marchant with Monique's story. See what his reaction is. If nothing else, we may scare him enough to make them back off Scott."

Thurman sat up straight and rubbed his face with both hands. With his hands still on his cheeks, he rolled his eyes at her.. "Okay, I'll let you go that far with it, but I'm going with you. If I don't see or hear something a little stronger, you're going to have to drop it, you hear?"

She shot from her chair, elated by his decision. "Yes, sir," she replied.

As they headed for Thurman's car, her hopes soared. At last, a first step toward an investigation of the alleged conspiracy.

38

O'Brien left the coffee shop angry and determined to fight back. He got in his Volvo, and drove toward Senator Pearson's house, out on Massachusetts Avenue, a couple of blocks inside the D.C. limits. Certain that Marchant and Frenchy had framed Pearson's widow, he still had to figure out how.

He didn't bother calling Mrs. Pearson since she probably wouldn't be answering the phone anyway. It seemed best to simply show up at her house and knock on the door, which is exactly what he did.

A plain, narrow-faced woman in her early forties, dressed in a maid's uniform, answered the door. She looked him over with a disdainful frown, as if he were a vacuum cleaner salesman. "Yes?"

"I'd like to speak with Mrs. Pearson, please."

"Ms. Pearson isn't taking visitors."

She attempted to close the door in his face, but he stopped it with an outstretched hand. "Please, it's in her best interest to talk to me. Can't you tell her that?"

The maid glared at O'Brien and kept pushing against the door. "I'm afraid it's out of the question. Mrs. Pearson gave me explicit instructions. She meant *absolutely* no visitors. Now, if you'll kindly—"

"Wait! I can help her. Go tell her I know she didn't do it."

The maid's eyes lit up, and she looked directly at O'Brien, as if seeing him for the first time. "Who are you?"

"I'm Will O'Brien. Tell her I used to be an investigative reporter for a paper in New York. And tell her I know she didn't murder her husband, but I need her help in order to prove it."

The maid stepped past O'Brien onto the porch, and glanced up and down the street, as if expecting to see a TV truck or a sidewalk full of photographers. "Are you alone?"

"Yes, and I'm not here for a story. I simply want to help her."

She slipped past him, back into the house. "Okay, I'll tell her you're here." She pushed the door almost closed and spoke through the narrow opening. "Tell me your name again."

"Will O'Brien."

"Wait here. I'll be right back."

She closed the door and O'Brien heard the deadbolt slide into place. He waited in the cool September air for what seemed like a long time, but when he checked his watch, he saw only five minutes had passed. It seemed more like thirty. Another minute dragged by, then, just as O'Brien raised his hand to ring the doorbell again, the metallic clank of the deadbolt broke the silence.

The door opened just wide enough for the maid to poke her narrow face through. The disappointment on her face foretold the verdict.

"I'm sorry, Mr. O'Brien. She called her lawyers and they told her not to talk to you."

He'd been afraid she'd say that. Now what? Obviously, the maid had hoped she would see him. "How about you? Will you talk to me?"

She seemed startled by his interest in her, and had to gather herself before answering. "Do you really believe she's innocent?"

"Yes, I do."

The maid tossed a quick glance over her shoulder before answering. "I'll talk to you, but not here."

"Great! Where?"

"I'll tell her I've got to pick up some groceries. There's a coffee shop next to the grocery store. We can meet there."

"Where's that?"

"It's in a small shopping center a few blocks from here, next to the American University School of Law."

"I know the place."

As he turned to leave, she reached through the narrow opening in the door and grabbed his jacket. "No! Not right this minute."

"Why not?"

"If I leave right now, she'll know what I'm up to."

O'Brien checked his watch. "It's ten-thirty now. How about lunch?"

"Won't work. I've got to fix lunch here for Mrs. Pearson."

"How about one o'clock?"

"That'll do."

With the meeting set, he drove away, trying to figure out how to fill in the time until one.

39

Zalva and Captain Thurman stepped out of the elevator on the PMC floor and approached the receptionist, a well-dressed, attractive blonde in her mid-twenties. Her name tag identified her as Wanda.

She greeted them with a bright smile. "May I help you?"

Thurman pulled the front of his coat aside, revealing the badge clipped to his belt. I'm Captain Thurman of the D.C. Police Department."

Wanda's smile vanished. "What can I do for you?"

"We'd like to speak with Mr. Marchant," said Thurman.

"Is this an official visit?"

"Yes," he replied.

"One moment please. I'll inform his secretary you're here." Wanda punched a number on the phone and spoke to someone named Shaunda—a name which Zalva recognized as the one Monique had originally given O'Brien as her own. Wanda motioned toward the waiting area. "Please have a seat. Mr. Marchant's secretary will be with you shortly."

They seated themselves and Zalva thumbed through a magazine while waiting for Shaunda. Within five minutes, a tall, African-American woman in a dark business suit entered the lobby from the hallway. She walked straight to them, with a face devoid of expression and no greeting. "Mr.

Marchant will see you now. Please come with me."

Shaunda led them down a long hallway lined with closed doors. She stopped at one, knocked softly, and opened it.

Zalva stepped into an enormous office with darkly stained plank flooring. An expensive-looking Oriental rug hugged the floor in front of an impressive, leather-topped executive desk on the left side of the room. A pair of high-backed leather wing chairs faced the desk. A sitting area to the right contained a leather couch, more leather chairs, and a glass-topped coffee table. Original paintings of the impressionist period lined the walls. Dozens of plants filled every nook of the room and screened the desk area from the sitting area.

A man in his mid-forties, brown hair, medium height and build, and dressed in a dark, European-cut suit, rose from his throne behind the desk. He waved them toward the sitting area. "I'm Donald Marchant, head of the Washington office of PMC."

Thurman flashed his badge for Marchant. "I'm Captain Thurman and this is Detective Martinez."

Unfazed by the badge, Marchant motioned toward the sitting area at the far end of his office. "Please have a seat."

"I detect a slight accent, Mr. Marchant. What is it?" asked Zalva.

Marchant regarded her with narrowed eyes for a moment before responding. "French-Canadian."

They stepped over to the sitting area and Thurman and Zalva seated themselves on the couch. Marchant took one of the leather side chairs and sat with his legs crossed, appearing to be completely at ease. "Now, what can I do for the D.C. Police Department?"

Thurman nodded his head for Zalva to do the talking. She gathered her courage and looked Marchant squarely in the eye. "Was Monique Norris an employee of PMC?"

A look of sudden understanding flashed across Marchant's face. "Ah, that's why you're here."

"You know what happened to her?"

"Yes, my secretary informed me about her, first thing this morning. Such a terrible waste."

"Was she an employee?"

"Of course—at least until yesterday afternoon."

"Yesterday afternoon or yesterday evening?" asked Zalva.

"Her employment was terminated yesterday afternoon."

"Terminated? Like in *fired*?"

"Yes."

"For what reason?"

"Drug abuse."

"While at work?"

"Yes. Shaunda, my secretary, spoke to Monique sometime after lunch, yesterday, and noticed she seemed confused, as if drugged."

Thurman cleared his throat. "Was that the first time?"

"Unfortunately, no. Shaunda had suspected Monique might be taking drugs for some time, and had confronted her about it. Monique claimed to be taking a prescription medication that made her drowsy, and said she'd ask her doctor for a substitute prescription without that side effect. Neither Shaunda nor I noticed anything strange after that, so we assumed she spoken the truth. Apparently we were mistaken."

"She worked directly under Shaunda?"

"Yes, but since she filled in for Shaunda often, I had substantial contact with her."

"And you confronted her again yesterday?"

"Yes. I called her to my office and questioned her in Shaunda's presence. Monique denied taking drugs but looked and acted spaced-out. I asked her to submit to an immediate drug screening—which she refused to do. So I terminated her employment and had her escorted from the building."

Thurman shifted uneasily on the couch and looked over at Zalva with a wrinkled brow. Undeterred, she continued pressing. "I'd still like to see Monique's personnel file and speak with Shaunda."

Marchant's face took on a sour expression. "What's this all about?"

"This is just a routine—"

"Excuse me," interrupted Marchant in a harsh voice. He rose to his feet and glared down at Zalva with unblinking eyes. "I don't believe this is a routine visit. Monique was found in her apartment in Virginia, which, if I'm not mistaken, is *outside* your jurisdiction."

"That's true," said Thurman. "But if you'll sit down, I'll explain why we're here."

Marchant glowered at Thurman for a moment, then down at Zalva, before resuming his seat.

Thurman hunched forward on the couch and told Marchant what Monique claimed to have overheard through the air conditioning vent, and how subsequent events had led O'Brien to believe her. Marchant listened intently, and his facial expressions appeared to reveal genuine astonishment at what he heard.

When Thurman finished, Marchant sat staring from Thurman to Zalva and back again. "I . . . I don't know what to say. That's the most preposterous story I've ever heard. But it certainly explains what O'Brien was doing here yesterday. We caught the conniving rascal snooping around, and had to throw him out of the building."

Zalva pressed on. "Mr. Marchant, did a meeting like the one Monique described ever take place here at PMC?"

"Well . . . yes . . . I suppose. I'm a heavy supporter of the Democratic Party, and Walker Gibson calls on me often for assistance. But we've certainly never plotted to assassinate anyone."

"Have you ever referred to Senator Gunter as the Traitor?"

"Oh, yes. Many times."

Zalva started to ask another question, but Thurman spoke first. "Have you and Gibson ever had any discussions in this building, regarding Senator Pearson and Senator Gunter, in which you mentioned getting them out of the way or getting rid of them?"

"We've had many meetings here in my office during which we discussed the possibility of losing control of the Senate. I can't recall everything we said, but I'm sure we talked about how convenient it would be if Pearson resigned in time for a new candidate to be appointed and how great it would be if Gunter resigned or even passed away. I assure you though, no one ever mentioned getting rid of them or getting them out of the way, at least not in a context that could be construed as meaning assassinations."

"Did you put a lot of pressure on Pearson to resign?" asked Zalva.

"Of course we did. Every Democratic senator talked to him at least once, but the old mountebank thought he had a chance of winning until just before his death. Two weeks ago, I offered him a position with PMC as an inducement for him to resign, but he turned it down on the spot. Then, on the day before his death, he called me and accepted the offer. So why would I have him killed?"

"You have any proof he accepted that offer?" asked Thurman.

Marchant's lips curled into a wry smile. "Of course not. That kind of thing would be politically embarrassing if it got out."

"Did you tell anyone else that Pearson had accepted the deal, prior to his death that is?" asked Zalva.

"Well, yes. As soon as Pearson called me, I notified Walter Gibson."

"Did you tell anyone else?"

"No, but I'd be much surprised if Gibson didn't tell others about it, that same day. Go talk to him. By the way, didn't you arrest Pearson's wife for his murder?"

"She claims someone framed her," replied Zalva.

Marchant stood up, and Thurman and Zalva both rose, as well. Marchant straightened his tie and spoke, with a sharp edge to his voice. "Seems to me you two are way out on a limb, coming in here like this. Pearson's wife killed him for his insurance money, and you've charged her with it. Gunter was gunned down, along with a couple of other people, by a two-bit hood who was robbing a convenience store for drug money. My secretary's drugged-up assistant misunderstood a muffled conversation she overheard through an air-conditioning vent, told a cheap tabloid reporter with a history of falsifying news reports that we were planning assassinations of senators, and you come running in here like you believe it."

Thurman held both hands up, palms out. "Now I didn't say we believed Monique or O'Brien. It's just that O'Brien said Monique told him Gunter was going to get it, and he did. And both Monique and Lezette, the woman in the hotel room with Pearson, died of cocaine overdoses. A lot of coincidences to think about."

"There must be dozens of deaths from cocaine overdoses in D.C. every year," retorted Marchant. "I wouldn't think it that much of a coincidence."

"You're absolutely right," agreed Thurman, grabbing Zalva's hand. "We'll be on our way now."

Zalva pulled her hand free. "I'd still like to speak with your secretary and the security guard who escorted Monique from the building, and review Monique's personnel file, if you don't mind." She wasn't going to let Thurman drag her out without at least doing that.

"As you wish," responded Marchant dryly. He stepped over to his desk, followed by Zalva and Thurman, punched the intercom, and asked Shaunda to bring Monique's personnel file to his office.

"A moment ago, you said O'Brien had a history of falsifying news stories," said Thurman. "Were you referring to his articles in the *National Probe*?"

Marchant appeared astonished by Thurman's question. "You mean you don't know about him?"

"What's to know? Isn't he's just a sleazy scandal sheet reporter?"

Marchant chuckled softly. "That explains why you came here. You didn't know any better." The tension seemed to drain from Marchant and he sat down on the corner of his monstrous desk. "I incorrectly assumed you knew the story about O'Brien, since everybody in the news industry does."

With a casual wave of his hand, he invited them to sit in the two wingback chairs. Once they were seated, he began. "Well, here it is. At one time, O'Brien was a rising star reporter for a hot New York daily paper owned by PMC. He wrote a series of articles about a ring that lured teenage girls from eastern Europe into being smuggled into the U.S. and enslaved as prostitutes in New York City. Our paper published his story, which created quite a stir.

"O'Brien won a Pulitzer Prize and the city created a special task force to investigate the matter. O'Brien had a paid informant as his source of information, and had given him a cover name, but refused to identify him for the government. The authorities slapped him in jail for his refusal to disclose his source, but a federal judge ordered him released almost immediately.

"Later, O'Brien's alleged source tried to extort money from the paper under threat of exposing the story as a hoax. The paper refused to pay and notified the authorities. It turned into a nasty mess. O'Brien's source claimed O'Brien invented the whole story and simply used him to launder money paid by the paper. O'Brien denied it, but it was just one liar's word against another's. O'Brien somehow avoided prosecution, but the paper fired him and he forfeited the Pulitzer. And, of course, no reputable news organization would touch him after that."

Shocked by Marchant's revelation, it took Zalva several seconds to speak. "I wondered why he worked for a grocery-store tabloid—considering his intelligence and education."

"And now, it seems he's fabricated another hoax, apparently to get revenge on PMC," asserted Marchant.

Zalva sneaked a quick glance at Thurman, and found him glaring at her again. He rolled his eyes toward the ceiling and shook his head slightly.

Nevertheless, he waited patiently while Zalva talked to Shaunda and the security guard, both of whom backed up what Marchant had told them about Monique's drug abuse. Monique's personnel file contained a document dated two months earlier, and signed by Monique, confirming she had been warned about the company's policy regarding drug abuse on the job. Zalva thanked Marchant for his time and apologized for the intrusion. Then she and Thurman departed, with Zalva feeling like a shamed dog with her tail tucked between her legs.

Thurman drove them back to precinct headquarters in silence. After parking, he turned to Zalva, put his arm across the back of the seat, leaned his left arm on the steering wheel, and looked her squarely in the eyes.

"I want you to drop O'Brien's nutty conspiracy story right now. Don't spend another minute on it."

"You don't believe Monique was murdered?"

"No, I think she was just another drug user who went too far. Besides, it doesn't matter to you, since she died outside our jurisdiction."

"And you don't believe O'Brien was kidnaped either?"

"You see him kidnaped?"

"No, but I saw him afterward. Saw his skinned-up knees and hands, from jumping out of the car."

"You see him jump from a moving vehicle?"

"No."

"Use your head, Zalva! The sleaze-ball probably did that to himself just to fool you. Look at what he did in New York. You can't believe anything he says. He'll do anything to sell a story."

"He had a witness of sorts. Carla, a woman who left the pub with O'Brien, backed up what he said about two guys approaching them outside Finigan's."

"He could've hired those guys. Remember what Marchant said about his informant in New York?"

"Yes, but Marchant could have a reason to tweak it."

Thurman threw up his hands in exasperation. "You interview her?"

"This morning."

"Did she hear them say they were from the FBI, or see them flash badges?"

Zalva sighed. "No, she was sitting in O'Brien's car. Didn't see any badges and couldn't hear what they said."

"Did she see O'Brien get conked on the head and shoved in the back seat of their car?'

"No, she was inside Finigan's by then."

"You got no witness, Zalva."

"How about the third senator Monique warned O'Brien about? Senator Scott from Maryland. Don't we have some responsibility to make sure that doesn't happen?"

"It's not going to happen because there's no damned conspiracy, Zalva. Even if there was, it'd be the FBI's problem—not ours. And didn't you tell me O'Brien had called the FBI and warned them about Scott?"

"He said he did."

"Good. Then it's out of our hands."

"How about the possibility Pearson's wife might have been framed? That ball's in our court, isn't it?"

"That's for her lawyers to prove. You leave it alone."

Realizing she faced a stone wall, she caved in. "Okay, if that's what you want."

"Good. We've got enough real problems to deal with. And speaking of that, let's go on in and see what's happened while we've been wasting our time on this wild goose chase."

40

O'Brien picked up his laptop and other personal items from the *Probe* and drove to the little shopping center suggested by the maid. He skipped lunch, deciding to eat a couple of muffins at the coffee shop; that would hold him until dinner. These little neighborhood coffee shops were always full of good-looking women. Maybe one might even find him interesting.

In the shop, O'Brien ordered a cup of Brazilian Santos, two bran muffins with raisins, and a large piece of chocolate cheese cake. Loaded down, he selected a table where he could watch the service counter and the front door, and ambled over to it. From that position, he'd easily spot the maid when she arrived and could scope out the female customers. He needed something to keep his mind off the stark reality of his unemployed status and girl-watching would at least do that, even if nothing came of it.

He opened his computer case and found a brand new laptop inside. Not surprising, since they couldn't be certain all traces of his files could be removed from the old hard-drive. At least one good thing had come of losing his job: the new computer was a much later model than his old one, faster and with more capacity. He didn't waste time mourning the lost files. Instead, he busied himself recreating files from memory.

The time passed swiftly. After what seemed only minutes, he glanced up from his computer to see the maid entering the shop. She'd exchanged her maid's uniform for faded blue jeans, a turtleneck sweater, and a corduroy blazer. She looked like most of the other women he'd seen that afternoon—just another housewife killing time before the kids came home from school. She bought a cup of coffee at the counter and joined him.

O'Brien stood up to greet her, noting she didn't look quite as plain now, as she'd put on makeup and pulled her hair back into a ponytail. The blue jeans revealed she even had a decent figure, but her narrow face didn't appeal to him. She suited someone, though, because she wore a wedding band. "Thanks for coming," he said with a smile.

She nodded, took the chair across the table from him, and got right down to business. "What makes you think Mrs. Pearson is innocent?"

"First off, what's your name?"

"Sylvia. Sylvia Reynolds."

"Sylvia, did the police interview you?"

"Of course."

"Can you tell me what they asked you?"

"Well, they asked if I had ever seen any Maxual in the house or in Mrs. Pearson's possession."

"Did you?"

"Yes. I saw a packet in Mrs. Pearson's drawer in the master bathroom about a month before the senator died."

"In *her* drawer? You sure it wasn't his drawer?"

"Oh, no. It was in her drawer—on the right side of her sink. I'm certain of it."

"What else?"

"They asked if I had seen her grinding up any of the tablets."

"Had you?"

"No. I never saw her do anything with them."

"What else did they ask?"

"They showed me a small cereal bowl and a little rod with a rounded end, and asked me if I'd ever seen it before."

"Had you?"

"The bowl came from the kitchen, but I'd never seen the funny-looking rod before."

"How about other people in the house?"

"There was nobody else in the house. Just me and the two of them."

"I mean other people coming and going."

"After his troubles started, they never had company any more."

"Any other employees?"

"No. I cleaned the house, did the laundry, and cooked all the food."

"Sylvia, I believe somebody got into the house and planted the evidence the cops found in Mrs. Pearson's closet. Are you sure they didn't have any visitors, maybe someone who came one evening after you went home?"

"If they did, I never saw any sign of it when I came in the next day."

"Could someone have broken in, one night while they were out?"

"They didn't go out—at least she didn't. I stayed overnight about once a week, because she was sick a lot, and he always came in real late—or not at all."

He leaned back in his chair and studied her for a moment. Surely someone got into the house and planted the damning evidence. But who? Their eyes met briefly; she shifted uneasily in her chair, and looked away.

Aha, he thought. *She's not telling me everything.*

"How about a repairman? Anybody come to fix something, like a leaky faucet, garbage disposal, dishwasher?"

"Not in the last couple of months."

O'Brien leaned across the table and looked into her eyes. "Sylvia, you're not being completely honest with me, are you? You have a boyfriend who visited you at the Pearson place?"

Sylvia recoiled and sucked in her breath. Tears welled up in her eyes and she tried to speak, but her lips trembled and her mouth moved without any sound coming out. She gave up trying to speak, buried her face in her hands, with her elbows in her lap, and sobbed.

A direct hit! O'Brien sat back in his chair and waited for her to regain control. Now he was getting somewhere. She had a lover who visited her at the Pearson's home! The police hadn't asked her the right questions, and she hadn't volunteered anything, fearing her husband would learn she had a lover.

While she struggled with her emotions, O'Brien rose and went to the serving counter to refill their coffee cups. A couple of elderly female customers had noticed her sobbing, and glared at him from their tables. They probably assumed he was being mean to his wife. He winked at one of the women casting an evil eye at him. The woman's mouth gaped wide open and she jerked her gaze away. Her friend turned up her nose in a show of disgust.

He placed Sylvia's coffee cup in front of her and patted her gently on the shoulder. "Take a couple of sips of hot coffee. It'll help you."

She took his advice and sipped at her coffee between sobs and sniffles. Finally, she gained enough control to speak again.

"I met a man—here in this very coffee shop. We met here every day, and just talked. Innocent conversation, at first, but later, he started talking about . . . about . . . wanting to make love to me . . . and I wanted him, too." She pushed her face forward, as if seeking his approval. "You've got to understand. I love my husband, but he's so cold and unemotional. Alain was different: handsome . . . sophisticated . . . warm. Just being with him made me feel alive—like a real woman. But he wanted me to spend a weekend with him, and I told him I couldn't get away that long."

"How did he take that?"

"I thought that was the end of it, because he became angry and walked off." A sad smile flitted across her face. "Then a strange thing happened."

"Yeah?"

"Mrs. Pearson received an invitation to a reception and luncheon in honor of the French ambassador's wife."

Surely, wives of senators received invitations like that often, he thought. "What was unusual or strange about that?"

"She hadn't been invited anywhere in months, because of his reputation and all."

"She'd become a social pariah?"

"What's that?"

"An outcast. So, Mrs. Pearson received an unexpected invitation?"

"Oh, yes. And you'd have thought she'd won the lottery, the way she acted. She couldn't wait to see the inside of their mansion."

"Whose' mansion?"

"The Rulons."

That name rang a bell. O'Brien remembered seeing it in the society section of the paper often, relating to events like the one Sylvia mentioned. "Mrs. Pearson had never been invited to the Rulons' place before?"

"Oh, no. Only special people got those invitations."

"I see what you mean. One day an outcast, and the next day elevated to the pinnacle of Washington society."

"That's right."

"Wasn't she suspicious about the invitation?"

"Oh, yes. She assumed they were going to try to get to her husband through her, in some way, but she decided to go anyway. And the very next day, I saw Alain here in the coffee shop again."

"Still wanting your body?"

Sylvia looked down at her folded hands. "Yes."

"You tell him about the invitation?"

"Yes. The invitation stated that the reception was to begin at eleven and go through two in the afternoon, meaning Mrs. Pearson would be out of the house for several hours. He wanted to come to the house while she was gone."

"And you agreed?"

"Oh, no."

"You got cold feet?"

"Yes."

"He get angry again?"

"No. He said he understood, and let it go. But on the day of the reception, less than fifteen minutes after Mrs. Pearson left the house, Alain showed up at the front door with a bottle of champagne."

"And you let him come in, of course."

She lowered her eyes and spoke in a voice barely above a whisper. "I couldn't help myself."

She began sobbing again, and O'Brien took a break to fetch fresh coffee. The pieces of the puzzle were falling into place now, but he still needed a handle on Alain. By the time he made it back to their table, Sylvia had regained a measure of control.

"So, you let him in. Then what?"

"We went upstairs to the spare room I use when I stay overnight. We drank a couple of glasses of champagne, and made love."

"Was he ever out of your sight while he was in the house?"

"I don't know."

"What? How can you not know?"

"I fell asleep after we made love—because of the champagne, I guess."

More likely because he drugged you, thought O'Brien. "What time did he leave?"

"I don't know. I didn't wake up until late afternoon, when Mrs. Pearson knocked on the bedroom door."

"That invitation came at a convenient time for you and Alain, didn't it?"

She answered without looking at him. "Yes."

"By any chance, did you ever mention anything to Alain about seeing the Maxual in Mrs. Pearson's drawer?"

Her face paled at his question. "Why, yes . . . I believe I did."

That explained why the killers used Maxual on Pearson. Thanks to Sylvia, they knew Mrs. Pearson had some in her possession and that it would probably be traced back to that source. Through Sylvia, they got access to the house, switched the fake NazinX tablets for the senator's real ones, and planted the evidence in Mrs. Pearson's closet.

"He . . . he . . . used me," mumbled Sylvia in a voice barely above a whisper. The unwelcome truth had finally dawned on her.

"Gee, you really think so?" he quipped.

She bit her lips at his sarcasm and looked away.

"What's Alain's last name?"

She answered with her head lowered, not meeting his eyes. "He told me he was a writer and his last name was Duramat . . . and that he was in D.C. to research material for a book."

Obviously an alias, and not even a clever one. "Did he give you a phone number or an address I could use to find him?"

Sylvia burst into tears again and buried her head in her hands on the table top. He reached over to console her and caught movement out of the corner of his eye.

A tall, broad-shouldered woman who would've made a formidable pro defensive tackle loomed over the table with her hands on her hips. A fat handbag dangling from her thick wrist. She glared down at O'Brien as if looking at a cockroach. "Why don't you leave your poor wife alone, you bully?" she growled in a harsh voice.

O'Brien stood up, fearing the woman might strike him in the head with her enormous purse, which she now held by the strap, as if ready to swing.

"Look, ma'am, this lady isn't my wife. The poor woman's simply telling me about something traumatic that happened to her. She'll be relieved once she's talked it through, and everything will be fine."

Sylvia looked up with tears still running down her narrow cheeks. "It's okay. He's not bothering me."

The behemoth glared skeptically at O'Brien for a moment, as if contemplating striking him anyway, then reluctantly retreated to her table.

O'Brien resumed his seat and let out a breath of relief. "Whew, that was close."

"I'm sorry," murmured Sylvia. "I'll try not to cry anymore."

"Don't worry about it. Now, can you tell me how to find Alain?"

"No. He's gone."

"Gone where?"

"I don't know. I haven't heard from him since the day he came to the house."

Not surprising, since his mission was accomplished, thought O'Brien. "Did he tell you where he was staying?"

"He said he had a suite at the Palmyra Court Hotel, on Wisconsin Avenue. But, after Senator Pearson died, I called the hotel and they'd never heard of him. And they'd had no long-term French guest, either."

"Alain was French?"

"He said he was, and he had a French accent."

Interesting, thought O'Brien. The unidentified man in the PMC meeting had a French accent. Lezette, the girl who ran from Pearson's hotel room—the same hotel Alain said he used—was French. Rulon was a French name, as sure as O'Brien was pudgy, and Sylvia's lover was French. What did it mean, if anything? Alain might provide some answers, assuming he was still alive, but only if O'Brien could find him. Well, Lezette had worked at the French embassy. Maybe Alain did, too. He made a mental note to ask Zalva to get some photos of the men assigned to the embassy, for Sylvia to look at.

"And you'll tell the police or FBI what you told me?" he asked.

Sylvia sat up straight and clasped her cheeks. "Oh, no! Will I have to do that?"

"If you want to help Mrs. Pearson, you will."

"But my husband will find out about Alain. He'll kill me!"

O'Brien felt like saying she should've thought about that before cheating on her husband, but he didn't. Instead, he said, "Maybe not. If you can identify Alain, they may be able to get enough evidence on him that you won't have to testify in court."

The facile lie seemed to make Sylvia feel a little better. "What now?" she asked.

Now comes the hard part, he thought. He took her hands in his and looked her in the eye. "You've got to be real careful now. So far, everybody that could've been a witness is dead."

She snatched her hands out of his and looked at him in horror. "What?"

"It's all part of a conspiracy, and it runs deep. Four people are dead and more are targeted."

Sylvia recoiled from his words. "Oh, my God! You think they'll try to kill me?"

"I'm amazed you're still alive."

She starred at him with wild eyes, like an animal caught in a trap. Finally, she found her voice. "Maybe . . . maybe it's because I haven't been home. I've stayed with Mrs. Pearson since the night her husband died."

"That's it. They wouldn't do anything at Pearson's house—cops might begin to wonder."

Her face had become pale and she wrung her hands. "What am I going to do?"

He sipped his coffee and studied her for a moment. She'd been lucky up to now. But with his snooping around PMC and talking to Zalva, they might decide to risk a move on her at the Pearson home. They could kidnap her while she was running an errand and kill her someplace else. They might even kill Sylvia in her sleep and frame Mrs. Pearson for that, too. Or vice versa. They'd certainly been experts at camouflaging their murders, up to this point.

"Maybe you should go on an extended visit to a friend or relative Alain doesn't know about, and don't tell anybody but me where that is."

"What about my husband?"

"Don't tell him where you're going—they could make him talk. Tell him you've got to get away. Better yet, don't tell him anything. Don't even go home or back to Pearson's place. I know a police detective who'll explain things to your husband after you're gone—without mentioning your little affair."

With the fear of death hanging over her, he didn't have to spend much time convincing her to hide somewhere. They exchanged cell phone numbers and she promised to call him when she reached a safe haven.

He walked her out to her car, watched her drive off, then left for the library and an internet connection. It was time to do some research on Rulon.

41

Zalva returned from lunch and found a note on her desk from Captain Thurman. She walked down the hall, knocked on his door, and entered, at his gruff invitation. She pulled a side chair around to sit down.

"No need to do that," Thurman said, holding his hand up to stop her.

"What's up?"

"We've got a probable suicide over in the Cathedral Heights area. I want you to check it out. Talk to the guy's wife. Make sure it smells right."

"Ginny already there?"

"Yeah, she left about twenty minutes ago."

Zalva picked up the street address from the dispatcher and left for the scene. The visit to PMC that morning had dampened her spirit considerably, and she felt relieved to have something to occupy her time.

The suicide victim's residence turned out to be a row house tucked in with several others on a short side street, conspicuous with all the police and emergency vehicles parked in the drive way and on the street. She parked about a hundred feet past the house and trudged back.

Zalva slipped on booties and a pair of latex gloves from boxes by the front door before entering the house. A uniform showed her to the room where the body had been found. Evidently a study, the small room, gloomy for lack of adequate lighting, contained a desk with a computer, a couple of printers, shelves loaded with books, and the body of the victim.

She saw a middle-aged man in a dark business suit slumped over the computer desk, with his head lying in the crook of his left arm. His right arm dangled at his side, and his index finger pointed at the chalk outline of a pistol on the floor.

Ginny was standing by the body, writing in her notebook as a member of her crew called out measurements to her. She noticed Zalva in the doorway and nodded to her.

Zalva stepped over to the body and saw a small hole in the right temple, where the bullet had entered, but no exit wound. She looked up at Ginny. "Small caliber pistol, huh?"

"A Sig .25 caliber semiautomatic loaded with soft ammo. Bullet probably fragmented on entry and tore his brain to pieces."

"He leave a note?"

"Haven't found one."

"Who was he?"

"Frank Pazotti."

The name didn't ring a bell with her. "Who found him?"

"His wife found him when she came home from her fitness center. She went back to her bedroom after making her statement."

Zalva left Ginny to interview Mrs. Pazotti. She knocked on the door to the master bedroom, heard a muffled response she took to be an invitation, and entered. She found Mrs. Pazotti lying on her back on the king-sized bed, with a wet washcloth covering her forehead. She still wore her black workout tights, a red, sleeveless T-shirt, and tennis shoes. She looked to be around fifty, but in good shape, and her closely cropped, light brown hair showed signs of greying. Her body had withstood the ravages of ageing better than her face, which had the marks of too much exposure to the sun over the years.

"Mrs. Pazotti, I'm Detective Martinez. I know you've already given us a statement, but I'd like to ask you a few questions, if you feel up to it."

Mrs. Pazotti held the wet cloth in place with one hand and sat up on the edge of the bed. She wiped her face with the washcloth, tossed it on her night stand, and rose to her feet.

"I'm okay now, but let's go into the living room to talk."

Zalva followed her into the small living room at the front of the house. Mrs. Pazotti motioned for Zalva to take the heavily cushioned love seat, took the side chair next to it for herself, and dabbed at her eyes with a tissue paper.

Zalva plopped down on the love seat and sank so low that her knees were almost level with her face.

Mrs. Pazotti cleared her throat before speaking. "There's not much to tell. I came home from aerobics class and noticed Frank's car parked in front of the house. He'd left the front door unlocked, which wasn't like him. I thought maybe he didn't feel well and came home for some rest, but he wasn't in bed. I saw the door to his study was closed and thought he must've come home to get something off his computer. I opened the study door and . . . and . . . you know what I found."

Although a little unsteady, Mrs. Pazotti appeared to be quite calm, under the circumstances. Zalva wondered about her relationship with her dead husband. "Mrs. Pazotti, did you see this coming?"

"Absolutely not. I never dreamed he'd do something like this."

"What could have prompted him to take his own life? Were you having marital problems?"

"Well, you might as well know, we weren't getting along very well. In fact, we've been on the verge of getting a divorce several times in the past two years."

That explained why she remained relatively composed. "What else could've bothered him? Do you have financial problems?"

"Yes. That was one of our big problems. He gambled heavily on college and pro football games."

"And lost often?"

"Oh, yes."

"Did he owe money to any bookies?"

"No, not that I'm aware of, but he often let our bills go unpaid in order to cover his bets." She shrugged her shoulders and blew out a deep breath. "The house is mortgaged to the hilt, and lately, we've been practically living on credit cards."

"How much do you owe on credit cards?"

"Close to a hundred thousand, I'm sure."

"Wow! And with interest at twenty-five percent?"

"Probably."

That would be enough to depress the hell out of anyone, thought Zalva. She marveled that Mrs. Pazotti hadn't already killed her husband. "How were things with his job?"

"Great—I suppose. At least, he never mentioned any problems."

"Where did he work?"

"He was editor-in-chief of the *National Probe*."

Damn! Pazotti was O'Brien's boss! Momentarily stunned, Zalva finally managed to stammer out a question. "Do . . . do you have the phone number for the *Probe*?"

Mrs. Pazotti rattled off the phone number and Zalva punched it into her cell phone. After a couple of rings, a recorded message told her the tabloid had ceased operations, and gave instructions for creditors seeking payment.

What an astonishing development. Maybe that was why the poor sap killed himself. It also meant O'Brien was out of work. She wondered why the tabloid had been shut down . . . but she could find that out later. Right now, she had a job to do. "Did you know the *Probe* was shut down today?"

"What?"

"Your husband's paper was shut down, today. Did he know it was coming?"

"Why, no . . . at least . . . at least, he never mentioned anything about it to me."

"Did your husband's job mean so much to him that he'd kill himself over losing it?"

"It's possible . . I guess. The only two things he cared about were his job and sports betting."

"Did he have any enemies?"

"A lot of people hated him for printing stories about them in the *Probe*."

Pazotti probably *had* ruined a few lives with his scandal sheet, thought Zalva. If it turned out his death wasn't a suicide, a review of the tabloid's past issues would certainly be in order.

She jotted down what little Mrs. Pazotti knew about the mechanics of her husband's sports betting and the name of the company that issued his life insurance policy, then got the names of witnesses who could testify as to where she'd been that day and the time she'd left to come home. Finished with Mrs. Pazotti, she went back to the study in search of evidence of Frank Pazotti's sports betting and to confer with Ginny.

The body had been removed and Ginny was talking to one of her associates. Zalva stood to the side until Ginny finished with her assistant, then approached her. "What about it? Suicide or murder?" she asked.

Ginny ran her hand over her face before replying, as if wiping away all her doubts. "Well, I found gun powder residue on his right hand and shirt sleeve, right where it was supposed to be and in the right pattern. The gun was on the floor in the correct position for it to have fallen from his hand. There was powder residue in his hair around the entry wound, which you would expect from a shot at close range. We found the invoice for the gun in his desk drawer. He bought it in his name five years ago. There were no other prints, no signs of a struggle, and no sign of a forced entry. In short, I see no physical evidence to contradict suicide."

"Mrs. Pazotti said the front door was unlocked when she came in. A couple of guys could've held him while another one put the gun in his hand and forced it against his head."

"True, but there's no evidence of that."

"Doesn't mean anything either. They could've tidied up before they left."

Ginny shrugged her shoulders. "Like I said, no evidence to support that."

Ginny was right. If the victim had been murdered, the perp or perps had left no obvious evidence. "You got uniforms checking with the neighbors in case one of them saw someone come and go today?" asked Zalva.

"Already done. No one saw anything. No one even heard the shot."

No surprise, since the pistol was only a .25 caliber and wouldn't have sounded like much more than a loud pop beyond the walls of the house. "Well, he had some reasons to end it all. He lost his job today, his marriage was on the rocks, and they owe about a hundred grand on credit cards because of his gambling."

Ginny put her hands on her hips, clicked her tongue a couple of times, and nodded her head. "Yep. Seen it all before. People make their own lives miserable, then can't take it. Well, all that remains now is to check out the wife's alibi, the gambling story, and the debts. If those check out, we've got a routine suicide."

"You are taking the computer, floppies, and CD's, aren't you?" asked Zalva.

"Absolutely. I'll have Richard go through all the computer files and check out his record on internet gambling."

"Grab any tip-sheets, magazines, newsletters, or other stuff related to sports betting, while you're at it."

Ginny signaled an okay, and Zalva left her to her work. She found Mrs. Pazotti again and asked for the family's bank statements, credit card statements, and other financial records, which they reviewed together. The records backed up what Mrs. Pazotti told her about the debts. Mrs. Pazotti went over her husband's cell phone bills with her, and pointed out the numbers of local bookies he'd used.

After gathering that information, Zalva thanked the newly-minted widow and headed for Mrs. Pazotti's fitness center, to check the time she said she left there. From there, time allowing, she intended to pay a visit to the *Probe*.

42

At the library, O'Brien signed onto the internet and found the PMC website. After several minutes, he pulled up a roster of officers and directors, scrolled down the names, and found Rulon listed as chairman of the board. He let out an involuntary yelp of glee at his discovery, feeling like a safecracker with a stethoscope, who'd just heard the first tumbler on a combination lock click into place. He clicked Rulon's name for a short biographical sketch.

Rulon's bio came up and he leaned forward to study it. Although born in the U.S.A., Rulon had spent most of his life in France, was educated in Paris and, under the last Democratic president, served as the U.S. ambassador to France. That bit of information sent a loud and clear message. To get that position, Rulon must have given untold millions in contributions to the party or to the president's campaign.

Curious to learn how much stock Rulon owned, O'Brien pulled up the latest annual report and scanned it, looking for disclosure of those who owned more than five percent of the outstanding company stock. Since Rulon was listed as chairman of the board, O'Brien wasn't surprised to find that he held controlling interest of PMC: a whopping thirty-five percent of the total outstanding stock.

After another thirty minutes on the internet, O'Brien spent a couple of hours going through microfiche of D.C. newspapers and various magazines, searching for articles on Rulon. He discovered that the man was indeed a heavy contributor to the Democratic Party. In fact, over the past fifteen years he'd been its largest contributor—not even counting the funds which O'Brien assumed the rank-and-file employees of PMC and the companies it controlled were politely pressured to donate.

A passionate Francophile, Rulon had married a wealthy French woman, maintained a second home in Paris, and was a close friend of Geroux, the French president. Interesting, since Geroux had opposed everything the U.S. had tried to accomplish in world affairs.

Rulon inherited most of his PMC stock from his mother, who inherited it from her third husband, the original owner, who had no children and was at an advanced age at the time of the marriage. Rulon, eight years old at the time, had been a rich kid during his school days.

He stood on the outermost fringe of liberal politics, supporting socialized medicine and a progressive income tax that would reach ninety percent on earnings above two hundred grand—which would, of course, prevent anyone else from ever becoming wealthy from their own efforts. The only way anyone would ever join Rulon's elite circle of the rich and powerful would be through inherited wealth, as in the days of feudalism. He supported confiscation of all personal firearms, not just handguns, a reduction in American armed forces, the elimination of all U.S. military bases in foreign countries, and pretty much a total submission to decrees of the United Nations.

"Wow!" he exclaimed aloud at Rulon's extremism. What a loose cannon. And dangerous, too. With his wealth, political clout, and control of PMC, he had all the necessary tools with which to promote his agenda. O'Brien regarded himself as a middle-of-the-road liberal. People on the far left, like Rulon—or the far right, for that matter—made his skin crawl.

He sat back in his chair in studied reflection. Ironic, he thought, how often scions with vast amounts of inherited wealth became ardent socialists, despising and working feverishly to destroy the very economic system that had spawned their billions. Even more puzzling was the fact that people like Rulon controlled much of the media. Everyone, especially people working in the media, should revere the freedom of the press guaranteed by the Constitution. A freedom that would quickly vanish under the heavy hand of a socialistic government. *Be careful what you wish for, he thought. You might get it.* He shook his head, leaned forward and continued his research.

O'Brien found numerous articles on the social affairs of Rulon and his wife in past issues of magazines and the society pages of old newspapers, as might be expected for a billionaire living in D.C. He found one article particularly surprising. Rulon's wife was an accomplished artist. She maintained a studio in their mansion and was widely exhibited. Her paintings hung in some of the finest homes in Washington, Paris, and New York. The article even had a couple of photos taken in her studio. According to the article, she made her own pigments, even grinding the minerals herself. One of the photographs depicted her grinding a pigment with a small bowl and pestle.

After completing his research on Rulon, he remembered his intention to research ownership of Celebrity Press, and logged on the internet again. He found the website but it disclosed nothing about ownership. He returned to the PMC website and began searching for a listing of subsidiaries. Within minutes, he learned that PMC had acquired all of the outstanding stock of Celebrity Press, owner of the *Probe,* earlier in the year.

Although O'Brien had expected that news, the weight of understanding was depressing. How likely was it that Rulon was the French guy in the meeting Monique overhead? About as likely as Michael Jackson grabbing his crotch during a live performance.

O'Brien left the library and headed for Finigan's, anxious to see Zalva. He wanted to hear what her boss said about the conspiracy, and tell her about Rulon. Maybe now, with what he'd learned from Sylvia and from his research on Rulon, she'd back him up if he went to the FBI again.

43

Zalva pushed her chair away from her desk and leaned back with her hands clasped behind her head, mentally exhausted from spending the entire afternoon on the Pazotti suicide. And it was a suicide, after all.

Mrs. Pazotti's personal trainer confirmed the time Mrs. Pazotti had said her session ended, and according to Ginny, postmortem lividity had progressed too far to have begun after Mrs. Pazotti returned home from the fitness center.

Ginny found no fingerprints or other evidence at the scene to indicate foul play, nor had any of the neighbors seen anyone come or go. That in itself didn't mean much, as the neighbors hadn't been looking for anyone. According to Mrs. Pazotti, she'd found the front door unlocked when she returned home. But if Pazotti came home with suicide on his mind, he probably went directly to his study, in a daze, not realizing he hadn't locked the front door behind himself.

The back door and all of the windows were locked, which could only be done from the inside. There were no signs of a forced entry. But the killer, or killers, could have rung the front doorbell and forced their way in when Pazotti answered it. If so, they seemed to have left no physical evidence. So, unless the autopsy revealed something unexpected, Mr. Pazotti's death would be ruled a suicide.

A security guard had let Zalva into the *Probe* offices, after she flashed her badge, and had guided her to Pazotti's office. The office was bare, and the security guard informed her all of Pazotti's personal effects had already been packed into boxes and shipped to his residence via UPS. She'd wandered down the hallway glancing into the other offices, and had noticed that they were untouched, as though everyone had simply left for lunch. She'd asked the security guard to show her O'Brien's office, which she found had been cleaned out like Pazotti's, computer and all.

She called Mrs. Pazotti, told her not to open the boxes when UPS delivered them, and left for the day. As she made her way to her car, a question tugged at her mind. *Why had only Pazotti's and O'Brien's offices been emptied?*

44

Needing to unwind, Zalva opted for Finigan's instead of her apartment. She wanted to ask O'Brien about the *Probe* closing down, and wanted to hear what O'Brien had to say about the New York incident that had ruined his professional reputation. If it turned out he really had been trying to fool her in order to create an investigation to support a false conspiracy theory, she just might shoot him in the ass, right there in the pub.

She made it to Finigan's at ten after five and relaxed with a brew at the bar. When Mary Kate served her and lingered to chat, Zalva decided to probe her about O'Brien's alleged trouble in New York.

"Mary Kate, has O'Brien ever mentioned anything about New York to you?"

"You mean that bit about the Pulitzer Prize?"

"Yeah. Someone told me about it today, but it was someone who could have an agenda, so he might've given it a little spin."

"We talked about it when he first moved back to D.C."

"Can you tell me his side of it?"

"Why don't you ask him?"

"I'd rather not open an old wound."

Mary Kate shrugged her shoulders. "Not much to it, really. He just got taken in by a con artist."

"You know the details?"

"Pretty much. According to Will, a ratty-looking guy approached him with a story about forced prostitution of illegal female immigrants from eastern Europe, mostly young girls. Will had to pay for the information, though, and his paper agreed. So, over a period of several weeks, the guy dribbled info to him in exchange for some pretty good money. He even took Will to some of the underground places, where he met a few alleged sex slaves.

"I guess Will was too eager for a big story and didn't do enough checking. After the story was published and Will won the Pulitzer, his source told him the whole thing was a hoax and threatened to expose him if he didn't pay up."

"And O'Brien didn't pay?"

"Oh, he paid up—the first time."

"The first time? The guy came back for more, huh?"

"A lot more. The first time, he only asked for ten grand. Will depleted his savings to get the money. A couple of weeks later, the guy came back, but asked for fifty grand."

"O'Brien couldn't pay that, right?"

"You got it. And when he didn't pay, the guy tried to extort money from the paper, and they went straight to the police."

"It must've hit O'Brien hard to lose his career like that."

"It crushed him."

"The guy who told me about it said O'Brien fabricated the story from the beginning, for glory and to embezzle money from the paper."

"That's what O'Brien's source said when he turned on him. He claimed to have kicked back most of the money from the paper to O'Brien, and he had proof O'Brien paid him the ten grand to shut him up, so everybody believed the worst. O'Brien barely escaped going to jail over it."

"He doesn't strike me as the type to try a hoax like that."

"Yeah, he's a good enough guy. I razz him a lot, but I love him."

"Does he have a lot of friends?"

"Everybody around here likes him, but his only close friend is Jason."

"How about women?"

Mary Kate rolled her eyes at the ceiling. "Now that's another story."

"Tell me about it."

"Not much to tell. They just seem to fall all over him."

"Why? He's certainly no hunk."

"It's his personality. He doesn't take much seriously, especially relationships. He has fun and makes no demands, attaches no strings, and lets go easily." She paused for a moment, as if reflecting on O'Brien's relationships with women. "It must have hurt him to the core when his wife left him, after his New York trouble. Wounded him to the point he's afraid of close relationships now."

"So, he has no steady girlfriend, just a lot of short affairs?"

"That's it. And mostly younger women."

Zalva sighed. "Too bad about New York. He's much too intelligent to settle for tabloid work."

Mary Kate slung the bar towel over her shoulder. "If you ask me, I think he does it as self punishment." She turned and sauntered down the bar to wait on a new customer.

A few minutes later, a tall, skinny guy slipped in beside Zalva at the bar. He nodded to Zalva and signaled something to Mary Kate. Mary Kate pulled a draft and brought it to him without any sort of verbal exchange. As she turned to walk away, he called out to her, "Is Will here?"

Mary Kate glanced back over her shoulder. "Haven't seen him."

The man gulped down half the mug of beer with one pull, set his mug down on the bar with a bang, and let out a long sigh. With a smug grin, he glanced down at Zalva. "First one's always the best."

"Yeah, and if the rest were as good as the first, we'd all be drunks. Speaking of drunks, you looking for Will O'Brien?"

"Yeah. You seen him tonight?"

"Not yet."

The man took a closer look at her face. "Hey! You're the detective woman, aren't you?"

"Afraid so," she answered.

"You looking for him, too?"

"Maybe."

"Gonna arrest him?"

"Hadn't planned on it. Should I?"

"Nah, just kidding."

"You must be Jason."

"Yeah, how'd you know?"

"Mary Kate told me his only friend was named Jason, and since you asked about him and she answered, I figured you had to be Jason."

Jason's mouth spread into a wide grin. "You're a detective all right."

"What line of work you in, Jason?"

Jason had raised his mug to finish it off, and stopped at her question. He placed the mug on the counter without drinking and frowned. "Why?"

"Just curious. You know what I do. I just wanted to know what you do."

"I'm a chemist."

Zalva sipped her beer and watched Jason toying with his mug, turning it around and around with his finger in the handle. All of a sudden, when she asked about his work, he'd become nervous. Then it struck her like a lightning bolt. *Jason had access to laboratory facilities. Jason could perform chemical analyses!* That's how O'Brien had known about the Maxual in the tablets in Pearson's hotel room. The brazen asshole had taken a tablet from the scene of a murder and had Jason analyze it.

Her face and ears burned red hot as she seethed at O'Brien's audacity.

Jason turned and sneaked a step away from the bar, obviously trying to escape before Zalva figured things out. She reached out and grabbed the back of his belt, stopping him so abruptly that beer sloshed out of his mug and splattered on the floor.

He turned with an indignant look on his face. "What's the—"

"You're not going anywhere just yet, Jason. We've got unfinished business."

"Hey, I've got to get back there and commandeer the snooker table—before someone else does."

"Not just yet you don't. Look at me, Jason." Reluctantly, he leaned over and looked her in the eyes. "Did you analyze a tablet for O'Brien?"

The look of guilt on his face was answer enough, and he didn't deny it.

"Shit!" she blurted.

"I didn't know where he got it, honest. I didn't know he took it from the hotel until afterward."

She doubted that, but let it go. "You realize how much trouble O'Brien could be in, for removing evidence from a crime scene?"

Jason's face took on a worried look. "You gonna arrest him now?"

Zalva drew a deep breath and exhaled slowly. "I don't know what I'm going to do."

She paused to think for a moment, and another thought hit her like an electric shock. The pill count was wrong! Mrs. Pearson had been given only one sample pack of Maxual containing twelve tablets according to her doctor, and all had been accounted for. Now, with another fake NazinX tablet surfacing, more than one sample pack of tablets had to be involved. It was just a coincidence that O'Brien's actions had made the pill count work out.

"How much Maxual did you find in the tablet you analyzed?"

"About two hundred milligrams."

Zalva was angry about the evidence being taken from the hotel. On the other hand, it could mean that Pearson's wife hadn't kill him. But if someone else killed Senator Pearson, was it pure coincidence that they used Maxual or did they know about the Maxual packet Mrs. Pearson's doctor gave her? And if they knew, *how* did they know? Was Mrs. Pearson's doctor involved?

These were all questions she couldn't answer. And now, she'd have to tell Captain Thurman about the tablet O'Brien took and the implication someone else could be involved—even if it meant O'Brien would be charged.

Mary Kate broke Zalva's concentration by plunking two full mugs down before her and Jason, who had been nervously watching her while she sorted things out in her mind. She grabbed her mug and turned it up.

"You guys figure out how the lapis lazuli got in the tablets?"

Zalva choked on her beer, as if she'd swallowed a bug, and spewed it all over the bar. When she continued coughing, Jason slapped her on the back to help. It was a full minute before she could speak.

"What did you say?" she asked.

"I said, did you guys ever figure out how the lapis lazuli got in the tablets?"

"You found something in the tablets besides Maxual?"

"Yeah, flakes of lapis lazuli."

"What's lapis lazuli?"

"It's a stone—a mineral. Sometimes people wear it as jewelry. You don't see it much anymore, but in the old days, artists used it to make blue pigment."

She didn't remember seeing anything about lapis lazuli in the lab report, but that didn't mean it wasn't there. She'd read the report quickly, focusing on the part about Maxual, and could easily have overlooked other details.

"It must've been in the bowl the tablets were ground up in, or maybe on the pestle itself, and came off when the tablets were crushed," she suggested.

"Sounds likely," agreed Jason.

She'd have to check the lab report out again first thing in the morning. If the report mentioned lapis lazuli, another search of Pearson's house would be in order. And if the source of lapis lazuli couldn't be found in Pearson's home, it could mean Mrs. Pearson had been framed, after all.

Another unexpected twist. It seemed that, every time she'd about decided to toss O'Brien's conspiracy story, something turned up to arouse her suspicions all over again.

45

O'Brien stepped through the doorway into Finigan's and froze at the sight of Zalva and Jason together at the bar. Jason spotted him, frowned, and nodded his head toward the door. He took that as a signal to beat a hasty retreat, but Zalva must've seen Jason's little nod, because she turned to see who he'd signaled to.

When she saw O'Brien, a fierce scowl spread over her face. Jason grimaced behind her back and shook his head, as if saying it was too late to exit now. The expression on Zalva's face, coupled with Jason's attempt to warn him, could only mean one thing: Jason had ratted him out about the tablet he'd taken from the hotel.

O'Brien hitched up his pants, swaggered over to the bar, and joined them. He slapped Jason on the back and nodded to Zalva, pretending not to notice her smoldering eyes and Jason's guilty expression.

Zalva jumped to her feet, snatched her mug off the counter with one hand, grabbed him by the belt buckle with the other, and stalked off toward a corner table, dragging him stumbling after her. When they reached the table, she slung him down into a chair.

"What in the hell is eating you?" he asked.

Zalva banged her mug down on the table, snatched up a chair, and sat across the table from him. She leaned forward with her face close to his.

"Don't you know it's a felony to remove evidence from the scene of a murder?"

He decided to play dumb a little longer, just to let her play out her anger. "What are you talking about? What evidence?"

She slapped her hand down hard on the table top. "Knock off the phoney acting job. Jason told me all about it. You took one of the fake tablets from Pearson's hotel room and had him analyze it."

"Jason told you that?"

"After I twisted his arm."

O'Brien realized there was no point in trying to delay the admission any longer. He leaned back, put his arm over the empty chair next to him, and cocked his head to one side. "Okay, so I did. So what?"

Zalva's mouth gaped open in astonishment. "So what? That's all you've got to say?"

"Where's the rub? I left one on the night stand for you guys to analyze."

Zalva simply glared at him for a moment, presumably formulating a response. While she stewed, Sheena placed a mug of Guinness Stout in front of him. O'Brien snatched his up and took a heavy pull.

Zalva eyed him stonily as he drank. When he put his mug down, she leaned over the table again, and spoke in a low voice, enunciating each word carefully as if speaking to a deaf mute who had to read lips.

"I'll tell you what the harm might be. Jason said the tablet you gave him had flakes of lapis lazuli in it. I can't remember seeing that in the crime lab report. And if it's not in the report, it might be because the tablet you lifted contained the first two tablets that were ground up. Any flakes that might have been in the bottom of the bowl, or on the end of the pestle, may have been absorbed in the first fake tablet. And since you removed that particular tablet from the scene, the chain of custody of the evidence was broken. Now, even if we find out where the flakes came from, we can't use the evidence in court."

If what she said was true, he'd screwed up big time. He ran his fingers through his hair in frustration. "Jason didn't say anything to me about any damned *lapis lazuli* flakes. What exactly is that, anyway?"

"It's a mineral used to make blue paint."

Her words rang in his mind like the clanging of a church bell. "Paint? Paint like artists use?"

"Yeah, according to Jason."

O'Brien bumped the heel of his right hand against his forehead. "Jesus! That figures."

Zalva gave him a puzzled look. "What figures?"

"Artists. Rulon's wife is an artist. Even grinds her own pigments."

Zalva squeezed her eyes shut and shook her head for a second before looking him in the eyes again. "Who's Rulon?"

"He's the guy with the French accent in the conspiracy meeting Monique overheard."

"What?"

"He's chairman of PMC's board of directors and he owns controlling interest. He's also the largest single contributor to the Democratic Party, served as ambassador to France under the last Democratic administration, and is so far to the left he's fallen off the chart. On top of all that, he grew up in France, was educated there, maintains a second home in Paris, and is married to a French woman—who by the way, is an accomplished artist who makes her own paints."

Zalva looked stunned. "How . . . how did you come by that?"

"I did a little research at the library. I also talked to Pearson's maid today, and guess what else."

Zalva slumped down in her chair, apparently overwhelmed. "Okay, what else?"

"Just before Senator Pearson was killed, his wife got a surprise invitation to a shindig in honor of the French ambassador's wife at Rulon's mansion."

"A surprise invitation?"

"You bet. Even though Senator Pearson was a social pariah, she got invited to the home of the cream of Washington society."

"So?"

"So, it seems Pearson's maid had taken on a mysterious French lover, who banged her bong in the Pearson house while Pearson's wife hobnobbed with the big-wigs at Rulon's place. And according to the maid, her French lover slipped her a mickey, had the run of house and could've switched the tablets and planted the evidence in Mrs. Pearson's closet. And—"

"And the lapis lazuli Jason found could have come from Rulon's wife's studio," said Zalva.

"Give the lady a cigar!" he quipped, clinking his mug against hers.

"This French lover have a name?"

"Alain Duramat, so he said—obviously bogus, at least the last name."

Zalva sat erect in her chair and wiped her face with both hands. "This is just too much. Where is he now?"

"Sylvia, that's the maid's name, said she hasn't seen him or heard from him since the day of the Rulon's shindig."

"Damn! Another missing piece of the puzzle. How about the maid? Where's she now?"

"I told her to get lost."

"What?"

"The way people are dying around here, I was afraid they might kill her, too."

"You don't know where she is?"

"No, but she's supposed to call me when she figures she's safe."

Zalva grabbed her beer, leaned back in her chair, and finished it off. She set the empty mug on the table with a clatter, and looked O'Brien in the eye. "Well, since you've got absolutely no credibility with *anybody*, I've got to hear it directly from her."

He detected a kind of disappointed bitterness in her voice. "Who've you been talking to?"

"Captain Thurman and I visited PMC today to follow up on Monique's death. Marchant told us all about your misadventure in New York."

"Care to hear my side of it?"

"One day, but not right now. It's just another obstacle for us to overcome."

"What about Monique? What did Marchant say about her?"

Zalva waved her hand in the air. "Oh, they had everything nailed down tight. She was fired yesterday afternoon for drug abuse on the job. Had prior warnings in her personnel file and witnesses who testified she was doped up at the office that day."

"But you know she was murdered, right?"

"It didn't seem so this morning . . . but now . . . "

"Well, it's clear enough to me. After Roscoe saw her with me at the deli, they put two and two together, and got rid of her."

Zalva sat back in her chair and tapped her fingers on the table for several seconds. O'Brien took the opportunity to finish off his mug of stout, watching her out of the corner of his eye.

A change came over her. Her eyes took on a sad look and the corners of her mouth sagged slightly. She leaned toward him and clasped her hands on the table top. "Look, O'Brien. I'm sorry you lost your job, but—"

"How did you know I lost my job today?"

Ignoring his question, she asked, "You heard about your boss?"

"Slick? He lost his job today, just like I did."

"There's more to know than that."

"What's to know about Slick?"

"He killed himself."

Her words were like a slap in the face. "Say again?"

"Slick committed suicide this afternoon."

"Suicide? Slick? No way!"

"He put a bullet in his brain, sitting in his study."

O'Brien pushed his chair away from the table, instinctively trying to distance himself from what she said. "Who told you that?"

"Nobody. I saw it for myself."

"You saw him do it?"

"No, I answered a call from his wife. She came home from her fitness center and found him."

O'Brien sagged in his chair, thinking about the last few minutes he'd spent with Slick. He hadn't known Slick very well; nobody had. That was the way Slick had liked it. He always kept his distance from O'Brien and the rest of the tabloid staff. But he sure as hell wasn't despondent when they left the coffee shop together. If anything, he was fired up: angry about the way the paper was closed and the reason given.

"Did he leave a note?"

"No, but he was deep in debt, his marriage was a failure, and the loss of his job could've pushed him over the edge."

"Bullshit! He wasn't depressed when we left the coffee shop this morning. He was angry; ready to fight back."

"You think he was murdered?"

"Abso-fucking-lutely!"

"Why would they kill him?"

"I kept him informed. He knew as much about the conspiracy as I did."

"If he was murdered, there's no way to prove it. Just like Lezette and Monique, all the tracks are covered," said Zalva.

He threw his hands up in frustration. "They're going to get away with another one."

"Why was the tabloid closed?" she asked.

"Economic reasons—they said. But Slick said that was a lie. He'd been to board meetings in New York, and nobody had ever mentioned any financial problems to him."

"That's curious."

"They just came in, confiscated my computer and all my files, and had security guards escort me and Slick to the street."

"That does seem a little melodramatic."

"Oh, yeah? Well guess who owns the company that owns the *Probe*?"

"Who?"

"PMC."

Zalva's jaw slackened. "You sure of that?"

"Yep. Looked it up on the internet."

"Then PMC closed the *Probe* down to keep you from exposing their conspiracy," said Zalva

"You got it."

"But why kill Slick after the tabloid was shut down?" she asked.

"He planned to shop the story around to some of the other tabloids and magazines."

"How would Marchant or Rulon know that?"

"Maybe he called the wrong person. Or maybe his phone was bugged."

Zalva folded her arms and studied O'Brien. Finally, she leaned forward with her elbows on the table, clasped her hands, and bumped her knuckles against her chin for a few seconds, apparently pondering all he'd told her. After a long pause, she spoke again.

"It's obvious there's something to this conspiracy, since the coincidences are stacking up faster than Chris Moneymaker's chips in a poker tournament, but my hands are tied."

"What you mean by that?"

"Captain Thurman ordered me to lay off. He's convinced, after talking to the FBI and Marchant at PMC, that you've cooked up the whole conspiracy idea just to take advantage of a string of unfortunate coincidences, and to get revenge on PMC for New York."

"How about the attempts on *my* life?"

"Thurman maintains the BMW incident was some drunk feeling his oats and that you skinned up your own knees and head to make the fake kidnaping look more real. I talked to Carla on the phone and she told me she didn't see the two men flash any badges and couldn't hear anything they said because the car windows were up. Without the fake FBI agents, or some witnesses, we're not going to change his mind."

"Okay, forget about me. How about all these suicides and overdoses? And PMC owning the *Probe* and shutting it down? And Pearson's wife going to Rulon's reception, while the maid slept with her French lover who drugged her? And the lapis lazuli flakes in the tablet and Rulon's wife grinding her own pigments? All of these are independent coincidences?"

Zalva laid a hand on his. "I'll bring all that up with Captain Thurman in the morning." She paused for a moment. "Of course, I'll have to tell him about you taking the tablet from Pearson's hotel room."

"Jesus, Zalva. You gotta tell him about that?"

"Don't have any choice."

"What'll he do?"

"Who knows? Might charge you, might not."

"How about the maid and her story—the probability her lover planted the evidence against Mrs. Pearson? What will he do about that?"

"Probably nothing."

"Why not?"

"Pearson's wife is going to court. If I know Thurman, he'll leave it up to the lawyers to settle."

"What if her lawyers don't know about the maid's story?"

"Maybe you should make sure they do know."

What good would that do? he wondered. To Zalva, he muttered, "The maid won't ever make it to court. Rulon and Marchant won't take a chance on their plot being exposed by defense lawyers prying into all these *coincidences*, or in a courtroom by a credible witness in a trial that'll be watched by half the world."

"That's another reason you need to talk to Mrs. Pearson's attorneys. If they believe the maid's story, they can arrange for her protection."

O'Brien shrugged and threw up his hands. "I've tried calling her cell phone, but she's turned it off. Not much I can do until she calls me back."

With Zalva resolved to speak to her boss again in the morning, they agreed to leave the topic alone for the rest of the night, and ordered sandwiches which they ate at the table. Zalva switched to iced tea, while O'Brien continued to drink Guinness Stout.

After eating, they adjourned to the pinball machines for an hour. Zalva was a lot of fun, lively and witty, and seemed to warm up to him, touching him playfully on the arms and back, and brushing against him occasionally.

Eventually, Zalva began to fade. "I'm ready to call it a night."

"Me too," admitted O'Brien.

"Have you been back to your place since the kidnaping?"

"Yeah, I went by this morning for a shower and fresh clothes."

"Aren't you afraid those guys will be laying for you?"

"Yeah, I am. Jason said I could stay with him for a couple of weeks, but now Carla's at his place. I'd best stay away from there."

She studied him for a few seconds, then she spoke softly, with a thin smile. "Well, you can stay at my place again tonight, if you want to."

More grateful than he cared to admit, O'Brien accepted her offer, and they left for her apartment.

46

At Zalva's apartment, O'Brien made himself comfortable on her couch, prepared to zonk out for the night. He heard Zalva puttering around in the kitchen and thought she might be putting some things away before going to bed. The noise from the kitchen ceased and he heard the padding of her bare feet on the carpet. It sounded like she was coming toward the couch.

He sat up and was surprised to see her come around the couch with a bottle of red wine and two glasses. "I thought you were going to bed."

"Not just yet. Scoot over and give me room."

O'Brien slid across the couch making space for her.

She eased down on the far end of the couch, poured two glasses of wine, and handed him one. "Don't get any ideas, now. I just want to relax a few minutes before going to bed."

O'Brien smiled to himself. He'd heard that one before. And in his experience, it usually meant, *I can be had but you've got to work for it and be damned careful how you go about it.*

She sipped at her wine, and studied him for a moment. "How are your knees?"

"Still touchy, but I'm getting used to it."

She pointed with a nod of her head at the coffee table where the ointment and bandages rested. "Be sure to use the Neosporin again tonight."

"You gonna help me again?"

"Not tonight. Now, tell me about New York."

He took a deep breath, let it out in a rush, and gave her the whole story; baring his soul to her scrutiny. While he talked, she sipped at her wine and, between sips, peered into the glass with the concentration of a fortune teller reading a cup of tea leaves.

When he finished, he drained the rest of his wine in one gulp. She refilled both glasses, emptying the bottle. She twisted her mouth and gave her head a slight shake. "Looks to me like your biggest mistake was not going to the law when the rat asked for the ten grand."

How many millions of times had he thought the same thing? "Enough about me. How about you? What's in your past?"

She curled her feet up under her on the couch. "Not much, really. I grew up in a barrio in New York. I managed not to get pregnant, never screwed around with drugs, and got a degree in Criminal Justice. I joined the NYPD right after college."

"Ever been married?" he asked.

"No. Came close though. You?"

"Yeah, to my college sweetheart, but she left me when I lost my job in New York."

"Did you love her?"

"Of course."

"Ever get over her?"

Once that question would've brought tears to his eyes, but the years had hardened him. "Yeah. Took a while though."

Zalva became silent, staring into her glass again, deep in thought. "How did you come to be in D.C.?" he asked.

She looked up at him with a faint smile. "I had to get away from Dwayne, my old flame. He was a cop who helped me a lot when I first joined NYPD. We ran around together for a while, then it kinda progressed to living with him. At first, I thought I loved him, but as time wore on, I realized I didn't. He was a real macho kind of guy—wanted to dominate me, and I couldn't take that. And I realized all my spare time was being spent around cops. I'd lost touch with ordinary people, and I needed to get out."

"But why D.C.?"

"I wanted to work homicides, and D.C. happens to have the highest per capita murder rate in the country. So I applied for a job here and was accepted."

They sat in silence for several minutes, contemplating their pasts.

Zalva finished her wine and placed the empty glass on the coffee table. O'Brien slid across the couch, intending to put his arm around her, but she stood up, grabbed the empty bottle with one hand and the empty glasses with the other, and turned to walk away.

He stood up with her and reached for her shoulder to turn her around.

She deftly evaded his grasp and walked quickly to the kitchen. He watched as she placed the empty bottle and glasses on the kitchen counter; then she padded into her bedroom, never looking back.

Puzzled, he stood watching her bedroom door. Last night she'd practically rubbed her tits all over him, after threatening to make him sleep on the balcony if he got out of line, and seemed disappointed when he didn't make a play for her. Tonight, she wouldn't let him touch her.

He stared at her bedroom door for long minutes, wondering if he should step over and try it. Finally, he decided against it—something in the back of his mind told him, *not yet*.

He let out a deep breath, and collapsed onto the couch. But sleep came slowly.

Friday

47

O'Brien stood in the darkness of the theater wings quietly watching the action on stage while waiting for his entrance cue. But as he listened to the lines being spoken on-stage, a horrible realization crept over him: The actors were speaking French! That was all wrong. He couldn't speak French. Why would he be in a play where all the lines were in French?

Nevertheless, he was standing in the wings, waiting to go on stage. But what about rehearsals? No play was produced without rehearsals, yet he couldn't remember going to any. Perhaps if he found a script he could memorize a few lines quickly, or maybe even carry the script on stage and read his lines. If he was real slick with it, maybe the audience wouldn't notice.

He scrambled around backstage looking for one and saw a tall African-American lady sitting by an electrical panel, holding what appeared to be a script. As he neared the woman, he saw she was Monique. Happy to see Monique alive, he rushed to her. But when she lifted her eyes to him, he found she was Shaunda.

Shaunda held the script up for him to see. "This what you're looking for?"

Angry that it was Shaunda and not Monique, he snatched the script from her hand and turned to walk away.

"It won't do you any good," Shaunda called out after him. "You'll see."

Anxiously, he opened the script, and groaned in dismay when he saw it wasn't a script, but an appointment book. Marchant's appointment book! Excited, he flipped through the pages, looking for the date of the meeting Monique overheard. He found the right date and ran his finger down the page, looking at the various notations by the time slots. As he read the entries, the words suddenly shifted from English to French. To his dismay, he now held a French script instead of Marchant's appointment book.

He screamed and threw the script against the wall. Now Shaunda appeared before him, laughing in his face. He shoved her away and looked around wildly for an exit. It was Time to get out of Dodge.

A woman wearing earphones and dressed in black intercepted him on his way to the exit. The title of Stage Manager was printed in large, white letters across the front of her shirt. He recognized Alice White, his old stage manager from the Shakespeare company he'd toured with, after college.

She blocked his path and put both hands on his shoulders. "Where are you going? Didn't you hear your cue?"

"Alice! Boy am I glad to see—"

"Shut up and get on the stage," she yelled in his face.

"But I don't know—"

Alice grabbed him by the shoulders, spun him around, and whispered into his ear, "You should've come to the rehearsals, you arrogant fool." Then she pushed him across the floor and shoved him out of the wings onto the stage.

He squinted his eyes against the glare of the stage lights. Two men and a woman were arguing down stage. They stopped arguing and stood gawking at him. To his horror, he recognized Roscoe and Henri, from the PMC building. What an absurdity! Those guys couldn't be actors.

The woman asked O'Brien a question in French. Dumbfounded, he stood with the stage lights beating down on him, starring at her like a man bereft of his senses.

The woman ran to him, grabbed him by the shoulders, and yelled in his face, again in French. As he gaped at her in confusion, her face shifted and she became Mary Kate. He struggled to pull out of her grasp, but her fingers dug deep into the flesh of his shoulders. As she screamed at him, her speech migrated from French to English. "Wake up, O'Brien! Wake up!"

Wake up? He wasn't asleep. Or was he? Was he dreaming? He took another look at Mary Kate's face, which blurred and shifted to become Zalva's.

Zalva? Finally, he opened his eyes, free of the nightmare. Zalva loomed over him, shaking him by the shoulders. He looked around the room in bewilderment.

Zalva stepped back from the couch. "You awake now?"

He blinked his eyes against the bright overhead light, sat up, and swung his legs off the couch. "Yeah. Finally."

"Know where you are?"

O'Brien rubbed his face vigorously with both hands, took a deep breath, and let it out slowly. He looked up at Zalva, and ran a hand through his bushy hair. "I didn't at first, but now I do."

"You okay?"

"Yeah. Just had another one of those accursed anxiety dreams."

Zalva stood over him with her hands on her hips. "Anxiety dreams? Like what?"

"I'm haunted by two of them. One's about missing a final exam that's going to keep me from graduating from college, and the other's about being in a play and not knowing my lines, or even what play it is."

Zalva sighed knowingly. "I have the college one, sometimes. It's pretty common, I'm told."

"So is the theater dream, but it still tortures me two or three times a month."

"Well, I've got to leave for work now. Put your shoes on, freshen up, and I'll drop you off at Finigan's."

Her mention of leaving made him notice she was dressed for work.

"What time is it?"

"Almost eight."

"Uh-uh. Way too early for me, since I don't have a job to go to. I'll take a cab later, if you don't mind."

"Well, suit yourself. Just be sure to lock the door when you leave." Zalva headed for the door, where she paused and glanced over her shoulder at him. "See you at Finigan's tonight?"

"You bet."

"Until tonight," she said and slipped through the doorway.

For a moment, O'Brien was tempted to stretch out again and sink back into sleep, but fearing the nightmare would return, he struggled to his feet and stumbled back to her bathroom.

48

On her way to the station, Zalva reflected on the miserable night she'd had. Haunted by O'Brien's conspiracy, she tossed and turned all night, and woke several times. She couldn't have slept more than three hours, the entire night.

Everything he'd said was plausible, yet no physical evidence existed to support him, at least none presentable in a court of law—with the possible exception of Pearson's maid. Even if the conspiracy was real, the conspirators had covered their trail well. She doubted a conviction could be gotten—short of an outright confession by a key player, like Marchant.

She wondered what O'Brien would do, now that he was out of work. In answer to her own question, she thought about his manuscript and the promise it showed. Maybe he'd turn to a writing career in earnest.

At the station, she went to her desk, intending to review her copy of the lab report on the medications taken from Pearson's hotel room. To her chagrin, the report was no longer on her desk. Thinking Ginny might still have a copy, she went back to the lab, but found she wasn't in. Frustrated, she started back to her desk, but paused at Thurman's wide-open doorway.

Thurman sat at an angle to his desk with his back to her, feet propped on the credenza under the window. He appeared to be absorbed with a report. She drew in a deep breath, exhaled, and rapped sharply on the open door.

Thurman glanced over his shoulder. When he spotted her, he rolled his eyes as if she were a cat that had found its way home after being dumped in a swamp. He blew out a deep breath. "Yeah?"

Zalva made no move to enter the office. "Can I talk to you for a moment?"

Thurman grimaced and made a noise which she took to be permission to enter. She pulled up one of the side chairs and sat directly in front of his desk.

Thurman swung his feet off the credenza and spun his chair around to face her, with a sour look on his face. "What's up?"

"It's about Will O'Brien."

Thurman's eyes became slits. "I thought I told you to drop that."

"You did, but I saw O'Brien at Finigan's last night and found out some things you ought to know."

"Finigan's? What were you doing at an Irish pub?"

"That's where O'Brien hangs out."

"So you've started hanging out there now?"

"It's a nice place—good food, good beer."

Thurman's brow furrowed. "You getting chummy with O'Brien?"

"I wouldn't exactly call it chummy, but I have gotten to know him a little."

"You'd better be careful. He'll use you like a ten-buck-an-hour sparring partner."

"I'm a big girl."

"Well, you've been warned. Now, what ought I to know?"

She filled him in on all O'Brien had told her about Mrs. Pearson's surprise invitation to the Rulons', the maid's mysterious French lover being inside the Pearson's home, and the possibility he'd drugged her, substituted the fake tablets, and planted the evidence. She told him about PMC shutting down the *Probe*, the confiscation of O'Brien's computer, and his suspicion that it had been done to stop his article on the conspiracy.

Thurman barely lifted an eyebrow at that.

Zalva finished with the results of O'Brien's research on the Rulons, and his belief that Rulon was the third man Monique overheard in the meeting at PMC. But, when the moment came, she found that she couldn't bring herself to tell Thurman about O'Brien taking evidence from the hotel scene and Jason finding lapis lazuli in the tablet.

During her presentation, Thurman sat sideways to his desk with his right arm resting on the desktop, head tilted back, and eyes closed. When she finished, he remained in that position for several seconds, twisting his mouth from one side to the other, drumming his fingers on the desk top. Finally, he opened his eyes, looked askance at her, and muttered, "So?"

Stunned, Zalva moved her lips to speak, but nothing came out.

Seeing her speechless, he twisted his chair around to face her and leaned across his desk. "I don't know why you're surprised. What'd you think I'd say?"

"I guess I was suffering under the delusion that you might be interested in justice," she retorted.

Thurman slammed his meaty fist down on the desk with such force she winced. "Watch your mouth!" He glared at her for a few seconds while he brought his temper under control. "Justice is not our concern."

Zalva shot from her chair. "What? How can you say that?"

Thurman rose, spread his hands out wide on the desk, and loomed over it, glaring down at Zalva. "Justice is the court's business. It's the responsibility of the judges and the lawyers and the juries. Our job is to find the evidence, make an arrest, and let the rest of the system sort it out."

She placed her hands wide on her side of his desk, mirroring his position, and leaned over it until her face was mere inches from his. "It's obvious there's a chance Mrs. Pearson may have been framed. Aren't you the least bit interested in that?"

"We've made our arrest."

"Shouldn't we at least talk to the maid?"

"Now what in the hell would the jury in the Pearson trial think if her lawyer told them we continued looking for other suspects, on the assumption she'd been framed, *after* we charged her?"

"If we follow up on this, there might not be a Pearson trial."

"We're not gonna follow up on it! If there's a possibility somebody framed her, it's her lawyer's job to exploit it."

Zalva stepped back in distress, putting both hands on her cheeks. "I can't believe I'm hearing this."

"You'd better by-God believe it! I'm giving you a direct order. Don't spend any more time on O'Brien's half-baked conspiracy theory."

Zalva's arms and legs trembled in anger. She wheeled and marched toward the door.

"Zalva!"

She stopped in the doorway, paused with her head down for a moment, then slowly turned to face Thurman.

"Take a couple of days off. Find something interesting to do. Something to get your mind off O'Brien and his trumped-up conspiracy."

"How about—"

"It's an order. Now go home."

49

O'Brien took a quick shower, brushed his teeth with his finger, and donned yesterday's clothes again. Driven by a gnawing hunger, he searched the fridge and came up with a lone English muffin, which he split and popped into the toaster. He found Zalva's daily newspaper on the kitchen counter next to a pot of coffee she'd left for him. When the muffin was crispy brown, he poured a cup of coffee, picked up the muffin and newspaper, and returned to the couch.

He found the remote on top of the TV, turned it on, switched to one of the local news channels, and made himself comfortable.

O'Brien breathed a sigh of relief at seeing nothing about Senator Scott on the front page of the paper and on the morning news show. Maybe the senator had gotten his e-mail and taken precautions. That thought brought a cynical sneer to his lips. If Scott had taken the warning seriously, it would be the first thing that had gone right about this whole mess.

He wondered why Sylvia hadn't called him as she'd promised. She was the only person left who could back up part of his story. What if she hadn't made it? What if they had followed him to the Pearson's home and to the little shopping center where he met with her? What if they'd been waiting in the parking lot and followed her when she drove away? He cursed himself for not escorting her to safety.

No, it won't be his fault if they got her, he told himself. To the conspirators, she'd been a loose end since the day they planted the evidence in Pearson's home. It was a miracle they hadn't finished her off before he got to her . . .

No, not a miracle either. Sylvia had stayed at Pearson's home with the widow, consoling her and hoping to prevent a suicide. Her death on the Pearson's grounds would surely raise questions, especially since he'd poked about, stirring the pot.

O'Brien rose from the couch and started for the kitchen for another cup of coffee. He stopped abruptly at the mention of Senator Scott on the TV. He stood halfway between the couch and the kitchen and watched what turned out to be a short human-interest blip about a surprise birthday party his staff had sprung for Scott, the previous afternoon.

Although his birthday wasn't until today, they gave him the party early. The reporter asked him what he planned to do on his birthday, and he admitted he planned to spend the day at his little getaway place on Bear Creek, near Nanticoke, Maryland. He hoped to get in a little fishing on Tangler Sound before the cold weather set in. He always fished alone; that way, he could quit when he wanted and not at someone else's convenience.

The man's got shit for brains, thought O'Brien. Alone all day, out on the wide open sound—easy prey for assassins. He felt frustrated and angry, too, knowing the danger Scott faced yet unable to do anything about it. Zalva couldn't help, even if she believed him. And if he called the FBI again, they'd probably arrest him or worse, cart him off to St Elizabeth's.

The news program faded from his awareness as he pondered the situation and reached an unpalatable conclusion: he just couldn't sit idly by and let Scott be killed.

He jumped up from the couch and began looking for his shoes. He'd do the only thing he could do—drive to Nanticoke, find the senator's place and warn him in person.

O'Brien called a taxi and had it drop him off at Finigan's so that he could pick up his car. He checked the Volvo out for bombs again, even though he doubted the assassins would kill him in such an obvious fashion. Afterward, he sat behind the wheel, wondering if he could risk going by his place for some foul-weather gear, in case he had to go out on the Bay.

He decided not to risk it. His field jacket and campaign hat were in the Volvo and that would do in a pinch. He figured he could make it to Nanticoke in a little over an hour. Once there, he could ask around at convenience stores for directions to Scott's place. He turned the key, waited for the car to warm up, and drove off toward Nanticoke. He snorted aloud when the image of Don Quixote tilting at windmills, popped into his mind.

"Yeah, that's me," he muttered, and hunched over the steering wheel.

50

Shortly after leaving Thurman's office, Zalva drove down Connecticut Avenue, wondering what to do with herself. Having a weekday off was a strange sensation, since she'd had damn few of them since moving to D.C. She spotted a coffee shop and decided to stop for coffee and a Danish.

She found a parking spot on a side street and walked the three blocks back to the coffee shop. At the counter, she picked up a cinnamon roll with extra icing and a cup of Mocha Java. She settled down at a table with a good view of the teeming sidewalk, took a bite of the cinnamon roll, and smiled at the taste. She took a larger bite loaded with icing, closed her eyes, and leaned back to savor it.

When she opened her eyes, she spotted a newspaper lying on a nearby table. After waiting several minutes to see whether anyone returned to claim it, she took it into protective custody.

Zalva lifted the coffee cup to her lips and scanned the front page story about 'Slick' Pazotti's suicide. A smaller headline caught her attention and she dropped her gaze down to the article. The article discussed the candidates likely to be substituted for Pearson and Gunter, their near-certain chances of success in the election, the impact that would have on the balance of power in the Senate, and the long-term ramifications on the judicial system.

At least O'Brien wasn't alone in his assessment of the consequences of the two senators' deaths. She laid the paper on the table and turned the pages while enjoying her coffee and cinnamon roll. She came to a section on world affairs and scanned the first page, looking only at the dark print. One of the articles had a photo of Geroux, the French president. She read the first sentence of the article which read, "Geroux lauds probable change in outcome of U.S. mid-term elections."

Interest piqued, she put her coffee mug aside to read the article, wondering what made the French politician comment on American politics. At a press conference, Geroux had been asked what he thought about the unexpected deaths of the two American senators and their last minute replacements. While Geroux lamented the deaths of the senators, he was elated at the prospect of the liberals maintaining their control of the Senate.

On further questioning, he had elaborated, claiming President Thompson was preoccupied with foreign affairs and was living in the past. According to him, neither Europe nor Asia needed or welcomed American hegemony any longer. From what he'd seen of the polls reported in the American press, the Democrats had been on the verge of losing control of the Senate. That would have allowed President Thompson to be more aggressive in foreign affairs, increasing the level of his unwanted and dangerous interference in the Middle East.

Geroux believed the new candidates would be successful in the coming election, allowing the liberals to retain control of the Senate and thwart Thompson's ambitions." The rest of the article was full of his insults about American culture and its brand of capitalism.

Annoyed by Geroux's condescending attitude toward America and its culture, she tossed the paper aside and grabbed her coffee mug. The article caused her to recall what O'Brien had said about Rulon being a Francophile, and the French presence that permeated the conspiracy. Rulon had strong ties to France, Marchant was from Quebec, Lezette was French and, according to O'Brien, the maid's lover was French.

Lezette worked for the French Embassy and perhaps the maid's lover did, too. A sudden thought made her gasp. *Was it possible they were French agents assigned to the embassy in Washington for the purpose of assisting Rulon with the assassinations?*

She recalled what she'd seen on TV in recent years about Franco-American relations. France had openly opposed U.S. policy in the Middle East, before, during, and after the invasions of Afghanistan and Iraq. Secretary of State Hederly had even alleged that France was building a political and military alliance with Germany and Russia for the express purpose of counterbalancing U.S. influence in the U.N. and around the globe.

And there was the unforgettable *Oil For Food* program for Iraq, supposedly overseen by the U.N., where billions of dollars had been siphoned off by Saddam and used to bribe a multitude of officials from the U.N. and foreign governments—perhaps even Geroux, although he wasn't president at that time—and purchase banned weapons from them.

But was it possible the French government would take such a drastic step as tampering with U.S. elections? As she pondered the question, she remembered that many countries in past decades had accused the U.S. of doing exactly that to them or their neighbors.

As her suspicion about French government involvement in the conspiracy grew, so did her anger. They couldn't be allowed to get away with it. But what could she do? The FBI didn't believe in the conspiracy, and Captain Thurman didn't care.

She stewed over the dilemma for several more minutes. Then she slammed her coffee mug down on the table and jumped out of her chair. In spite of Thurman, she'd do what she could—even if she got fired for the effort.

But what could she do? The maid was on the lam, and Zalva couldn't go to Mrs. Pearson's home for an interview or call her, not without her attorney being present. She pondered the matter for a couple of minutes. Then she decided to go directly to Rulon's home, interview his wife, and scope out her studio. She got Rulon's address from the dispatcher and headed in that direction.

51

Zalva cruised slowly down Foxhall Road, looking for Rulon's mansion. She passed several she thought were impressive before she found the right address. The brick driveway into the estate was gated, with a small sentry house posted in the middle of the split driveway. She gained entry after identifying herself and showing her badge to the guard.

As she drove toward the mansion, it seemed she'd been teleported to the south of France. She'd never been there, but Rulon's home and grounds resembled the pictures of French country manors she'd seen in magazines.

Zalva parked right in front of the door, as the wide circular driveway had plenty of room for other vehicles to get around her car. A carriage house stood apart from the manor. The doors were open, revealing a uniformed chauffeur vacuuming the interior of a black limo. She rang the doorbell, and a maid in the traditional black uniform and white apron answered the door.

"Oui?"

Zalva pulled her badge from her inside coat pocket and clipped it to her belt, making sure the maid got a good look at it. "I'm Detective

Martinez of the D.C. police department. I'd like to speak to Mrs. Rulon. Is she in?"

"*Oui*. May I tell her the purpose of your visit?"

"Just that it's official police business."

The maid pouted at her response. "Very well, ma'am. *Entre, s'il vous plaît.*"

Zalva stepped into the foyer and followed the maid across the marble floor to a richly furnished sitting room. She recognized an original Cezanne and a Monet adorning the walls. The place reeked of opulence.

The maid motioned for Zalva to be seated. "I will announce you to Mrs. Rulon," she said, and left Zalva to study her surroundings.

After several minutes the maid returned and beckoned to her. "Madam will receive you now, in her studio. Come with me, *s'il vous plaît.*"

Perfect, thought Zalva. She could get right to the core of the matter immediately. The maid led her through the house and out the back door. They crossed an enormous brick patio cluttered with life-sized sculptures of Napoleon, Voltaire, and others she imagined were French notables from history, to another building.

Obviously designed as an artist's studio, the building consisted of a single cavernous room with a vaulted ceiling. The north-facing wall was mostly glass, with windows stretching from almost floor level to within a foot of the ceiling. A couch, two side chairs, and a coffee table occupied one end of the studio. The other was cluttered with finished and unfinished canvasses.

With her back to them, Mrs. Rulon stood before a monstrous easel almost as tall as the ceiling, working feverishly on a huge canvas. She wore faded blue jeans, a man's blue oxford shirt that hung down to her knees, sneakers, and a baseball cap. A long pony-tail of light brown hair, streaked with gray, protruded through the gap in the back of the cap. A table next to the easel held the subject of her painting: an arrangement of fruit, flowers, and wine bottles.

She heard their approach and tossed a quick look over her shoulder, her ponytail swishing like the tail of a frisky filly. Then she put her brush down, wiped her hands on a rag, and turned to face them. She was thin as a fashion model, at least fifty, and still attractive; the only tell-tale signs of age were the tiny lines at the corners of her eyes.

"*Je vous présente Mademoiselle Martinez,*" announced the maid. At a nod from Mrs. Rulon, she turned and left them alone in the studio.

"I'm a detective with the D.C. Police Department," said Zalva, since it didn't seem to her that the maid had made that clear.

"*Oui,* but what on earth do you wish to discuss with me?"

"I'm working on the Pearson case and—"

"Senator Pearson? *Il s'est couvert de honte.*"

"Beg your pardon?"

"The awful man disgraced himself. What could I possibly know about such a pig?"

"Was your husband a close friend of Senator Pearson?"

She winced at that question. "*Mon Dieu!* Of course not."

"Was Mrs. Pearson a friend or acquaintance of yours?"

Mrs. Rulon looked down her nose disdainfully at Zalva. "Heavens no."

"You didn't travel in the same social circle?"

"I should say not. I barely knew her, and Pearson was a crude peasant."

"For some reason, I had the impression you and Mrs. Pearson were close friends."

Mrs. Rulon's back stiffened. "What on earth gave you such a notion?"

"Didn't you invite her to a reception in honor of the French ambassador's wife, a day or two before Pearson died?"

Mrs. Rulon's mouth opened wide. "*Mon Dieu!* I had forgotten about that. *Oui,* I did invite her."

"Why'd you do that, if you didn't like her or her husband?"

"My husband's idea. I did not wish to, but he insisted."

"Did he give a reason?"

"Something about trying to get Pearson to resign, I believe. *Oui,* that's it. He and other party officials had already talked to Pearson—without result of course. He felt he might have better luck with Mrs. Pearson."

"You mean he intended to pull her aside at the reception and try to get her to work or her husband?"

"*Oui.* I believe he had something like that in mind."

"Do you recall seeing him talking to Mrs. Pearson during the reception?"

She rolled her eyes and patted her lips lightly with her fingertips. "*Non . . .* come to think of it . . . I did not see them together."

"Did you know Lezette, the young woman who worked at the French Embassy?"

"*Oui.* Why do you ask?"

Zalva politely ignored her question, parrying it with another of her own. "Had she ever visited your home?"

"Many times. My husband adored her. She was like a daughter to him. We don't have any children of our own, you know."

"Did he meet her in France?"

"*Oui.* I believe he requested she be assigned to the embassy here."

"He must've taken her death very hard."

She frowned and nodded. *" Cette tragédie l'a frappé cruellement."*

"Pardon?"

"I said her death was a cruel blow to him."

"Did Lezette attend the reception for the ambassador?"

"Certainly. She was a lively girl and popular, too."

"Does the name 'Alain' mean anything to you?"

"*Non . . .* no, I don't know anyone by that name."

"Thank you for answering my questions. You've been very helpful. But before I leave, would you please show me some of your work?"

Mrs. Rulon's face brightened. "My pleasure." She waved her hand around the studio and said, *"J'adore la peinture impressionniste."*

Zalva assumed that meant she loved the impressionist style of painting, since the original paintings she'd seen in the house and all the paintings in the studio were of that style.

Mrs. Rulon gave her a tour of the studio, discussing each piece in detail. An abrupt change had come over the woman; her haughtiness and formal rigidity were replaced by a relaxed manner and an eagerness to talk about her art.

Thank God that Art Appreciation 101 was a required undergraduate course, thought Zalva. She was able to draw upon her memory of the course to make at least a few intelligent comments during the tour.

Mrs. Rulon prated on and on about her work and all the places where she'd been shown, and the ribbons she'd won, alternating between French and English in her enthusiasm. For the most part, Zalva tuned her out, letting her mind wander back to other aspects of the conspiracy. Suddenly, however, her mention of pigments caught Zalva's attention like the pop of a balloon.

"And this is where I grind the minerals," said Mrs. Rulon, waving a hand at a work table covered with at least a dozen small, shallow bowls, along with pestles, jars of minerals, and assorted knives and tools.

Striving to appear casual, Zalva surveyed the array of items on the work table. Her heart leaped into her throat when she saw that one end of the long table contained a couple of clay busts and several modeling tools. *The fragmented clay mold found in Mrs. Pearson's closet could well have been made at this very table!*

Zalva had to struggle to suppress her excitement. "Are you a sculptor, too?"

"Oh, I toy with it occasionally. Whenever I'm working on a troublesome painting, I find it relaxing to work in clay for a change of pace. One doesn't have to worry about hues, values, or pigments with clay."

"I find it interesting, but also puzzling, that you make your own pigments when inexpensive, ready-mixed oils are available at art supply stores."

Mrs. Rulon shook her head in obvious disdain. "Commercial paint makers cannot match the pure hues I make. All the great masters mixed their own pigments, you know."

Zalva walked around the table, grateful for the excuse, inspecting each bowl in turn. She left the bowls and examined the various colored minerals and powders on the table. She picked up a small piece of deep-blue, rock-like material, about an inch thick, which she suspected to be lapis lazuli. "What is this stuff?"

"Lapis lazuli. I use it to make ultramarine blue."

"It's a beautiful blue," said Zalva. She'd already noticed that one of the small bowls contained traces of deep blue powder in the bottom. "You grind each pigment in a different bowl?"

"*Oui*. It is quite necessary, in order to achieve a pure hue."

Zalva casually ran her eyes over the work table surface and saw smudges of blue powder, as well as other colors, here and there on the table. Her heart pounded with excitement and she feared Mrs. Rulon would hear it, too. If the fake NazinX tablets had been made here in this studio, and whoever smashed up the Maxual tablets—most likely Lezette she figured—had gotten a little careless, she very well could have picked up traces of the lapis lazuli from the table top or from a bowl—and perhaps even left traces of NazinX behind.

Zalva lingered for another ten minutes, half-listening as Mrs. Rulon talked about the shows where she'd exhibited, the important people in the area who had purchased her paintings, and where those paintings had subsequently been hung. Eventually, she thanked Mrs. Rulon for her time and departed, ecstatic that something O'Brien had told her had finally been confirmed.

52

Zalva drove away from the Rulon mansion convinced the conspiracy ran deeper than even O'Brien dreamed. Now she had to read the lab report again. If it mentioned finding particles of lapis lazuli in the tablets, Thurman would have to change his mind. And if he wouldn't, maybe the FBI would.

She couldn't go back to the office though, because Thurman had ordered her to take the day off. Since it was nearly noon, maybe she could get Ginny to meet her somewhere for lunch and bring the lab report.

Using her cell phone, she called the station and asked for Ginny. A few seconds later, she heard the familiar squeaky voice on the phone.

"Yeah, Ginny here."

"Hi. It's Zalva."

"Zalva? What are you doing calling the office? I heard Thurman sent you home for a couple of days."

"He did. That's why I'm calling you."

"What've I got to do with it?"

"Can I buy you lunch today?"

"Sure, but what'd I do to deserve that?"

"It's what you're *going* to do."

"Uh-oh. I don't like the sound of that."

"It's okay. I just want you to bring me your copy of the lab report on the Pearson case."

"Why? Isn't that over except for the trial?"

"I'll explain over lunch."

"Where's your copy?"

"It wasn't on my desk this morning. I think Thurman took it."

Ginny paused a few seconds before responding. "Okay, I'll do it."

"Great."

"Can you pick me up out front?"

"Yeah, but can you walk down the street to the corner? I don't want Thurman to see you get in the car with me."

Ginny hesitated a few seconds before replying. "I don't like the sound of that, either."

"It's nothing to worry about. You won't get into any trouble, I promise."

"Well . . . okay then. I'll meet you at the corner to the north of the station. But don't leave me dangling, down there."

"I won't," Zalva promised. Another thought occurred to her. "Hey, Ginny . . . "

"Yeah?"

"You think maybe you could get photos of all the men assigned to the French Embassy, say, between the ages of forty and fifty-five?"

"Zalva, what are you up to?"

"I'll explain later. Trust me."

Ginny sighed. "All right. It'll take a while, though."

"What time do I pick you up?"

"Better make it late . . . say . . . one-thirty."

"Great. See you at one-thirty."

Zalva put her phone down and checked her watch. Only eleven-thirty now, leaving her some time to kill before picking up Ginny. She decided to drop by the library and do a little research of her own—on Franco-American relations.

• • •

Zalva picked Ginny up at the corner at precisely one-thirty. They discussed choices for a restaurant for a few seconds, decided on Italian, and opted for Giorgio's.

At Giorgio's, Ginny ordered fettuccine with Alfredo sauce and chicken, while Zalva chose lasagna and a glass of red wine. When the waiter left, Ginny pulled two large manila envelopes from her satchel, and placed them on the table in front of her. She leaned forward with her elbows on the envelopes and her chin resting on her intertwined fingers. "Okay, girl. Spill it."

Zalva told her all she knew, including the part about O'Brien removing evidence from the hotel room and the results of Jason's analysis. Ginny recoiled at that, but remained silent until Zalva finished.

Ginny leaned back in her chair. She studied Zalva for a moment before speaking. "What'd Thurman say about O'Brien removing evidence?"

Zalva swallowed hard. "I haven't told him yet."

Ginny leaned forward with a look of concern on her face. "And why not? You're risking your career for that bum."

"That's why I have to read the lab report again."

"You're hoping it mentions lapis lazuli, aren't you?"

"You got it. If it does, we've got a substantial break."

Ginny's brow wrinkled in concentration. She opened one of the envelopes and pulled out the lab report. "Well, here it is, but I don't remember seeing anything about foreign particles in the tablet."

Zalva took the report from Ginny and anxiously flipped through the pages, scanning them carefully. As she'd feared, the report failed to mention lapis lazuli. Bitterly disappointed, she sighed and let her shoulders sag.

Ginny took the report from her limp hands and shoved it back into the envelope. "O'Brien screwed it up good, didn't he?"

Zalva nodded her agreement. The damage was done, but maybe they could still salvage the situation with what they had. She remembered the photos she'd asked Ginny to bring with her. "What if the Pearson's maid can ID her lover as one of the embassy staff, and we find him?"

"Since the only fingerprints on the evidence were Mrs. Pearson's, he's just the maid's casual lover—unless he signs a confession, of course."

Fat chance of that, thought Zalva. She slumped back in her seat, dejected. The arrogant thugs! They were going to murder three senators—along with who knew how many other innocent victims. Worse yet, they were going to change the course of U.S. and world history, and get away with it.

But Senator Scott hadn't been killed yet. Maybe they could at least save him.

She reached into her purse and brought out the material on Rulon and his wife that O'Brien had given her. "Here," she said, offering it to Ginny.

"What's that?"

"Some info about Rulon and his wife. There's even a photo showing her studio and an article that says she grinds the materials to make her own pigments."

"And I'm supposed to do what with it?"

Zalva reached out and grabbed Ginny's hands. "Look, Ginny, you've been in this business a long time. You've got credibility with the FBI. Go to them. Tell them everything I've told you. Go over Rulon's obsession with France, his socialistic leanings, and his heavy political involvement. Tell them about the lapis lazuli flakes in the tablet that O'Brien stole, and how that connects back to Rulon. Maybe they'll believe you."

"Even if they do, they still won't have any more evidence than you've got."

"That's true, but they can do wiretaps—matter of national security and all. And they can spend unlimited time on it. Maybe even save Senator Scott."

Ginny reluctantly took the material from her and handed over the envelope containing the mug shots of the French Embassy staff. At that moment, the waiter arrived with their food and they fell to eating in silence.

After lunch, Zalva dropped Ginny off at the same corner. Before closing the door, Ginny poked her head into the car. "I'm gonna pay a visit to the FBI, but unless the conspirators screw up down the road, there's little the FBI can do because the only real evidence you have is tainted."

"I know. It makes me sick, too," said Zalva.

"What are you going to do now?" asked Ginny.

"I'm going home to study some material I picked up at the library and do some research on the internet. Maybe, later, we'll hear something from the maid and we can talk to her. Show her the mug shots."

"Keep your cell phone on. I'll call you after I talk to the FBI."

Zalva agreed, and Ginny pulled her head from the window, turned and hurried up the street toward the station.

53

O'Brien stopped for gas at a convenience store on the outskirts of Nanticoke. While the gas pump was running, he entered the store for coffee and directions to Senator Scott's place. A squat, grey-haired, wrinkled crone sat on a stool several feet behind the counter, with her back against the wall.

He gave her his best smile. "Good morning."

She didn't budge from her stool, or return his smile or his greeting. She blinked her bulging eyes a couple of times and spoke in a hoarse, raspy voice. "What you need?"

"Coffee and a snack," he replied. He turned away from the counter and wandered through the isles until he found a familiar brand of powered doughnut, then located the coffee pot. He poured a cup of vile-smelling coffee thick enough to make asphalt. Business appeared to be slow at the store, so he figured the coffee had to be several hours old, having been made early that morning. Better than nothing, but barely.

He approached the counter where the woman remained on her stool like a gargoyle, suspiciously eyeing his movements around the store. Waiting until it was absolutely necessary, she slid off the stool, grunting with the effort, and waddled toward the counter. She rang up his goods and muttered, "Dollar ninety-eight."

O'Brien gave her two ones and held out his hand for the change. Without looking at him, she dropped the two pennies into a small bowl on the counter for customers who needed pennies to avoid breaking bills, and turned toward her stool.

He spoke quickly, before she got back to her stool, fearing she wouldn't come back once she made it. "Ma'am, could you tell me how to get to Senator Scott's place?"

The old crone turned slowly and regarded him with narrowed eyes. "Who wants to know?"

"I'm Will O'Brien, a reporter from D.C."

She raised one eyebrow and raked him up and down with a piercing gaze, taking in his campaign hat, field jacket, wrinkled khaki pants, and dirty tennis shoes. "You don't look like no reporter to me."

"Well, I am. I'm dressed like this because I might have to go out on the Bay."

"Un-huh." She waddled back to her stool, resumed her perch, and eyed him with a look of dour suspicion. "What business you got with *His Majesty*?"

"An interview for my paper, naturally."

She rubbed her mouth and chin, then folded her arms and croaked, "Don't know where his place is. He ain't never invited me out there."

O'Brien couldn't decide whether she actually didn't know where Scott's place was or just didn't trust him. He gave up and took his coffee, such as it was, and his snack out to his car. As he drove away from the store, he glanced in his rear view mirror and saw the old woman standing in front of the store, watching him drive off while jotting down his license number. *What's she going to do,* he thought, *call the police?*

He mulled over the ramifications if she did. The worst result for him would be temporary detention by the local police, and possibly missing an opportunity to see Scott. On the other hand, if he told the local police about the conspiracy and the impending danger to Scott, they might decide to pass it on to him. O'Brien shrugged, deciding not to worry about it until it happened.

After stopping at two more convenience stores, he scrapped his plan to get directions to Scott's place by asking locals. Either no one knew where the senator's place was or they just wouldn't tell. Probably the latter, he concluded. Tight-lipped bunch of folks around Nanticoke.

He knew an alternative, though, and set about it. He drove the short distance to Salisbury, the county seat. He found the Wicomico County Tax Assessor's office, and asked to see the tax roll—specifically the alpha listing. He found Senator Scott's name and the location of the parcel of property, then asked to see the tax map, located the parcel, and found the name of the access road and the nearest intersection. After leaving the tax assessor's office, he picked up a local map at a convenience store and sat in his car, studying the map while sipping a freshly brewed cup of coffee. With the directions fixed in his mind, he tossed the map on the back seat and headed for the senator's place.

Senator Scott's property was situated on a small creek that emptied into the Wicomico River, between Nanticoke and Salisbury. The Wicomico River ran into Tangler Sound, off Chesapeake Bay. O'Brien had to navigate a maze of back-road turns to get there. By the time he finally reached the road on which Scott's cabin was located, he'd decided it was highly probable the people he'd asked for directions probably didn't know how to reach it.

According to the tax map, Scott's parcel was the eighth one from the last intersection. He counted the driveways until he came to the eighth one. A rusty mailbox rested on a weathered post by the road but didn't have a number or name on it. Unless one of the parcels between Scott's and the intersection hadn't been developed, it had to be Scott's driveway, so he turned in and drove toward the house. He followed the gravel-covered dirt lane about a hundred yards on its winding path through the high grass to a small, salt-box-style house standing on stilts, about fifty feet from the water.

He spotted a dark-blue Lincoln Navigator with D.C. plates, parked by the cabin, and pulled in behind it. Leaving his Volvo, he stepped around the SUV, and surveyed the house and grounds.

A weathered, two-bay boat shed projected into the creek behind the house. A small aluminum fishing boat, with an outboard motor attached, occupied one bay and the other was empty. The missing boat indicated that the senator was out fishing, but O'Brien decided to knock on the cabin door anyway, in case Scott had brought a relative with him. He didn't want someone in the cabin to see him hanging around and call the sheriff.

He ascended the steps to the back porch, grimacing when the lacerated skin on his knees stretched, and rapped on the door. After several seconds, he knocked again. Still no answer. With a heave of his shoulders, he turned, descended the steps, and trudged out to the boat shed.

A steady wind, occasionally gusting thirty knots, kept the tall marsh grass bent southward. It was unlikely the senator would stray far from his house today, with the wind kicking up rough whitecaps on the sound. With that in mind, O'Brien mulled over the idea of taking the senator's aluminum boat out and searching the river upstream from Scott's cabin, and maybe downstream to the sound. With any luck, he'd find Scott before the assassins did. Surely, Scott wouldn't be angry about the boat after hearing about the conspiracy.

Convinced his cause was just, O'Brien turned the hand crank that lowered the boat, but as it settled on the water, he noticed a chain and padlock secured it to the boathouse. "Rats," he muttered to himself. Seemed like everything in the world was conspiring against him. He stood with his hands on his hips and surveyed the horizon, wondering what to do.

As he stood in the boathouse, staring out at the water in exasperation, a thought came to him. Wouldn't it be likely the senator would leave the key to the padlock in the house, rather than keeping it on his key chain? After all, why keep one on his key chain that he only used when at this location? Thinking the key might be hanging on a nail just inside the doorway, O'Brien went back to the house and climbed the rear steps to the back porch.

He'd never done it himself, but he'd seen doors unlocked with credit cards in the movies, so he decided to try it. He pulled a card from his billfold and approached the back door. To his consternation, he found it more difficult than Hollywood made it appear in the movies. He pushed hard, trying to force the plastic card to bend around the strip of wood on the door frame. Finally, just as he thought his credit card was going to split, he felt the bolt give.

He pushed the door with his shoulder and it swung open with a creepy groan of its hinges. He slipped the credit card back into his pocket and tossed a quick glance over his shoulder, to make sure no one was watching him. Then, swallowing hard, he stepped into the house and pulled the shut behind himself.

The cabin interior was pitch black. From the depths of the darkness, the floor creaked, and a rustling sound made his heart skip a beat. He froze in mid-step, like a soldier in a combat zone who, with his last step, heard the ominous click of a mine being armed. It sounded as though someone leaning against a wall had shifted his weight from one foot to the other and brushed the wall with his clothing. Was someone in the house? Was an assassin already here, waiting for Scott to return?

O'Brien peered into the darkness, held his breath, and strained to hear over the pounding of his heart. He eased his right foot to the floor and held that position for what seemed like several minutes. Nothing but silence. Maybe the sounds he'd heard were the result of a change in air pressure due to his opening the door, or maybe a slight gust of wind had stirred a curtain.

O'Brien kept his feet firmly planted and, with his left hand, groped along the wall for a light switch. He found the switch but, like a character in a horror movie, hesitated to flip it, fearful of finding himself face to face with an axe murderer poised to lop off his head. Still, he couldn't wait indefinitely. He swallowed again, flipped the light switch, and let his eyes dart all around the lighted room.

The overhead light revealed him alone in the room, and he breathed a deep sigh of relief.

He scanned the wall near the door, looking for a nail with keys hanging from it, but didn't spot one. Disappointed, he thought about searching the kitchen drawers for the key, but discarded the idea. Taking a single step into the house was one thing; rummaging through drawers was quite another. O'Brien turned the light off and backed through the doorway. He closed the door firmly, descended the steps, and went to sit in his Volvo while waiting for Scott to return.

After nearly two hours, he finally detected a boat easing up the creek. The lone occupant was an elderly man dressed in blue jeans, a flannel shirt, a fishing vest, and a foul-weather hat. O'Brien assumed it was Senator Scott, and hurried down to the dock to greet him.

As the boat approached, he saw that it was indeed Senator Scott, who eyed him with a frown of annoyance. O'Brien smiled and waved, hoping to ease Scott's apprehension at seeing a stranger waiting on his dock. Scott turned the engine off and the boat floated up to the dock, with its wake washing up against the pilings.

Scott was slightly chubby, over sixty, with a face lined from years of political haggling with unreasonable people. He allowed the boat to drift into the bay and, without mooring it, turned his attention to O'Brien. "What are you doing here?" he asked with a scowl.

"Don't be alarmed, Senator Scott. I'm Will O'Brien, a reporter, and my intentions are good."

"Christ! Can't you guys let me have a day off? It's my birthday, you know."

"I'm truly sorry, sir. But didn't you get my e-mail, the other day?"

Scott shook his head. "All my e-mail is screened by my staff, and they haven't given me anything from anyone named O'Brien."

"Until yesterday, I worked for the *National Probe*."

"The tabloid?"

"That's right. And I'm the one who found Senator Pearson's body at the hotel."

"The paper said the bellhop found him."

"I was with the bellhop at the time."

"Okay, so what's your business with me?"

"You know Pearson was murdered, don't you?"

"Yeah, by his wife."

"No, she was framed. Pearson was assassinated."

Scott tossed the tackle box he'd just picked up onto the dock and scowled at O'Brien again. "Are you out of your mind?"

O'Brien gave Scott a shortened account of the assassination plot and told him about the deaths of Lezette, Monique, Rashid, and Slick. Wrapping up, he said, "And that's why I'm here. To warn you so you can get some protection."

While he'd talked, Scott remained in the boat, keeping some distance between himself and O'Brien. Now they both turned toward the canal at the sound of a small fishing boat as it puttered by, a grizzled old guy at the helm. Scott turned back to O'Brien and waved off his concern. "That's the craziest yarn I've ever heard."

"But it's true."

"Then why hasn't the FBI warned me?"

"They don't believe me, since I can't produce any concrete evidence. They say all these deaths are a string of unrelated coincidences."

"If the FBI doesn't believe you, why should I?"

Exasperated, O'Brien threw up his hands. "Believe me, don't believe me—it's up to you. Either way, it couldn't hurt to take a few precautions, could it?"

"Like not coming out here alone?"

"Exactly. I could've been an assassin."

Scott frowned and nodded his head. "You've got a good point there. Okay, I promise to be careful, so accept my thanks and let me put up my boat and get out of here."

O'Brien left Scott at the boat house and returned to his car. As he waited for the engine to warm up, his stomach growled, signaling that he'd missed feeding time. He turned the Volvo around, drove up the long driveway to the road, and headed for Nanticoke. He'd spotted a Burger King earlier, and could pick up something to eat on his way back to D.C.

Mission accomplished, he told himself.

Maybe.

54

Back in D.C., O'Brien drove slowly by his townhouse, contemplating stopping and running in for his toothbrush and a change of clothes. The sight of an unmarked white van with tinted windows parked across from his house, about four doors down the street, changed his mind. Could be nothing, but could be a stake-out waiting for him to come home. Caution ruled and he passed his house by.

He checked his watch and saw it was a little after five. Zalva was probably still at work. He tried her cell phone number and got no answer. Figuring she was tied up with a case, he began thinking about a place to hang out until she returned his call. He decided to camp out at a bookstore with a coffee shop, figuring that it was unlikely anyone would try to assassinate him or forcibly abduct him from one of those in broad daylight.

He chose Tally Hall, a bookstore and coffee shop on Connecticut Avenue a couple of blocks up from Dupont Circle, and nestled between two trendy Vietnamese-style restaurants. Tally Hall did a brisk business and was usually full of good-looking women, and while there was some truth to the adage about safety in numbers, it was a nice perk if most of those numbers were female.

He found a parking spot a block off Connecticut and three blocks from Tally Hall. The sidewalks were packed for a Friday afternoon in September, but he liked it that way. Many times during the tourist season, he would walk from his place to downtown, just to meander up and down the churning sidewalks, observing the faces and body types that passed, trying to imagine what kind of people they were and the secrets they harbored.

At Tally Hall, O'Brien picked up a piece of carrot cake and a mug of Brazilian Santos at the counter. Then he settled down at a table where he could observe customers at the serving counter. As he unpacked his computer, a shapely, thirty-something brunette took the table next to his. He watched her remove her thin, fall overcoat and saw she was dressed in a form fitting black dress with a slit up the side. She glanced over her shoulder, saw him watching, and flashed an inviting smile.

He returned the smile with a grin and her gaze lingered on him for a moment before she turned and began reading a magazine. He busied himself setting up his laptop, keeping a watchful eye on the friendly brunette.

While waiting for the computer to warm up, he found himself wondering why he was making the effort. Nobody believed him, including Zalva. And with the elections imminent, the Democratic Party had already decided on substitute candidates for Pearson and Gunter, jumping on the opportunity like defensive linemen pouncing on a fumble at the goal line.

Even if he exposed the conspiracy, by the time the FBI could find enough evidence to prosecute the conspirators, the elections would almost certainly be over. The Democratic Party would have retained their majority, and the effects on presidential appointments and world policy would be long-lasting.

He leaned back, clasped his hands behind his head, and pondered the matter. The Democratic Party, although not involved in the conspiracy, would be the collateral beneficiary anyway. The replacement candidates would be legally appointed and duly elected. No matter how or why Pearson and Gunter had been killed, the election results would stand.

But what if the new senators, upon learning Pearson and Gunter had been assassinated in order to create vacancies for them, simply resigned? Special elections would be held, certainly. But since both districts were heavily Democratic, the party would win the two seats again, still maintaining the upper hand in the Senate.

The new senators could abstain from voting on matters where the vote fell strictly along party lines, or could elect to vote with the Republicans, out of a spirit of respect and remorse for the dead senators. He scoffed at that bit of reasoning. The new candidates were dedicated and honorable men who would be duly elected by their constituents. They would certainly vote as their philosophies dictated, which would be with the rest of the Democrats.

No matter how you tried, what had been done couldn't be undone. The important things now, were to save Senator Scott and to expose the conspiracy. Best to develop the article and seek another publisher. Maybe one of the houses that had recently published some of the conservative-leaning, nonfiction books would be interested. If not, he could incorporate the conspiracy into the plot of a suspense novel, or maybe put it on the internet. He could set up a website loaded with the conspiracy story, for people to read or download. He could even send e-mails to every member of Congress, the State Department, the attorney general, and anybody else that could do something. He just might stir up enough interest for the public to demand an investigation.

A movement caught his eye, and he looked up in time to catch the brunette rising from her chair, exposing the inside of a well-tanned thigh. All thoughts of the conspiracy vanished, as if he'd accidentally pressed a delete button. As he watched, she stepped in his direction with her head down, fumbling in her purse.

Absorbed in her search, she bumped into O'Brien's table, sloshing coffee out of his mug onto the table top. "Yow!" she yelped.

O'Brien scooted his chair away from the table, stood, and moved away from the scalding coffee dripping over the table edge.

"Oh, my goodness. I'm so sorry." She put her hand on O'Brien's arm. "I hope I didn't ruin your work."

"No, it survived." He moved his laptop to a chair, yanked a handful of napkins from the holder, and began wiping the table.

She laid her purse on one of the chairs and grabbed his napkin-filled hand. "Here, let me do that for you. It's the least I can do."

Her warm, soft touch made his heart skip a beat, and he felt a stirring in his loins. He released the napkins and watched as she leaned over the table and began sopping up the spilled coffee. The top of her dress billowed open, exposing exquisite breasts with large nipples, to which his eyes were drawn like missiles to laser-painted targets.

She glanced up while wiping the table and caught him before he could tear his gaze away. Her provocative mouth twisted into a sly grin. "No harm, I guess, if I didn't get *you* or your computer wet."

"No, my computer's fine," he croaked in a hoarse voice. "How about you? Your leg okay?"

"It stings a little. Probably bruised, too. Let's see."

He stifled a gasp as she parted the slit in her dress and hiked it up on her hip to inspect the injury, carelessly exposing thin red panties and a dark patch of pubic hair beneath them. "It's a little red—probably be blue by tonight." She looked up at O'Brien, ran her tongue along her upper lip, and allowed the dress to fall back into place. "Good thing I'm not married. I don't think a husband would believe my explanation, do you?"

"Probably not," he said, trying not to choke. "I don't think I would."

She offered her hand. "My name's Pauline."

He took her slender hand, which felt hot. "I'm Will O'Brien."

She glanced down at his table. "I've ruined your little work station here. Why don't you have a seat at my table so we can chat.

Is this my lucky day or what? thought O'Brien. Pauline was practically begging to be picked up, and he was just the man to do it. "I believe I'll take you up on that offer. Give me a minute to gather my stuff and I'll be right over."

She returned to her table and O'Brien hurriedly packed his computer. Finished, he went to Pauline's table, placed his computer under the table, and took the chair next to her.

She leaned toward him with her hands on the table, near his. "What were you working on?" she asked.

"A little story I hope to sell."

"Oh, you're a writer?"

"That's right."

Her eyes widened in awe. "A novelist?"

He opened his mouth to say he was unpublished, but said, "Yes," instead, lying with a smile on his lips, feeling absolutely no guilt. After all, how many men wouldn't have lied in his position? One in a million—maybe.

She put her hand on his arm, leaned over, and spoke softly into his ear, "You've just got to tell me about your writing."

Before he could respond, the cell phone in his pocket vibrated. He pulled it from his pocket and saw Zalva's number. As much as he wanted to, he couldn't ignore the call; she might have important news. He looked into Pauline's willing blue eyes and forced himself to speak. "I've got to answer this call. It's urgent." As if his need for Pauline wasn't.

Pauline released his hand with a thin smile and fluttered her long eyelashes. "Hurry back now."

O'Brien stepped away from the table and answered the call. "Zalva?"

"O'Brien, where are you?."

"At a book store. What's up?"

"Guess where I went this morning?"

"To work?"

"I interviewed Mrs. Rulon at her home."

"Mrs. Rulon? I thought this deal was off-limits for you."

"Officially, it is. Captain Thurman ordered me to take some time off, so I used it to advantage."

"What'd you find out?"

"Not on a cell phone. Exactly where are you?"

"Tally Hall on Connecticut Avenue."

"I'm already on Connecticut. I can be there in less than ten minutes."

O'Brien turned to look back at Pauline, who flashed him a smile, along with another shot of her exposed thigh. "Can't we get together tonight, instead?"

There was a short pause before Zalva answered. "Are you with someone?"

"Well . . . yeah . . . kinda."

There was a longer pause before Zalva spoke again. "You're trying to pick up a woman, aren't you?"

"Give me a break, Zalva. I'm suffering from *opportunity interruptus*. The last three times I tried to make it with a woman, something got in the way: Pearson at the hotel, the BMW in front of Finigan's, and bogus FBI agents."

Zalva cleared her throat. "For an investigative reporter, you've got your priorities a little out of order, haven't you?"

She was right, of course. He was thinking with the wrong head. He sighed deeply. "Okay, okay. I'll wait here for you."

"Good. I'm headed toward Dupont Circle, so wait on the sidewalk across from Tally Hall and I'll pick you up."

He agreed and returned to the table. Pauline sat with one arm draped over the back of her chair and the other on the table, tapping her fingers impatiently. She saw the glum look on his face and her smile vanished.

He remained standing and took her hand in his. "Bad news I'm afraid."

"Oh?"

"The call was about a story I'm working on. A situation has developed and I've got to go."

Pauline removed her hand from his, frowned, and slumped in her chair. "If you must, I suppose you must."

"Give me your phone number and I'll call you later tomorrow," offered O'Brien.

"I have a better idea. You give me your number, and I'll call you later this evening."

He couldn't suppress the grin that spread across his face, and quickly jotted his name and cell phone number on a napkin and gave it to her.

She took it with a broad smile, and said, in a low, sexy voice, "I'll be in touch."

O'Brien picked up his satchel and departed, with vivid images of Pauline's nude form dancing in his head. At the door, he glanced back over his shoulder and saw her making a call on her cell phone.

O'Brien went down to the corner, crossed Connecticut at the traffic light, and walked back up the street to stand directly across from Tally Hall.

He spotted Pauline exiting the coffee shop and watched as she walked to the edge of the sidewalk, apparently waiting on a taxi or someone else to pick her up. His mind churned, fantasizing about how his encounter with Pauline could have been, and still might be, later in the day.

Then, as he watched, a white Audi pulled to an abrupt stop directly in front of Pauline.

She ran to the front passenger's window and spoke to the driver. The rear door popped open and Pauline jumped into the back seat. The Audi roared away, leaving O'Brien staring after it with his mouth gaping open.

A white Audi! The French broad in Pearson's hotel room had driven a white Audi. Suddenly his knees got weak, and a hollow feeling hit the pit of his stomach. *She'd been a trap!* No wonder Pauline had come on to him. They must've picked him up when he drove by his apartment and followed him to Tally Hall where they'd improvised and sent her in to lure him to a hotel room where they could kill him. Or maybe they knew his weakness for women, knew he liked to hang out at bookstores, and planned the trap after the kidnaping failed. And it would've worked, too. He'd have been dead meat if Zalva hadn't called.

O'Brien's fear turned to smouldering rage at their audacity. He clenched his teeth, seething at their attempt to exploit his weakness for women. But anger turned to frustration as it dawned on him that he hadn't even thought about taking down the license number of the Audi; he'd been too preoccupied with trying to see the people inside.

"Son of a bitch!" he shouted.

Passers-by looked askance at him and detoured as far away as they could on the crowded sidewalk. He stood with his hands on his hips, furious at his mental lapse, and stared blindly in the direction the Audi had taken.

55

A car horn beeped beside him, and O'Brien turned to see Zalva waving for him to get in. He hurried to her car, tossed his computer onto the back seat, and slid onto the front seat beside her. O'Brien flipped the driver off who was honking his horn behind her, and Zalva eased the car into motion again.

"I can't believe you went to Rulon's house," said O'Brien.

"Neither can I. I'm way out on a limb on this."

"You see Rulon?"

"Not now. I can't talk and drive at the same time in this traffic. Let's get your car first, and you can follow me back to my apartment. I'll tell you everything when we get there."

"I'm parked about three blocks on the other side of Tally Hall."

A few minutes later, she pulled up next to his parked car. He opened the door and got out, then stuck his head back in the car. "By the way, I drove by my house earlier this afternoon and I think I picked up a tail in a white Audi. Might be nothing, but—"

Zalva's face clouded with concern, then brightened. "That could be a break. You know how to get to my place?"

"Of course."

"I'll move on up ahead and wait for you to pass, then follow several car lengths behind you. If anyone tails you, I'll spot them."

"Sounds like a plan to me."

• • •

They didn't catch the white Audi, or anything else, following him. At Zalva's place, they settled down on her couch with a couple of cold Coronas. O'Brien draped his right arm over the back of the couch, and twisted around to face Zalva. "Okay, spill it."

Zalva shifted to mirror his position and began to relate the details of her visit to Rulon's mansion. O'Brien noticed her fingers were scant inches from his, on the back of the couch. Although tempted to reach out and touch her hand, he remembered how she'd reacted the night before. Instead, he listened intently as Zalva recounted the details of her visit with Charlene Rulon.

He was elated to hear about the lapis lazuli flakes all over Charlene's work table. "How about the crime lab report? Did it mention lapis lazuli?"

"Not one iota."

"Damn! I screwed up big-time, didn't I?"

She didn't bother confirming his screw-up. Instead, she reached for a folded newspaper she'd placed on the coffee table when they sat down, and tossed it onto his lap. "Here. Read what I've circled."

He saw that it wasn't a whole paper, just the World News section, with an article circled with a pen. The article was about Geroux, the French president, and some comments he'd made about mid-term congressional elections in the U.S.

O'Brien scanned the article and looked up at Zalva. "What an arrogant asshole!"

"He's that for sure—and maybe more," responded Zalva.

The implication began to dawn on him. "You mean he might be involved in Rulon's conspiracy?"

"Maybe. Didn't you tell me he and Rulon were good friends?"

"Yeah, according to the research I did on the internet."

Zalva leaned toward him, supporting herself with a hand on his knee. "Lezette was French, and the maid told you her lover was French. Rulon's wife even told me that her husband had specifically requested that Lezette be assigned to the French Embassy. At first I thought possibly Rulon used her simply because he was close to her. But now, after seeing this article, I wonder if Lezette, and maybe Alain, and possibly others, were assigned to the embassy specifically for Rulon's use."

Zalva's hand on his knee was distracting, and he had to struggle to keep his attention on what she said. "I suppose it's possible."

She removed her hand from his knee and draped her arm on the back of the couch again. "I spent a good part of the day researching France's role in world politics, and I found a few things I was unaware of."

"Like what?" he asked.

"France has always been sort of a renegade with respect to the rest of western Europe—always trying to be the wild card, playing one power against another."

"I don't remember much about history. You've got to give me some specific examples," he said.

She compressed her lips in contemplation for a moment, composing her thoughts. "How about the Ottoman Empire?"

"The what?"

Zalva gave him a disdainful look. "You know, the old Turkish empire."

"Yeah . . . I remember something about that."

"Well, one of the books I found in the library today had a chapter about France and the Ottoman Empire. The Sultan granted France exclusive trading rights throughout the Ottoman Empire, and protectorship status over all Christians within its domain. Of course, France didn't do anything to earn that except try to block every alliance the European Christians put together to fight the Turks. France even signed a mutual assistance treaty with the Sultan and allowed the Turkish fleet to dock at one of its ports when it was at war with Venice."

Astonished, O'Brien asked, "Why did France do that? Didn't the

Turks slaughter or enslave tens of thousands of Christians in eastern Europe, and force hundreds of thousands to choose between converting to Islam or being slaughtered?"

"France didn't want the Holy Roman Empire, under the Hapsburgs, to dominate Europe. So it welcomed the presence of the Ottoman Empire in eastern Europe as a counterbalance against the Holy Roman Empire."

"That's incredible."

"I thought so, too," Zalva admitted. "But later, when it was clear the Ottoman Empire was in decline, France used Russia the same way. And then, when Russia became powerful and ambitious, France sided with England and the Ottomans against it."

"Playing both ends against the middle," said O'Brien.

Zalva nodded in agreement. "They did the same thing to Germany, in the years leading up to World War I. And after World War II, as soon as the last of the Germans were out of France, de Gaulle saw the U.S. as the new super power and insisted that we withdraw from France. He began to oppose us at every turn, even refusing to allow France to join NATO."

"They're in NATO now," he replied, "I know that because I remember they voted against NATO being involved in keeping peace in Iraq after Saddam was brought down."

"Yeah, they're in, but only on the non-military side."

"That's crummy," said O'Brien. They've reaped the benefit of NATO's protection since it was formed."

"True, but being in NATO would've put them in one of the two major camps, limiting their ability to play one side against the other."

"And now that the Soviet Empire is gone, they don't need us any more," said Will.

"Right," agreed Zalva. "To them, the U.S. is now the power that needs to be reined in, controlled, and isolated. That's pretty obvious from the way they opposed us in the Middle East. They wouldn't let our bombers fly over their territory during Desert Storm, and tried to keep us from invading Iraq to depose Saddam."

O'Brien took a sip of his beer and thought back over the many news stories on TV and newspapers over the past years about France and Iraq.

"I think it's all about economics. France has lost billions of dollars in trade with Iraq since the first Gulf War. They're totally dependent on foreign oil—hence their Saddam-Iraq connection. It also explains why they were soft on the old USSR and are such good friends with the Russians now, because of it's huge oil reserves."

"So you think they're just looking out for number one?"

"Right." O'Brien shook his head in disgust. "And they claim *we're* a problem. I even saw an anti-American protest in Paris on the evening news, and the protesters were wearing T-shirts with 'What are we going to do about the U.S.?' printed on them.

"According to Secretary of State Hederly, what they're trying to do about us is establish an alliance with Germany and Russia to counterbalance us, politically and militarily," said Zalva.

O'Brien pondered Zalva's history lesson in silence for several minutes before speaking again. "Even with everything France has done to oppose us, isolate us, or whatever, I still can't see them risking a war by helping assassinate three senators."

"How do you explain the embassy connection then?" asked Zalva.

He paused to gulp down the last of his beer, and she did likewise. He studied his bottle for a moment, then continued. "Geroux has reasons of his own to prevent the shift in control of the Senate."

"Surely you don't mean his friendship with Rulon?"

"Hardly. I'm talking about the old *Oil For Food* program scandal that's never been fully resolved, and the nuclear proliferation that's taken place over the last twenty years. Independent US investigators have alleged that Geroux took millions in bribes from Saddam and helped Iraq buy contraband weapons instead of food with the proceeds of oil sales, and that he was involved in black-market sales of nuclear and missile technology to India, Pakistan, North Korea, and Iran. Thompson's administration is hammering the UN to prosecute him for violations of sanctions against Iraq and violations of the U.N.'s prohibitions on nuclear technology, under threat of withholding dues again."

Zalva frowned. "But that was years ago and Geroux wasn't president of France back then."

"True, but he held an important post in the French government, had nothing when he went into politics, and is wealthy now."

Zalva scoffed at his last remark. "You could arrest thousands of elected officials in this country, based on that logic." Then her expression became solemn again. "So you think Geroux's helping Rulon's party get control of the Senate because he thinks it will block Thompson's effort to force the UN to investigate and prosecute him?"

O'Brien shrugged his shoulders. "That's the best I can do. Even so, his participation is probably limited to nothing more than seeing that appropriate personnel and state-of-the-art spy technology are available for Rulon's use."

"That would make him an accomplice, if he knew what Rulon's plans were," said Zalva.

"I wonder what the President Thompson would do if the FBI could prove Geroux was an accomplice in the assassinations of two senators," O'Brien mused aloud.

Zalva let out a long sigh and rose to her feet. "We'll probably never know, the way things are going. You ready for another Corona?"

He glanced at the empty bottle in his hand, then back at Zalva. "I'm always ready for another brew."

She slipped her shoes off and turned to go back to the tiny kitchen. O'Brien watched the rise and fall of her perfect behind under her black slacks as she padded away from him on the soft carpet. He was beginning to like her a lot. She might be the only woman he'd ever met who could hold his interest beyond the bedroom.

A growl from his stomach reminded him he'd eaten nothing but a small hamburger for lunch and a piece of carrot cake at the coffee shop. He called out to her. "Hey, you got anything to eat here?"

She opened the pantry and leaned on the door while inspecting the contents. "Don't see anything," she called back over her shoulder.

O'Brien pushed himself off the couch and strode back to stand behind Zalva, still peering into the pantry as if hoping something would materialize on the shelves.

With her right arm still on the pantry door, she turned slightly in his direction, pressing her body against him. "See for yourself."

He moved closer and leaned his head forward to see into the pantry. Zalva didn't retreat from the body contact. Her hair smelled of green apples, and the warmth of her body sent his pulse racing.

She twisted her neck to look at him over her shoulder, her face only inches away, and her beautiful brown eyes gazed into his. "You see anything you'd like to have?"

She let her moist lips part and O'Brien lost all restraint. He put both arms around her and pulled her against him. She came willingly. Their lips touched with a spark and she pulled back momentarily, then smiled and renewed the kiss. Her lips parted and his tongue sought hers with a hunger he hadn't experienced in years. Her body trembled against him, and as his dick stiffened, she clutched his butt with both hands and pulled herself hard against him.

Suddenly, O'Brien felt a vibrating sensation against his leg. Startled, Zalva broke away from him. "What's that?" she asked in a hoarse voice.

"My damned cell phone! Forgot it was in my front pocket. I'd better answer it—could be Pearson's maid." O'Brien's hand shook so badly, he had difficulty removing the cell phone from his pocket, but managed to get it out before the caller gave up. He glanced at the caller ID and saw Sylvia's number. He nodded to Zalva, indicating it was the maid.

"Sylvia?"

The sound of her voice confirmed it. "Mr. O'Brien?"

"Yeah, it's me. Where are you?"

"I'm at my old high-school friend's place in Virginia."

"Are you okay?"

"Yes."

"Did you have any trouble getting away?"

"No . . . not really."

The pause in her speech made him suspicious. "What do you mean, 'not really'?"

"My husband was furious."

"What'd you tell him?"

"I didn't tell him about Alain . . . or you. I lied. Said I had witnessed something that might prove Mrs. Pearson didn't do it and the police were taking me into protective custody for a few days while they sorted things out. I told him I didn't know where I'd be."

"Your husband know where your friend lives?"

"Oh, no. He doesn't even know who she is."

"Good," replied O'Brien with a sigh of relief. "But how about your friend? Is she married? What'd you tell her?"

"Yes, she's married. I told her I had to get away from Howard for a few days. Meg knows how that is."

"They're going to know something's up when we get there."

"They're not here. Her husband is from North Carolina and they left this morning to go to North Carolina's football game with Duke tomorrow."

"I've got Detective Zalva Martinez with me. She needs to hear your story and she's got some photos for you to look at."

"Photos?"

"Yeah. One of them might be Alain."

"Can you come tonight, while my friend and her husband are gone?"

"Absolutely. We need to get this over with as quickly as possible."

"That suits me."

"Where does your friend live?"

"In the country, not far from a little town called Rixeyville. Alice's husband operates a small logging business."

O'Brien repeated the name of the town aloud.

Zalva hurried to a small bookcase in the living room and pulled out a large book that O'Brien took to be an atlas. She stepped back to the couch, sat down, and opened the book on the coffee table.

O'Brien joined her on the couch, this time sitting close to her with his arm around her neck and his hand on her shoulder.

She flipped through the pages until she found the map of Virginia. With her index finger, she traced a path from D.C. across into Virginia. "Got it," she said, holding her finger on the map and looking up at O'Brien.

O'Brien leaned over for a closer look and saw a tiny dot with 'Rixeyville' printed over it in small letters, at the end of her fingertip.

They could take a four-lane most of the way, but the last fifteen or twenty miles would be on a two-lane country road, with the last five miles on an unpaved road. It looked like about a two-hour drive. From the directions Sylvia gave him, it wouldn't be a problem finding the house once they made it to Rixeyville. He put the phone back to his ear. "Sylvia?"

"Yes."

"It's going to take at least two hours for us to get there, and we're probably going to grab a bite to eat before we leave. Expect us around eight, okay?"

"I'll be here." With that simple response, she hung up.

O'Brien put the phone down, pulled Zalva against him, and kissed her.

They maintained the kiss for several long minutes. Finally, Zalva broke it off and, with her face still close to his, whispered, "We've got to get moving, Babe."

"I bought us a little time to play in," he replied, pulling her back and kissing her again.

The way her tongue met his and the way she pulled at him led him to become bolder. He pulled her polo shirt out of her pants and slipped his hand underneath, seeking out her breasts. He found them and ran his a fingernail across one nipple, which hardened immediately. In response, she unbuttoned his shirt and ran a hand beneath it, rubbing his chest and playing with his hair.

After several minutes of heavy petting, he slipped his left arm under her knees and stood up, lifting her off the couch. Still maintaining the kiss, he stumbled around the couch and headed for the bedroom with Zalva in his arms. Suddenly, Zalva straightened her legs, slid from his grasp, and turned to walk away.

"Hey! Where you going?"

"We don't have time for this right now," she replied over her shoulder. She went to the kitchen and grabbed her gun and badge off the counter.

"I told her we'd be late getting out there," he offered.

"Let's take care of business first," she said, approaching him again.

"Come on, Zalva. Can't we get take care of our business first?"

She smiled and patted him on the cheek. "You're thinking with the wrong head again."

She was right, of course. Zalva needed to see this witness—the only one left. He let out a heavy breath, rolled his eyes at her, and said, *"Now comes the sweetest morsel of the night, and we must hence and leave it unpicked."*

"Cut it out, Falstaff." She gave him a teasing wink, then went to the couch, picked up the atlas, and tucked it under her arm. "We'll have to go in your car."

"Why mine?"

"I can't take my unit into Virginia."

"You drove into Virginia the night we found Monique."

"That was still in the metro area, just across the river—and I hadn't been ordered to lay off."

O'Brien shrugged his shoulders. If it had to be, it just had to be.

As they pulled out of the parking lot in O'Brien's Volvo, Zalva's cell phone rang. She pulled it from her jacket pocket and looked at the caller ID. Her face paled instantly. "Damn! It's Captain Thurman."

"Why's he calling you? Didn't he order you to take a couple of days off."

"He was adamant about it, to be precise. He must've found out about my visit to Rulon's mansion."

"Rulon must've called him," said O'Brien.

"I'll just have to let it ring, because if I turn it off now, he'd know I saw his number," said Zalva. She let out a long breath and shrugged her shoulders. "Probably wouldn't make any difference, though—I'm going to be fired anyway, for disobeying orders."

56

Once underway, O'Brien told her about seeing Senator Scott in Nanticoke. Afterward, she filled him in on her conversation with Ginny and her promise to present the case to the FBI, which seemed to please him. Thurman tried to call her three more times before she finally turned her phone off. Screw him! He could chew her out in person Monday morning, if he didn't have a heart attack when she presented the maid to him.

Eventually, their conversation segued to his year spent playing Falstaff with the touring company. He became much more animated, gesturing wildly as he talked, and turning to look at her instead of watching the road.

"I can see you loved the stage. Why'd you quit?" she asked.

"Actually, it became boring at the time."

"Boring?"

"Yeah. We only did the one play, *Henry IV:* over, and over, and over again—just in different places."

"I guess I never thought about that," she said.

"Yeah, neither did I until I did it. In college theater, we usually only had three or four performances."

Her thoughts drifted back to the one production she'd participated in. It had been a lot of fun, even the rehearsals, but by the time it ended, she'd grown tired of it. "I can't imagine doing the same play for five or ten years, like some of the big-time productions in New York."

"Me either," replied O'Brien. "That's why I decided to give it up. I knew I didn't have the patience to stay with a long-run production, or the talent and looks to make it in the movies, not to mention the long years of struggling, so I dropped out."

Time passed quickly and they soon passed a small country store with a big sign over the door declaring it to be Joe's. Obeying Sylvia's instructions, O'Brien turned off the highway to the right, onto a dirt and gravel road. "Just five more miles," he said.

Although only five more miles, they were tough ones, with the sandy road imitating an old-fashioned washboard. O'Brien's Volvo shook and rattled to the point where Zalva feared it would come apart at the seams. O'Brien finally slowed down to twenty miles per hour, which helped considerably. The countryside consisted mostly of gently rolling hills until they got off on the dirt road. After about two miles, they descended into some swampy lowlands.

They followed the winding road through the swamp for about a mile, rounded a curve and mounted a sharp little incline to find themselves astride a railroad crossing. Luckily, no train erupted from the darkness and they crossed in safety.

"Damn!" exclaimed O'Brien. He darted a glance at her. "That was a thrill I could've done without."

She glanced back at the crossing, noted that it was without a warning light, and shook her head. "You got that right. A car could round the curve, top the hill, and get creamed by a train roaring out of the swamp."

She returned her concentration to the road ahead, alert for deer crossing the road. Another mile, and the road emerged from the swamp, back to gently rolling hills, half farmland, half forest.

A little farther down the road, O'Brien leaned over the steering wheel, peering at his odometer. "Sylvia said her friend's house was exactly 5.5 miles from the country store. We just passed the five mile point, so we should see lights from the house any second now."

As the words were out of his mouth, they rounded a curve in the road and spotted the lighted window of a house less than a mile ahead. As they approached the house, she saw that it looked about fifty years old and had clapboard siding. The house rested four feet off the ground on brick pillars. The only light came from the front room.

As O'Brien turned onto the wide, gravel driveway, the Volvo's headlights illuminated a large, fully-loaded logging truck parked in front of a metal maintenance barn on the far side of the house. A Nissan Altima with a D.C. license plate, presumably Sylvia's, was parked on the grass to the right side of the house.

With the house isolated, Zalva expected to see someone checking them out from a window, but no one appeared. She turned in her seat and pulled at the car door lever, but O'Brien stopped her with a hand on her shoulder.

"Hold on a minute."

She looked back at him. "Why? Something wrong?"

"Dogs. They've got to have dogs, out in the middle of nowhere like this."

Zalva scanned the part of the yard lit up by the Volvo's headlights, listening for barking or growling. "I don't see or hear any."

O'Brien sneered at that. "Sometimes, the bastards hide under the house and wait till you're out of the car before they show themselves."

"Sounds like you've got experience."

O'Brien muttered something under his breath and peered into the darkness for a few more seconds. Finally, he grunted an okay and opened his door.

They stood by the car with the doors open for a few more seconds, ready to dive back into the car if dogs came after them. None came, so they crossed the yard and stepped up onto the wooden front porch.

O'Brien knocked on the door while Zalva stood to the side. No one came to the door and O'Brien knocked again, but still no one answered.

Zalva became uneasy, and the skin on the back of her neck prickled. She'd approached enough houses as a police officer to sense when something was awry. "I'm going to walk around the house," she said. "Stay here and keep knocking."

She turned to start down the steps and froze. "Shit!" she blurted. A tall, slender man, dressed all in black, stood on the ground at the bottom of the steps, peering up the gaping barrel of a shotgun pointed directly at her face.

57

Zalva heard O'Brien turn to see what had startled her and heard him gasp. "Snake Eyes!"

The front door squeaked open behind her, and O'Brien spoke again with a strangled voice. "Roscoe!"

A deep, ominous voice rang out from behind her. "Well lookie here, Henri. It's the big-shot reporter and the nosy bitch cop that showed up at Rulon's place this morning."

Zalva kept her eyes on the shotgun, but recognized the name of the goon at PMC who had manhandled O'Brien. *Not good!*

The light from the open doorway highlighted a malicious grin that spread across the thin man's narrow face. He spoke in a reedy voice with a thick French accent. "Good surprise though, *non?*"

Zalva thought about going for her gun and tensed up; the muscles in her arm twitching in anticipation. *Don't do it,* something inside her warned. Henri had the face of a stone-cold killer and couldn't miss at this range.

"Where's Sylvia?" demanded O'Brien.

Henri ignored O'Brien's question. "Hands on the porch railing, both of you." He waved the shotgun at Zalva. "And get her gun."

Roscoe shoved both of them against the porch railing. "Bend over and grab the rail," ordered Henri.

Zalva stepped back from the railing, leaned over and grabbed it with both hands, as did O'Brien.

"Spread your legs!" ordered Henri. "Back a little farther!" he ordered again, motioning at O'Brien with the shotgun.

His intent was for them to lean so far forward to grab the railing that they couldn't use their hands to resist without falling down; standard police procedure. But Zalva knew that he'd made a serious mistake. Unlike O'Brien, her center of balance was below the waist, giving her the ability to lean farther forward and still be able to use her hands without falling. And Henri hadn't noticed and made her move further back!

"Now get her gun," said Henri.

Her heart pounded with an adrenalin rush as Roscoe stepped closer, a little behind her to the right. She wore her Glock 27 in the standard police fashion, holster tilted forward, so the grip would be easier for her to reach. In order to grasp the gun from behind her, Roscoe would have to reach over the gun with his wrist bent at a severe angle.

Roscoe lifted the tail of her blazer and she felt the weight of his hand on the grip of her gun. With a lightning fast move, she grabbed his right hand with both of hers, threw her ass under his center of gravity, pivoted on her toes to her left, and tried to throw him over the railing on top of Henri. But although he was thrown off-balance, Roscoe held fast to her blazer, and the best she could do was sling him toward the railing as he dragged her with him.

They crashed through the porch railing and hit the ground with a thud, Roscoe on the bottom and her on top. She heard the breath whoosh out of him. She rolled off him to her right, whipped out her gun, and rose up on her knees. Then the cold barrel of Henri's shotgun pressed hard against the back of her head.

"Drop the gun, bitch!"

No way she could get a shot off now, before he took her head off. Frustrated, she dropped the gun and cursed through clenched teeth. "Fuck!"

Henri stepped around her, keeping the end of the shotgun barrel within an inch of her head, and kicked her gun further out into the dimly-lit yard. He grinned down the barrel of the shotgun at her. "Be calm now, *mon chéri*, and we'll be good to you—a pleasurable reward, perhaps."

If his intent was to frighten her, it didn't work, since she figured Roscoe and Henri were going to kill them anyway. But why hadn't O'Brien reacted when she threw Roscoe? She tried to turn her head far enough to sneak a glance at the porch to check O'Brien out, but Henri bumped the shotgun barrel against her forehead.

"Don't look back! You just stay right there on your knees." Henri took a quick glance over his right shoulder at Roscoe, who remained on his hands and knees facing away from them, gasping for breath.

"You okay, Roscoe?"

Roscoe rose to his feet, turned and lurched toward them, massaging his right wrist. He glared at Zalva with hate in his eyes. "The bitch almost broke my wrist."

"You're too damned careless," replied Henri.

Roscoe gave him a dirty look but took the barb in silence.

Zalva heard a scraping sound on the porch, followed by a low moan from O'Brien. Roscoe looked past them up at the porch. "What's with him?"

"He tried to jump me over the railing. I caught him in the head with the butt of my shotgun."

Zalva remained motionless, alert for any lapse of vigilance by Henri.

"Get her handcuffs," ordered Henri.

Roscoe moved to stand behind her and Henri put the shotgun barrel within inches of her forehead. Like most cops, she kept her handcuffs on the back of her belt. Roscoe reached over her shoulders, grabbed her blazer by the lapels, and pulled it over her shoulders and off.

"Hold on to the jacket," said Henri. "We'll throw it in the trunk with her when we're through."

Before or after they kill me, she wondered.

Roscoe removed the handcuffs from her belt. "Hands behind you," he ordered.

She complied and Roscoe clamped the cuffs over her wrists. The metallic click of the lock snapping shut sent a cold shiver down her spine. All wasn't lost, though, as long as they didn't find her spare key.

Roscoe stuck his hands in her pants pockets, searching for keys and weapons, but found nothing but some folding money, which he stuffed into his own pocket. He began patting her down. She winced and sucked in her breath when he groped between her legs.

"She's got a backup gun somewhere," said Henri. "Probably in an ankle holster."

Roscoe ran his hands over her thighs, between them, and down to her ankles. He found the snub-nosed, .38 caliber Smith & Wesson in her ankle holster, and grunted in satisfaction. "Got it." He straightened and slipped the gun into the outside pocket of his jacket.

"She didn't have any keys in her pockets?" asked Henri.

"No, just some cash."

"Check out her jacket pockets."

Zalva's heart began racing again. Roscoe hadn't found the spare key to her handcuffs hanging on the chain around her neck. Maybe he wouldn't search her again, after shifting his attention to her jacket.

The material of her jacket rustled as Roscoe went through the pockets. "Yeah, here they are," said Roscoe. He jingled the keys for Henri.

"No one who carries handcuffs keeps just one key," said Henri. "Search her again, and check between her tits."

Her heart sank at Henri's orders and she took a hard swallow. Roscoe stood over her again, bent down, and ran his hand down the front of her blouse. He made a big deal of running his rough hand all over her breasts, and pinched one of her nipples.

"You bastard!" She tried to twist away from him, but he grabbed a handful of hair and yanked her back.

"*Ça suffit!*" yelled Henri.

"Speak English, you cretin frog!" retorted Roscoe.

"Just find the key, moron!" yelled Henri. "You can play with her later."

Roscoe angrily tore her blouse open and shoved his hand down between her breasts, actually searching this time. He found the key hanging there, yanked hard, and broke the chain.

"Fuck!" cried Zalva, her hopes for escape shattered.

"What? You disappointed or something?" mocked Henri.

Roscoe stood over her, staring down at her exposed breasts. "You ever had a Puerto Rican woman, Henri?"

"Not before tonight."

"They're hot stuff," said Roscoe. He leaned over and blew in her ear.

Zalva twisted her head away from him, but he snatched her back by the hair again. "They like it too. She'll fight it at first, but later, she won't let you stop."

"Leave her alone!" yelled O'Brien.

Roscoe released his grip on her hair and she heard him step up on the porch, followed by a sickening splat of fist against flesh, and a groan as O'Brien fell to the porch. Roscoe growled, "That'll teach you to keep your trap shut!"

"When he can get up, take him inside," ordered Henrie. He pulled Zalva to her feet by her hair, and steered her up the steps onto the porch and into the house.

58

As Henri shoved Zalva through the doorway into the house, O'Brien pulled himself to his feet, gasping for breath through his broken nose. He steadied himself against the porch railing and wiped the blood from his eyes and nose with the sleeve of his jacket. He'd seen Henri kick Zalva's gun away from her, and so he sneaked a quick glance at the dimly lit area of yard just off the porch. He figured they were going to be killed anyway, so he had nothing to lose by risking a try for the gun.

His heart leaped when he saw the muted reflection of light off metal in the short grass about fifteen feet from the bottom of the steps, but before he could make a move for the gun, Roscoe grabbed him, twisted his arm behind his back, and forced him into the house.

As O'Brien stepped into the front room, Roscoe tripped him and shoved him to the floor beside Zalva. His looked into her face and saw that her eyes were filled with despair. No damned way she could get them out of this mess now, and once they bound him, all hope would be lost.

"Get the duct tape out of the bag and tape his hands behind his back," ordered Henri.

O'Brien glanced up to assess Henri's exact location, with the idea of making a move on him while Roscoe was looking for the duct tape. Henri was to his left and near enough, but the Frenchman was anything but inattentive, with the shotgun pointed directly at his head.

He decided to wait until Roscoe came back before making a move, hoping he could catch Roscoe between them, so Henri couldn't fire the shotgun. He conjured up a vision of him forcing Roscoe across the tiny living room into Henri, with the shotgun going off into Roscoe's back, and wresting the shotgun from Henri's grasp.

"Got the tape?" asked Henri.

"Got it."

"Then here's what you do. Put the slick side against his wrists, wrap it around a couple of times and cut it. Then put the glue side against the tape already on his wrists, and make a couple of more turns with it."

"What in the hell is that about?" complained Roscoe.

"Don't want any glue residue on his wrists for a coroner to find," explained Henri.

Roscoe muttered something under his breath and stepped over to where O'Brien lay. He figured Roscoe was likely to put a knee on his butt to control him while taping his wrists. Even worse, Henri would probably move closer and put the gun barrel to his temple until Roscoe was done. He and Zalva were both going to be killed, no doubt about that. And once they taped his wrists, the game would be over. He set his jaw and resolved to go down fighting.

O'Brien felt the toe of a shoe against the inside of his thigh as Roscoe straddled one of his legs in the process of kneeling to pin him with a knee.

O'Brien winked at Zalva, swallowed hard, rolled to his left, and kicked Roscoe behind the knees with the back of his right calf. Roscoe's knees gave way and he collapsed in the direction of Henri. At the same time, O'Brien rolled to his hands and toes, and charged Henri like a defensive lineman after a quarterback.

"*Merde!*" yelled Henri, leaping out of Roscoe's way. Bug-eyed with surprise, he attempted to bring the shotgun barrel down to shoot O'Brien.

Instead, O'Brien rammed into him, grabbed the barrel of the gun with his right hand, and forced it upward before Henri could fire. Still holding the barrel of the shotgun, O'Brien grabbed the stock behind Henri's trigger hand and pushed him back against the wall, trying desperately to wrest the shotgun from his grasp.

As they struggled for the gun, noise behind him signaled Roscoe was getting to his feet. Damn it! There was no way he could handle both of them.

Suddenly, there was a loud thump behind him and the floor shook. "Fucking bitch!" roared Roscoe.

Zalva must've rolled into him and tripped him again, buying more for O'Brien to deal with Henri. With renewed hope, he fought harder. Much heavier than Henri, O'Brien kept him pinned against the wall, but couldn't break his grip on the gun. Henri tried to knee him in the groin but got the front of his thigh instead. O'Brien twisted his hips just in time to avoid another knee, and caught the blow on his hip. He ignored the pain and hung onto the gun, knowing their lives depended on it.

He heard the loud smack of fist against flesh behind him, and a scream from Zalva. Another sickening smack of knuckles against flesh and Zalva's screaming ceased. With Zalva down and out, O'Brien had to overcome Henri quickly, before Roscoe attacked him from behind.

Still holding the shotgun, he pushed against Henri more fiercely, causing him to push back. As soon as he did, O'Brien jerked hard and fell backward, pulling Henri with him. As he went down, he planted his feet in Henri's chest, and propelled him into the far wall, head first.

Now in possession of the shotgun, O'Brien twisted his body around to get a shot at Roscoe. At that instant, something hard crashed against the back of his skull, stars burst before his eyes, and darkness overwhelmed him.

59

Awareness came back to O'Brien with excruciating pain. It felt as though the top of his head had been crushed, and he labored for breath through his broken nose. He tried to breath through his mouth and discovered he was gagged with something that tasted like a dirty sock. Nor could he move his hands, which were bound behind his back.

He arched his back, twisted his head to his right, and looked directly into Zalva's eyes, only two feet away. Like him, she was lying face down on the floor. Her hands were cuffed behind her back and a strip of duct tape covered her mouth. Her face was swelling rapidly, and large bruises were forming on her cheek and around one of her eyes. Zalva's eyes were wild with fear and she shook her head in a gesture of hopelessness.

"They're both awake now," called out Roscoe, as if Henri was in another room.

"About damn time," yelled Henri from a distance. The floor vibrated with his footsteps as he returned to the front room.

"Do it now?" asked Roscoe.

"No, not just yet," replied Henri.

"Why not?" complained Roscoe. "Why don't we just screw her now, waste both of them, and bust outta this puke hole?"

"Because it's what *the man* told us to do," replied Henri.

Then the entire house began to vibrate and the air was filled with the deafening chop-chop noise of a helicopter landing near the house.

"It's the damned law!" cried Roscoe. He rushed to the window for a look.

"No," said Henri, "it's Rulon and Marchant."

"What in hell are they doing out here?" asked Roscoe.

"Came to gloat over these two," answered Henri.

The chopper blades stilled and the engine settled into a neutral drone. A few seconds later, O'Brien heard footsteps on the porch. The door squeaked open and the two men entered the house.

"Excellent!" said one of them with a moderate French accent. "Still alive and conscious."

O'Brien arched his back, enabling him to lift his head, which he turned in the direction of the man's voice. He saw a medium-sized guy with brown hair—most likely Marchant—and a tall, slender, silvered-haired aristocrat who had to be Rulon. Both were attired in dark slacks, dark, turtle-neck shirts, and dark blazers.

"Pull that television over in front of them where they can see it," ordered Rulon.

Roscoe lifted a small TV off its stand and placed it on the floor in front of them.

"Now turn it to PMCN."

Roscoe did as Rulon ordered and stepped back to watch.

"A big-time investigative reporter like you, O'Brien, should find this fascinating," sneered Rulon.

A streamer across the bottom of the screen indicated that PMCN was in the middle of a breaking news story. The grave face of Peter Blaine, the evening news anchorman, dominated the screen. "We're now going back to Andrea Wallace, our field reporter on the scene in Nanticoke, Maryland."

The face of Andrea Wallace, an average-looking, dark-haired woman in her mid-thirties, appeared on one side of the screen.

"Andrea, have you learned anything new in the last few minutes?"

"Yes we have, Peter. I've got Mr. John Collins here with me now. As I reported earlier, Mr. Collins is the man who found Senator Scott's body and notified the authorities."

The camera view widened to show a gray-bearded, gnome-like, man of at least seventy, standing next to Andrea. He was dressed in rubber boots, faded, thread-bare jeans, a soiled flannel shirt, and a greasy baseball cap.

Andrea looked down at the old man and asked, "Mr. Collins, could you tell us about finding the senator's body?"

"Yep. When I went down this here slough to fish, there was a man on this here dock, arguin' with another man standin' in the boat. And when—"

"How could you tell they were arguing?"

"Well, they was wavin' their arms while they talked, like this." The old guy waved his hand in the air in imitation of what he'd seen the two men do.

"Could you hear what they were saying?"

"Naw, couldn't hear nothing on account of my old motor."

"Tell us about finding the senator's body."

"About two hours later, I was a comin' back up the slough here, when I saw this boat driftin' around loose. It didn't look like nobody was in it, so's I steered over to it. Then—"

"And exactly where was the boat when you found it drifting loose?"

"Right here behind the cabin."

"What did you think when you first saw the boat."

"Well, I figured it floated out from that there boat house—like maybe he done forgot to chain it."

"Tell us what you found."

"When I got to it, I seen the man who was standin' in the boat earlier, layin' in it, with blood all over him and the bottom of the boat."

"And what did you do then?"

"I poked at him with my fishin' rod, but he didn't budge, so I figured somebody done killed him. I tied his boat to mine and pulled it over to the dock. Then I used the cell phone my daughter give me to call the sheriff."

Andrea thanked the old man and turned her face back to the camera.

"Andrea, it's Peter again. Have you been able to set up an interview with the sheriff?"

"Yes, Peter. Give me a few seconds and I'll find him."

The scene shifted back to Peter Blaine in the PMCN studio. "Again, the top story of the moment is the murder of Senator Scott of Maryland. A local fisherman found the senator's body in his boat, drifting in backwaters of the Chesapeake Bay within site of his fishing retreat. This brings to three the number of senators murdered within the last eight days. As you will recall, Senator Pearson was poisoned and his wife has been charged with that crime. Senator Gunter was killed in a convenience store robbery, along with three other people. And now Senator Scott has been stabbed to death."

Blaine stopped and cocked his head to the side for a second. "Hold on. Andrea now has Sheriff Simpson of Wicomico County with her for an interview, so we're going back to the scene at Nanticoke, Maryland."

Andrea's face reappeared on the screen.

"You there, Andrea?"

"Yes, Peter. Sheriff Simpson has graciously consented to an interview and I've got him with me now." The view widened to show Sheriff Simpson standing by her side. The Sheriff's massive body loomed over Andrea. Large-boned and heavy, he had a wide face, bushy eyebrows and heavy jowls, and he looked to be in his forties.

"Sheriff, can you tell us what you know about the senator's death?" asked Andrea.

The sheriff's heavy eyebrows knitted in concentration. He spoke in a deep, growling voice. "As best we can figure, it looks like Senator Scott had been out fishing and, when he came back in, somebody met him at the dock and stabbed him repeatedly with a long-bladed knife. They must've hit him when he first got in, 'cause he never had a chance to tie up his boat."

"Can you tell how many assailants were involved?"

"No, at least not right now." Sheriff Simpson waved his hand at the area around the dock and boathouse where they were standing. "As you can see, all this area around the dock and up to the back porch and the driveway is covered with gravel. It's impossible to get tire tracks or foot prints from it."

"How about fingerprints?"

"Well, we did find one set of prints that we lifted and scanned into a computer. The FBI's running a check on them right now, while we're talking."

"Where did you find them, specifically?"

Sheriff Simpson nodded toward the boathouse. On the crank handle that lets the little aluminum boat into the water. Looks like the perp was trying to steal the boat. Scott must've come up while he was lowering it into the water."

"Have you found anyone who might have seen something?"

"I had deputies question everyone living on this road, and they found a witness who drove past this place on the way back from town about midafternoon. She reported seeing an old, orange Volvo pull out of Scott's driveway, but she didn't notice the license plate. Then there's—"

The sheriff stopped in mid-sentence and looked at someone off camera. He handed the microphone back to Andrea. "Let me see what my deputy wants."

Andrea and Peter Blaine tossed speculative comments back and forth while they waited for Sheriff Simpson to return for the rest of his interview. After a few minutes, the sheriff came back to stand by Andrea.

"Anything new, Sheriff?"

"We've just gotten two major breaks. Since the story hit the TV news, a convenience store worker called in, saying a man in an orange Volvo had asked her how to get to Senator Scott's place. She wouldn't give him the information and, suspicious of the stranger, wrote down the license number as the man drove away. Our dispatcher ran a computer check on the tag and found it belonged to William O'Brien, a tabloid reporter who works for the *National Probe*. As soon as the owner of the Volvo was identified, my people gave the name to the FBI, in case they had his prints on file."

"Did they?"

"Yep, and they matched the ones we lifted from here."

Peter Blaine reappeared on the screen. "The footage you've been watching is a rerun of our earlier news report. Since that time, a lot more has been learned about William O'Brien, the tabloid reporter now regarded by the FBI as the primary suspect in the murder of Senator Scott of Maryland."

Two windows popped up on the television screen, presumably from remote cameras. A bearded, broad-faced man with thick black hair appeared in one box and a younger, well-groomed, man O'Brien recognized as Agent Barnes, one of the FBI agents he'd met with after being thrown out of PMC's offices, appeared in the other.

Blaine spoke again. "The faces you see on your screen are, from left to right, Dr. James LeBlanc, who is a consulting psychologist for PMCN, and Special Agent Barnes of the D.C. office of the FBI. If you don't mind, Agent Barnes, we'd like for you to go first."

"Of course," replied Barnes with a smug expression.

"Can you tell us something about this O'Brien?"

"Yes, I can. O'Brien came to the Bureau earlier this week, Tuesday afternoon to be precise, alleging he had uncovered a conspiracy to murder three senators, Pearson, Gunter, and Scott."

"But Pearson and Gunter were already dead," interrupted Blaine.

"That's correct, Peter. And according to O'Brien, Senator Scott was to be the next."

"Why didn't you believe O'Brien's story?" asked Blaine.

"Several things initially made us more than a little skeptical. First, his source of information was a mysterious woman who worked at PMC and told him she'd overhead two high-level executives of PMC plotting to kill senators, yet he couldn't name her or reach her again. Claimed she gave him a false name.

"Second, the idea that two wealthy, high-placed executives of the world's largest media conglomerate would plot to kill senators merely to hold on to a slim margin of control in the Senate for their favorite political party seemed far-fetched.

"Third, O'Brien said the informant told him the conspirators referred to the intended victims as the *Satyr*, the *Traitor*, and the *Rogue*. We thought that a bit melodramatic; something a tabloid reporter would do—not media executives.

"And most important of all, Pearson's wife had already been arrested for his murder and we all know Gunter was shot down, along with other innocent bystanders, during a convenience-store robbery. So, we felt that O'Brien was being an opportunist, a tabloid reporter trying to make a big conspiracy story out of a couple of totally unrelated events."

"What did you tell him?" asked Blaine.

"Let me give you a few more facts first," replied Barnes. "As soon as he signed in, requesting to meet agents on a matter of national security, research on his background was automatically initiated. While we were in the meeting with him, the results of that research were relayed to us."

"Did you find anything interesting?" prompted Blaine, with a voice and facial expression that indicated he knew full well what the research had revealed.

"More astonishing than interesting," replied Barnes with a smirk. "Several years ago, O'Brien was fired by a large New York newspaper for fabricating a news story that won him a Pulitzer Prize. Incidentally, that's how we were able to match his fingerprints. During the investigation of his bogus story, the New York Police arrested him for refusing to reveal his source for the story. That's how his prints got on file."

"Well!" remarked Blaine, pretending to be surprised. "Do you know who owned the newspaper?"

"PMC."

Blaine frowned, rubbed his chin, and said, "Interesting. Anything else to add, before we go to Dr. LeBlanc?"

"Yes. O'Brien is also wanted for questioning regarding the disappearance of Sylvia Reynolds, the late Senator Pearson's maid."

"How does she tie in to this?"

"Don't know for sure, yet, but O'Brien showed up at the Pearson home Thursday morning claiming to know Mrs. Pearson was innocent and asking to see her. Mrs. Pearson wouldn't see him and had her maid sent him away. After lunch, the maid left to pick up some groceries and never came back. Mrs. Pearson called the maid's husband, late Thursday night, figuring she'd decided to spend the night at home instead of staying with her, which she'd been doing since Senator Pearson's death.

"The maid's husband told Mrs. Pearson his wife wasn't there. Said she'd called him at about three o'clock that afternoon, and told him she was being taken into protective custody because she knew something that would prove Mrs. Pearson didn't kill the senator. Mrs. Pearson, thinking the police no longer believed she killed her husband, called her attorney, who called the police, who denied it.

"Mrs. Pearson's attorney, concerned that the maid may have been abducted, called us. During a routine check at the shopping center near the Pearson home, employees of a coffee shop confirmed the maid did in fact meet with a man fitting O'Brien's description, early Thursday afternoon. They said O'Brien must have said some harsh things to her, as she spent most of the meeting in tears. The two left the coffee shop together, and the maid hasn't been seen since."

With a somber face, Blaine said, "Thank you Agent Barnes." The popup window of Barnes vanished and the one with Dr. LeBlanc, who'd been studiously listening to Agent Barnes, grew larger. "Dr. LeBlanc," began Blaine, "now that you've heard Agent Barnes, could you enlighten us on what may be going on in the mind of O'Brien and whether that may have driven him to murder Senator Scott, and possibly Sylvia Reynolds?"

Dr. LeBlanc drew himself up, squared his shoulders, cleared his throat, and spoke in a nasal voice. "I won't bother with all the medical terminology that's so often used in our profession to describe a person like Mr. O'Brien. Clearly and simply, he's a man who's obviously snapped under the pressure of trying to be somebody special without having the requisite abilities. He craves fame, apparently as a renowned investigative reporter, but is unwilling—or for various reasons unable—to achieve that fame through honest efforts. So, in New York, he tried a short-cut that backfired, causing the legitimate newspaper industry to cast him out as being unworthy.

"Still ambitious to be that special person, he stayed in reporting, but had to take the only job he could find—working for a tabloid. He probably blamed his fall from grace on PMC, instead of himself, and his hatred of PMC has festered within him for years.

"As you know, he was one of the two people who found Senator Pearson's body in the hotel room. He claimed he went there on a tip, to get a scandal story for his tabloid. He had exclusive photographs and didn't share them. But that wasn't enough for him. In a play to be great again, he embellished the story by claiming Senator Pearson had been poisoned. I can only imagine how amazed he must have been when that assertion turned out to be true.

"This success, although accidental, spurred him into thinking he could make a comeback. When Senator Gunter was killed, he hit on the conspiracy idea, and went to the FBI, trying to sell them on it. If they took it seriously, it would give his articles immense credibility. Of course, the FBI didn't believe him and threw the New York affair in his face again.

"Compounding his misery, PMC shut down the *National Probe* on Thursday for economic reasons. To his warped mind, PMC had struck again. It had persecuted him in New York and now in Washington. He fought back the only way his warped mind could, and continued to push the only thing that might bring him back into the limelight: the alleged conspiracy.

"Whether he planned to kill Senator Scott when he went to Nanticoke, or merely hoped Scott would believe the conspiracy story and ask for federal protection; thereby giving him credibility, we'll probably never know. Possibly, Scott ridiculed O'Brien or said something that set him off. He went berserk, grabbed a scaling knife or something similar, either from Scott's boat or off the dock, and went to work. The fact that Scott was stabbed more than a dozen times is a sure indication of an enraged assailant."

"Le coup de grâce!" declared Rulon, clapping his hands together.

"Turn it off," ordered Marchant.

Rulon stepped between the TV and O'Brien, and looked down on them. "Did I not tell you it would be fascinating?"

60

O'Brien had watched the news in disbelief, which now turned to anger. He'd played right into their hands, giving them a way to kill Scott and pin it on him. The suspicious noise he'd heard in Scott's cabin must've been Roscoe, or Henri, if not both, or maybe another one of Rulon's henchmen. Since he left his fingerprints all over the place, they cooked up the scheme to frame him for Scott's murder. They waited until he left, probably overpowered Scott on the porch, forced him back out to the dock and into the boat, and stabbed him to death.

But how did they know where Sylvia was hiding? And how did they know he and Zalva were coming to see her? Had Pauline put a bug on him at Tally Hall? The answer hit him like a punch in the gut. *He gave Pauline his cell phone number earlier, in the coffee shop!* That's why she said she'd call him, instead of him calling her. What a fool he'd been. He gave Pauline his number, which somehow enabled them to intercept the cell phone call from Sylvia, probably with some sort of hi-tech equipment provided by French Intelligence, and beat them out here.

Henri's voice broke O'Brien's concentration. "Look what we found in his coat pocket." Henri handed Rulon the pamphlet Aaron had given him.

Rulon studied it for a couple of minutes, turning the pages slowly. He gave the pamphlet to Marchant.

"I've seen it before," said Marchant casually. "The old fool almost got it right, but he missed the motive by a mile."

O'Brien wrinkled his brow, puzzled by Marchant's comment. Rulon noticed his look, pulled a chair away from the wall, sat in front of O'Brien, and gazed into his eyes. "You didn't really believe the part about Satan, did you? No? But you still don't know why, do you?"

O'Brien moved his head from side to side in response. *Keep gloating,* he thought. *Spell it out for me.*

"Since you're history now, I don't see any harm in telling you. The old man's right about a few things. We have been systematically promoting the worst aspects of American culture and undermining authority of all kinds—making billions along the way, mind you. And I've poured much of that into campaign coffers so politicians would be obligated to appoint the crazy judges that ruined the judicial system, and vote for the bills my people proposed.

"Still puzzled? Think about it. A nation is held together by its institutions. Destroy them and you destroy the nation. We've driven wedges between parents and children, between liberals and conservatives, between whites and ethnic groups, and between the religious and non religious. We've all but destroyed feelings of patriotism and blocked all attempts to stop illegal immigration, improve border control, and establish a national language. And with our nationwide campaign of law suits, we've stretched the Constitution almost beyond recognition."

Rulon paused to study O'Brien's face. "Don't see it yet? The tremendous influx of Hispanics will ultimately result in large portions of Texas, Arizona, New Mexico, California, and Florida being dominated by people speaking English only as a second language, or not at all. Add the immigration—legal and illegal—of Muslims from Africa, the Middle East, and eastern Europe, with all their cultural baggage, and you've got real *diversity*. Lack of respect for the incompetent central government, along with language, religious, and cultural differences, will loom more and more significantly as time goes on. Eventually, a few of those states will break away from the U.S., and federal government will be powerless to stop it.

"The rest of the country, thanks to our efforts, will be so divided, with so many problems, that it will say 'Good riddance,' and the federal government won't dare use force to stop it, because France, Germany, Russia, and China won't let it. My organization is working on that now, by the way. Once a couple of those states make a successful break, other sections of the country will follow. Just as the old Soviet Union fell apart in a matter of days, so will the U.S.—and most of the world won't shed a tear."

O'Brien closed his eyes for a moment. Rulon was obviously out of his mind, but still hadn't explained the *'why'* of it all; why he, or the mysterious *'we,'* was striving toward that end. He looked into Rulon's face and raised his eyebrows questioningly.

Rulon leaned forward, reached out a hand, and slipped the gag out of O'Brien's mouth. "You have a question, no?"

O'Brien had to lick the roof of his mouth and his dry lips before he could speak. "What does all that—even if it did come about—do for you?"

Rulon sighed and gazed at O'Brien for a few seconds, gathering his thoughts. "Once, France led the world in culture, economics, learning, and the arts. With the powerful U.S. splintered into several countries, each going its separate way, France will regain its former prestige. It will once again be the acknowledged world-wide center for arts, culture, and learning. France will assume its rightful place as the political and economic leader of the world."

"I can see why a lot of French people would like that, but why you? You're a U.S. citizen and you owe all your wealth to U.S. capitalism."

Rulon shook his head at O'Brien's words. "I grew up in France and am able to see the world in a way you could never understand."

"You keep ranting about *'we.'* Is it Geroux? Is the French government involved in your conspiracy?"

"You'd be amazed to know who and how many believe in our cause," replied Rulon.

"Cause? You don't have a cause, you blithering idiot! You're just like every other megalomaniac that's come along. I'll bet what you're really angling for is to be set up as puppet ruler of one of the countries you think will come out of the chaos—Emperor of New York, or of Virginia, maybe."

Rulon pursed his lips and stuffed the gag back into O'Brien's mouth. "Typical crass, overweight American's reaction to something he doesn't understand." He rose to his feet, looked at Henri, and gestured toward the front door with his head.

O'Brien watched as Rulon, Marchant, and Henri stepped out onto the front porch and closed the door.

Roscoe kneeled in front of O'Brien, grabbed the hair on his head, stuffed the gag back into his mouth, and pulled the binding strip of cloth back over his mouth.

After several minutes, Henri returned and spoke to Roscoe. "Go get the knife we used on Scott and the woman."

So they had killed Sylvia. With his face on the floor, O'Brien felt the vibration of Roscoe's heavy footsteps as he walked back to the bedroom to fetch the knife used to dispatch Scott and Sylvia. Then the whoop-whoop of the helicopter blades signaled Rulon's departure. The noise and vibrations from the engine masked Roscoe's returning footsteps and he seemed to materialize out of nowhere, with the knife in his hand.

Henri placed the shotgun barrel against O'Brien's head. "Get his prints on it. But first, get his car keys out of his pocket."

Roscoe approached O'Brien from the side, this time, avoiding his earlier mistake. O'Brien felt Roscoe's knee in his back and felt his hand digging into his pants pocket. Roscoe found the keys and stuffed them into his own pocket. When Roscoe tried to slip the knife into O'Brien's hand, O'Brien clenched his fists in resistance. Roscoe pulled at O'Brien's fingers and succeeded in prying a couple loose, but couldn't get them all open at once.

"Son of a bitch!" Roscoe yelled, then slapped the back of O'Brien's head with an open hand.

"Now what?" asked Henri.

"I can't get all his fingers loose at the same time."

"Then break his fingers, you stupid troll."

Ignoring the slur, Roscoe gleefully pried O'Brien's little finger loose and bent it back until it snapped. O'Brien screamed as pain shot up his arm, down his side to his toes, and back again.

Roscoe leaned over and put his mouth by O'Brien's ear. "Hurts like hell, huh? Don't worry though, 'cause you won't ever use that finger again anyway." He grabbed the next finger and repeated the procedure, doubling the pain.

O'Brien shrieked again, but still kept his unbroken fingers tightly curled, determined to resist in anyway possible.

But Roscoe easily pried his unbroken fingers loose, placed the hilt of the knife in O'Brien's palm, wrapped his hand around O'Brien's, and squeezed, making sure all O'Brien's fingertips touched the hilt.

"Done, by God," growled Roscoe. He grunted from the effort of getting on his feet and took a deep breath. "Now what?"

"We'll put the knife in the glove compartment of his Volvo and lock her in the trunk."

"But I thought we were—"

"Change of plans. Coming over that railroad track in the swamp on the way here gave me an idea. I called Pauline and had her run down the train schedule. Train's going to barrel through there in about thirty minutes at seventy miles an hour."

"And hit his car, with them in it?"

"You got it. It'll look like he brought the detective out here to talk to his bogus witness. The cops will figure the detective heard about Scott on the radio and tried to arrest him. He overpowered her, cuffed her, and killed the maid. They already believe he was deranged, or he wouldn't have killed Scott. It's not much of a stretch to believe that, in his twisted state of mind, he wouldn't see or hear the train coming.

"But why wouldn't he just leave her body here with the other one?"

"Who knows? Maybe he had a romantic attachment to her. They'll find out he was staying at her place, you know. And that guy on TV did say he was nuts and couldn't think straight. Now let's load them up and get to the tracks."

Roscoe protested, "But that doesn't give us time to do her."

"Can't be helped. Besides, there may be enough of her body left for a coroner to discover she'd been raped. You wouldn't want them to have a sample of your semen to track you with, would you?"

"I've got some con—"

"Damn it, Roscoe, forget it!"

Roscoe muttered something inaudible and kicked O'Brien in the side, out of frustration.

"We've got to get moving ," said Henri. Put her in the trunk of his car and follow me to the railroad crossing. Park his car right on the tracks. We'll put him in the driver's seat and take the duct tape off his wrists and the gag out of his mouth. Then we'll wait on the other side of the tracks, where we can see the collision."

"But how are we gonna keep him in the car until the train hits, without the duct tape on him?"

"Don't worry about that. I've got a little bottle of something in the car that'll do the trick. It breaks down quickly and won't leave traces. But it will only last for a few minutes, so we'll have to wait until we hear the train coming before we use it. And remember to put her ankle gun in his jacket pocket after we zap him with the drug."

"Why?"

"So they'll think he took it away from her. It'll make our ruse more believable."

"Yeah, I get it." Finally satisfied with the plan, Roscoe stooped over Zalva, grabbed her hair with one hand and her cuffed wrists with the other, and yanked her to her feet.

"After you put her in the Volvo trunk, come help me get him into my trunk."

Roscoe mouthed a surly reply and marched Zalva across the room and out the front door. Henri laid the shotgun down long enough to pull O'Brien to his feet, then marched him through the house and out the back door to where their white Audi was parked. O'Brien fought against being thrown in the trunk and succeeded until Roscoe reappeared. The two of them managed to cram him into the trunk and slammed the lid down with a sickening thud.

O'Brien attempted to roll from his side to his back, hoping to put his feet against the trunk lid and force it open. No good! In the cramped space, his bent knees were in the way. Nor could he roll completely over to his other side in order to search the trunk with his hands.

In the darkness, O'Brien rued the ten minutes they had lingered at Zalva's apartment while he tried to get her into bed. Those precious minutes had allowed Henri and Roscoe to beat them here and prepare their trap. And before that, he'd made a major mistake by giving his cell phone number to Pauline. *What a fool he'd been!* Now both he and Zalva were going to die, all because of his weakness for women.

His arms and legs went limp, and his stomach felt queasy, like he was about to retch. He fought the urge to throw up and thought about poor Zalva. She'd tried to help and he'd led her into a trap. What a time to die, when he'd finally found a woman who might be right for him.

He heard one of the doors open and felt the car receive the weight of someone, presumably Henri, on the driver's seat. The engine started, and the Audi moved across the back yard toward the road, carrying O'Brien toward his date with Zalva and the freight train.

61

The trunk lid of O'Brien's Volvo banged down over Zalva with a dull thud, but instead of sinking into despair, her spirits soared. The old Volvo had a large trunk—large enough, she was sure, for her plan to work. She wasted no time. Quickly rolling to her back, she brought her heels up to her bottom and slipped her cuffed hands over her heels. Then she ripped the tape off her mouth, unbuckled her belt, arched her back to take pressure off the back of the belt, and slipped it off.

She held the prong of her belt with her finger tips and twisted her hand back to insert the prong in the lock of the handcuffs. She couldn't see the hole in the dark and had to feel for it with the tip of the prong. Her fingers were still nearly numb, and she dropped the belt, found it, and tried again. Finally, she found the keyhole, inserted the prong, and stifled a cry of joy when she heard a click as the lock released.

Now she needed to find something in the trunk that would enable her to pop the lid. Most car jacks came with a tire tool that served as a lug wrench, a jack lever, and a tire tool. The tool would be L-shaped, with a socket on the short arm and a long arm that tapered to a flat point. Hopefully, O'Brien's was like that.

Zalva groped frantically along the floor of the trunk for a ring or finger hole for lifting the lid off the spare-tire well, where the jack would be stored. She found a smooth metal ring mounted on the floor, hooked two fingers through it, and pulled. Then she ran her hands over and around the tire until she found the tire tool wedged between the spare tire and the side of the tire well.

She had to get out of the trunk now, while Roscoe and Henri were separated, and while she was near her gun, which she hoped was still lying in the front yard where Henri had kicked it. If she could get the trunk unlocked in time, she could wait until Roscoe closed the driver's door before escaping. That way, he'd have to stop and get out of the car to chase her. It might just be enough of an edge for her to reach her gun before he caught up with her.

Zalva pulled the tire tool from the well and repositioned her body, not an easy task in the tight space, to get at the trunk latch. She took a deep breath to calm herself, and explored the catch mechanism with her fingers, trying to determine where to insert the point of the tire tool before applying pressure.

The Volvo sagged with the weight of Roscoe's huge frame on the driver's seat, and the front door slammed shut, rocking the car. *Time was running out!* Within seconds, the car would be moving at forty or fifty miles an hour. If she leaped from the trunk at that speed, she'd be seriously injured, maybe killed.

The engine sputtered for a few seconds before the vehicle lurched into motion. Roscoe backed onto the gravel road and drove off toward the railroad crossing, picking up speed quickly, then slowing, due to the bumpy road.

Zalva had forgotten how bad the road was until her head banged against the trunk lid several times before Roscoe slowed down. The wash-board road was a real life-saver. Now she had a reasonable chance of escaping the car without breaking her neck. She found the catch mechanism on the lock, guided the point of the tire tool to it, and applied pressure. The lock gave with a sharp twang and the lid sprang open.

The sudden release sent her off balance, and she banged her head on the underside of the open trunk lid. With her heart fluttering, she grabbed the bottom lip of the trunk opening with both hands, got her feet under her, and leaped from the trunk like a frog leaping from a lily pad.

Drawing on her judo training, she hit the road hands first, tucked her head and rolled, with the back of her shoulders taking the brunt of the force. Even though the car was only going about twenty miles an hour, it was still a serious impact to shake off.

Even as she picked herself up, the car slid to a stop. Roscoe must have heard the trunk lid pop or seen the lid pop up in the rear-view mirror.

She had to make a quick decision: run into the woods, hoping to lose Roscoe, or sprint for the house and her gun, only about two hundred yards away. Hiding in the woods wouldn't help O'Brien. At some point, they would cut their losses, shoot O'Brien, hide the body, and come back after her with dogs. PMC had private helicopters and could get them out here in a hurry.

"Stop right there bitch!" yelled Roscoe.

His yell startled her into an automatic decision, and she broke into a sprint down the dirt road toward the house, expecting him to chase her in the car, backing up because he couldn't turn around quickly on the narrow road. Instead, she heard the pounding of his feet in pursuit and grinned grimly at his mistake. He wasn't built for speed, probably never jogged, and wasn't running for his life. With the lead she had, she'd beat him to the house for sure. *But would she have enough time to find her gun?*

62

Zalva's lungs burned with pain as she ran, with Roscoe right behind her. The pounding of his big feet were gaining on her, but she didn't dare risk a glance over her shoulder to gauge the distance between them, fearing it would slow her down.

Only halfway to the house, she realized Roscoe, with his longer legs, was going to catch her. *Stupid mistake!* She should've run into the forest, where she could've lost him in the trees and brush. Now she'd have to deal with the big man out in the open and barehanded. Her long hours of training were of little use now: Roscoe was simply too big, too strong, and too agile. *Mobile, agile, and hostile.* She'd heard the cliche many times, but now she had a keener appreciation of what it meant.

Suddenly she remembered being in the same situation as a little girl in grammar school, running for the school-house door while trying to escape a bully. She'd realized she couldn't outrun the bully to the door, so she'd pulled a playground trick. Would it work on Roscoe? Would it buy her another few seconds to put distance between them?

In desperation, she decided to try it. Timing was the key. She had to wait until he was almost within arms length of her for the trick to be effective. Still, she didn't slow down to allow the gap between them to close; after all, there was a slim possibility he'd run out of steam before reaching her.

The moonlit tree trunks along the roadside flashed by like pickets in a fence, and still Roscoe came, so close now she could hear his labored breathing above her own. She detected a shift in his breathing, as if he was stretching an arm out to grab her. She dropped to the road and rolled into a ball. Roscoe slammed into her and launched himself into the air like a steeplechase rider whose horse had balked at a jump.

He uttered a surprised yelp, then a loud grunt as he hit the road beyond her. She scrambled to her feet and darted past him.

"You'll pay for that, you smart-ass bitch!" yelled Roscoe. Then she heard the pounding of his feet as he resumed the chase.

But the ploy had worked; she'd gained nearly fifteen yards on him, and the house was looming closer. She was going to make it!

But with pure rage fueling him, Roscoe closed the gap again. As Zalva ran off the road onto the gravel driveway, he made a lunging tackle at her ankles, like a defensive back making a last-gasp try for a ball carrier at the five-yard line.

She twisted her body as she fell, and took most of the impact on her shoulder. The force of her impact with the ground bounced her out of Roscoe's grasp. She rolled to her back and saw Roscoe scrambling toward her on his hands and knees.

Zalva pulled her knees up and kicked out at his face with her heels. The blow caught him in the nose, and blood spurted from his nostrils. Roscoe wiped at the blood with his sleeve and glared at her, his eyes wild with anger. "You bitch!"

She rolled to her knees and, in the dim light coming from the living room window, frantically scanned the yard for her gun. Her heart leaped when she saw the glint of reflected light off her gun, no more than twenty feet away.

She scrambled across the driveway toward the gun, ignoring the sharp gravel that tore into her hands and knees, with Roscoe crawling after her. She covered the ground quickly and stretched out her arm for her gun. But just as her hand was about to close on the gun grip, Roscoe's strong hands closed on her ankles and snatched her backward. She screamed in frustration and tried to flail out with her feet, but Roscoe had them secured in his powerful grasp.

He twisted her ankles, forcing her over onto her back. Pulling her under him, he pinned her to the ground by sitting on her knees. His face was demonic, his eyes glowing like coals with reflected light from the house. His mouth twisted into a malevolent grin as he made a fist and drew back to strike at her. She closed her eyes and threw her arms up to protect her face.

Roscoe delivered the blow to her rib cage instead, sending a stabbing pain through her lungs. "How's that, bitch?"

Gasping for breath, she squirmed and twisted from the waist up, trying to get out from under him. He drew his fist back to deliver another blow, but this time she kept her eyes open. The blow descended, aimed at her chin from the side, and she managed to get an arm in the way, but the blow was too powerful. His fist crashed through her guard, slammed into her jaw, and sent her mind reeling into darkness.

63

O'Brien lay in the dark trunk of Henri's car, muscles aching from the cramped position of his body. Suddenly, Henri slammed on brakes and the car slid to a dead stop, dragging at the road gravel under the tires. The car sat in the road with the engine running for long seconds, and he could hear Henri muttering to himself in French.

O'Brien heard a loud splat, as if Henri had slapped his hand on the dash with force, and Henri yelled in a voice full of frustration. *"Merde!"* A few more seconds passed and Henri slapped the dash again. *"Maudit soit-il!"*

The Audi stirred into motion again as Henri executed a series of tight back and forth movements of the car, apparently turning it around in the narrow road, and started back toward the house.

Something's gone wrong with Henri's plan! Hope surged through O'Brien. Zalva must've figured out some way to stop Roscoe, or else Roscoe had decided to rape her after all.

The Audi sped down the dirt road then slowed dramatically, and cut slightly to the right. The front bumper banged against metal, Henri steered back to the left, and the car picked up speed. He dodged something in the road, thought O'Brien, maybe his Volvo. If so, the metal object the car nudged could've been the driver's door, standing wide open. *But why? What was happening?*

• • •

Awareness came back to Zalva with a shock of pain. She was still in the yard, on her back with Roscoe on top of her. The knockout had lasted only seconds, but Roscoe had been busy. She was naked from the waist down, and Roscoe was on his knees between her legs with his pants down, about to mount her. Just as that realization came to her, his left hand closed on her throat, almost blacking her out again.

He grinned at her with glinting eyes. "To hell with the train wreck. I'm going to screw your eyeballs out and then we'll burn the car up with both of you in it. There won't be enough left for an autopsy."

In stark terror, she grabbed his hand with both of hers, struggling to free her throat. But he was too strong, and he tightened his grip in spite of her efforts. His right hand probed violently between her legs, stabbing her with pain. He shifted his position and then, with a grunt, entered her.

She let out a stifled cry, but then an eerie calmness settled over her, and she no longer felt the pain of his wild thrusting, as if her mind had closed a door on what was being done to her. With her thoughts detached from the terror, she realized that Roscoe's primal preoccupation with her body had given her an opportunity. After each of his wild thrusts, she twisted her hips and pushed with her heels, inching her body across the yard toward the gun.

Mistaking her movements for arousal, Roscoe muttered huskily, "You fucking whore! I knew you'd like it."

She moaned and wiggled harder, moving further with each twist of her hips. Stretching her arms out behind her, she swept the ground for her gun.

The pace of Roscoe's wild thrusting changed, and he began grunting like a bear with every thrust. He was nearing his climax, and the closer he got to it, the harder he squeezed her throat. The lack of air was paralyzing. *This is it!* Zalva thought in despair. *He was going to crush her throat when he came, any second now.*

Suddenly, the fingertips of her left hand found the Glock, and a whimper of joy escaped her lips. As her hand wrapped around the handle, she looked up at Roscoe's face, now tilted back with his eyes closed, his pose unmistakable. *He was about to blow!* She shoved the barrel of the Glock under his chin, pointed at his brain, and pulled the trigger.

"That good for you, too?" she yelled.

• • •

Over the engine and road noise, O'Brien heard a muffled gunshot. Then Henri slammed on the brakes and the car slid to a stop on the gravel driveway. A car door opened and the Audi lifted slightly, free of Henri's weight, as he screamed a command. "Throw down the gun, bitch!"

O'Brien's heart pumped so hard he could hear the blood squirt through his arteries. *Zalva was loose with a gun!* Maybe she even killed Roscoe with that single shot he heard.

• • •

Roscoe's limp body lay across Zalva's chest and shoulder, pinning her gun hand to the ground. In that awkward position, she couldn't raise the weapon to fire at Henri, or switch the gun to her other hand, or even roll Roscoe's body over to act as a barrier between her and Henri. She had no choice but to roll Roscoe toward the house and crawl over him for protection. Mustering all her remaining strength, she forced Roscoe's body into motion and tried to roll over him.

Henri fired his shotgun before she got over Roscoe's body and she screamed as pellets tore into her right side and neck with searing pain, as if she'd been gored with white-hot pokers. She rolled off Roscoe's body onto the ground and scrambled into firing position. She switched the gun to her left hand and rested it on Roscoe's motionless chest.

Blinded by the Audi headlights, she fired into the glare, aiming at where she thought Henri might be standing behind the open driver's door, but with no result. She saw the flash of the shotgun as Henri fired for a second time, and felt Roscoe's body absorb the impact. She capped off two quick rounds at Henri's muzzle flash and was rewarded by a grunt from Henri as the bullets hit home. Then she heard him whimper, and heard the shotgun clatter off the hood of the car, followed by a soft thump as Henri's body sagged to the ground.

It was over! She'd won! She tried to get up, and shrieked in pain. She couldn't move her right arm and, with every breath, a sharp, piercing pain stabbed deeply into her rib cage. Warm blood flowed from another wound in her neck and ran down her breasts.

Trembling, she pulled her knees under herself and struggled to her feet. Naked from the waist down, her blouse torn open at the front, and bleeding badly, she stumbled toward Henri's car to make certain he was dead.

64

O'Brien lay helpless, in an agony of suspense, as he listened to the exchange of gunfire. He heard Zalva scream then a grunt from Henri, followed by a whimper, then the clatter of something falling on the hood of the car. *Was it the shotgun? Did Zalva nail Henri? Is she hit, and if so, is it bad?*

He cocked his head and strained for the slightest sound, but heard nothing. Minutes dragged by and still no sound. *Were they both dead?* He wanted to scream in frustration, but the gag in his mouth prevented it.

O'Brien heard shuffling footsteps crunching on the gravel driveway. Silence again, then the Audi rocked slightly, as though someone had sat in the driver's seat. Suddenly, the trunk lid popped up and the trunk light came on, forcing him to close his eyes momentarily. He opened his eyes but still saw no one. The car faced the house, so his field of vision was confined to a portion of the road.

The Audi lifted slightly, and the gravel crunched again as someone took halting steps toward the rear of the car, shuffling along as if using it for support. O'Brien cringed, steeling himself for the worst. Then a small hand gripped the edge of the trunk opening.

Zalva!

She loomed over the open trunk like an apparition from a horror-movie, blood all over her face, neck, shoulder, and torso. She had one hand pressed to her side, as if trying to hold herself together. In the other hand, she held the knife Roscoe had forced him to hold.

Zalva didn't say anything, just gestured with the knife for him to roll over so she could cut the duct tape binding his wrists.

He did his best, but there just wasn't room for him to get in a position where she could use the knife properly. Gingerly, she took her hand away from her side and pushed him in the rear with it, trying to get more room to get at the bonds.

Finally, she spoke. "I . . . I've got to cut the tape . . . while I have the strength. Might cut . . . your . . . arms."

He nodded that he understood, and felt her go to work. She must be in terrible pain, he realized, as she fumbled with the knife and his bonds. He felt the sting of the blade, but couldn't tell what the damage was.

"Done," she gasped. Then she sagged to the ground behind the car, out of his field of vision.

65

O'Brien climbed out of the trunk, ripped the rest of the tape off his wrists, untied the knot, and snatched the gag out of his mouth. Quickly, he knelt beside Zalva to examine her wounds. "Where are you hit?"

She labored for air, taking rapid, shallow breaths. She winced, coughed up blood, and pointed to her wounds with her good hand.

As best he could tell in the dim light from the trunk, the neck wound was superficial. The shoulder hit was a little more serious, and the wound in her side was definitely bad. It appeared that at least one buckshot pellet had penetrated her lung.

O'Brien looked in the Audi, and found Henri's cell phone on the front seat, along with a roll of duct tape. He reached for the phone, but jerked his hand back when it rang. He starred at the ringing phone in horror, realizing it was probably Rulon or Marchant, following up with Henri.

"To hell with them!" he yelled. He snatched the cell phone off the seat, pushed the send button, followed by the end button to kill the call, keyed in 911, and punched send again. He gave the 911 operator his name and a quick description of the events and Zalva's condition.

O'Brien shoved the cell phone into his pocket and returned to Zalva.

He used the knife she'd freed him with to cut long strips of duct tape, which he used to bind up her side. As he put the last strip of tape into place, he heard a distant sound that sent a shudder down his spine. The sound was unmistakable and definitely getting closer. Rulon and Marchant were coming back!

Now he'd have to deal with Rulon and Marchant and no-telling-how-many of his bodyguards, without Zalva's help. Their only hope was to hide until the 911 responders arrived, but he couldn't risk running through the woods with Zalva over his shoulder. The jarring motion might kill her.

Moving on pure instinct, he lifted her off the ground and placed her gently in the trunk of Henri's Audi. Then he ran around to the driver's door, snatched the keys from the ignition, and locked the doors. Zalva was unconscious, but he spoke to her anyway. "I'm sorry baby, but this is our only chance." He slammed the trunk lid down, grabbed her pistol and Henri's shotgun, and sprinted for the maintenance barn adjacent to the house.

With the helicopter almost overhead, he dropped to the ground and crawled under the logging truck. From there, the Audi was within range of the shotgun and the truck afforded some protection.

The helicopter settled onto the dirt road about fifty feet away, slinging dirt and gravel up under the truck, where it pinged off the undercarriage and peppered O'Brien's face and hands like bee stings. With a tightened jaw, he endured the assault and kept his eyes focused on the chopper.

Two men, neither of them Rulon or Marchant, left the chopper, stooped low, and ran out from under the rotor blades toward the Audi, with weapons drawn. They found Henri's body and one of the men watched the other's back as he examined the body. Then they moved into the yard and repeated the procedure over Roscoe's body.

They stood over Roscoe for a long minute, apparently talking things over. O'Brien watched them, unable to hear them over the noise of the helicopter engine. Then they turned abruptly and ran into the house. It didn't take them long to search it and return to the yard, where went to stand over Henri's body.

One of the men pointed down the dirt road toward the main highway and yelled something to the other, who nodded his head in understanding. Abruptly, they broke off the conversation and moved back to the helicopter in a crouch, even though the rotor blades were stilled.

O'Brien breathed a sigh of relief, then crawled toward the front of the truck for a better view. Apparently, they thought he and Zalva had escaped in the Volvo. The two men jumped into the chopper, which didn't depart immediately. The henchmen were probably reporting to Rulon and awaiting his decision about further pursuit.

As he lay under the truck, watching the motionless helicopter, O'Brien noticed a large metal hook attached to the end of a cable dangling past the front bumper of the truck, just inches from his face. It was a winch line, used to pull the logging truck out mud when it got bogged down.

A sudden, daring thought flashed into his mind. The chopper was positioned ahead of him, making it difficult for the occupants to see behind them. Without a second of hesitation, he crawled out from under the truck, released the brake on the winch, grabbed the winch line and dragged it out to the helicopter, where he hooked it to the undercarriage. Wild with a perverse glee, he ran back to the truck and pulled another fifty feet of line off the winch. Then, with his arms aching from overcoming the resistance of the winch spool, he scrambled back to his hiding place beneath the truck.

Several long minutes passed, then the rotor blades began turning again. The helicopter rose slowly and paused, hovering about ten feet off the ground. "Damn!" he cursed sharply under his breath. He'd hoped the chopper would take off quickly, increasing the effect when the winch line played all the way out to its limit. O'Brien chewed his bottom lip nervously and watched. Then a horrible thought occurred to him. *What if the damned thing crashes down on top of the Audi? Or the truck?*

Suddenly, the chopper lurched upward, ascending some fifty feet before being snatched to an abrupt halt. The nose was jerked downward and the tail pointed into the sky. The front end of the truck lifted about a foot off the ground and slammed back with a thud. Still, O'Brien couldn't take his eyes off the chopper, which seemed to hesitate, standing on its nose in midair for an endless second before plummeting straight down to the dirt road, where it crashed with a wrenching, metallic groan. The rotor blades pounded the ground with a fearsome whump-whump-whump, again slinging gravel and dirt everywhere.

On his stomach, O'Brien covered his head and face as the loose gravel pelted him. Finally, the rotor blades tore apart, and the engine shut down. He risked a peek at the crash site and saw nothing but a dense cloud of dust and smoke. As he watched, a lone figure stumbled out of the cloud, dragging one leg, took a few crippled steps, then collapsed. Afraid the helicopter was going to explode, O'Brien remained under the logging truck, keeping an eye on the lone survivor lying motionless on the driveway.

Several minutes passed, and O'Brien decided the helicopter wasn't going to explode. He crawled from underneath the logging truck, dragging the shotgun with him. He checked out the unconscious survivor and found that it was Marchant. A sharp piece of bone protruded through a gaping wound on Marchant's right thigh and a nasty gash ran across the top of his skull, bleeding profusely.

With the shotgun held at the ready, O'Brien approached the helicopter warily, and peeked inside. He saw four mangled bodies heaped in a pile against the side of the copter lying on the ground, with arms, legs, and necks turned at unnatural angles,. Blood was spattered all over the interior of the helicopter and covered the heads of all four men. He watched carefully for signs of breathing but saw none. Satisfied that all were dead, he lowered the shotgun and hurried to the Audi to release Zalva.

66

O'Brien lifted Zalva from the trunk and laid her out on the ground where she'd originally fallen. She was still alive, although unconscious, and her pulse was weak. He sat on the ground beside her and cradled her head on his lap. For the first time, he noticed that she'd tied the sides of her torn blouse together, in an attempt to cover her bare breasts.

He heard a faint sound from far away, as if another helicopter was approaching. He twisted his head around to look toward the sound and spotted blinking lights in the distant night sky. As he watched the lights grew larger and the familiar sound of a chopper engine became louder. Within seconds, a medivac helicopter settled on the dirt road, a safe distance in front of Rulon's craft.

Medics sprinted from the medivac with a stretcher and waved him away from Zalva so they could check her out. While two of them were tending to Zalva, a third medic checked out the chopper, then tended to Marchant, who was still alive.

While the medics worked, O'Brien trudged over to Roscoe's body, to make sure he was dead. When he reached the body, lying face up, he saw that Roscoe's pants were bunched around his ankles and his dick was streaked with blood. *Zalva's blood! The bastard had raped her!*

O'Brien's knees went weak and he felt a pain in his abdomen, as if someone had sucker-punched him. He realized that, despite her intense pain, Zalva had taken the time to put her slacks on before rescuing him. He stumbled away from Roscoe, his mind reeling, overcome by a flood of emotion. He bent over with his hands on his knees, and retched until it felt like his stomach had turned inside out.

As he recovered, two county patrol cars, with lights flashing and sirens wailing, slid to an abrupt halt behind the wrecked chopper, turning sideways in the process. The doors popped open, and several uniformed men burst out. A tall, lanky figure O'Brien assumed to be the sheriff pointed at the downed chopper, and two deputies sprinted for it. He directed other deputies toward the house, then turned his attention to O'Brien.

The tall man stalked menacingly toward him. The strobe lights from the patrol vehicles and the Medivac prevented O'Brien from looking directly at the man, but a quick glimpse revealed him to be about forty-five, with a long face, high cheek bones, and a hooked nose.

"You O'Brien?" he asked in a gruff voice.

"Yeah, and I need—"

"There's a warrant for your arrest, boy. Turn your ass around and put your hands behind your back."

"Let me expl—"

"Turn your ass around like I told you or I'm gonna lay my gun up side your head!"

O'Brien did as commanded, deciding to let the sheriff vent his anger before speaking again.

The sheriff slapped a pair of cuffs on O'Brien, grabbed him by the shoulders, and spun him back around. "I'm Sheriff Porter and this is my county. You boys think you can just come over here and have a private war in my county?"

"I can explain everything if you'll give me a chance," retorted O'Brien.

Before the sheriff could reply, the lead medic called him aside, where they huddled in conference for a couple of minutes. While they conferred,

Zalva and Marchant were loaded on the chopper. The lead medic left the sheriff and jumped on the chopper, which took off and sped away into the night.

Sheriff Porter watched it disappear then turned his attention back to O'Brien. Spreading his legs, he put his hands on his hips, and glared. "Okay, Bud. You said you had an explanation."

O'Brien launched into a brief narrative of events, from finding Senator Pearson dead at the hotel to the sheriff's recent arrival at the scene of the final showdown.

When O'Brien finished, Sheriff Porter dispatched a couple of deputies to the Charlottesville hospital, where the Medivac chopper was headed, to maintain custody over Marchant. O'Brien was placed in the back of a patrol car while Sheriff Porter and his crew examined the crime scene. After what seemed like hours, Sheriff Porter opened the front door and slid into the driver's seat.

"Okay, O'Brien. Everything you told me about tonight seems to check out."

"Then how about taking these cuffs—"

"Can't do it," replied Sheriff Porter, cutting him off. "What you told me about what happened out here checks out, but I don't know shit about that murder warrant. I'm getting you some first aid, then I'm holding you till the FBI gets here."

Tuesday

67

Zalva opened her eyes and realized that her mind was functioning properly again. She thought she'd been awake several times before, but couldn't be sure because she'd been heavily sedated and couldn't distinguish reliably between dreams and reality. But now, with the increased awareness came pain. Her face and head hurt from the blows Roscoe had given her, in the house and out in the yard. That was minor, though, compared to the pain in her side when she breathed.

She glanced at the empty chair by her bed, half-expecting to see O'Brien sitting there, as he'd been each of the previous times she'd gained consciousness. But he wasn't there now. She wondered if his presence had been real or a figment of her drugged state of semi-awareness.

With a perfunctory knock on her door, a stocky, middle-aged nurse entered the room. When she saw the awareness in Zalva's eyes, she grinned. "Well, look who's awake!"

"Am I really awake or am I dreaming again?"

The nurse busied herself checking the IV apparatus and other equipment by the bed. "I'd say you're really awake this time. We've cut back considerably on the pain killer."

Zalva wanted to turn onto her right side, but realized she couldn't, due to the wounds to her shoulder and side. She tried to roll to her left, winced from the pain on that side, and remembered how Roscoe had slugged her there with his fist. He must've broken a couple of her ribs, she thought.

The nurse noticed her squirming and grabbed the control button for the bed. "You want to sit up some?"

Zalva nodded her assent. The nurse raised the head of the bed slowly, to a point where Zalva was sitting halfway up. Her side still hurt with each breath, but nothing like when she'd freed O'Brien from the car trunk.

The nurse noticed her wincing with each movement. "Honey, you need to stay as still as you can, for now."

Zalva forced a slight nod of understanding. "Has a man been sitting in that chair or did I just dream it?"

The nurse gave her a knowing smile and a sly wink. "He's been sitting there, Honey." She pointed to a cheap-looking, plastic-covered couch against the wall and added, "And sleeping on that."

"Then where is he now?"

"I think he went down to the cafeteria to get some breakfast. Should be back any second now."

As if on cue, O'Brien appeared in the open doorway, shaggy-headed and unshaved, with nasty bruises on his cheeks and forehead, and a huge bandage on his broken nose, wearing clothes he'd obviously slept in.

To her, he looked wonderful.

His face lit up at finding her sitting up with her eyes open. Apparently not certain how she'd feel about him, he approached her bed timidly. "You really awake this time?" he asked.

She managed a weak smile and nodded her head.

The nurse turned, smiled to O'Brien, and exited the room, pulling the door closed behind herself. Zalva held out her hand for O'Brien, and noticed the bandage on his arm and the splints on his fingers.

"I cut your arm, didn't I?"

"Didn't hurt none," he protested, widening his eyes in mock-denial.

"What happened after I passed out?"

O'Brien released her hand, stepped over to the chair where she'd seen him sitting so many times in her semi-conscious state, and pulled it close to the bed. He settled into the chair and gently took her hand in his. Then he described everything that had happened after she passed out.

"What day is it now," she asked when he finally paused for breath.

"It's Tuesday morning. You've been here three days and four nights."

Zalva sighed. She'd had no idea she'd been out that long. "Is Marchant still alive? Did he implicate Geroux?"

"He died in the Charlottesville hospital sometime Sunday morning, according to the FBI, for what that's worth. After spending the rest of Friday night and all day Saturday with the FBI, I've been cut out of the loop. Nobody will talk to me. I think the D.C. police are out, too. The FBI has pulled everything in, close to the vest."

At least the bastards were dead. She found some consolation in that, although it would have been much better to see them convicted in a court of law.

Still, there were many others involved. "How about the French Embassy? Weren't some of the embassy staff involved?"

"Apparently so, since some of them were unexpectedly recalled on Saturday, before the FBI decided the conspiracy was real. The French government won't allow them to be questioned either."

"Has the FBI finally acknowledged the conspiracy publicly?"

"Oh, yeah. They even named Rulon and Marchant as the masterminds. But not one word has been said about Geroux or the French government being involved."

How frustrating, thought Zalva. How maddening, to be in on something, then be pulled away before the conclusion. "What's on the news this morning?"

"Don't know. I haven't kept up with the news, the past few hours. Didn't want to bother you with the TV in here."

"Turn it on now. It won't bother me."

O'Brien lifted the TV remote from the over-bed table, clicked it on, and turned to the Fox News channel—in the middle of a commercial, of course. They watched in silence, waiting for the news to return. The regular program finally resumed: a four-way panel discussion about which party was likely to be in control of the Senate after the coming election.

As they watched in silence, a 'breaking news' banner began to stream across the bottom of the screen. Abruptly, the panel discussion was replaced by the face of Rich Shelton, the morning anchorman. Shelton appeared puzzled as he listened intently to something on his earphone. He looked into the camera and spoke. "We interrupt our coverage to bring you this special report on events taking place in France. We're taking you now to Sally McDonald, our foreign correspondent in Paris."

Shelton's image shrank to the left half of the screen, while the right half dissolved to show an attractive blond woman in her mid-thirties, with the French Capitol in the background. Shelton asked, "Sally, what's going on over there?"

"Rich, the entire French nation is stunned. About fifteen minutes ago, President Geroux resigned and walked out of his office."

"Amazing! Has he given any explanation?"

"None at all. Just called the TV news cameras in, announced his resignation in a single sentence, and walked out of the building. Now, there may—"

"Is there any clue as to what induced him to resign?"

Sally looked a little miffed at Shelton's interruption, but smiled gamely and replied, "As I was about to say, he had an unscheduled meeting with his foreign minister and intelligence minister shortly before he resigned. The meeting was brief—only ten minutes long."

"That sounds ominous. Any idea what the meeting was about?"

"Not at this moment, Rich. But I'd guess it had something to do with Secretary of State Hederly's surprise visit to Paris last night."

"Hederly made an unscheduled trip to Paris?"

"Yes, but he was only here for two hours and never left the airport. It seems now that some kind of top level meeting must have taken place out there."

"Do you know who attended?" asked Shelton.

"We know who he met with, and it's mystifying, if not astounding."

Rich Shelton looked a little exasperated. "Can you please elaborate on that, Sally?"

"Certainly, Rich. First, he met with the foreign minister and the intelligence minister. After that, he met with the leader of Geroux's opposition."

"A secretary of state meeting with an opponent of the head of a foreign government? I've never heard of that happening before." He paused, gathering his thoughts. "Sally, any chance Hederly's visit had anything to do with the continuing fall-out from the old U.N. *Oil For Food* scandal?"

"No way to tell right now, Rich. No one in the French government will answer our questions. Now if I—"

She stopped in mid-sentence and appeared to concentrate on what someone was telling her over her earphone. Her face took on an expression of disbelief and she shook her head from side to side as she listened.

"What's wrong, Sally?" asked Shelton.

"Rich, the news continues to be astonishing. I've just received word that President Geroux's armored limo was struck by some sort of anti-tank missile."

Shelton asked, "Was Geroux—"

"No survivors Rich. Geroux, his body guards, and the driver are all dead."

News of Geroux's demise didn't seem to bother Shelton at all. "Do French authorities have any idea who's responsible?"

"A minor Muslim terrorist group calling itself the *Gaulic Jehad* has already claimed responsibility."

"How fitting," mumbled Shelton with a sarcastic grimace, apparently believing he was no longer on camera. Then, the view shifted to the scene where Geroux had just been killed.

Zalva heaved a deep sigh, wincing with the effort, and looked at O'Brien. "Turn it off. I've seen enough." O'Brien had been standing, watching the news. He clicked off the TV and sat down at her bedside again.

"Another amazing coincidence—Geroux being killed, isn't it?"

"More like an assassination," answered O'Brien. "Marchant must've implicated Geroux before he died after all. The secretary of state must've had some kind of evidence and laid it on the line for the French, forcing Geroux to resign. Then, either the CIA or French intelligence got to Geroux and they're covering it up by blaming it on Muslim terrorists."

"Either way, it's over now, isn't it?"

He took her hand in both of his, sighed, and nodded his agreement. "There were more underlings involved, but I'd lay odds they won't last a year."

She studied his bruised and battered face in silence for a few seconds, while he studied hers in turn. She remembered he was out of work, and asked, "What are you going to do now—about your career, I mean?"

"I've had a lot of time to think about that, sitting here in this chair, waiting for you to come around. Did you mean it when you said my manuscript was good, or were you just humoring me?"

She hadn't lied. His manuscript was excellent. "It's the truth, O'Brien. You missed your calling."

"You promise you won't laugh at me?"

"Of course."

"I'm not going back to being a reporter. I'm going to stay home and write. I've got one manuscript finished, and we just lived through my second."

"That's great, but what will you live on?"

"My grandmother left me a little money along with the house. I've been hoarding it, thinking I might buy a small town paper someday . . . but now I think I've had enough of the newspaper business. What about you? What are you going to do when you get out of here?"

"If they'll let me, I'm going back to being a detective."

O'Brien tightened his grip on her hand and seemed to be mulling something over in his mind. She studied his face for a clue to his thoughts, but couldn't read him. After a few seconds of silence, he leaned closer, his face inches from hers.

"Even after you get out of here, it's going to be a good while before you can take care of yourself properly, let alone go back to work. Come home with me, Zalva. Stay at my place. Let me take care of you for a while. I'll be home writing, anyway."

His invitation caught her completely by surprise, and she had to take a few seconds to absorb it. While waiting for her answer, his face tensed up, and the corners of his mouth twitched slightly, betraying his anxiety.

"You don't have to answer right this minute," he blurted, apparently fearing she was on the verge of declining.

"Are you making this offer because you feel you owe me something?" she demanded.

"I do owe you, Zalva. But that's not the reason. I asked you because I've come to like you . . . well, more than like you . . . and I want to know you better."

"No more pick-ups in bookstores and taverns?"

"None."

"On your honor as a journalist?"

A broad grin spread across his face. "Absolutely."

She rolled her eyes at the ceiling in mock dismay. "Well then, since you've pledged your honor as a journalist, I accept."